Dear Reader,

Just between you, me, and the henhouse, you would be doing yourself a disservice by not reading *Candle in the Wind*, Book I of the *Chronicles of the Ladder Society*, the book that precedes this one. With just a synopsis you would be unaware of many of the nuances that surround each player, nuances that form the foundations of the characters. I'd put the complete story into one volume but it would be so thick you couldn't turn the pages.

But should you need something to spark your memory, this is it:

Bad Moon Rising

by
t connor michael & T. Burchell

The Chronicles of
the Ladder Society

Book 2

Dobermann Enterprises LTD
Black Hawk, Colorado
www.tconnormichael.com

Publisher's Note: This is a work of fiction. Names, characters, places, and incidents are a product of the author's imagination. Locales and public names are sometimes used for atmospheric purposes. Any resemblance to actual people, living or dead, or to businesses, companies, events, institutions, or locales is completely coincidental.

Cover Illustration and Design © 2020
by Michael Molinet

Book Layout by YellowStudios

Bad Moon Rising / t connor michael

ISBN Paperback: 978-1-7360158-1-0
ISBN eBook: 978-1-7360158-2-7

Other Titles by the Author

Here Know Evil
Heed No Evil
The Lost and Found Department
Driving Miss Sandy

The Chronicles of the Ladder Society
Book One: Candle in the Wind
Book Two: Bad Moon Rising
Book Three: The Gales of November
Book Four: Crow's Raven
Book Five: The Last Architects - A Love Story

Ways to Connect

Sign up for email alerts about
new releases, sales, and bonus content at
www.tconnormichael.com

or follow the author on Facebook at
www.facebook.com/tconnormichael

WHAT HAS GONE BEFORE

In a small town in Maryland 15-year-old Elizabeth Feye lives with her single mother Mary. Elizabeth is burdened with myopia, braces, excess weight and limited stature, all of which is balanced by being a brilliant student whose IQ is beyond measure. She lived a mundane life until one day she is taunted by her physical education teacher, causing Elizabeth to direct a volleyball at her teacher, concussing her. Stunned, Elizabeth finds an ally in the form of Mr. Jack Hawkins, the enigmatic gymnasium janitor at Edgar Allan Poe High School. From Hawkins she begins to learn that she has abilities beyond that of normal people and she has been protected from before the day she was born by a mysterious organization known as *The Ladder Society*. She finds out that Hawkins, her Vice-principal Jackson Barrett Sawyer, and Bandy Wolfe, the proprietor of the curio shop *The Jack in the Box*, are all high-ranking members of the society.

As one accepts Good, one must acknowledge Evil. Members of the Ladder Society are bound by oath to thwart Evil in all its forms. The members are called *Jacks*. But as there are *Jacks*, there must also be *Anti-jacks*, those that support Evil as fervently as the Jacks defend Good. It is the most ancient of struggles. Long have the Anti-jacks looked for Elizabeth and her mother but a geas was laid upon them years ago so as to camouflage them from evil eyes. The summoned will of strength and accuracy that allowed Elizabeth to spin the volleyball at her teacher bent the geas and started a physical transformation as Elizabeth's body adapted to optimize her new abilities. But it also released energy that Evil could possibly detect, and in doing so perhaps give them a new starting place for the hunt to find and kill Elizabeth.

Elizabeth is also burdened by strange dreams, dreams so realistic that they seem real. Although she has a friend named Holly, she cannot confide in her because of Holly's lack of restraint; she was truly incapable of keeping a secret. But after the incident in the gym two senior girls befriend Elizabeth—LaTisha Wood and Amy Shestack. The three schoolgirls bond quickly and become allies. These allies become important as Evil searches for Elizabeth, using local students as pawns. Directing the search is the Anti-jack called Jack Daws, a malevolent soul that the society has come up against in other times. As Daws' (or Crow as he is known) search narrows, Jack Hawkins calls Elizabeth and her mother for a meeting. It is there that Elizabeth learns that her father, Arthur Council Dodge, was killed by the Anti-jacks in the act of saving her and her mother from a deranged homeless woman who was being directed by the Anti-jacks. Elizabeth and her mother are amazed to learn that Arthur Dodge was at the time of his death the High Clan Chieftain of the five hundred member Ladder Society.

As the spell binding Mary Feye begins to weaken she finally comes to realize that she has great lineage behind her, and as astonishing as it seems, she is descended from the race of elves. But more to the point, she learns what the members of the Ladder Society already know: That her daughter is predestined to be the ruler of the ancient race of elves and must be protected at all costs, because it is only her special abilities that can prevent the emergence of an Evil that intends to rein on Earth.

The tableau is set: The Bear, the Wolf, the Hawk, Mary Feye (*An Bheannaigh Go Specisialta*) and her daughter, (*An Bronntanas o Dhia*) are at the Jack in the Box. The tale commences just seconds after the three members of the Ladder Society bow in homage to the once and future *Ruler of the Elves* . . .

1

"I need another drink," was the first thing that came out of Mary Feye's mouth. The first thing that came to Elizabeth's mind was that she wished she were old enough to have a drink, too.

"I . . . it really freaks me out when you bow like that. Could we maybe not do that anymore?" Elizabeth said with embarrassment.

"I think that can be arranged, Milady," said The Hawk with a smile. "I realize that all of this must be overpowering, and I wish we could do this slowly, but events are pushing us. We had planned on two more years of time to prepare but you have made hash of that; we must go forward *now*. Let me continue with the history lesson." Hawkins cleared his throat and went on:

"Elizabeth, your father knew that your mother was special, and it was hoped within the Ladder

Society that he and your mother would marry. Dodger made it very plain at the start that he would woo your mother only if there was a reciprocal attraction. In other words, Mare, he would not deceive or subvert you, even for the sake of the Ladder Society. Luckily for all concerned the attraction was mutual. Once married, Dodger was tasked with making sure that your mother remained hidden. This he accomplished. His other work took him away, but his main interest was always your mother. When he realized that his time was short, he knew that it was time for *An Bronntanas o Dhia*. You were always to be, Aubrey. Only the time of your coming was in doubt."

Elizabeth spoke up: "Okay, so my father believed in planned parenthood. But I've seen you do things, and heard about other things involving you, and you Mr. Sawyer, and you too, Bandy. What makes you think just because of a prophecy or something that I can do what you can't?"

"Since I'm the teacher here I'll answer some of this," said Sawyer. "Aubrey, do you know what the population of the world is?"

"I'd guess about 6 billion. Why?"

"Last time I checked it was about 6,400,000,000 give or take a million. The reason I ask has to do with percentages. We'll get to the math later. I see you brought your radio. May Wolf work on it while we talk?"

"Sure." Elizabeth got the radio and handed it over to Wolf, who took it to his workbench and started tinkering with it as Bear resumed: "Historically, the existence of Elves has been documented in just about every culture in the world. Their names are varied, be it fairy or sprite, brownie or whatever, and as different as the country in which they are found. But the life form is basically identical across the board. When something lasts as long as this in the collective consciousness it usually has a basis in truth. As you may or may not be aware, music and song are an integral part of the elfish legend. It is by this medium that the elves express themselves, just as the dwarves were known for their mastery of the forge. Tell me, Aubrey, do you enjoy music?"

"Yessir, very much."

"What type of music do you like?"

"All types, really. Some more than others."

"Does any one type of music call out to you? Are there musical instruments that you especially like? Mare, you may want try this too. I feel your thoughts will coincide nicely with that of your daughter. Just for fun, we three will state beforehand what we think your answers will be. Wolf, what say you?"

"Aye, 'tis the fiddle I'm thinking of. And the bagpipe second."

"Hawk?"

"The pipes, and the flute. And you, Bear?"

"My guess is the drums. Ladies, how did we do?"

Mare answered first in astonishment: "Not *how* did you do, but how did you *do* it! Elizabeth?"

"Mom, they are right on the money. How could you know what instruments we would like? There are so many to choose from!"

"It's a given, Aubrey. These are all instruments of power, more power than most, for all music has magic to it."

"Aye, lass. Think anyone could stand hearin' the pipes if there were no magic to 'em?" said Wolf from the workbench.

Bear continued: "Given that these are special, that all music is special, think how music seems to transport us to other places. Singing in the shower, choral groups, campfire songs; they all have magic to them in one form or another. And that's what we want to talk about. Let's get back to the math. Aubrey, can you tell me what 96% of 6,400,000,000 is?"

Elizabeth quickly did the math in her head: "6,144,000,000".

"Very good. What this number represents is the approximate percentage of people that are calmed or excited by simple music. At over six billion, it is obviously the majority of the world's population. Now, Aubrey, give me 3% of the world population."

"One hundred and ninety-two million people."

"I'll take your word for it. This represents the number of people that are susceptible or inspired to do something good or evil by music. That is what we call a *rang a dhá,* or Class Two. "

"Okay, next we take 1% of that total, which equals about 1,920,000. That is still a very significant number. This figure represents the people that are transported mentally into a song, and for a brief moment they are part of, or one with the song. That is a *rang trí* or Class Three."

"Now it gets tricky. Less than 1% of that number, or about 19,200 people, are able to transport themselves into the song. In essence, they are in the song, watching what goes on, sort of like a third person invisible point of view. That would be a *rang a ceathair,* or Class Four."

"*Class Fives*, or *rang a cúig*or, which are statistically about .25 percent of Class Fours, number about 50 or less, and are able to be physically transported into the song, and actually interact with the characters in the story."

Mary Feye quickly interrupted: "Oh come on Mr. Sawyer. Please. How gullible do you take us to be?"

"Give the Bear a chance to finish, Milady. Twas it not minutes past that ye dinna believe in the fairy folk?" queried Bandy. "Slow as he is, he will still get to the point before sunrise."

Mary Feye sat back down and nodded to Sawyer, who continued as if there had been no interruption, save an exasperated glance at Bandy: "Wherever or whenever the song is, that person is able to go to that place or time period. They are also able to move outside the boundaries of the song itself. They are known to us as a *imoibreoir,* or a Reactor." Bear let the two women think about that for a brief time before going on.

"Let me explain that further: Let's say you listen to the song *Molly Malone.* A *Reactor* would be able to talk to Molly, even help her sell her fish. But you could also move around in the time period depicted by the song. You wouldn't be constrained to the street where Mollie was pushing her cart. You could go anywhere . . . if you have the training and the ability."

This got Elizabeth's attention. "I've been having dreams like that! I had this one crazy dream where I was in a car with some old woman that drove like a maniac. It seemed so real! It was like I was back in the nineteen- sixties."

"Aubrey, do you remember any of your other dreams?" asked Hawk.

"Yes, I do. There was one where I went to a party with a bunch of monsters, and I was in a mine where there was a cave-in, and I dreamed I was on a boat that was in trouble. I think it sank in the ocean. There were probably others but I don't remember them, at least not as well as the ones I just mentioned."

"And you felt as if you were right there?" asked Hawk.

"It was so real that I have trouble believing they were just dreams."

"So Aubrey darlin', do ya think ye qualify for bein' a *Reactor* then?" asked Bandy from his workbench.

"Well . . . I guess so. What do all of you think?"

"Did you have any music playing the times you dreamed?" asked Bear.

"Yes, I think so. At least, when I woke up the radio was on."

"Did you feel part of the dream?"

"Yes."

"Did you interact with people in the dream?" asked Hawkins.

"Yes."

"Did you recognize any of the songs?"

"No, I don't think so."

"If you knew the name of one of the songs, could you tell if you went beyond the song's boundaries?" queried Sawyer.

"Yes, I think so," said Elizabeth.

"Give us a rundown of one of your dreams, then," asked Hawk.

Elizabeth recounted the story of riding in the souped-up car with the hot-rodding old woman.

The three men and Mary Feye all looked at one another. Hawk was the first to speak: "I think we have enough clues to name the song. It sounds to me that what you were listening to was a song made popular by the Beach Boys and Jan and Dean called *The Little Old Lady from Pasadena*. The type of car, Colorado Boulevard, the carnations, the physical description of the woman; all that coincides with the song. I want you to notice that you didn't just witness events; you participated in them. And you did and saw things that are not mentioned in the song itself."

"So that means I'm what you call a *imoibreoir*, Mr. Sawyer?"

"Yes . . . and no. You certainly qualify as a *Five*, but your math quiz isn't over. If you multiply the number of *Fives* by .01% you reach the highest class that we are aware of, *aisghabháil*, or one that *recovers*. Looking at the percentage, you can see that not every generation will produce a Class *Six* individual," said Bear. "Colloquially within the society they are known as *Retrievers*."

Mary Feye asked the group of men the obvious question: "So what exactly are these Retrievers? Surely the reference is not to dogs."

Wolf looked up from his work: "A picture 'tis surely worth the breath it takes to talk about it. Bear, would ye be so kind? I've still a minute o' work to do here."

Sawyer walked over to the bench and picked up the box that Elizabeth had carried with her. "You brought this with you, and I can see you didn't open it. Have you any idea what it contains?"

"No sir. I remember the box, though; the radio was packed in it. I remember the markings. But I have no idea what's in it."

"Mare, have you a clue?"

"I have my suspicions but I think I will keep my own council for the moment. No doubt you will enlighten us."

Sawyer handed the box to Hawkins, who slit the tape, opened the lid and addressed Elizabeth: "Aubrey, I'm going to show you a few things. Please, before you answer, think with your mind, just like you did in the gymnasium, and do not let your emotions overbear you. Will you try and do that for me?"

Elizabeth nodded, more curious than ever, now overlaid with trepidation.

With a look of caution to The Mare, Hawk pulled out the first item and tossed it to Elizabeth. Elizabeth tried to catch the small sphere with her left hand, but bobbled it and dropped it to the floor where it rolled to the feet of her mother. The Mare picked it up and examined it. "It looks like a gearshift knob." She handed it to her daughter. Elizabeth just looked at it, confused.

"I don't get it. It says *HURST* on it. Who's Hurst?" asked Elizabeth.

Hawk laughed. "Strike one. Okay, try this. Mare, maybe you should be the designated catcher." This time he threw another small object to Elizabeth's mother, who deftly caught it left-handed. She handed it over to her daughter.

"Do you recognize it, Elizabeth?" asked Hawk.

"I don't recognize it, but I think I know what it is. It looks like the handle off a teacup or coffee mug. Should I recognize it?"

"With practice you would. We don't expect miracles this early in the game. Strike two. Careful you don't strike out!"

This time Hawk didn't throw anything, but retrieved a bundle of black cloth from the box, and placed it in Elizabeth's lap. In a voice as soft as velvet, Hawkins said: "Third time wins for all, Aubrey." The old man sent a small look of warning to Mare.

Elizabeth carefully opened the heavy cloth, and spread it out. It wasn't until she turned it over that she saw the crimson lining, and knew what it was she held in her hands. Her mother was supporting her before she realized how lightheaded she had become.

"I . . . I know this. I remember being cold, and Brad putting this over my shoulders . . . but that can't be! That was all just a dream!" Elizabeth remembered something, and felt the bottom hemline. "The lead shot. It's there . . . "

"Yes Aubrey, just as it was at the party when the Count loaned it to you." Hawk reached into the box one last time. "One time more, Aubrey, just as proof of what is possible." He walked over and placed a ring into Elizabeth's hand.

Elizabeth dropped it like it was white-hot, and started crying into her mother's shoulder as the wedding band rolled to a stop by the coffee table. The assembled group found reasons to leave the room to the two women, and patiently waited.

2

Elizabeth was finally able to pull herself together and speak to the gathering: "Jonathan gave me that in the mine just before he died. Was it a dream, or wasn't it? I'm not understanding any this."

Sawyer answered her question: "Your dreams, Elizabeth, are a bit different from ours, but a dream nevertheless. But that is indeed the ring that Jack gave to you at the bottom of that pit."

"Aye, Big John, now there was a man for ye," said Wolf. "The world lost a hell o' a man when he crossed over."

"He was real?"

"Aye, did he no feel real to ye? Is the ring you see there not real? Aye, he was as real as anything in this world or the next, and a finer man you will never meet. Sorry that he's gone, I am. Even if he wasn't Irish."

Elizabeth picked the ring up off the coffee table and examined it. "A *Class Six* then . . .?

"Exactly, Milady. As far as we can see, and please realize that all things are not visible, you are about the only person on this earth at this point in time that is able to carry things back with you from a song-inspired dream. There has not been a new Retriever for more generations than I care to count," explained Hawk.

Sawyer spoke: "So you can see why you were to be guarded, Aubrey. Should the others ken you, and find you, they would try to turn you to their purpose, and failing that, eliminate you. You are that train we talked about earlier; the best and the brightest–the combination of your mother's hidden talents and your father's abilities."

Elizabeth was thoroughly confused. "Even seeing all this, holding Jonathan's ring, it just doesn't seem real. I remember the dreams, all of them. And–say, that's where I got this cut on my forehead! In the mineshaft with Jonathan! But I'm alive . . . and he's dead."

"Yes he is, but his death was not wasted. By his sacrifice twenty people lived. And you made a friend, albeit for a short time. I helped with that dream, Aubrey, to start you into it. Big John had a lesson to teach you." Hawk studied Elizabeth. "Did you learn it?"

"I . . . think I learned two lessons. One was compassion, when John was kind to me when we ate. The other was sacrifice, sacrifice for the good of all?"

Sawyer answered her: "Sacrifice, yes, but not a needless one. Big John showed you that the loss of one is justified if it saves the many. It was what your father did to save you, your mother, and many more."

Hawk continued the theme: "Your father didn't throw his life away. In fact, no one should. Your father weighed his life against the future, and made a decision. Much as we miss him, it was the right and true course."

Mary Feye spoke up: "I need to get some things straight here. We have before us physical proof that objects can be brought back from a dream, however incredulous that may seem. But listening to Elizabeth, it seems she is unaware of bringing them with her, and she has no memory of putting them in the box. Is all this just random collecting, like a pack rat?"

Hawk answered: "Absolutely not. And absolutely true! The piece of coffee mug from the *Edmund Fitzgerald* was random, as she had a mug in her hand at the time the ship went down. The cape was placed on her shoulders, and the ring put in her hand. Her hand must have been on the gearshift knob at the end of the car dream. Aubrey, since you had no prior knowledge of what you could do, you did not seek out to retrieve an artifact. The articles were on you or with you when the dream terminated. In this context, it was random. Had you gone into the dream looking for a piece of coal, and put a chunk of it in your pocket, you would have returned to the *Now* with the coal. Again, lack of knowledge and inexperience works against us."

Mare broke in: "What about the box? How did the items get inside it?"

The Hawk looks sheepish. "Some of my doing, I'm afraid. I believed it to be too great a shock for Aubrey to awaken wearing a vampire's cloak. I placed a mild wreaking, that's a spell, on Aubrey that allowed her to place the items in the box without conscious knowledge. Aubrey, with practice you will be able to pick and choose the artifacts you wish to return with, and with full knowledge."

Mary Feye wouldn't let go: "How real is this *Field of Dreams*? Is it dangerous to be wandering around inside these songs?"

"As dangerous as real life," said Sawyer, "and you need to walk as softly in that realm as in our own. Witness the scratch on Aubrey's forehead; it is real enough. We don't know everything about this other world—no one does. But you can be hurt, and hurt seriously."

"But", said Elizabeth, "I was in at least three situations where I could have been killed, but I'm still here."

"True enough, lass," said Wolf as he rolled in and joined the group, "but ye dinna die. We think there is a failsafe switch somewhere that pulls ye back to the *Here and Now* before you kin die in the Otherlands. But think on this: What if ye got yerself stook in the stomach with a blade, and then ye transport yerself back? You'd be alive, sure, but you'd still be having your insides on the outside. We're thinkin' ye can't be killed outright in the *Otherlands*, but you can be hurt bad enow so that ye'll die in the *Here and Now* if the timing be bad."

Sawyer took over: "In a dream, if you fall off a cliff, don't you always seem to awaken before you hit the ground? It is no coincidence that people say that if you don't awaken before you smack the ground you'll die. It is an old wives' tale that actually is valid: you *can* die if you don't awaken. I believe that each time you have awakened a split second before you could die in your dreams."

Elizabeth thought that bit of information over. "Then I wouldn't be in any more danger there than I would be here, right?"

The three men looked at one another, and Hawk answered: "Truth be told, the danger is greater by a magnitude of at least two. No, wait; I'll explain: The *Otherlands* are in part constructs of people's imaginations. Therefore the normal limits of time, space and physical law do not always apply. An example would be Peter, Paul and Mary's *Puff the Magic Dragon*. In the *Here and Now* no such creature exists, yet in the *Otherlands* it is as real as an elephant, and just as potentially dangerous. Puff may well be a peaceful creature, but if he accidentally coughed up a fireball the burns would be real. For all intents and purposes whatever is encountered in the *Otherlands* is real."

"The other problem is that in the *Otherlands* you would not have the assistance of the Ladder Society. As with the rest of the world population, few are able to access the *Otherlands*. More importantly, you go to the *Otherlands* naked, that is, stripped of your abilities. You would be just plain Elizabeth Feye. *Here and Now* powers do not operate in the *Otherlands*. We have no idea why they do not. Just know that it has been tested, and found to be a valid tenet."

"Seems to me that there isn't much on the plus side for even going to these *Otherlands*," said Mary Feye.

"An there ye be takin' a wrong turn, Milady. There is much to be learned in the songs, and much more behind 'em. Look at the past, ye can, and to distant places. Learn that which no one else knows."

"Wolf is right," said Sawyer. "Better yet, time has no real meaning in the *Otherlands* as it relates to the *Here and Now*. A day there might be a second here. It would be as if the Library at Alexandria was recovered from the desert sand and placed at your disposal. You would have almost unlimited time to study. If the right song is found, you could visit anyone, anywhere, at any time."

"If ye can go into the *Otherlands*, and knowing what you want to do there, ye could learn a language in one night, or could find many a lost treasure, if that be yer goal," added Wolf.

"But," said Elizabeth, "somehow I don't think you want me to go on a treasure hunt. You said something about time being against us, that we were being *pushed*. What's the hurry, and who is doing the pushing?"

All eyes gravitated to Hawkins. "Yes, Aubrey, the timing is bad for us. It is very bad in fact. As disturbing as it is, we must tell you a tale about a right evil person. Even as we sit here, he is seeking us. Seeking us in general, and you in particular. Make yourselves as comfortable as possible, for this is not a comfortable tale and will take time in the telling. When you are ready I will tell you the story of Jack Daws." Drinks were replenished, and Elizabeth and her mother waited expectantly for the story.

3

Hawkins started the narrative with a question that needed no answer: "To begin, I hope you realize the value of that which we have spoken? Can you imagine the price one would put on such an ability that Aubrey holds? Or to what lengths someone would go to gain control over such a gift, or barring that, preventing someone else from accessing that gift?" said Hawkins. The stillness that followed that thought was prolonged. "Please keep that thought foremost in your mind as I relate what we know."

Hawkins began the story: "As there is Good, so there is Evil. And do not look surprised. In this context Evil comes with a capital E. Each side has its own hierarchy, with followers, mid management, and leaders. At one time Daws was just a follower, but that was a long time ago. He excelled in his work, and because of this he rose in the infrastructure of Evil. If I were to give him the dignity of rank, he would be called a Captain in their service. He commands his own minions now, many of them unaware and unwitting slaves to his whims, easily paid off with worldly desires. He has power, much sly skill, and his share of brute strength. Yet still he answers to a lower Power. He takes his orders from another, and has little freeboard in what ultimately takes place. He himself is not mindless. He knows that disobeying a command would be the end of life as he knows it. So he does what is dictated to him, and a very good and diligent servant he is. He takes his name from the jackdaw, so it is by *The Crow*, or *Crow,* that he is known on the street and to us."

Hawk continued: "In the past, Crow worked his Evil by mischief, subterfuge, and misdirection. It wasn't until this period of time that he has become a serious threat. His success has emboldened him, and his little crimes have increased exponentially. Death and destruction are his companions now and he poses great harm to you, for we feel that he has been selected to find, and destroy, *An Bronntanas o Dhia*."

Mare spoke up: "You're saying that this *Crow* has been appointed to kill Elizabeth?"

"Not necessarily kill. He has been appointed or directed to eliminate *the power* that your daughter possesses. If she is killed in the process that is but a happy bonus for him. Whether he was selected, anointed, or marked is of no consequence. It all leads down the same road. We believe that his sole point of existence at this time is the elimination of Aubrey as a threat to the AntiJacks. Should he fail, his existence will probably be forfeit in her stead."

"So why can't you just catch him, or trap him, or something, and, you know, do something with him?" asked Elizabeth.

"Easier spoke than accomplished," replied Sawyer. "There is balance in the world, and as each of us have special skills so do the servants of the Dark. Crow is quite adept at concealment and disguise, and when cornered will fight like the rat he is. But he is not to be underestimated: I bear grim testimony of his skill."

Saying that, Bear removed the patch over his eye, revealing an empty socket where his right eye should have been. It was a shocking sight to the two women. "He is overquick with a knife, a stiletto being his weapon of choice. At our first meeting I thought him overrated, and forfeited half my sight to that conceit."

"Doan be such an actor, scaring the ladies, ye gigantic side of beef!" yelled Wolf in admonishment to his big friend. "Pay him no heed, Miladies, for it's sympathy he's wantin' and sure to be gettin' it with that performance. When tha' happened he was but a stripling; their second meeting was a different story. The Crow was stirring trouble as usual, 'twas the Sixties, and he was feelin' invincible. He was doin' his dirty deeds in The City of Angels, down in Watts. It were no place for the likes of Hawk and meself. But Bear blended right in if you're takin' my meaning. Bear found Daws incitin' the locals to loot and burn their own neighborhoods. Daws had grown lax and vain with his power, and Bear caught him alone and without his minions, way up in an abandoned apartment building. It were a bloody brawl, it were, and Bear had the best of it, but barely, excusing the pun. We came in under cover of night, and carried yon moose to hospital. Daws learned a mighty lesson that day: Crow may be his name but fly he couldn't; Bear had tossed him out a fourth story window."

Elizabeth couldn't wait: "So what happened to Crow?"

Sawyer answered: "I'm sorry to say now that he must have survived the fall. According to Hawk here he bears the marks of our meeting." Sawyer glared at Bandy. "You should have finished the job then."

"And how would we be doing that, you daft bugger, with you lookin' like a sad scrap of mutton tossed on the floor, and us havin' ta carry you over a mile to hospital, never mind the three flights of stairs, and you bleedin' over me best shirt every step o' the way?"

"You should have worried less about me and more about the job at hand!" replied Sawyer.

"Gentlemen! Enough! Forgive them, ladies. As you can see, this has been a bone of contention for many a year." Looking at both men, Hawk said, "And it is high time that it be laid in the past!" Both Bear and Wolf had the decency to look embarrassed.

"Crow lives, and that's the true of the matter, and we must deal with that fact before it deals with us. Aubrey, I'm guessing you've seen the Terminator movies?" Elizabeth nodded. "Crow is more like the T-1000 in the first sequel. He is devious and sly as opposed to all brute force. Good at blending into the world. But make no mistake. Once tasked with your elimination, like the Terminator, he will not rest until the job is marked paid. No pity, no remorse. But he does enjoy his work." This harsh reality made both women shudder. "As much as it grieves me to say it, we cannot sit idly by and allow events to come to us. We must confront Crow, and eradicate him from this realm."

Mare spoke: "What are we to do? Surely you don't expect Elizabeth to take this Daws person on head to head?"

"It is not a total impossibility," said Sawyer. "Two years from now I would not hesitate to suggest it. But now . . ."

"Agreeing with Bear I am, Milady. Methinks young lassie is no match for Crow at this time, not in a face-off, if ye take my meaning."

"To a certain point, I also agree," said Hawk. "But it is better to err on the side of caution. Aubrey, you are our greatest asset, and our biggest liability. We cannot afford to lose you, but unless we employ you, we will lose you by default. There are lives at stake here, and not just ours."

"Do you mean that last sentence in a rhetorical sense?" asked the Mare.

"Unfortunately not, Milady. Have either of you been keeping up with the local news? If you have, then you must have heard about a number of murders in the city, all of them depressingly familiar? Young women, workers, runaways, prostitutes, all with their throats cut?"

Elizabeth spoke: "I remember hearing about two or three of them on the radio. Didn't two happen just this week?"

"Yes, and sorry to say they have a pattern to them that eludes the local police. If this were occurring in England the connection would already have been made, however wild the accusation. Not that anyone would believe it."

The Mare's face drained to white. "Oh my God! Mr. Hawkins, please tell me I'm wrong, and that it's not possible! No, it can't be."

"Would that I could, but it would be a lie."

"But how can it be so? That was a century ago! No man could live that long!"

"What are you two talking about?" asked Elizabeth.

"Aubrey, do you not remember your history? Think! London, prostitutes, murder weapon a knife?" quizzed Sawyer the teacher.

This time it was Elizabeth who was stunned. "Oh, come on! That isn't possible! Is it?"

"It is not only possible, but probable. As we all know, the killer was never apprehended, the murders never solved. If we were to have the forensics before us I believe they would match exactly. By whatever means Darkness has at its employ, Jack the Ripper once again stalks the streets. But this time he visits his carnage on the New World."

4

The room remained silent for a long time, each inhabitant alone with their own thoughts. It took the Mare to break the impasse. "There isn't much I've understood tonight, but it stretches my imagination to the breaking point to believe that a homicidal serial killer from the nineteenth century is out and about in Baltimore, killing prostitutes at will."

Sawyer responded to her question: "Let me give you an outline of the entertainment business and the Ripper. The first Ripper story to make it to film was *The Lodger* in 1926. Another followed in 1944. A movie called *The Man in the Attic* appeared in 1954. The BBC did a program called simply *Jack the Ripper*. Christopher Plummer and James Mason starred in *Murder by Decree* in 1979. That same year *Time after Time* premiered. A personal favorite of mine, that. Just recently we had Johnny Depp in *From Hell*. The

Ripper has voyaged on the Starship Enterprise and visited Babylon 5. This is just a sample of the films made about him. There are many others less known and countless knockoffs using a Ripper-like character. The books and articles about him would fill a small library. In a figurative sense the Ripper has always been alive. Why not in a real sense? Vampire stories never end, either. I can only state that something that stays in the collective consciousness of an entire world for so long must have its basis in fact. Maybe our very thoughts and actions keep him alive. I'm not a philosopher. Yet the man doesn't die.

"Mare, you have proof before you that physical objects can be retrieved from a dream. In less than a week your daughter has changed drastically. You yourself are coming to realize that your lineage is far from mundane. If all the above can be accepted, then why not the premise that a slayer of women can still be alive in some form one-hundred years since last he was heard from?" Which is the more outlandish: The Ripper still being alive or you and your daughter being descended from the race of Elves?"

Mary Feye thought about all Sawyer had said. Putting the unbelievable proof to one side, she assailed Sawyer with logic. "I can understand the police not catching him back then, but science has progressed, and so has crime solving. Surely the police of the 20th century would be able to apprehend someone from the 19th century?"

"Aye, and would that it be that easy, Milady. But it stands to reason that as the constables have gotten smarter, so has our boyo. Smart as a whip, he is, and slippery as a weasel," said Wolf.

"Think how our society stands at this moment in time," said Hawk, "especially in an urban city environment. There is poverty, overcrowding, and unemployment. All the ingredients are there for a violent society. With few exceptions, there is not much difference between Baltimore today and the London of the 1880s. The Ripper fits right in. To be sure, it would take time to adapt, but what if he has been here awhile, just studying, waiting, and planning? It would not take long for him to update himself on today's procedures of crime detection. Just by watching television he could learn much on how not to get caught. To be blunt, we just don't know for sure, and must assume that the local law enforcement agencies will continue to fail."

This time it was Elizabeth that was first to speak: "I'm probably wrong on this, but doesn't it strike anyone odd that the Ripper appears here in Baltimore? I mean, the world is a big place. And there are a lot of cities with bigger populations that he could hide in. Why here of all places?"

Sawyer replied: "Sad to say but that is a question we have already debated, and we have a theory. It's not a pleasant one. Our consensus is that the Ripper was called to this place, and at this time, for a reason."

The Mare didn't let him finish: "It's a trap, isn't it? This Crow, or someone else, is using Jack the Ripper as a Judas goat, and I bet we all know what they are trying to trap."

"Yes," replied Hawk. "That's the nut of it. It is a win-win situation for the AntiJacks. The Ripper goes about his grisly business in this time and place, happy as a clam at high tide. If the Ladder Society does not respond, the AJs add another victory with each dead girl. If the Society does respond and eliminates the Ripper, all Darkness loses is a foot soldier that loves to kill. But if we respond we expose ourselves, and leave a trail for Daws to follow, and follow he would, right back to Aubrey. Again, Darkness wins. Ultimately, we believe they wish to use the Ripper to flush us from safety, and lay bare the exact whereabouts of you, Mare, and by extension, Aubrey, and anyone else their net can snare."

"Then what are our options? More to the point, do we *have* any options?" asked the Mare.

"The Ladder Society has come up with a plan. It is the reason why we have asked you here tonight. It involves great danger for Aubrey–no, wait; please hear me out. But we all feel the alternatives have even greater danger attached to them, maybe not now, but surely in the long run, and for the rest of the world," said Hawk.

Elizabeth's mother broke in: "You're telling me that my daughter is between a rock and a hard place and that we have to pick the lesser of two evils! Oh, forgive me, that's evil with a capital E! I'm sorry if I seem to have a one-track mind, but my concern is for my daughter, right *here* and right *now*. All of you can afford to take a worldview of things but Elizabeth *is* my world, and having her involved in something that quite honestly is beyond my comprehension does not fill me with warmth and satisfaction. Is there no way to just let this entire thing pass over her until she is better able to deal with it? For that matter, until *I* am able to deal with it?"

"With all due respect, Mare, you hear but do not listen. Nothing would make the three of us happier than to let all this wash by. But it will not, no matter how hard the wishing. I cannot minimize the danger that threatens Elizabeth, or all of us for that matter. Mare, even you are in a dangerous place. Evil has a long memory, and do not doubt that there are forces that would love to destroy that which The Artful Dodger held most dear. We hold the worldview because if we do not there will *be* no world as we know it. I am at a loss as how to convey the importance of all this in the overall scheme of the world," said Hawkins. "America's seventh president once said: *"Take time to deliberate, but when the time for action arrives stop thinking and go."* Aubrey, who was that president?"

"It was Andrew Jackson. *Jack*son! Was he a–" Hawkins cut her off. "Absolutely. A great man in his own way and a credit to the Ladder Society." Hawkins paused for a moment, then turned and looked at Wolf, then to Sawyer. Something passed between them, and Sawyer took over the conversation.

"Aubrey, you have Mrs. Hurd for American History, correct?"

"Yes sir, second period."

"Do you like the class?"

"Yes, very much."

"And Mrs. Hurd?"

"Of course. She's great."

"Good. She is an excellent teacher, and a good person who truly cares about what she teaches, and who she is teaching it to. Would it interest you to know that she has only been at The Poe for two years?"

"I guess so. But wha . . ." Elizabeth's brain caught up with her mouth. "Are you telling me that—"

"I'm not telling you anything. I'm merely saying that not everything has to be the way you initially perceive it. And that not all assignments are serendipitous."

The Mare broke in: "You've lost me."

"It's about my history paper, mom. Remember when I told you how Mrs. Hurd does that *What if* thing? What if this happened, or what if this was different? My paper is about something like that. What if the Nazis had left the Jews alone during

World War Two? Would the outcome of the war been the same? I think I see what they are saying—that one decision at the right time can change everything. Am I right?"

"Yes, Aubrey, although this is an extreme example, and a worldview one at that. While it may be hard for your mind to encompass the mass misery that prevailed at that time, you may find it easier to relate to a single story. Ask your new friend Amy to help you. She can lead you in this."

Hawkins took up the narrative from Sawyer: "Mare, Aubrey, I realize that we, the Society, are asking you to take what we tell you on faith alone. Your rational self dominates, and naturally rebels against talk of Elves, and the Otherlands, villains that do not die and forces that you cannot see. But just because you cannot see them does not preclude their existence. You cannot see the wind, yet it also exists. It can be harnessed to move a ship across the sea, yet let it build and the November gale will destroy that same vessel. I, we, ask, in the name of the man that we all held dear, that you suspend your doubts, and heed us. You must believe that the course we lay is right and true . . . and more the pity, the only path open to us." Hawkins retired to the bar and poured more wine. The silence lengthened until finally Mary Feye stood up and spoke.

"Perhaps you also hear but do not listen. My concern is not for the world, but my daughter. If I could I would sacrifice myself in her stead but you tell us that she is what is needed. In essence, you have backed me into a corner. Let me talk to my daughter alone for a moment. Go in the other room and hatch plots while we talk." Realizing they had been dismissed the three men made their way out of the room and shut the door.

5

"Jaysus, I'd hate ta be around if she was really angry!" laughed Bandy as they stood talking in the outer room.

"No argument there, Wolf," said Sawyer. "God help the soul that gets between her and Elizabeth. I pray it's never me. Well Hawk, what do you think?"

"I think we all know what the ultimate outcome will be. Just now it is a matter of how painful the transition will be. Mare struggles to reconcile her love for her daughter against the knowledge of what is right and true."

Wolf interjected: "Won't the geas restrain her from seeing this?"

"I think the fog will dissipate for her in spite of the geas. It is a potent spell at its center, but in this particular area I believe it will part. Truth be, if

The Mare puts her mind to it the whole geas would splinter like wood under an axe."

"Hawk, are you that sure the geas would not hold?" asked Sawyer.

"Bear, the power that small woman holds within her is undiluted from the very source. You know her family line runs like an arrow back to the union of Graenbrae and Wallace. The geas has the power dampened down to a mere degree of heat, but fan that coal and I would care not to be in her way. She is the distilled essence of wood and fen. Light the flame and the whole forest will be naught but ash. Wolf, you are of her lineage, though of a different branch. Does she not carry the fire of the Irish and the Scots?"

"Aye, and then some, I'm thinkin'. That can be a worrisome thing, the temper. Bear, you have been the nearest to her. Do ye think Elizabeth will be as explosive?"

"No . . . I think she was influenced by her father in that respect. She flares like her mam, but while the fire is as hot, it is also banked."

"She burns with a sharper flame from what I have witnessed," said Hawkins. "But it burns with a blue-white light. Her mother burns full of the reds and oranges and yellows of passion. It is wider and more encompassing, but Aubrey's power is more direct and focused. It is our job to make that light the flame of a cutting torch. I fear we do not have the time to transform her into a laser."

"Aye, but is the torch enough for the problem at hand? I canna abide sending her into the Otherlands unarmed, let alone bein' here without power enow to keep her safe."

"It will have to be. Do we really have much of a choice? Without her ability to bring back what is needed we are stymied. The work of the AntiJacks would continue unabated, and another piece of the future will be lost forever. You know as well as I that we could surround the women with a hundred Watchers if we had them to spare, and still it would not be enough. Mundane means will not suffice here. You know that. Rule must follow rule in this instance or we will not prevail. We *must* use *An Bronntanas o Dhia* to thwart Daws and his master. Otherwise she will be lost to us, and the world. I cannot let that happen so soon after losing Dodger, even if it means putting Elizabeth into the match ahead of schedule. Besides, if we do nothing, we will in all likelihood lose her anyway. No, we go as planned, and let the Devil chase *us* for a change." Hawkins was flushed from speaking.

"Be at ease, Hawk. We are with you. We just worry, as do you. But be careful you do not let it become a personal thing that clouds your judgment."

"Bear, you know it will always be personal for me, and why. But I take your meaning, and I heed the warning. Thank you."

"Hawk, can ye be tellin' more o' Daws and what he is about? Were ye able to find out more?"

"Not much more than you already know. After Bear launched him out the window Jack Daws has not been heard of, or felt. Sorry I am that we were unable to retrieve the body so that we would have known, but who could foresee he would survive the fall? Small victory, Bear, but his face is a mess, not that he was any great beauty to begin with. And as I said, his right arm is injured, or seems so. I feared to search for him myself as I felt he would know of it immediately. I did contact one of us from out of town, and had her send forth an *imperative*. She used a blanket rune-cast, and she tells me he was quickly aware that someone was searching, but only knew the source was from afar, and weak. Why he is here for sure is anyone's guess. Moreover, I do not know for sure if he is connected to that which we three are bound, or just has a separate agenda of finding Elizabeth. Either way, he complicates the issue enormously, and we will ultimately have to deal with him."

"Since I did not finish the job the first time then it is only right that I do it now," said Sawyer.

Hawkins replied to this statement quickly and with force: "Bear, who was it that just admonished me about this thing becoming personal? Heed your own words man! Jack Daws will be dealt with as the need arises, and by whomever is able. Besides, the caster relates that the power tailings from Daws is stronger than she has encountered in two score and ten, including that which was on record for Daws himself. It seems he has gained ability in the interim since his fall, or someone else is endowing him. This is not the Crow we knew, Bear. It is an improved version. Beware!"

Sawyer hung his head. "You are right as always, Hawk. The good for all. I apologize."

"Not needed, Bear. Just a warning to us all to take nothing for granted."

"One thing ye can take for granted, boyos, an' that be women will jabber forever if let to themselves. Bear—go knockin' on yon door and hurry the ladies."

Bear laughed sardonically. "If you're in such a damn hurry, then wheel yourself over to the door and pound on it yourself. But don't ask me for a fire extinguisher if the door catches fire, and you with it!"

"On second thought, maybe we should be givin' the ladies a few minutes more!" laughed Wolf.

6

At the same time the two groups separated Amy Shestack was in her bedroom preparing for bed. As usual her homework was long since done. Now her only desire was a hot bath and bed. Like Elizabeth, she too had a full-length mirror, and as she stripped off her clothes she looked at her reflection. It wasn't the first time she wondered why, with a nice-enough body and a pretty face that she seemed never to have any dates. Was there such a thing as being too smart? She didn't feel like she intimidated boys, but maybe she did. Her dad being a cop probably didn't help much either. Of course being Jewish in a town this size was a drag and it cut more than one way: the pool of boys of Jewish faith was very shallow indeed, and limited her choices to about five boys her own age, none of whom appealed to her. And since everyone knew she was Jewish, and because there were no Jewish girls her age attending The Poe, she was a novelty, and that was something teenage boys avoided. Old Uncle Ephraim was right when he said teenagers were the most conforming of all the age groups. Not for the first time did she wonder what life would be like if she was a blonde with a pert little upturned nose. Turning sideways to the mirror she pushed up the end of her nose to see the effect: *Not bad. Maybe there was a nose job in her future!*

As Amy ran her bath she had the oddest feeling come over her, as if someone was staring at her. The sensation was so strong that she actually turned around and looked to see if someone was behind her. Of course, there was no one there, but the feeling remained. Amy wasn't a cop's daughter for nothing. She doused the bedroom light and allowed her eyes to adjust to the darkness before sidling over to her window and gently parting the drapes a fraction of an inch. From her upstairs window she had a panoramic view of her back yard and the yards to each side. She could detect no movement anywhere, yet the feeling persisted, although it was not as strong as before. She could not see anyone watching her, but somehow she *felt* someone's eyes on her. *Strange. No peeping tom would be able to see into her room with the drapes drawn—which they had been. Just because she looked at herself naked didn't mean she wanted the rest of the world to look!* Yet she still felt as if, well, as if she had *company*. Easing back from the window Amy pulled her phone into position by the window and dialed up LaTisha. Amy was very grateful that LaTisha answered the phone herself. She knew that after a certain hour LaTisha's parents would not let her talk on the telephone. "Tish, it's me."

"What's up girl? You just got under the wire. Ten more minutes and you would have been in the *no call zone*."

"LaTisha, listen to me, please? I've got the creepiest feeling that someone is outside watching me. I was just getting ready to take a bath and I felt like there was someone looking at me."

"Girl, who would want to look at your skinny butt? Besides, who could see it up there on the second floor?"

"I know, I know, and the drapes were drawn tight. But it still feels like someone is watching me!"

"Easy girl. Where are you at now?"

"I'm still in my room. I killed the lights an' peeked out the curtains but I can't see anything suspicious out back. Mom and Daddy aren't home yet, Shelby is staying over but she's already asleep, so it's just Granna and me. I'd feel foolish calling the cop house; my Dad would never hear the end of it if it were a false alarm. Do you think I should call down to the station anyway?"

"Are all the doors locked? What about the alarm?"

"LaTisha, how many nights you sleep over? You know my dad doesn't let Shoebox out to pee without locking the door after her. This place is like Fort Knox."

"How soon 'til your parents get back?"

"Half an hour, maybe less."

"Then what's to worry? No one can get in, and this isn't some horror movie where you're dumb enough to go outside. Just chill and wait until your Dad gets home."

"You don't think it's Parker or one of the others, do you?"

"Amy, how would I know? It could be, I guess. If it is then I don't think you have much to worry about."

"I don't know what to think. But some really strange stuff has happened since we hooked up with Elizabeth."

"Hey, what about the you-know-whats?"

"What are you talking about?"

"Amy, you know, the things we got on the ramp!"

"What about them?"

"Jeez, do I have to draw you a picture?"

"There's no way I'm going to try and use that! And what good would it do? She's across town, and I could just as easily telephone her!"

"Amy, shut up a minute and listen for a change! Maybe it's good for things other than what Elizabeth said. What if you could use it in another way?"

"How would I know? Do you?"

"Well, why not get it and see? It's worth a try, isn't it? Just don't concentrate on her name or mine, okay?"

"All right, hang on and let me get it off the dresser. Okay, I've got it. What now?"

"I don't know, maybe just look out the window and see if you notice anything suspicious."

Amy held the gold jack in her hand and eased back the drapes. She scanned the entire area but saw nothing that she had not already seen.

"Nothing, LaTisha. Nothing at all."

"Well, it was worth trying. Anyway, your parents should be home soon. I have to go. My mom wants to use the phone."

"'Tish, wait! I just remembered that we were supposed to use our *left* hand to hold it. I was using my right. Let me try again. And 'Tish, do you have yours nearby?"

"Left is right and right is left, Amy, and no, I put it in my jewelry box. Why?"

"Just a hunch. Go get it while I take another peek."

Amy's ear reverberated as LaTisha dropped the phone on her way to her dresser. Holding the jack in her left hand she once again looked out the window. This time things were different. The world outside was bathed in a soft blue light, punctuated in places by dim objects outlined in scarlet. It took Amy but seconds to realize these were objects radiating heat, having been allowed to look through her father's infrared nightscope last summer. She was so engrossed that she had trouble recognizing that the irritating noise she heard was LaTisha who was back on the phone.

"Oh, wow, 'Tisha, you won't believe this! It's like daylight out there. I can see everything! Wait! Let me try something! Yes! As soon as I release it everything goes back to dark. Try yours!"

"Amy, nothing happens. I can't see any difference at all."

"Maybe it works different for yours. Is it in your left hand?"

"Yeah, left hand."

"Damn. Wait. Let's try something else. Try closing your eyes. Does that do anything?"

"Yes, yes it does. Now I can't see."

"Okay, okay. What if you try closing your eyes and thinking my name?"

"Come on, Amy, my mom needs the phone. This isn't a Ouija board."

"Just try it!"

"Okay! Amy, this is-OH SHIT!"

"'Tish, what's wrong!"

"Girl, I ain't believin' this! Wow o wow o wow! Did you know your neighbors have a raccoon rummaging around in their garbage can?"

"'Tish! How do you know that?"

"'Cause I can see it, dummy! And I'll bet you a dollar you're looking at it right this second!"

"I am!"

"Look to your right. Yeah! Amy, it's like I'm hooked up to cable! Everything you look at I see too. When you looked to your right the picture in my head swung right. It's like I'm looking through your eyes. This is just too cool. Man, wait'll we tell Elizabeth!"

"The ja-thing must be a transmitter of some kind. I wonder if it can do anything else?"

"Girl, who cares? I don't know about you but I'm never letting this thing out of my sight!"

"Me either. 'Tisha-look! Past the chain link fence in back. In that row of pine trees. See the red barely sticking out halfway down the row?"

"Yeah, I see it. Something's there all right. Amy, try concentrating harder on the pines. Maybe it will–Yes! This thing's got a telephoto lens!"

"'Tish, look! It's not a man; it's a woman! She's looking right at us, I mean me! And she's grinning!" Amy was so unnerved that she lost her balance at the windowsill, and in doing so dropped her jack. Instantly the contact was lost. Once again the back yard was dark.

"Amy! What happened? Are you okay?"

"I'm fine. I dropped the, I mean *it*, and lost the connection."

"I dropped off-line, too. But we saw her, right?"

"You bet we did! That was something else. Hold on . . . 'Tish, my parents are home. I'm gonna have Daddy go look out there. I'll let you know what's what tomorrow. Thanks for being there."

"Tomorrow. And Amy? Nothing to nobody, right?"

"Right! Love you!"

"Ditto!"

As Amy went down to talk to her father she couldn't get over the feeling that the mysterious woman had known Amy could see her, even though Amy was two stories up in the air, two-hundred feet away, and the woman hidden by the trees and the darkness. It was not a happy thought.

7

With the three men in the adjoining room Mary Feye found it only slightly easier to talk. "Elizabeth, I would be lying if I said I knew what to say. I thought having to talk to you about sex was tough. But this! I need a bigger brain because the one I have isn't capable of holding all of this."

"Mom, I know better, and so do you. Thanks for trying to make it easier for me, but I think we both understood everything that was said. You probably knew most of this already—you just couldn't access it with that *geas* on you. And you're starting to remember stuff, aren't you? I can see it in your eyes! That geas thing isn't as strong as they think it is, is it?"

"Would that it were, Elizabeth. I have a feeling that I'll be remembering too many things best left forgotten. But right now you are my only concern. I appreciate how high the stakes are when we talk of Good and Evil. The Baptist Church was at least good for that! But this *damned if you do and damned if you don't* ideology is not to my liking. There must some middle ground for us somewhere."

"Mom, doesn't the idea of fighting on the side of Right excite you?"

"Yes, but it would excite me a hell of a lot more if my only daughter wasn't on the varsity and designated to be the one fighting."

"It's really funny you should say that. LaTisha and Amy said I qualified to be on their varsity as a friend, even when I thought I only deserved JV status. But I think I'm varsity material now. Mom, I can *do* things! Wonderful things. And I feel good when I'm doing them. I'm through being a doormat. I've been the victim in school as long as I can remember. It's time to switch categories. If I can make a difference, then I want to do it, even if it is dangerous. Mom, I'd rather make a difference in the world at fifteen than live to be a hundred and not count at all."

Mary Feye looked with love on her daughter, the only living relative she had, and not for the first time saw the father reflected in the eyes of the child. But this was the first time she had ever seen that part of her husband that was The Artful Dodger in her daughter. It was this above all else, seeing the grey-green eyes sparkling with crimson flecks that decided her course of action.

"Okay, Elizabeth. If you are indeed the *An Bronntanas o Dhia*, Aubrey, Ruler of the Elves, then we best make sure you are prepared to accept the position. But before we call the *three wise men* back I think we should decide what questions need asking, before too much smoke and too many mirrors are placed in front of us."

"O . . . kay, how about asking more about this Jack Daws? And what I'm supposed to be bringing back, or from where I'm to be going? How will I get there? How does the whole process work?"

"Good start, Aubrey. I think I want to ask a question or two about your safety, and what the LS will be doing while my daughter is putting her life on the line. I think I'd like to know more about the Ladder Society itself, too."

"Mom, what did you mean by smoke and mirrors? Don't you trust them?"

"Trust is something I don't give lightly, Elizabeth. I sense that there is still much to know and that they are intentionally keeping us in the dark. I feel they do it for our own good; to protect us because we are women, because they are of the old school and of a different generation. If we are of high birth, then let us ask for that which is our Right. If truth be ours, then let it not be hidden from us." Mary Feye's eyes were molten green liquid.

"Mom! Where did that come from?"

"Aubrey dear, something tells me the Ladder Society has gotten themselves more than they bargained for. Call the blackguards in!"

* * *

While Sawyer or Bandy were still arguing over which one of them should knock on the door to hurry up the women it was opened by Elizabeth. She held the door as the three men made their way into the room and arranged themselves.

"Miladies," started Hawkins, but was quickly interrupted by Mary Feye.

"Thank you, Mr. Hawkins, for the additional time so that my daughter and I could compose our thoughts. At this point I would like answers to several questions before we make any decisions. We prefer direct answers, however brutal. Can we be served in this manner?"

Hawkins looked at his two companions and smiled. Turning to Mary Feye he said: "Absolutely, Milady Feye. Ask what you would of us."

"First off, please tell us what you know about Jack Daws in the current sense."

Hawkins complied: "I have just returned from a reconnaissance mission. Aubrey, I followed an acquaintance of William Parker's by the name of Harold Yoder. He is one of the three boys that were harassing you. Through Mr. Sawyer's efforts we were able to ascertain that he was behind the incidents at the bus stops. Young Mister Yoder led me to a man called Spratt, who led me to Jack Daws. I was able to positively identify the man. He is alive, and searching for the trail. I have no doubt that soon his minions will lead him to you."

"How soon, seeing as how he now has information about Aubrey?" asked The Mare. She watched The Hawk intently for his answer.

"As of now the scent is weak. I fear he did not receive the information he wished for this night, but surely he will redouble his efforts if no results are forthcoming."

"I sense you withhold something, Mr. Hawkins, but I believe that it is of little import here. Please continue."

"There is little more to tell. For the moment, The Crow is thwarted. I doubt he will show himself personally unless absolutely necessary, and then only when all options are exhausted and all assets expended. I would hazard a grace period of three days, maybe more if luck is with us."

The two women absorbed that information, and it was comparable to a reprieve from the governor. Mary Feye nodded to her daughter, allowing her to pose their next question:

"Mr. Hawkins, where is it you want me to go?"

Bandy took a deep breath and answered the question for Hawk. "'Tis not only a where but a when we be wishing for. We need ye to go back to Whitechapel in Londontown. We need ye there in August of 1888."

Mary Feye was out of her chair in an instant. "Now wait one damn minute! You don't really think I'd allow my daughter to return to 19th century London when we *know* Jack the Ripper is alive and working the streets, do you? You must think I'm a complete idiot!"

"Milady, there is scant difference between then and today, for The Ripper is among us in the Here and Now. Let me lay out the details and state our case, and see if I can allay some of your fears," said Hawk.

Mare sat back down with a grace that did little to mask her anger. "Make it good, Mr. Hawkins."

"Point one: If we do nothing, the killing will continue unabated. This the Ladder Society is most sure of. Point two: If we do not turn the tables on the AntiJacks and smoke them out then surely they will smoke us out. Point three: We believe that at this time we are a step ahead of the AntiJacks, and hold the upper hand. More to the point, the AntiJacks think *they* are playing the tune, and that works for us. Point four: We feel we have a window of opportunity where we can slip Aubrey in, and out, without anyone being the wiser. By the time the AntiJacks realize they lag the field we will have what we need. True, the window is very small, but a window nevertheless, and available to us. If we do not avail ourselves of it, sooner or later Aubrey will slip and use her abilities and the hounds will follow the trail to your very doorstep when you least expect them. We prefer to know when the hounds are coming."

"Mom, Mr. Hawkins is right. At least this way we can see them coming. I don't want to have to worry about people or things coming after us every minute from now on. Besides, I don't want to think that others are being killed because of me, or because I was afraid. Please."

Four individuals with one purpose looked to Mary Feye. They could only guess as to what emotions came and fled within her, for she had closed her eyes as soon as Hawkins started speaking. When her eyes opened there was but little of Mary Feye in them. At first they seemed lifeless, but slowly from their depths there came a fire of kelly green, and then the descendant of the Hidden Kingdom stood before them, and spoke: "Hear this: If I give up my daughter to The Ladder Society, in the name of Wallace, and Graenbrae, and the line that produced me, then which of you would stand for Arthur, her father?" The three men and Mary Feye's daughter were momentarily stunned by the transformation they had witnessed as The Mare's eyes hardened into jade as she surveyed the men in the room.

Hawkins hesitated but a second and immediately stood and faced Elizabeth's mother: "Milady Meriam de la Feye, greatdaughter of Meridrill, Lady of the Misted Forest, and Eldriss Fenmaster, I stand for Arthur, The Dodger: Slain Clan Chief of The Jacks; brother clansman, friend, husband and father."

The air in the room shimmered with waves of power, and had not Hawkins made sure the wards were set and a shield placed over the building the very walls would have exploded. As it was, they seemed to bend outward like bellows. Elizabeth stood stock-still, both afraid and in awe of the show of power. She watched as her mother locked eyes with Hawkins, and colored lines of power transversed between them; green from her mother and cerulean blue from Hawkins. The colors met and clashed in the space between them, piling up and spilling into one another, neither color gaining dominance over the other. Unable to achieve advantage, they formed two walls, one of forest-green wood and the other of blued steel. Their eyes never blinked, nor left the eyes of each other. Sparks spit from the point of contact. The lights in the room went out, and all that remained visible were the warring colors, each hue throwing miniature lightning bolts at its opponent. After minutes of contact, the two walls began to crumble, but the lines of force did not retreat. Then, amazingly, each color extended a tendril across the neutral zone, and followed the opposing color to its source. The lines thickened, and then they began to intertwine, until the offshoots were bound together like twisted cords of hemp making rope. The color of the *rope* was green and blue, and yet neither. It was a color that defied definition. It held tight for a few moments longer, burning with brilliant light, then faded into the dark without a trace . . .

From the darkness Meriam de Feye spoke again: "With this you are bound to that which is mine, and was his. I acknowledge your honor, and your duty. I accept your TwinningOath as proof of integrity and purpose, and that you will care for my child as if one of your clan. Protect my daughter, and the mists of the fens will forever shield you."

The Hawk followed with words of his own: "As if one of my Clan will I watch over your daughter. Five hundred strong are we, and with one voice I speak for all: My sword is hers, my life for hers, my soul for hers. Let it be done! Hawkins looked at Elizabeth. "Aubrey de la Feye, stand and face us!"

Elizabeth had no choice but to obey. She was instantly bathed in a violent swirling tornado of supple twisting vines of green and taut cables of steel blue and grey. The colors engulfed her yet did not so much as stir her hair. The colored lines of force seemed to speak to her in a language she could almost but not quite understand, yet still letting her know that she would never walk the earth alone from this moment forward. Slowly the lights and the sirocco surrounding her slowed, and dimmed, and faded into the darkness of the room.

When all was still the room seemed to shrink, and the lights regained their luminance. As the light in the room rose, the fire in the eyes of The Mare and The Hawk subsided.

"I think I could use a drink," said Hawkins, and walked over to where the liquor was laid out. As Hawkins passed by Mary Feye, Elizabeth thought she overheard her mother whisper to herself: "Who *are* you?"

* * *

Elizabeth was not sure, but she believed she had just witnessed a ritual that had its roots buried deep in time, a time before lawyers, and contracts. The ceremony was more binding than any legal document could ever hope to be. Strangely enough, it all seemed familiar and *right* somehow. More importantly, she was coming to realize that even though she had spent almost every day of her life with her mother, she did not know her. She always knew her mother to be strong. As a single parent she had to be. But this! *One thing for sure: that geas thingy was on thin ice!*

The room was quiet for a while, yet still tingled as if filled with static electricity. Hawkins fixed himself a drink and brought a fresh glass of wine to Mary Feye. "It is done, and well done, Milady. Let us proceed, as time grows short this night. We have only started on our path, and have miles to go. I ken that one evening will not answer all your questions, so we must make do with some now, and save the rest of your questions for the morrow. Already the hour is late, and the Little One needs her rest."

"Mister Hawkins!"

"Sorry, Aubrey. I forget myself! But sleep you do need, in more ways than one. Now, what questions can be answered in our time remaining?"

"What about my radio?" asked Elizabeth.

"Wolf, I think this is your question," said Bear.

"Aye," said Bandy, and wheeled to the table where the radio had been placed. "Be a good lad and plug the thing inta the wall. It'll need warmin' up."

Bear quickly did as instructed, only pausing to give Wolf a look when he said *good lad*. After a minute–less three seconds–the speaker was humming and the tubes hot.

"Now gather round all of ya and I'll go over this slowly, so even the vice-principal can get the use of it!" Bear started to say something but got an elbow in the ribs from Hawk for his trouble. Bear held his tongue.

"This bit o' Marconi magic, or Tesla magic if truth be told, has at its heart a super heterodyne receiver–a radio to the vice-principal here. Electricity makes it work, but the tubes give it a soul no transistor can hope ta match. There is naught one like in the civilized world, Aubrey, so please try not ta knock this one off the night table. The Ladder Society handmade this set over three quarters of a century ago, and it lay fallow 'til called for. Its special *qualities* are sentried against use by other than those of Jack lineage: should the wrong person try to avail themselves of its abilities the innards would melt to dross. As ye can plainly see, the ward is visible on the grill; the wee jackrabbit sitting there as calm as a clam.

"As to what it can do, I canna demonstrate that. I can only tell ye: See the four wee buttons at the bottom, the presets? If ye have the knowledge, a person can set them to single out a particular song tha' floats on the airwaves, and magnify it just a wee bit so it takes precedence over the other songs, if you take my meaning. Say ye be wantin' to visit that dear ol' lady in Pasadena again. What ye do is set it to listen for that song, and when it is played it will single it out, and help ye get inta the song."

"How does it do that?" asked Elizabeth.

"'Tis surely all manner of magic, Aubrey," said Wolf.

"That and Bandy's doctorate from MIT," muttered Bear.

"However it happens, the fact that it *does* is more important that the *how* of it. It provides us with a valuable research tool, and that is what matters. Go on, Wolf," said Hawk.

"Think of this as an amplifier, or directional beacon, if ye take my meaning. It gets ye where ye be wishing to go."

"But I was getting to places before I had this radio! I told you about my dreams."

"Indeed you were, Aubrey, but did you have any control over when you would go, or where? You see, you have the ability to travel to the Otherlands. But this radio is the vehicle that gets you there," said Bear.

Mary Feye spoke for the first time: "Okay, I think we grasp the concept as stated. Aubrey, or any Retriever, or Reactor, for that matter, can go into the Otherlands. They are limited in that they have to be asleep and hear the song, correct? So why can't you just take out a cassette tape and play *The Little Old Lady From Pasadena* over and over again?"

"Nothing is that easy, Milady," said Hawkins. "For whatever reason, and I can think of several, the music must be broadcast and received over the airwaves. All recorded forms of music such as records and CDs do not work unless broadcasted. However, live music does have the same properties as broadcast songs. In many cases it is actually a more potent transmitter. No, unless we want to hire musicians to serenade Aubrey to sleep we must use the radio."

"I hate to play Devil's Advocate, but let's say you need to hear a particular song on a particular night. What are the odds of that happening? Unless of course the song is a Top Forty hit?" asked Mary Feye.

Hawkins saw that Aubrey knew the answer. "Aubrey–can you answer that for your mother?"

"Mom, you could make the song a request! Even if the station doesn't have a regular request time I'll bet a bored DJ would play anything at three in the morning!"

"I'm getting old. I had forgotten about that."

"If that didn't work, I think the Ladder Society could come up with a way to *persuade* a disc jockey to play a special song for a special someone," said Sawyer with a smile.

"Aye, where there be a will, there be a way!" laughed Wolf.

"I think we have time for maybe one more question?" said Hawk, looking at his watch.

Meriam de Feye looked from one man to the next until settling her eyes on those of The Hawk. "How are going to protect my daughter? I feel that the LS can take care of her in the Here and Now, and maybe she can take care of herself a little bit, too. I think that I might even be able to assist on that score. But what about the Otherlands? She won't have the abilities there that she has here. How can she be protected with the small amount of time left to us?"

Wolf answered the question for Hawkins: "There be yer mistake, Milady Feye. Ye be thinkin' in terms of mundane time. Yes, here we be havin' only three days befor' us. But in the Otherlands we have almost all the time in the world!"

Hawk allowed that concept to sink in before speaking: "It is true that we could never train Aubrey in the time remaining to us. Even if we had six months it would not be enough. But time in the Otherlands has no relative meaning as we know it. This works for us, and is at the core of our plan. Wolf, the radio."

Wolf turned the radio so that Meriam de Feye and her daughter could see it.

"What Wolf has done is programmed four songs into the presets on the receiver. Each song has the ability to send Aubrey to a place that will assist her and accelerate her learning curve exponentially. Aubrey need only set the timer for midnight and go to sleep: the radio is already tuned to the station of choice. The timer will turn the radio on at the correct time and with luck she will go where the transmitter leads her."

"And the songs?" asked Mary Feye.

"Will be played sometime before 7:00 AM," said Hawkins.

"How can you be sure?" asked Aubrey.

"Ah, we have an *arrangement* at that particular radio station," said Sawyer with a bit of a Cheshire cat grin.

"So, what are the songs then?" asked Aubrey.

"Some things are better left to the imagination, Aubrey. I don't want you lying awake thinking about them. Besides, there is a good chance that you will only visit one, maybe two of the sites in one night. No sense getting excited or apprehensive about something that may or may not materialize. You will be better sensitized to the songs if you do not anticipate them," said Hawkins. Just then the phone rang. Bandy rolled out to the showroom to answer it.

"I think it would be wise to adjourn for the night. It grows late and there is much for all of us to think about and do. I might add that it is a school night and the Little One needs her sleep," said Hawkins. He laughed and apologized before Elizabeth could protest his choice of words.

"Aubrey honey, would you like to drive us home? I feel okay but no sense taking chances when drinking," said Mare.

"Sure Mom. No problem."

"Here are the keys. Go warm up the bus. Don't forget the radio. I'll be right out."

Sawyer could sense that his presence was not needed. "I'll be with Aubrey, just in case. Goodnight, Mare." Sawyer picked up the box containing the cape and other articles and left the two alone in the back room.

"I'd ask, but I know that I would not get a straight answer from you," said Meriam de Feye. "You are alien to me, yet there is something about you that is known to me. Given time, I will place you. Will I have that time?"

"Milady, if all goes well we shall have time enough for stories. As for now, rest easy. One other thing I have not told your daughter is that she may be entering an area and an era where she is susceptible to disease. I have made arrangements for her to be inoculated on her next journey. As she is already covered against polio and diphtheria we won't worry about them but she will get inoculated against typhoid fever, tuberculosis, Hepatitis A, smallpox, and bubonic plague. Her exposure will be minimal, and as soon as she returns I believe her special immune system would cancel out anything harmful. As I am sure you have noticed, Aubrey has always been depressingly healthy. It is just a precaution but better to be safe than sorry. I'm sure she will be cursing me thoroughly when she finds she has a date with needles.

"As for you, please be careful of what *you* do. I am no fool. Although you have tried to hood it from my view, I feel that the geas is but featherlight on you. Do not let your anger overstep your good sense. I do not wish Aubrey to know, but from now on she is never alone. There are Watchers detailed to you both, and phantom your every move. You could feel them if you reached out, but I pray that you leave be, lest the reaching be felt by others. If in need, summon them. Do not slap at the insects—let my flyswatters do the work so that you remain hidden. I also tell you that Watchers now guard the Little One's two friends, the dark one and the child of Jacob's tribe. This also would I keep secret, though the three of them may glom on to it on their own."

"Why not tell them?"

"It creates a backflow of power. On a more mundane level, a minion of Evil who watched closely would notice someone looking back for their Watcher, and follow their gaze to the source."

"I understand. I will do my best to *contain* myself, but all bets are off if Elizabeth's life is in danger. You still do not tell all. For whose benefit I am not sure." Mary Feye stared hard at Hawkins, then turned and started walking to the front door.

"Meriam de la Feye, all things come to those who wait. I have sworn the TwinningOath. I will protect your daughter as if she were of my own blood."

By now they had reached the entrance. "I am most aware of that, Mr. Hawkins. I believe I was there. In parting I give *you* a warning: Beware of the consequences when you are willing to Star Trek us, sacrifice *one* for the *good of the many*. Until tomorrow, then." Meriam de la Feye opened the door to the *Jack-in-the-Box* and disappeared into the mist. The Hawk could only shake his head ruefully and smile.

8

After the two women had left the building the men reconvened in Wolf's living quarters. Sawyer and Hawkins drank tea while Wolf abstained, invoking the names of numerous deities as he cursed tea as a plot of the British to subvert the Emerald Isle, and fixed himself a cup of Irish coffee instead.

"Well," said Sawyer, "that was pleasant."

"Indeed, twas better than expected, I'm thinking," said Wolf.

"I'm still leery. The Mare holds much inside her, and it aches to be released. She does not trust us overmuch. Me especially," replied Hawk.

"Twas quite a show you put on, Hawk. Did ye think she would put ye to the test in such a fairy fashion?" asked Wolf.

"Truth, it was much unexpected, and I had to run to catch up. But had I not stood I feel she would have walked, and taken Elizabeth with her."

"Did she feel anything, do you think? What about her power? The lines of force looked to be of some magnitude," asked Sawyer.

"She felt something, yes. She remarked on it as she left. But she can't put her finger on what's puzzling her. She looks in all the wrong places, thank the Maker. I set blockers as I stood. As to her power, it steams like an untended crock of oats on a hot stove. The power is there–make no mistake! What she put forth as a testing this night wasn't all she had, only all that she could summon and command. I was full up trying to maintain the illusion of equality. Overpowering her now would not serve any useful purpose I can think of."

"'Twas quite a pretty sight, nonetheless. Did ye do the framin', or was it her doin'?" asked Wolf.

"I am happy to say that the images between us were hers and hers alone. I merely followed her lead. She has a gift for imagery, that one. I must admit that the cyclone presentation was mine, and she followed me weave for weave and twist for twist. Quite a woman, our Mare."

"And still she knows you not?" asked Sawyer.

"No, that doorway is shut and locked, and will remain so until better times are upon us," said Hawkins in a quiet voice.

* * *

Elizabeth was thrilled to be allowed to make the drive home, even if her mom *was* in the copilot's seat. She hoped her mother wouldn't be in her critical driver mode, especially tonight, as this would be the first time she had driven after sundown. She walked to the car and unlocked it, then put her radio on the back seat. She got behind the wheel, buckled herself in, and relocked the vehicle. She started the car, familiarizing herself with the gauges and dials, all of which looked different in the darkness. Elizabeth had hardly started her checklist when her mother appeared at the passenger door and motioned for her to unlock her door.

"Okay honey, take us home in safety!"

"You need to buckle your seatbelt, mom. Them's the rules."

"Okay, okay! I'm buckled already! Lead on, McDuff!"

Elizabeth checked her mirrors, put the car into drive and started the journey home. *Her mother was totally relaxed for a change. Or was she totally exhausted? Only one way to find out:* "Mom, are you okay?"

"I'm fine, Elizabeth. The wine just hit me a little harder than I realized. But you're doing well, I see. Your driving is much improved. I could almost fall asleep . . . but I won't!"

"Wow, thanks for the left-handed compliment! That's just what I need to bolster my confidence. But I am getting the hang of this, aren't I?"

"Yes, I admit it. So far you haven't hit anything expensive."

"Mom!"

"Elizabeth?"

"Stop!"

"Okay, okay. Hey, don't forget to turn on Highland Avenue. So, what did you think about our little get-together?"

"Gosh—which part? The thing with you and Mr. Hawkins was awesome! How did you do that? Why did you do that?"

Mary Feye took her time in responding: "The why of it is easy. I had to know if your Mr. Jack Hawkins was truly serious about you and what was going on around you. It was a test. Your Mr. Hawkins passed. He is serious enough to pledge the souls of five hundred people to protect you, and I don't doubt that he would place his soul at the front of the line. But the Ladder Society reminds me much of the Knights Templar, and I fear he would sacrifice much in its name just as they did. As to the how, I just don't really know. The power was just there, and I used it. Used it like it had been in my purse all my life. Funny thing is, the energy you saw tonight was a fraction of what's in the purse. I just can't seem to find the compartment that holds all the rest. What about you? What did you feel when the field centered over you?"

"Well . . . it was weird at first, but then it sort of mellowed out, and it was nice. I felt that no matter where I went there would be someone watching over me, sort of like a guardian angel."

"Good, that's good. Keep that thought because I believe it to be a true one."

"Okay, I will. Mom, what was all that about Mrs. Hurd? I had a little trouble following that. Do you think Mr. Sawyer knows everything that goes on in my school?"

"I wouldn't bet against it. But I think it goes a lot deeper than that. If we had a copy of the Ladder Society membership and did a roll call, I have a sneaking suspicion that when we got to the letter H, Mrs. Hurd would answer up."

"Mom, are you serious? Mrs. Hurd? But she's so . . . normal!"

"And your Mr. Hawkins the custodial engineer wasn't? Didn't one of them say that Mrs. Hurd had only been teaching at your school for two years? I'm beginning to be very wary of coincidences! I guess the moral of the story is to look twice, and question everything and everybody. It shouldn't be too hard for you to find out for sure. Just don't make it obvious. I think we both need to concentrate a little bit more on self-control. Put on your turn signal."

"I got it, Mom. I'll make sure I keep things locked down as best I can. If you can do it, so can I. At least I don't make the walls bulge!"

"True, but please stop the car before *you* make the garage door bulge with the bumper!"

"Oh Mom!"

9

"Hawk, Bear, 'tis forgetful I am: I dinna tell you who was on the wire just now. It was KatyJay from Philadelphia."

"She's the Watcher detailed to Amy, yes?" asked Bear.

"Indeed, and she were *made* while we stood here gabbin' away."

Hawkins was alarmed: "She's one of our best field agents. How could she let herself be compromised so early in the game?"

"Tha be the best part! It seems the young lass has already learned a thing or two about her gold jack! She used it to see KatyJay in the dark from twenty rods distance."

Hawk wasn't satisfied: "That still doesn't explain how she was made—only how she was found. Did KatyJay say anything about that?"

"Aye, that she did. KatyJay said she was *questing* to make sure the girl was inside, seeing as how a car left the house. Twas right past that when she felt that the small one was aware."

"Interesting, that. She picked up on a questing without help from the talisman. Bear, Wolf, it seems that there is a bit more to our little Amy than meets the eye. Bear, sometime tomorrow call EarthStar and have Rodney do some research, run a genealogy on her. Oh, while you're at it, have them run Ms. Wood. Tell Roddy it's a high priority for both."

"No problem. They're five hours ahead of us so I can call as soon as I get to work. Anything else we need to set up?"

"Yes, now that you mention it. Pull KatyJay off of Amy and have her join up with JohnPaul." Hawkins wrote something on a scratch pad. "Send them to this address, to the rear of the alley closest to that street number. Have them remove Spratt's body and dispose of it. Tell them to circle wide and check the area first, and to go in *only* if they can do what needs done without anyone being the wiser. Better to have the body found than to have them found *with* the body."

"Consider it done. That it?" asked Bear.

"One more thing: Have KatyJay come to me at school around noon. Not before. Let her get some sleep first. And switch JohnPaul to Amy until I say so."

"Isn't JohnPaul a bit young for that job? He's not much older than she is."

"I'm sure he's the prefect Watcher, Bear," said Hawk, smiling.

"Hawk, are you sure on this?" questioned Bear.

"Jaysus! How dense can one man be! No wonder ya doan have kids o' yer own."

Comprehension finally dawned on Sawyer's face. "Oh."

"Oh indeed! Now, any more *oh by the ways* and we'll still be here at sunup! Go home the both of ye. Get some sleep. All this will still be here on the morrow."

"True words, Wolf. I'm gone." Hawkins shuddered for a second. "I've dropped the shield, Wolf. Make sure the wards are set after we leave. Goodnight!" Hawk was gone before either man could reply.

The two remaining men just looked at each other. "Well, quite a lot for one night," said Sawyer, "but even though it goes well I don't think all is well with our friend."

"Ye noticed something too, did ye? I think I know what bedevils the man, but only because I'm closer to it, if you take my meaning. He masks it well, but he canna hide it from me."

"I agree, old friend. Since when does The Hawk trip over anything, let alone a tricycle? That limp was of far greater importance than Hawk gave it.

I think he will worry himself to death with the possibilities. But what will be will be. There is no changing that."

"Truth. He canna escape the fate."

"On that somber note I will leave. You okay cleaning up?"

"Aye, go on with ya. Tis little to do. We'll talk tomorrow."

"Good night, Wolf."

"God be with ye."

10

It was well past eleven before Elizabeth finished her nightly routine and was able to crawl into bed. She had already set up her radio on the nightstand, but waited until she had doused the lights before turning it on. After a minute the warm blues and yellows pushed away the darkness, and she was again transfixed with its beauty. Although the radio was on, there was no sound. Evidently Wolf had rigged the audio to come on when the correct song was received. No matter. She was happy just to see the illuminated jackrabbit sitting by her bed.

Elizabeth felt conflicting emotions as she buried deeper into the covers: excitement over what would happen as she slept, weary with all that had happened in the last twenty-four hours, and fear for what might lie ahead in the next few days. She realized that she was evolving into another person.

That much was evident. Living up to the person she was expected to be was another story. As she finally drifted off her last thought was how nice it would be to have a boyfriend to hold her and share her fears.

* * *

Elizabeth was disoriented by the heat of the sun when she awakened. *Awakened?* A ray of sunlight had pierced the ceiling of the room she was in, making a beeline for her face. Elizabeth moved her head from the white light and surveyed her surroundings. This was the first time she was actually aware of what was taking place when she was inside a song. She *knew* this was a dream. Still mentally muddled, she shook off the cobwebs and started to come to terms with what she saw. This was indeed a room if you used the broad sense of the word and had a sense of humor. There were walls, and a roof of sorts. The ceiling was thatched, or covered with sticks or small tree branches, and the walls were composed of crumbling plaster or adobe. The floor was hard dirt, with an old rug or two covering most of the space. There did not seem to be any windows. There was no door, just an opening covered by a blanket. Elizabeth could see no bedroom, kitchen, or bathroom. By the angle of the sun Elizabeth guessed the time to be around 10:00 AM or later. Knowing that just lying on the rug was not in anyone's game plan Elizabeth got up and pulled back the blanket covering the doorframe and stepped outside.

The sunlight outside was dazzling and hit her eyes like a camera flash; Elizabeth was immediately blinded. It took her a full minute to acclimate her irises to the intense light. When she could once again see Elizabeth was amazed at how *far* she could see. She was up high; how far up she couldn't guess. Below her stretched miles of semiarid land, desert almost. Looking to her left and to her right she concluded that she was probably on a butte or mesa of some sort. There wasn't much greenery, and the trees all looked stunted and, well, tired, as though living here was something that had to be endured rather than enjoyed. Even with her elevated position she could see no sign of human habitation save the place she had just come out of. Turning around she inspected the building again and she was no more impressed the second time around. The walls were definitely old, but the roof was recently redone. There was nothing to indicate a source of water or electricity. This was a very primitive structure in a very primitive land. Where, or when, had Bandy sent her? Elizabeth had no idea as to the *when*, but she guessed that the *where* was the American Southwest. She had no clue what she was supposed to do now that she was in this place. It did not seem terribly bright to go wandering far from the building, so she found a partially shaded spot up against a wall of the shack and hunkered down. She would wait.

Elizabeth's patience was rewarded not by the appearance of humans but by the creatures that lived in this harsh place. During the long afternoon she witnessed the emergence of lizards, insects, and the occasional bird, and the disappearance of many of these into the mouths of their waiting predators, much like her chess matches: insect to lizard, lizard to bird, bird to hawk. Unless you were at the top of the food chain Elizabeth could see that this was a very dangerous place for stupid or inattentive creatures. But instead of just being taken off the chessboard you forfeited your life. Even though Elizabeth considered herself to be as close to the pinnacle of the food chain as possible she still vowed to keep her wits about her. She did not want to argue her supremacy against a tarantula with delusions of grandeur. But that force of will could not compete with the baking heat of late afternoon and her precautions were for naught. Ultimately the sun won out. Elizabeth fell asleep. Some time must have passed because Elizabeth was no longer as hot as she had been. In fact she was now in total shade. She stretched and opened her eyes, and came face to face with a pair of cold black eyes with vertical pupils. Elizabeth froze. So did the owner of the eyes that looked back at her.

The snake tasted the air with its tongue, wondering what sort of creature this was, hogging all the shade. The snake was convinced of one thing; this creature was too big to eat. Now it's main concern was whether or not the creature could, or would, hurt him. Most Warm-bloods of this size were incredibly slow and extremely stupid. They almost never watched where they sat or put their feet, and the rattler did not care to be squashed. Deciding that discretion was the greater part of valor, the snake lifted its tail and vibrated its rattles. From experience this usually caused a big Warm-blood to quickly remove itself, the only danger coming from their inability to pick up their feet. But life was a crapshoot, and the snake had already rolled the dice. This time, however, the Warm-blood did not move at all, but remained motionless. Even so the snake felt a vibration nearby, and pulled into itself, facing halfway between the Warm-blood in front of him and the newly perceived threat. If the snake had learned nothing else it knew that rash acts had high costs. Patience was one virtue the snake possessed. He could wait.

While the rattlesnake was checking Elizabeth out she was ransacking her brain trying to remember everything she could about vipers. She could pretty much guess that this was a rattlesnake of some kind; she sincerely doubted the reptile had stolen the rattles on its tail from some other snake. Add the vertical pupils and the triangular-shaped head and she was sure that this snake was venomous. *So much for the identification stage. More important to the moment was what should she do?* The creature must be at least seven feet long. She therefore assumed it was a pretty smart animal to have been able to reach that size without being killed or eaten. The snake had checked her out with his tongue, and was looking at her with those impassive eyes. If it *was* smart then it probably knew better than to waste energy and venom on something it couldn't swallow. What Elizabeth didn't know was whether or not it would strike if she moved slowly away from it. Right now she was almost eyeball to eyeball with it, her head being on ground level. She remembered stories of how animals seemed to be hypnotized by the gaze of a snake, and she could well believe it. Right now she couldn't move a muscle. In essence, the rattlesnake decided her course of action, or lack of one. Since she couldn't move anyway she concluded that her only option was to wait it out. As she and the snake had their staring contest Elizabeth was reminded of the scene in *Raiders of the Lost Ark*, where Indiana Jones was face to face with a cobra. The only difference was that Harrison Ford had a piece of glass between him and the snake–she remembered seeing the reflection. But she had only air. There seemed to be no impasse in the contest . . . and then the snake blinked, figuratively speaking. Ever so slowly the rattler sat back on itself, and swung its head to a point perhaps thirty degrees to her right. The snake's right eye still looked in her direction even as the head was pointed in a different direction. Elizabeth did not sense the presence of the person who spoke softly to her, so mesmerized was she by the viper in front of her.

"You do well to imitate the stone, Little Sister. My brother has little tolerance for awkward mammals. I will talk to him, and let him know me. As I do this, slowly sit up. Do not talk–it will disturb us." The owner of the soft voice appeared from around the corner of the building. He approached the rattlesnake from an angle, softly talking as he walked. As for the snake, it merely watched the man's progress. When the man was within two feet of the snake he squatted down, continuing to talk in a soft singsong language that Elizabeth could not understand.

The big rattler watched the Warm-blood approach. It walked carefully. It would not step on him. He listened with his tongue, and felt the old words that were given to his kind in the early times. This was a Warm-blood that has not forgotten The Way. No harm will come from it–no harm will I do. The snake did not understand the word friend. One word did it know and understand: BROTHER. The grandfather snake rested his head, and waited.

The man laid out his hand, and the snake placed his head in his palm. More soft words were spoken. Then the snake uncoiled itself, and moved in Elizabeth's direction.

"Do not speak, Little Sister. Do not move quickly. My brother does not yet know you. Let him perceive you in his way. If your heart is pure no harm will come to you."

Elizabeth had no trouble obeying the request. She couldn't move if she wanted to. The rattlesnake came up to her, and flicked its tongue in her direction many times. Satisfied, the snake maneuvered its seven feet of length into Elizabeth's lap, and for all intents and purposes, fell asleep. Elizabeth didn't quite know what to do. She wasn't *snakeaphobic* but this was beyond the pale. "What should I do?" she asked in a very quiet voice.

The man smiled. "My brother is content to enjoy the shade with you, and share the warmth of your body. My brother is old, and tires easily. Let him rest."

"Can, may I touch him?"

The man spoke soft words that Elizabeth could not hear. "My brother would be honored. He now knows of you and feels safe. He wishes to know how you wished to be called so that he may tell his children's children of this day."

"My name is Elizabeth."

More soft words were spoken, and the man turned again to Elizabeth. "My brother says you are wise to give the name which others know. He asks that you keep your true name close to your heart, so that others may not learn of it and have power over you."

Elizabeth felt a tad foolish using someone she had never meant to interpret what she said to a snake, which was a paradox since snakes didn't have ears to begin with. But, when in Rome, or a dream . . . "Please thank your brother. I will keep my name close." Elizabeth took her left hand and slowly ran it across the snake's body, staying well away from the reptile's head. As her confidence grew she was able to appreciate the dry, elastic feel of the reptile's skin. With water at a premium in this arid land, slimy skin was not an option. As she became comfortable with the viper sitting in her lap she inspected the man in front of her. He still had not moved from his squatting position. Elizabeth wondered how he was able to maintain that difficult pose for such a long time. He was not overlarge, probably about six feet tall–it was hard to tell exactly with him squatting and the tall black hat he was wearing didn't make judging his height any easier. His clothes were rough, ranch-style, with western boots, jeans, and long sleeved shirt. He wore leather gloves that matched the color of his oddly shaped headgear. The nearest she could come to describing his hat was that it looked like the one Hoss Cartwright wore on Bonanza, only black instead of fawn colored, and adorned with a beaded band and a single feather. It was not the type of hat the average person could wear and get away with. On this guy it looked like it belonged.

As the hat was a mixture of cowboy felt and Indian beadwork, so the man seemed a composite of White man and Red man. His face was lined and beginning to seam from the wind and the heat but Elizabeth guessed him to be in his early to mid thirties. His face was round, and dark, but not the deep mahogany of pure Native American heritage. Although surely politically incorrect, the expression *Half-breed* sprang first to her mind.

"You have great power in your family, Little Sister. Grandfather Snake does not have much tolerance at his age. He has told me that you are welcome here, as were your ancestors before you. Your family is not unknown to his people. Nor to my people, either. I also give you welcome."

"Uh, thank you. Do you have a name? Or is that a secret?"

He smiled. "The local people call me Bill, or Billy. There are other names, but this will do for a time, as will Elizabeth for you. I must apologize for not being here to greet you when you arrived. I was . . . delayed in town."

"There's a town? Where? How did you know I was coming?" asked Elizabeth.

"Yes, there is a town, with lights, running water, and cars. The town lies about 12 klicks to the east. As to your arrival, yes, I was advised of your coming. The Hawk is well known hereabouts, and his name is honored. The Hawk has asked that I help you study. His words were: *"Teach her all that you are able in the time allotted us. Aubrey is stronger than she looks; she bends but does not break. Lead her to The Way, and show her the door. The rest shall be her's to choose."*

"Billy, Hawk never told me what it was that I was to learn! Do you know?"

"Yes, Little Sister: Everything!" Bill laughed and stood up. "Now, say goodbye to my brother. We should leave here while there is still some light left to us."

Elizabeth reached under the coils of the snake and gently laid him off to one side. She got up, then went back down to her knees and spoke to the serpent: "Grandfather, thank you for sharing your warmth with me. I will remember this time always."

The big rattler just seemed to lie on the rapidly cooling ground, watching as the Warm-bloods walked down the game trail to the base of the mesa. If Elizabeth had looked back she would have seen something no naturalist had ever witnessed: a rattlesnake that looked like it was smiling. *This Warm-blood was special,* thought the snake. *Because she is special she will find much trouble here. The Warm-blood called Billy Jack would be wise to train her quickly.* Letting his thoughts drift away like the dust in his trail, Grandfather Snake headed for someplace warm.

* * *

Elizabeth followed Billy down the trail to where he had parked his vehicle, an old jeep. They climbed aboard and bounced their way to a sheep trail that eventually led them to a county road. Billy did not say a word the entire trip. Neither did Elizabeth. The road was too rough for the kind of conversation she wanted to have. Intellectually she knew what was happening. She had fallen asleep, been induced to this place by a prearranged song, and was now living the song as reality. Only the reality was hard to believe. In reality, how often do you pet a rattle-snake like a Siamese cat? She couldn't remember a reality where snakes talked to you, either. Keeping all the pieces of *dream* reality separate from *awake* reality was a real pain. If the rules were different here she had better learn them quickly. The penalty might be too horrible to imagine.

After three miles of hard surface road a town came into view. It wasn't much of anything, just a common area in the center–irrigated no doubt–there was green grass, and maybe half a dozen streets going east/west and maybe ten going north/south. They didn't stop in town. With the sun mostly at their back they traveled another five miles, on and off road, finally stopping at the junction of Nowhere and Nothing. Billy Jack shut off the jeep and turned to Elizabeth. "This is home, Little Sister. Grab a bag of groceries and follow me."

If the jeep ride was painful, then the walk was torture by comparison. The bag of groceries (2 bags, actually) seemed to weigh 100 pounds by the time they had gone one hundred yards. Billy was likewise loaded down with supplies. He carried the additional burden of a knapsack and a rifle. Billy had the very annoying habit of telling her that his place was just up ahead, but every time they reached *up ahead* there was nothing there, only Billy Jack saying his place was just *around the bend*. Elizabeth wanted a break badly, but there was no way she would give him the satisfaction. She might pass out and be eaten by coyotes but she wouldn't ask to stop. After what seemed like ten miles–later she would learn it wasn't even two–Billy Jack stopped and waited for Elizabeth to catch up. She was breathing heavily, her wrists were welted from the twine handles of the grocery bags, and she was thirsty beyond belief. When she came up alongside Billy she wanted to cry. When she saw his *place* she thought better of crying and decided she might just as well drop dead on the spot. She didn't know what she had expected but this was definitely not it. With the exception of a better roof, a small bedroom inside and some extra square feet of interior space, Billy Jack's home was a clone of the building they had just come from. There was no door, nor was there glass in the windows. From the look of things there had *never* been glass in the windows. *What a dump!*

Billy Jack must have seen the disappointment in her eyes because he finally stopped and talked for the first time since they parked the jeep.

"What do you think of my home, Little Sister?" Elizabeth could not see him smile.

"It's, uh, very . . . nice, Billy."

"You aren't disappointed? Maybe hoping for a teepee?"

"Oh no, this is much better. Uh, does it have a bathroom?"

"Of course, Little Sister! Just follow the path around back."

"Thanks." Elizabeth walked around the adobe shack and hiked the trail to an outhouse set up against the hillside. After checking the toilet for indigenous life forms she sat down, and tried very, very hard to wake herself up.

11

Time passed for Elizabeth in this stark place of scorpions and reptiles, sun and heat, dust devils and sand. For the most part Elizabeth just did her best to try and survive the day. There did not seem to be any great hurry in Billy–his plans were his own and he rarely shared them with her. Billy Jack never came out and said: *This is what you are to learn*. Rather, they went on extended journeys through the countryside, Billy leading, Elizabeth trailing along. Billy would stop and point something out–a creature, a plant, sometimes just a rock. He would talk about it, what it was, what it did, how it meshed with the things around it. They went to watering holes to watch the animals that came to drink. They stood on mesas and watched thunderstorms stampede across the land. They walked everywhere. Elizabeth at first tried to keep track of the days but soon time melted into itself and she gave up the count. It was Billy himself who gave her a reference point, stating that they had used up their monthly supply of food and would need to get more in town.

Hiking the two miles back to the jeep was not nearly the chore it had been a month ago. When they reached the vehicle she was breathing normally. Even the rough ride into town did not feel as bone jarring as it had the last time. Elizabeth had thought the sight of civilization would be like opening a Christmas present. Instead the slightly down-at-the-heels town just depressed her. Billy Jack parked them in front of the small grocery store. They entered and she helped Billy pick out the groceries and load them back into the jeep. Billy asked if she minded waiting while he went over to the bank. Elizabeth said she was fine just sitting in the jeep.

Elizabeth didn't know what day it was but the town seemed pretty lively. *Perhaps it was Saturday?* There were people about, music played, and cars buzzed by. Just as she was about to doze off someone spoke to her.

"Hey, baby, whatcha doing in Billy Jack's jeep? You his new squaw? Ha ha!" The speaker was a boy about seventeen or eighteen, dark haired, and not bad looking in a *I know I'm a hottie* kind of way.

Usually Elizabeth did not answer creeps like this. If you ignored them they would just go away. But not this one. He decided to stay. "Hey, I'm talkin' to you. You gone deaf, squaw girl?"

Elizabeth looked out from under the beat-up western hat Billy had given her. "I can hear you. The way you're shouting they can hear you in the next county. Go away, please."

"Who you think you are, talkin' to me that way. You know who my father is?"

"Why, don't *you* know who your father is?" Elizabeth couldn't hold it in. The heat made her irritable.

The boy's face reddened when he realized what Elizabeth had implied. "Listen you, we don't take that kinda crap from Indians around here. Where the hell you think you are–California?"

"Actually, I don't really care where I am as long as it's away from you. And I'm not an Indian. Indians come from India, a subcontinent on the other side of Africa. But if you're a white boy then I think I'd rather be a Native American." This guy was a real ass.

"Native American? Right. You may think you can pass, and maybe you can in *Callyfornia*, but your red skin shows up real good here."

Elizabeth started to laugh but stopped. Now that this clown had mentioned her skin it became obvious to her that a month of outdoor living had darkened her skin to a burnished red. In the direct sunlight she could possibly be mistaken for someone with Indian blood. Having had her share of slurs from fat to ugly to smart she was in no mood to add a racial epithet to the list. "Move along, boy. You bother me. Hit the road before I scalp you."

"You don't talk to a Poser like that, bitch!" He swung his arm back and slapped Elizabeth across the face. *Jesus, did that sting!* Elizabeth tried to scramble out of the jeep as the boy pulled back to hit her again. At the top of his swing his arm stopped, and was immobile.

Grasping the boy's fist in his hand, Billy Jack smiled down on the boy: "Bernard, you just never give up, do you? Now what makes you think you can hit this young woman, a lady that's just minding her own business? Are you just inherently stupid, or do you work at it on weekends?"

"Stay out of this, Billy Jack. My old man will—"

"Will what, Bernard? Sanction assault and battery in the middle of town? Do you think even he would back your foolishness in this? Look around, Bernard. They call all those people who saw this *witnesses*." Billy increased the pressure on the boy's fist until he was forced to kneel on the ground. Billy wasn't even sweating.

"Elizabeth, are you okay?"

"I think the little bastard gave me a black eye. Who does he think he is, anyway?"

"He thinks he is the *Heir Apparent* to the Poser Empire hereabouts. What he is is a bully and a bigot and a coward. Bernard, I think you should apologize to Elizabeth. How about it?"

"I ain't"–Billy applied more pressure to his wrist-lock. "Okay, okay! I'm sorry." Billy pulled the boy up on his feet and whispered in his ear. Elizabeth couldn't hear what he said but it must not have been good news because Bernard's knees buckled slightly and his face went white. Billy released the boy. "Go home, Bernard. Go home now." Bernard went.

Billy Jack went over to Elizabeth: "Let me look. Hmmm . . . nothing a cold beefsteak and a week of time won't cure. Let's get out of here before Bernard remembers all the guns his daddy owns."

The ride back out was a reflective one for Elizabeth. She didn't like being hit–not one bit. It irked her not to know how to fight back. Did guys go to a school to learn how to slap a girl, or was it on-the-job training? She should put ice on her eye, but she hadn't seen any for a month. Already the swelling was starting to close her eye. As she sat nursing the pain in her eye Elizabeth thought about her father's side of the family. Her mom had said little about his ancestry, only that he was wise in Native American ways. *Maybe that boy was right. I might actually have some of that blood in me.* That thought alone was enough to ease the pain of her eye. Some of it, anyway.

Even with her eye throbbing Elizabeth had no problem carrying her share of the food up the trail to the hogan. By the time everything was put away it was near dark. Billy built a fire while Elizabeth put a match to the kerosene lantern, opened up some Dinty Moore beef stew, and laid out some dough on the Dutch oven. They talked as they waited for the food to heat.

"You didn't much like getting slapped today, did you, Little Sister?"

"No, and double no! It sucks! It's not just the pain part, either. It's like you just get whacked and you're powerless to do anything because the other person is bigger and stronger. No, I didn't like the feeling at all." Elizabeth stared into the fire.

"Do you think that it is something you must accept? Or is it something that you must endure because you are female?"

"Billy, that boy was twice my size! What was I to do? Get the tire iron out and break his arm?"

"If need be, Little Sister. There are very few things as a *fair* fight. Maybe in professional boxing, where the weights of the boxers are measured, and each boxer fights within his own weight class. But in the real world it is never equal. It is your job to make the contest equal, or better yet, to your advantage."

"So how does that happen, Billy?"

"Like anything of value, you must want it, and seek it, and sacrifice for it. Is this something you desire? Would you work to such a goal?"

Elizabeth thought for a moment. "If it meant not being afraid, of being able to stand up for myself, yes. I would work hard for that."

"So be it. We shall start tomorrow. Let's eat now. Tomorrow will come soon enough."

12

Tomorrow did come, and the tomorrow after that, and the next and the next. Elizabeth realized that she had never known the meaning of the word exhausted. At night she collapsed on her sleeping bag, hearing nothing until awakened by Billy Jack in the pre-dawn hour. The hikes never stopped. She carried rocks. She sweated until she felt like a dried fig. They climbed rock faces, with rope and without. This was Marine Boot Camp without benefit of solace from her fellow sufferers. Billy never yelled. Neither did he ever say a harsh word to her. He also did not wait for her. If she fell behind she caught up while Billy took a breather. Then they were off again. In the early morning hours she was given stretching exercises. In time she stretched parts of her body that had begged her to be left alone. What little fat that remained on her body dissipated, converted to energy. In the end all that was left was the frame that was Elizabeth, nothing more. It was with this framework that Billy Jack began her education.

"Little Sister, in the time we have together I cannot teach you all there is to know about *The Way*, only set you on the path and help you start the journey. If we were to have the luxury of years it would be simpler, but even here there are constraints of time. If things are resolved for you in a good way, then maybe you will return to this place, and learn more. Until that time I can only give you the bones of what you need, and hope for the best." Here Billy Jack paused, making a mental decision.

"In your world time is so very short. You must return there soon, with tools of survival. It is contrary to my wishes to teach you what you need to know without grounding you more firmly in *The Way*. One without the other is dangerous. You do not give a pistol to someone without first teaching them firearm safety. Nor do you throw someone in a lake without first teaching them to swim." Billy paused. "The Hawk has told me not to worry, that you will not drown. So be it. Let it begin."

Elizabeth didn't really understand what Billy was talking about. He seemed upset in one way, yet mollified that in the end everything would work out. For her part, she just felt lost.

Billy spoke as if to a great audience: "The Beginning has many tellers, as many as the tribes on this land. I cannot tell you which of the tellings is the true one, or if all of them are true. Whether the Great Spirit came to us riding on a turtle, spoke to us from a burning bush, or revealed herself through Trickster Coyote makes no difference. The end result is now, and forever has been, *The Way*. *The Way* does not advance with a Crusade. Its forward motion gains no speed by parades in Londonderry. You cannot serve it by planting bombs in churches, or synagogues, or burning crosses in the middle of the night. *The Way* has many paths, but they all lead to the same place. Violence, death, and pain are but detours, nothing more than blind alleys that harbor the dark and the Ungood. Little Sister, what I teach you is not an end unto itself; it is part of a larger whole. It is only of necessity that I give you the tools to survive your world. Please think on that word: Necessity . . . necessary. That which is *essential* for you. Listen well, Little Sister: *These tools will destroy you if you stray from the path!*" Billy Jack let that sink in, and then continued:

"The skills that you will learn, the techniques of self preservation, are used for defense. Use these tools in an offensive manner and they will subvert you in time. Go in a good way, and they will serve you. Turn your back on the Path, and you will be the servant." Elizabeth looked confused so Billy Jack tried an analogy.

"Think of your game of baseball. It is a sport of rare violence, one that uses strategy and skill as its hallmark. Where did most men learn this game? They learned in Little League, or school, or just in a pickup game played in a vacant lot or a city street. It is called the *game* of baseball. Something to enjoy, both as a participant and a spectator. Yet this too can be corrupted. When the object ceases to be enjoyment of the game itself, and becomes only about winning, you are lost. Little League coaches that yell at their young charges, parents that scream at the umpires–they no longer see the game, only the end result. Winning at any cost is not winning. Fighting for the sake of fighting is no coup, no matter what the Old Ones say. Do not fight or kill because you can. Do so only if you must. Do you understand the difference, Little Sister?"

Elizabeth had to think before answering. "Yes, I think so. That Machiavelli wasn't right; the end *doesn't* always justify the means? That if you lie or cheat or hurt people without thinking or caring, the end result you wish to achieve will be corrupted. You can't make a good tasting pie if some of the apples are rotten to begin with?"

"Yes, Little Sister. It is not a hard lesson to understand, only difficult some times to remember. Now we work."

They started with their stretching exercises, pulling, twisting, and arching until Elizabeth felt six inches taller. When Billy was satisfied that they were sufficiently warmed up he started the first day of Elizabeth's martial arts training.

* * *

If Elizabeth had thought she understood exhaustion she was overestimating her abilities of comprehension. What she had experienced before was a mere annoyance compared to the total weariness she now greeted at the end of every day. Even her hair was tired. That first week she quit a dozen times a day, and rehired herself a dozen and one. Every single thing she did correctly was offset by three mistakes in timing, balance, or technique. She wanted to scream at least once an hour, but to whom? Billy never so much as raised his voice at her. If she missed a kick, he shook his head. Poorly held arms, he placed them in the correct position. A bad stance, he quickly and efficiently swept her off her feet, then helped her up again. Being mad at Billy was like trying to cut silk with a wooden sword—he offered no resistance to her anger. Billy Jack gave her no incentive to excel. Executing her moves was the reward. It wasn't until her second week that she successfully achieved her first move, a correctly applied block. For this she did receive a reward of sorts. She was given an extra half-hour that evening to wash up at the natural tank they used as a water source. Elizabeth did not need prompting. She was out the door of the shack in seconds. She reached the rock outcropping and stripped immediately. Using the old pot they kept there as a ladle, Elizabeth poured water over herself half a dozen times before she got out her small bar of soap and lathered up. She washed everything that needed washing–which was everything–allowing the dying sun to dry her. Usually she was reduced to scrubbing away the sweat with sand, and that was so far from pleasant that you couldn't see it with binoculars. Water was a luxury in this part of Arizona, this natural cistern and spring being the source of life for much of the wildlife in the area. Because of this, as soon as Elizabeth was dry she headed back down the path, allowing other creatures access to the water hole that was upstream from the tank.

When she returned to the hogan Billy was nowhere to be seen. As he was want to do Billy disappeared for hours at a time. Elizabeth knew better than to ask where he went, but that didn't stop her from wondering. While she waited for his return Elizabeth took the time to stoke the cooking fire and start dinner. *What she wouldn't give for a microwave!* At least tonight the food was store-bought: the last two nights had been special-ties of the house, mainly tubers and things with names she was glad not to know. Waiting for the water to boil she brought Billy's Winchester into her lap and started cleaning it. Rust wasn't much of a problem here but sand was; the gritty stuff got into everything. Before this experience with Billy she would never have looked at a rifle, let alone fire and clean one. Billy had made her assemble and disassemble his weapons by feel. Having no electric lights, this was almost a necessity. He took her out to an improvised shooting range, letting her fire the weapons to experience the shock load of the recoil first, then working with her on sighting, stance, and accuracy. Since her eyes had improved she found it easy to hold and acquire the target, more often than not nailing what she shot at. On one level her skill pleased her. Elizabeth always liked to conquer new things. On another level she was disturbed by the utter impersonality of the bullet. A bullet would never veer away from its target on its own accord, no matter how inappropriate that target might be. Coming from fifteen years of being what Elizabeth considered a coward, now her preference for in-close fighting amazed her. Was this part of *The Way,* or just her natural inclination now that she had a choice?

Cleaning the Winchester repeater was calming in a strange, detached sort of way. She could feel the allure of the cold metal, the smooth feel of the ratcheting mechanism as she worked the receiver, the intense *weight,* real and imagined, of the rifle.

Even she was not immune to the siren's call of life and death: *Take me up and you can be a God!* The sensation was strong enough to make Elizabeth release the weapon from her hands. She studied it as it lay in her lap. Yes, in the wrong hands, in weak hands, this song could obliterate reason. Despite this, there was an underlying beat to the song, albeit soft, which stated: *I am but a tool* over and over again. Evidently there were two sides to this particular record. Clearly, it was up to the individual which song they listened to. Elizabeth hoped she would never make the wrong choice.

Elizabeth went ahead and finished preparing the evening meal, eating hers and leaving the rest for Billy. He would return when he returned, and not sooner. She banked the fire and settled into her sleeping bag, content to be alone in this land of stark reality and surreal existence. Fading into sleep, she willed herself not to fail.

13

Elizabeth's days had turned into weeks and the weeks to months. She knew she was in the *Otherlands* but still found it difficult to equate the time difference. While a second may go by in the *Here and Now*, perhaps a day could pass here. Yet how would she know? These were questions that were better answered in the *Here and Now*. Right now–which wasn't *Now*, really–she was here–which wasn't *Here*, really–not there, which really *was* the *Here and Now* . . . *never mind!!!!!* Elizabeth gave up trying. She started over. Right now she would just pay attention to the business at hand. Half of each day was filled with breathing exercises, stretching, running, climbing, and all manner of physical adventures. The other half of the day was spent learning everything Billy Jack could teach her about the science of martial arts. He was the ultimate perfectionist. He thought nothing of spending an entire afternoon on one move or one stance. Nothing less than the best was good enough. His philosophy was simple: *Know what you know and use what you know.* He never wasted time teaching her tricky moves or flying kicks or any of a hundred things she had seen teenage ninja turtles do or white-haired masters demonstrate in kung fu movies. She never had to *wax on/wax off* anything. He had explained all of this to her early in her training: "Little Sister, I will teach you very few things. Most of what I teach you has little flair and even less flamboyance. But when we are done, what you *do* learn you will know better than anyone you will meet in open combat. Others will show you the options. Here you get only the standard equipment!" Elizabeth had laughed at the analogy. It made her miss her driver education teacher, Mr. Petrotski.

Elizabeth knew her training was coming to its conclusion by the change in Billy Jack. He smiled more, his manner was more relaxed, and he stopped teaching her new things. Instead of new punches, he concentrated on refining the moves she thought she had already perfected. It was on their 5th trip into town for groceries that signaled the end of her time with Billy Jack. She hadn't seen it then but in retrospect it was obvious. The previous three times Billy had never let her out of his sight. Come to think of it, except for the first day, he had never left her side, even for a moment. This time things were different.

"Little Sister, will you fill the supply list while I make a quick trip over to the sheriff's office? I won't be long."

"Sure, I've got the list with me, Billy." Elizabeth quickly entered the store, grabbed a cardboard box, and started filling it with the listed supplies. As she worked she glanced out the window and was able to see Billy talking with Sheriff Cole in front of his office. Billy was the Law on Indian Land since he was a tribal policeman, but he had no authority here. The opposite was true for Sheriff Cole. Evidently there was mutual respect between the two lawmen.

The last thing on the list was a mineral block that Billy put out for the mustangs that ranged through the area. The store kept the heavy blocks on the back porch and since the clerk must have been seventy-five years old and someone's grandmother, Elizabeth said she would get it.

Sidling past the sacks and boxes stacked in the storeroom Elizabeth made her way out the back door to the rear overhang that served as protection from the sun. As she wrestled a block from the stack she heard voices yelling in the open lot behind the store. She looked up and saw two boys throwing rocks at a tree. Elizabeth was intrigued. She left the mineral block and walked up to where the two boys were standing. Now that she was closer she saw that the boys were older than she thought. They were at least eighteen, maybe older. The two were so intent on their rock throwing that they never saw her approach. She was almost beside them when she saw what the big deal was. Curled up around the tree were two small, bewildered rattlesnakes. They were ill equipped to defend themselves against flying rocks. As each rock landed they turned at the vibration only to be fooled again by the next missile. Elizabeth was still not especially snake-loving, but in this event the snakes were outmatched. Before she could think about what she was doing she ceased being a spectator and became a participant.

"Hey, come on you guys, they aren't hurting anyone," she said.

The two turned to her, startled. Then they laughed. "What's it to you, girl? Ain't nuthin' but a coupla rattlers," said the larger of the two.

"You're right. It's nothing to me. But it sure is something to those snakes over there. Just leave them alone and they'll go away on their own."

"Screw you ya little papoose. Didn't your daddy teach you that the only good snake is a dead snake? Or don't you know your daddy? Ha, that was a gooddun, weren't it Dino?"

Dino smiled but didn't answer. He just picked up another rock and chucked it at the snakes. It barely missed one of the rattlers.

"I asked you not to do that. Please." Elizabeth was becoming upset.

"So what you gonna do if we don't?" said the big one named Dino.

"Stop you."

"Yeah, right. Little ol' you gonna stop the three of us? That's a laugh!" said Dino.

Three? There were only two of–

"Well, well, well. Hello again, squaw girl. How's your eye?"

Elizabeth spun around and faced Bernard Poser. He had three bottles of Coke in his hands. "You and that mouth sure do get around. You know, I bet I can think of better things to do with it than talk." Because her attention was on Poser she failed to notice the other two boys moving behind her until they had each grabbed one of her arms.

By now Elizabeth's temperature had popped her internal thermometer. She owed this guy big time. She didn't need him to remind her of the black eye he had given her. But being provoked into something was not what she had been taught. She remembered Billy's words: *Never play on the opponent's home court if you can help it.* Good advice, but she'd be damned if she'd allow these punks to stone those two snakes to death just for the fun of it. Maybe she could get him to play on *her* court.

"You know, *Posey*, every time I see you all you ever do is talk, talk, talk. Boys, do you ever see *Posey* here with a girl? Or does he just like to hang out with the guys. Know what I mean? I bet he likes to spend a lot of time with you two, doesn't he?"

All three of them watched as Bernard's face turned bright red. When he dropped the two Cokes in his left hand it startled both of Elizabeth's captors. It was all the edge she needed. Targeting the boy to her right, Elizabeth executed a low sidekick to the right, making contact with the smaller assailant's left knee. The sideways force of the blow buckled the boy and put him to the ground. The swift move surprised Dino so much that he leaned forward to get a better view. That was the big youth's undoing. Ignoring the first boy, Elizabeth moved her right arm across her body and cupped the back of Dino's neck, forcing his head downward. At the same time she raised her right knee, which found Dino's nose. It broke on contact, forcing Dino to release Elizabeth's left arm. Using her now free left hand she grabbed his right palm and rotated it ninety degrees, breaking him down even further. When Elizabeth had Dino bent to waist level she slammed down on his exposed shoulder blade with her right hand. The sound of his shoulder dislocating was clearly audible. Dino's face was buried in the dust. He had been rendered ineffective in two seconds flat. Feeling her other attacker rising, Elizabeth spun in place and delivered a back-spinning hook kick. She laid it perfectly across the side of his head.

The sound it made connecting rivaled the pop of poor Dino's shoulder. The boy went down without a sound. Not waiting to admire her handiwork, Elizabeth regained her fighting stance and faced her last tormentor.

Bernard was furious and incredulous at the same time. *However did that little red bitch do that?* If he had taken just the tiniest bit of time to think he might have realized that if she could do that to the two of them *what could she do to him?* But he didn't. Bernard allowed his emotions to overcome what little good sense he had. It took two smacks against the table but the Coke bottle that was still in his right hand broke. Bernard put it in front of him like a knife blade and headed for Elizabeth.

Elizabeth backed up. *Oops! Time to switch tactics!* "Bernard, think about this a minute." Elizabeth was now speaking in a soft voice. "Before it was just a little fight. This is assault with a deadly weapon, Bernard. You could go to jail over this. Is that the smart way to go here?" Elizabeth was using all the charm she possessed.

"The only way I want to go is into you with this Coke bottle." Bernard's eyes were slightly less glazed but still unfocused.

"Listen, Bernard, I'm sorry, okay? I didn't mean what I said before. These guys know better, right? I'm sure you have plenty of girlfriends. You don't want to go to jail just because a girl made you mad, do you?"

Bernard stopped his forward motion. He didn't lower the bottle. Instead he just looked at Elizabeth. "You know, you're right. You ain't worth it. Not here, not now." He threw the bottle at Elizabeth's feet. He looked at her with contempt, spit in her general direction, spun around on his heels and ran smack dab into the chest of Sheriff Cole.

Billy Jack was leaning against a shed post. He was smiling at the boy. "Bernard, you have to be the luckiest little bastard on earth. Standing down is the first smart thing I ever saw you do. Come on, Elizabeth, I'll buy you an ice cream cone."

14

Biologists, botanists, and zoologists living in the 21st century have still not managed to solve all the riddles in the Kingdom of Life that resides on Planet Earth. One of the mysteries still to be revealed was the method in which communication from being to being is encoded and transmitted. How plants connected with one another, why cetaceans whistled, what one loon said to her mate are still puzzling enigmas to science. *But Grandfather Snake cared not a wit for enigmas or conundrums, or science, for that matter. Fact was he didn't know what a cetacean was. Nevertheless, within the hour he was aware of what had transpired in town. His time-sense was hazy but he surely remembered thinking that this particular Warm-blood would find trouble. Or was it that trouble would find her? That was the trouble with*

Age. If you were lucky you achieved wisdom. That was a good thing. The irony was you forgot what it was that made you wise in the first place.

Grandfather Snake didn't need to be a philosopher to survive. He knew his time on the Wheel was almost over anyway. But what he could do was pass on what had happened to his den-kin. From there it would spread to the lairs of all the tribes of his people. From generation to generation would it pass. Until such time as the Wheel stopped turning, the Nation of the Legless Ones would honor and protect the Warm-blood named Aubrey, and call her Sister.

Grandfather Snake headed for the denning place that served as hogan for his family. He needed to get something, and while he was there he wanted to talk to his den-daughter. He was pretty sure he had advised her not to let the twins go into town. He let out a long snake sigh. He couldn't remember. But when the twins returned, he thought he might smack his two grandchildren on the rattles just to be sure they remembered, even if he didn't.

* * *

That evening was her last with Billy Jack in his Arizona hideaway. He fixed a special meal for them— all store-bought food including canned pears for dessert. *Nothing like dessert in the desert with the stars as your night-light, thought Elizabeth.*

Although never totally satisfied, Billy at least seemed content. "Little Sister, your time ends here. I am very proud of what you accomplished in such a short time. If we were to quantify your work I would say we jammed five years of lessons into as many months. I don't have any colored belts to give you, and little enough ceremony unless you consider pears as ceremonial. Today you took your final exam. I could not be more pleased. Your decision to use reason instead of force, to subdue your desire for revenge was admirable. The sheriff will deal with the three young fools you encountered today. Sooner or later, and I would bet sooner, they will be back to working their little mischiefs. They are not immune to the turning of the Wheel. Overseas we had a saying: *Payback's a Medevac.* Your generation would say: *What goes around, comes around.* No matter what the wording the meaning is the same: You reap what you sow. Today Bernard has sowed a bitter crop. I fear he will harvest nothing but chaff. There is an old saying attributed to the Spanish that goes: *Revenge is a dish best served cold.* I would like to take that one step further and add *or not at all.* It is good advice. I only hope I am able to follow it myself." Billy seemed to drift off on his own thoughts, then returned.

"No matter! Too much philosophy can sour even the sweetest dessert. Little Sister, I have a little something for you." Elizabeth tried to protest but

Billy would have none of it. "Please honor me by accepting this token of respect."

Billy Jack got up and went over to an old army footlocker that he used for storage. He opened it, lifted out the inside tray and removed a package the size of a dinner plate. Billy returned with the gift and sat back down on the blanket that served as their carpeting. He handed the item to Elizabeth without ceremony, as if to say that the gift was nothing. Elizabeth took the offering with both hands. The box was wrapped in comics from the Sunday newspaper. On the top she could see Lucy trying to once again entice Charlie Brown to kick the football. The paper wasn't taped but rather held together with ribbons made of rawhide. She undid the knotted laces and set aside the funny papers and lacing and opened the box. Elizabeth knew what the present was immediately.

Using both hands she gently removed the kelly green hat from the box that held it. She could see that the original insignia had been removed. Another emblem had been embroidered and beaded in its place. Now the beret sported green shamrocks and a blue thistle, which intertwined over and around the horns of a buffalo skull. The patch was edged with the four primary colors of the Wheel: Yellow for fire, blue for water, red for earth, and white for sky. It was arguably the most wonderful thing she had ever been given.

"Oh, Billy, this is beautiful! However did you do it?"

Billy laughed: "We Injuns good at beadwork. Sorry, I can't take credit for it although I'd like to. I took it over to the Freedom School. Jean did it for me. And for you."

"But this is your beret, isn't it?" she asked.

"Yes, it was mine. I treasured it above all things once upon a time. Back when it's meaning was pure and bright. Through the years it got tarnished and its symbolism distorted. Now it has a new banner, and a new owner. Perhaps you can restore it to what it once was." Billy Jack faded off on her again to that other place, but not for long. "So wear it wisely, Little Sister."

"I will, Billy. I promise. Shall I try it on?"

Billy smiled mischievously. "Absolutely!"

Elizabeth lifted the green beret up to her head and when she did she heard the sound of a rattlesnake. She quickly put the beret down only to hear the sound again. Elizabeth looked to her left and right but could not see a snake anywhere. What she did see was Billy Jack laughing his butt off.

"Wha . . . ?" was all she could get out of her mouth. Billy Jack got himself back together, wiped his eyes, and pointed to her new headgear. "I forgot to tell you. There's another gift for you! Pick the beret back up!"

Elizabeth did as she was told. Securely tied to the rear of the beret by a six inch piece of black rawhide was a set of rattles. She lifted the rawhide thong and jiggled it; the snake rattles clattered away in a most menacing manner.

"Please! I couldn't resist. You don't have to wear them on the beret if you don't want to. Personally I think they go rather well. And before you ask I'll tell you. They are a gift from an old friend. Believe it or not they come with instructions. You have been inducted into the Snake Clan and have been named *QuickStrike* in the speech of the Legless Ones. They would have named you *Quickhands* but they have no word in their language for hands. The rattles you hold are sacred to the Clan. They are very, very old and contain great power. Should you have need you but have to shake the rattles. Those of the Clan that are able will come to your aid. This is very powerful stuff, Little Sister. In all of time there exists but four of these medicine rattles. One set has been lost. Two are in the world. You hold the fourth."

Elizabeth was stunned. "I can't take this, really. There must be a mistake somewhere. I'm not even sixteen years old! Why would anyone give this to me?"

"First off, it is not *anyone* that gives this to you. My brother, Grandfather Snake, is the Giver. Do you want to give the rattles back and tell him he has made a poor choice? I didn't think so. Secondly, it might please you to know that the two snakes you saved from being stoned today were his favorite granddaughters, a set of twins from the same egg. He and the Clan set great store by them. That in itself would be reason enough but there is also the *legacy* to consider." Billy Jack got up and yawned.

Elizabeth innocently played the perfect straight man to Billy Jack: "What *legacy*?"

Billy walked toward his room, stopped in the doorway, and smiled: "Yours, of course. Your father was the first Warm-blood in modern times to ever receive the medicine rattles. Good night, Aubrey. Pleasant dreams."

Elizabeth lay awake inside her sleeping bag, arms outside, holding the beret. She ran her hand across the green cloth and smooth leather, wondering what tales the hat could tell. As for the rattles, well, she was in awe of them. They were as light as popcorn. She held them in her hand and imagined that they warmed to her touch. As she finally found sleep her last thoughts were of her father. Sometime in the past he too had held rattles such as these. That was indeed strong medicine.

15

Baltimore lacked the fog, the smoke, and the smell of horse manure that enveloped London a century ago. You could get a pretty good mist if conditions were right and the wind came off the Chesapeake Bay, but that was rare. What this city gained in visual acuity it made up for with auditory overkill. The hours of darkness hardly muted the city sounds. Vehicles never stopped moving, ships came and went, people never shut up. *Heaven. Absolutely heaven. He would miss this place, this town. He would definitely miss the Inner Harbor, a Mecca to the entertainment-starved citizenry, drawing in the naïve and the unwary. My compliments to the chef.*

He found that one of the greatest attributes of this particular city was its indigenous population, many of whom were Hottentots. If you were colored you could expect trouble walking late at night, at least trouble from the Peelers. He wasn't 100% sure what racial profiling was, but it seemed to work in his favor. Because he was white he had never been stopped in his nightly walks through the city. He had never been stopped by a constable, that is. Two young kaffirs had accosted him once, something about being on their turf. It didn't amount to much; they expired before he could remember to ask them what grass had to do with anything. But that was days ago and he had more important things to think about.

Finding what he needed had taken only one night. Finding the best place to procure it took another. The third time pays for all. He practiced whistling on his way downtown. It was always good to whistle in the dark. Although he had checked out this place during the waning day and fullest night he still examined the area thoroughly once more, then once again. Since he had plenty of time he walked completely around the block and came in from the other side, just to see what lighting there was from that angle of approach. Better more light than too little. Really dark places were very, very, scary. Satisfied that all was well he vacated the premises. He knew of a nice all-night eatery that carried decent tea and biscuits on their menu. It was over a mile away but well worth the walk. Besides, you never knew what—or who—you might come across strolling through the city at two o'clock in the morning.

* * *

Looking back, he wondered what part Lady Luck played in the grand scheme of things. Was there a reason the diner had Earl Grey tea? How had he found the restaurant in the first place? Was he meant to go there all along, or was it just a lucky happenstance? As he hid behind the dumpster he allowed his mind to wander over his predicament. It was funny in one way, tragic in another. Funny that he should be hiding. Tragic for someone should he be found.

The walk to the diner had been most uneventful. He minded his business and everyone else did the same. He found a corner booth in the back of the restaurant and enjoyed his little snack. Ten minutes later a woman entered the diner, casually looked around, and joined him as if they had a prearranged meeting. He tried to calculate the odds on a streetwalker propositioning him on this night, but gave it up as hopeless. He did not really believe in Luck, but Fate was another thing altogether. He enjoyed the sexual banter with the woman who had plopped herself into his booth. She was no great beauty, but neither was she a hag. She retained all her own teeth but her wig was out of style. No matter. He wasn't interested in her hair. The ironic part of the encounter was that he had other plans. On any other night he would have obliged her willingness to display her charms. But not this night. He was as polite as possible but the harlot would have none of it. She would not leave be, hounding him out the front door and into the street. To the unwary this would have been the moment of their undoing. He doubted few people would have noticed the two deeper shadows to his right, and the one to his left. But he lived in the shadows. Quick assessment was part of his makeup, that special thing which helped keep him alive. As tempting as this little tête-à-tête was, even wanting to do the little wench who was still at his elbow harping at him, he could see little advantage. It wasn't that three to one odds were insurmountable; no, unless all of the shadows had guns he could take them easily. The problem was one of delay, and the diner waitress and the counterman. They could identify him if properly motivated. Was there a moving picture camera over the cash register? He couldn't remember. No, the odds were not to his liking. Quickly seizing his chance he grabbed the whore and walked her back into the diner. She tried to talk but he pinched the nerve in her elbow and the pain blocked whatever protest she voiced. Keeping her in front of him he walked her past the rest room doors, then into the kitchen and out the rear alley door. He pulled out one of his very sharp toys and put it to the slut's throat.

"Next time, doxy, don't try so hard. You scare the fishies off with all that bloody jabbering." With that he took his knife and slit the woman's blouse from neck to belt. Another quick slice and her brassiere was in two pieces. He looked at her naked breasts without the slightest lust. "Nice. Now get away from me before I cut them off and use them for ashtrays.

I don't have time tonight to play, my sweet little tart. But maybe you'll give me a raincheck? Go!" He opened the diner door, pushed the prostitute inside, and slammed the door behind her. He put away his knife and started running as silently as possible down the alley and out to the next street. He soon heard two heavy sets of footsteps. *He could stop and drop the pair right where he was but that would be incredibly stupid.* Instead he found a hiding place behind a dustbin. The two muggers pounded past his place of concealment. *Imagine, hiding from these moronic louts! Ah, America. He was glad to be home. But the things one had to do here to stay sane!*

* * *

His would-be assailants lost interest and breath after ten minutes, returning to their car that was parked near the diner. Jack watched them recount the evening's work. Wisely, they went off to greener pastures, but not before he was able to write down their license number. *One never knew when a raincheck might come in handy, that's what I always say.*

Keeping to the shadows just in case the fools were stupid enough to sneak back, he started retracing his steps toward Charles Street. He checked his pocket watch: 3:30 AM. Still plenty of time. He always allowed for the unexpected. Always better to hurry up and wait than be late, his mother was fond of saying. Not that she was saying anything these days. The tart that tried to shanghai him reminded him of his mother, what with her constant prattle. The more he thought of it, the more it looked like bad weather for his new girlfriend. Perhaps he could make it rain for her over the weekend. Of course, he'd have to check his appointment calendar, but things looked good, very good. For him, anyway. God, he did so love his work!

By his watch it was 4:35 AM when he reached his initial point. Hugging the dark places he found just the spot he wanted: A doorway deepened by shadow but with near one hundred and eighty degrees of visibility. He was in readiness; everything was in place. It always was. It was the details that got you killed. He remembered all the details and had done so for a long, long, time. He was the living, breathing proof of that lesson. It was easy, really. So easy that now he looked for tougher situations more worthy of his skills and abilities. Tonight was just such a situation that required a theatrical flair. He was in top form. The show must go on.

16

When Elizabeth next awakened, the hogan and the oppressive heat had disappeared. In its place was a chilling cold. She still held her beret on her breast. Marshalling her senses Elizabeth checked out her surroundings. She was on a cot in what was someone's bedroom, a boy's judging by the décor. She heard nothing in the way of sound or movement. Standing up, Elizabeth opened the door and walked down the hallway. Everything seemed normal. The floor was carpeted, and framed family portraits hung the length of the corridor. The passage emptied into a dining room. Upon the dining room table was every type of fast-food container known to man, including pizza boxes from five different companies. Counting the boxes Elizabeth calculated the pile of trash equaled at least a week's worth of meals. Then she finally heard a noise. It seemed to be the very low sound of a radio playing in the next room. She went toward the music.

Coming into the living room Elizabeth spotted a man sitting in a chair staring out the window. All the furniture had been pushed into a corner to make room for the mound of equipment the man had around him. Elizabeth recognized the binoculars and the audio-dish, the still camera and the film camera. Everything else was a mystery. As quiet as she was the man in the chair heard or sensed her presence.

"I thought you would sleep until noon. Pull up a chair." The man spoke in a vaguely British Isles kind of accent. He did not bother to turn her way but continued to watch through a small gap in the curtains. Now familiar with the way things seem to work here in the Otherlands, Elizabeth brought in a chair from the dining room and sat down as instructed. Peeking out the window she noticed that the vehicles going past seemed smaller. Their steering wheels were on the right side of the car, too. As she watched the cars pass each other on what to her was the wrong side of the road Elizabeth realized she was probably in Great Britain, or maybe Australia.

"We'll get right to it, then," said the man. "See the house across the street? We're keeping tabs on a man who goes by the name of Frederick Grossman. It's probably not his real name. So far he has been the model of decorum. He gets up, goes to work, comes home, reads and then goes to bed. Occasionally he eats out or takes a walk. He does nothing suspicious in any way. Which is why I am suspicious as hell. In a fortnight, other than receiving a few telephone solicitations, the man has not made or received a call on the phone. It just isn't natural."

"Maybe he makes his calls from work? To save money?" asked Elizabeth.

"We have a tap on his office phone. Nothing but business."

"Why are you watching him?" asked Elizabeth.

"Grossman has been seen in the company of Doctor Eric Drostric, professor of nuclear physics and one of the top men in the military application thereof. The professor has family still behind the Iron Curtain. We think that Grossman is putting pressure on Drostric to either return to the East or pass over research documents on nuclear fusion."

"Can't you just arrest him?"

"On what charge? The man has done nothing illegal. In fact, if he doesn't do something soon the wiretaps will be withdrawn. So, we just sit and wait. You don't play cribbage or gin rummy, do you?"

"Ah, sorry. I never learned." Elizabeth thought out the problem. "Could someone be relaying messages through the telemarketers, I mean the telephone sales calls? Maybe in code?" she asked.

The man swiveled in his chair to look at her with interest. "They said you were smart. They neglected to say *how* smart. Your name is Elizabeth, correct? Or do you prefer Aubrey? I favor Aubrey myself."

"Aubrey is okay with me. But I, I mean, nobody told me who you are," fumbled Elizabeth.

He smiled. "The name is Bond . . . James Bond."

* * *

Elizabeth was duly impressed. Now here was someone she knew about. James Bond, 007: Licensed to Kill. Spy, raconteur, expert in self-defense, driving, diving, and good living. Oddly, he did not remotely look like Sean Connery, or any of the other movie Bonds she was familiar with. The question must have been readable on her face.

"I see you are disappointed. You were expecting something more dashing I imagine. Sorry. What you see is what you get."

What Elizabeth saw was a man in his thirties with thinning brown hair, about five feet, eight inches in height, and slightly overweight. He was dressed in slacks and white shirt. If she had to describe him in one word it would be *drab.* This was not the way she envisioned the legendary James Bond. This revelation was also clearly legible in her expression.

"Oh, don't feel bad, young lady. I get this all the time. It's part of the job. The boffins at MI-5 went to a lot of trouble to create my persona. You see, the

Bond that you are familiar with might just as well paint a bull's-eye on his arse. He would be too easy to spot and dispose of. With me, well, no one sees me even when they look at me. I'm almost invisible. That quality makes me the perfect spy." Bond looked at Elizabeth closely. "I must say, you aren't exactly the way you were described to me, either. If I recall correctly I was to receive a shy mouse of a girl with glasses and braces on her teeth. You are much improved over that description."

Elizabeth blushed. She really didn't know what to say. Instead, she just smiled—sans braces—at 007 and nodded at the equipment. "Is all this used in your surveillance?"

"Oh yes, and then some. We record everything in and out of the telephone. We have listening devices in the master bedroom, front parlor, and kitchen. His car has a direction finder planted in the boot. Our people read the meter, deliver the post, cut the grass in his garden. About the only thing we don't do is flush the loo for him."

"Well, if someone else is doing all that what can I do to help?"

Bond smiled. "You could start by cleaning up the dining room."

All Elizabeth could think of was *here we go again!*

* * *

Indeed, some things remained the same. Elizabeth was the freshman member of the team, spending a great deal of her time running errands. In-between she was given information and instruction on how the spy game was played. The first assignment ended after three incredibly dull weeks. This was her first lesson: most surveillance work was composed of mind-numbing boredom. After those three weeks her James Bond fantasy vision was destroyed, replaced by a respect for people who could watch a door for three hours without falling asleep.

After that initial assignment her team was switched to tailing a suspect's vehicle. This was more interesting, especially since she was detailed to drive one of the following vehicles. No parking skills were needed. She learned about multiple car tails, parallel tailing, bracketing and all the variations of how to keep in contact with a suspect vehicle. She was even issued a set of wigs and hats to subtly alter her appearance when she was driving.

From that task her group was put onto individual tails, which were the hardest for her to learn. The procedures for following a single person were intricate, almost a ballet. It was never done singly but in a team, with an agent following, an agent in front, and people paralleling their course across the street. She learned how agents leap-frogged each other when following, used business glassfronts as mirrors, and made extensive use of radio communications.

All in all it was quite educational. When she wasn't working she tried to run and exercise. She didn't want to lose what had taken her so long a time to attain. The dim English sunshine allowed her tan to mellow out a bit so she wasn't as dark as before, although the difference from the old Elizabeth was still noticeable.

In the weeks that followed Elizabeth was immersed in the tradecraft of covert operations. She was sent to a shooting range where she was given basic instructions in the use of rifles, shotguns, and pistols. Having learned the fundamentals her teachers worked with her on the combat course, teaching Elizabeth how to use her skills in real life situations. She was even given a familiarity lesson on the Uzi 9mm machine pistol. Of all the weapons Elizabeth handled she did most poorly with the Uzi; the weight of the pistol with a thirty-two round magazine was too much for her to control. Her groupings were all over the target. Consequently her instructors concentrated more on the Remington twelve-gauge shotgun, .38 caliber and .357 magnum revolvers, the 9mm Beretta and the Colt .45 autoloader. Her marksmanship was superb with all the weapons although her shoulder was sore and bruised after a week of recoils from the scattergun.

After another two-week stint in the field with a unit dedicated to watching and following a female suspect Elizabeth was flown to California in the

United States. It was here that she attended a ten-day course in defensive driving usually taken by Secret Service drivers, chauffeurs, embassy drivers and the like. Of everything she learned this was the most fun. When she completed the course she was at the top of her class. Her confidence in her driving ability had soared with the training. Her skills were now on a par with professional adult drivers. The only thing they didn't teach in the course was, naturally, how to park.

When Elizabeth landed at Gatwick Airport Bond was waiting at customs. He ushered her through without a noticeable glance from the officials. Bond said next to nothing until they had loaded her luggage into his Mini Cooper and started towards London on dual carriageway A23. Elizabeth still had trouble adjusting herself to the incredibly small car. Weeks ago she had stopped looking for Bond to show up in an Aston Martin DB5. As James had told her, the flashy car was too obvious for spy work.

"We have a spot of work to do, Aubrey. I have been given permission for you to participate. Sort of a graduation exercise if you will. Care to join us?"

"Certainly, James. You know I'd love to. May I ask what the job is?"

"Don't know, really. At least not all of it. We are to shadow our old friend Mr. Grossman. It seems you were correct about the phone solicitors being part of the story. The same phrases were repeated almost word for word by different people. Our boys think they have decoded part of their message. Tonight they believe Grossman will finally receive documents from Doctor Drostric. Cut and dried, really; just follow the bugger, film the transfer and nab the villain in the act."

"What am I to do?" asked Elizabeth.

"Actually, we want you to drive the taxi cab Grossman has ordered up for 8:00 PM."

"Really? Me? But how do you–oh–the telephone! You heard him call the cab company."

"Righto. We'll bug the car of course. But in case he gets tricky we want someone in the vehicle with him. The people at headquarters think a woman behind the wheel will allay any suspicions he might be harboring. I quite agree. Are you up to it, lass?"

"Yessir! There's only one thing I need."

"What's that?" asked Bond.

"A really good street map of London. I'll need to know how to get where he wants me to go without fumbling around."

"Good as done. We have your ID already made up, and suitable clothes are waiting for you. Let's get you back so you can study." Bond stepped hard on the accelerator but unlike a DB5, the little car hardly changed speed at all.

* * *

Elizabeth spent the next five hours going over likely areas her fare might wish to go, concentrating on public areas where there would be lots of people, places favored for safe dropoffs. London cabbies were famous for knowing the streets of the city. By 7:30 PM Elizabeth was dressed and ready to go. Bond gave her last-minute instructions: "Try not to talk. If he asks about your accent tell him you're here going to school, that you work as a fill-in when a driver is sick to help pay your tuition. Don't elaborate. Simple, straightforward, polite. Questions?" Elizabeth had none.

"Good. We'll be close, but not too close. We're using six cars so he has little chance of losing us. Now head on out. And Aubrey? Do keep your head down."

Elizabeth opened up the door to the taxi, started it up, and headed for the pickup point. She still amazed herself that not only could she drive safely on the wrong side of the road but also shift the manual transmission. Her time in driving school had taught her how to use a clutch. The hour she had spent getting familiar with this taxi had also paid off. She felt comfortable moving the cab through the dark streets of London.

Arriving five minutes early, Elizabeth parked two blocks away and waited. She had been advised not to show up early for fear that Grossman would wonder about the prompt service. At five minutes past the hour Elizabeth rolled slowly past the address, slowing, then stopping as if searching for a street number. Then she did a U-turn and parked in front of the house she had watched for hours weeks ago. She hit the horn once as instructed and waited. She did not wait long. Frederick Grossman hurried out to the cab and let himself in. He hardly looked at Elizabeth, just gave her an address in downtown London and proceeded to look out the window. It wasn't until they were nearing their destination that Grossman spoke again.

"I need to pick up some things from the chemist shop. Pull over up there." He pointed to a pharmacy halfway down the block. "I'll just be half a mo'." Grossman bounded out and was gone. Elizabeth could do nothing but wait. Bond had decided it was too risky to put a listening device in the car itself so she had no way of contacting the following team. But she knew they would be out there watching.

Five minutes later Grossman returned. He carried no package. He spoke again to Elizabeth: "I have a few more stops to make. Take the next left, then the first right." Elizabeth did as she was told. "Stop up ahead at that fish and chips place." Again she did as instructed, Grossman got out, returned promptly. Again he carried nothing away from the store.

"Head towards Piccadilly Circus, please." Elizabeth just nodded and accessed the roadmap she had committed to memory, taking them directly to the roundabout. Before she could ask, Grossman gave her new directions: "Pretty at night, what? Let's go around a time or two and enjoy the view."

As Elizabeth did as she was asked Grossman spend the time looking behind them. After two circuits he told Elizabeth to head for St. James Square. Here they repeated the process. Seemingly satisfied that no one was following Grossman gave another set of directions to her: "Take Whitehall, then take Westminster Bridge, then back across the Waterloo if you please."

Elizabeth piloted the car across the bridge, up York Street then back across the Thames on Waterloo Bridge. Further instructions had her depositing him at the Savoy Hotel. As he got out he handed Elizabeth a wad of bills. "I have to see someone here for just a minute. Meet me around back of the hotel." Elizabeth drove through heavy traffic and made her way to the rear of the Savoy. To her surprise Grossman was already waiting for her. "Head for the Charing Cross tube station," was all he said. A quick drive down Strand and they were at the entrance to the Underground. Grossman told her to keep the change and was gone, leaving Elizabeth parked at the curb wondering what to do next.

Ten minutes passed before Bond appeared at the door and got in the rear seat. "Drive away, Aubrey." He did not look pleased. "Head back to our starting point. This has been a bit of a cock-up, I must say.

Grossman was either on to us or very, very careful. Each time you stopped we had to drop off people to follow on foot, then investigate where he was, like the chemist's shop. By the time we hit the Savoy we had lost half of our assets. When you dropped him at the tube entrance he disappeared before we could acquire him again. The boss isn't going to like this."

"Do you mean we lost him?" asked Elizabeth.

"Yes, for now. But he hasn't met up with the professor yet," answered Bond.

"How do you know that if you lost him?"

"I said we lost *him*. The professor is another matter. We have a whole other team covering him, and I doubt he is as agile as our Mr. Grossman." Bond was silent until they pulled up to their destination. "I suggest you get some sleep, Aubrey. I hope this will be useful to you in the future. If I don't see you before you leave, good luck, and stay in the shadows." Bond smiled and was gone.

Elizabeth got back to the flat they had provided for her, showered, and sacked out. It had been a long and seemingly fruitless day. Looking back on recent events she noted that not once did anyone draw a weapon or use physical force in the performance of their job. As she drifted off Elizabeth felt beneath her pillow for the pistol James had given her, remembering what the agent had told her: *Better to be prepared and not need it than the other way around . . .*

17

Elizabeth awoke with a start. She surveyed the room, her room, and its contents. She looked at the clock. The time was 7:15 AM. But what *day* was it? Everything seemed the same: her bed, her dresser, the computer on the desk. The only thing that seemed out of place was *her*. *For the first time in my life I'm awake and don't feel woolly-headed! In fact, she had awakened before the alarm went off. And that was always a good thing!* She was wide-awake and full of energy. Her mind seemed to be running at a much faster pace, and any number of issues marched through her brain, the first one being she had not done any homework. As she arose from bed she realized she was still gripping the pistol James had given her. Her beret was still stuck on her head although slightly wrinkled. She safety-checked the .25 caliber Beretta pistol just to be sure and placed it and the beret in her middle dresser drawer. Feeling quite smug with herself Elizabeth marched to the bathroom and after that she sat down at her desk. Within twenty minutes Chemistry, Biology and History were, well, history. She was surprised how easily the answers came to her considering it had been nine months since she had picked up a schoolbook. She could hear that her mother was up too, but not yet downstairs. Elizabeth would actually have time for a shower. Even though this room had been hers for years, this morning it felt different; unused, as if she had been absent for months instead of hours. The shower was already running before she even remembered she had a mirror. She stepped back from the tub and went over to the full-length mirror. She gasped! This was not possible! Not overnight. No way. The body that she was looking at was not the one she went to bed with! Losing some weight was one thing. This was above and beyond all reason. Elizabeth went over to the scales and weighed herself. The dial came up to one hundred and seventeen, not far from what it read the last time she weighed in. She went back to the mirror and looked again. It wasn't the difference in weight that amazed her. It was the tone of her body. Yesterday she had baby fat and zero definition. Today her body fat was a non-issue and she was now sporting muscles. Not little teenage-girl muscles, not steroid-induced bodybuilder slabs of beef, but hard, chiseled, flexible, usable muscles. Her triceps and biceps were laid out in perfect proportion to her deltoids and traps. The little flabby layer on her tummy was gone. In its place was a stomach ribbed with strength. Her thighs and calves looked like they had been melted down and then reforged into the legs of a marathon runner. That big caboose she called a butt no longer existed. What was left was tight and tidy. It seemed the only thing that hadn't changed were her breasts. Evidently big boobs didn't go with the rest of the ensemble. *Who cares!*

Elizabeth's first thought was to go to her mother, but she thought better of it. *Best to get herself ready for school. With the thought of school came a reality check: What in the name of God could she wear? No way could anyone see her like this!* After a frantic search through everything she owned Elizabeth gave up, wrapped a towel around herself and headed for her mother's bedroom.

"Mom, oh it's so good to see you again. I missed you so much!" Elizabeth hugged her mother for all she was worth.

"Elizabeth, it's only been eight hours."

"For you, Mommy, but it's been almost a year for me!" Elizabeth had started to cry.

"Easy, baby, it's okay. I'm right here. Are you okay? Did everything go all right last night?"

"It was hard and rough and wonderful and crazy all at the same time! I can't tell you everything now. I have a big problem!"

"Good morning to you, too. Problems seem to be our stock in trade here lately. What's up?"

"I don't have a thing to wear!"

Mary Feye laughed. "Honey, you're not supposed to use that line until you're in your thirties!"

"Mom, I'm not kidding! Look at me!"

Mary Feye pushed her daughter out to arms' length and surveyed her only child. Then she spun her around for good measure. Her baby was gone for good. In her place stood a toned athlete with a serious tan. "Okay, who are you and what have you done with my daughter Elizabeth?"

"Come on, Mom! This is serious! I can't let anyone see me like this and you know it. Hardly anything fits, and what does won't cover me up. Help!"

"Okay Honey, easy on the volume! Let's dig around and see what we can come up with. Here, stand beside me. Look at that–we're almost the same size now. This is absolutely incredible. Should I ask what happened last night or wait until tonight?"

"Wait, I think. It would take too long and I don't want to rush the story, okay?"

"I guess I can wait if you can. Now, I think a top with a long-sleeved sweater is the way to go. Here–try these on. Here's a pair of gray slacks that should fit you. They're loose in the thigh so it should be a good fit. I bet your underwear doesn't fit either." Mary Feye rummaged in her bureau and came up with matching panties and bra. "These should work for you today. I don't think we can both continue to use the same clothes so you better go to the mall after school and get some underwear, maybe a couple of tops, definitely some slacks, and a bulky sweater or two." Mary Feye reached for her purse and extracted a credit card and gave it to Elizabeth. "Be gentle with this. World crisis or not, I didn't exactly budget for this."

"Thanks, Mom. You're the best."

"Yes, I know. Now get out of here and go get dressed so I can finish making myself beautiful. I'll be down in ten minutes."

* * *

True to her word, Mary Feye was in the kitchen ten minutes later. For various reasons neither Elizabeth nor her mother was very hungry, so breakfast consisted of English muffins and orange juice. They said their good-byes, each promising to meet back at the house around 6:30 PM that evening.

Elizabeth wasn't one hundred percent comfortable in her mother's clothes but she had to agree they were better than anything that belonged to her. At least her shoes still fit. The trip to the bus stop was an enjoyable one. She felt like running. Her step was lighter and more purposeful, and her bearing was different, more attentive and self-assured. She was only half a block from the bus stop when she realized that if she could feel the change, other people could just as easily see it. With a sigh of resignation Elizabeth made herself slow down and slump down at the shoulders. Until now she had never grasped the simple fact that she slumped intentionally, tucking her head into her shoulders like a turtle. *Did she need shelter from the world that badly that she tried to physically retreat into herself? Well, not now. Now it would be pure camouflage.*

Elizabeth ended up being early for the bus, and spent an uncomfortable five minutes talking to the other waitees. In a way it was a blessing as she was able to blend into the old Elizabeth slowly with kids who did not know her well, not to mention working to shed her acquired Brit wordage. Obviously the big test would be with Holly. *Holly! What was she going to do about the relationship with her best friend?* Just then bus 81c pulled up and Elizabeth boarded and found her usual seat. Elizabeth devoted the rest of the drive thinking of scenarios. Holly had made it pretty clear that if Elizabeth didn't come clean and tell her what was up then their friendship was over. But there was no way she could tell Holly what was happening. *She really cared for Holly. Really. She and Holly had been friends for ages, yet she knew Holly could not keep a secret like this. Heck, Holly couldn't keep any secrets.* Elizabeth's face still burned when she remembered the time she confided to Holly that she wished she could get a tattoo of Tweety, and ten minutes later the whole 8th grade was laughing. *Nooo, telling Holly was not an option. So where did that leave her? They could tell when they lied to each other, so that was out. Should she tell her part of the truth? A half-truth? What about a glittering generality? The more she thought of it the less attractive talking to Holly became. They were just too close. It would only take one slip-up on Elizabeth's part to alert Holly. Then* something *would be all over school. Maybe not the real deal, but enough to red flag her if someone was looking for things unusual at The Poe. As unappealing as it was, and as potentially painful to both of them, Elizabeth would have to sever her ties with Holly, at least for the short term. When everything was sorted out and things returned to normal then maybe she could talk to Holly and explain. That is, if Holly would let her.*

* * *

Mrs. Davner delivered the contents of bus 81c to Edgar Allan Poe Senior High School in reasonably good order. Elizabeth piled out with the rest of the flotsam and forced herself to walk slowly to her locker. She put her invisibility shields up to maximum, and it wasn't until she was in C Building that she knew she was unconsciously putting up a *real* shield. That realization came only because she seemed to be dodging kids the whole way down the hall. She stopped, took a deep breath, and relaxed.

The corridor sharpened in focus ever so slightly. *Wow. That was really stupid! This was exactly what she and her mother had discussed! So here she was, diddybopping down the hall like a road flare. Get a grip! You can do this. It's like driving: just pay attention to business. Tinkerbelle, how did you ever do it?*

As luck would have it–or lack of same depending on the outlook–Elizabeth found Holly at her locker, dropping her jacket and swapping out books. There would never be a good time for this so Elizabeth hitched her determination up a notch and headed for the lockers.

"Hi, Holly."

"Hullo."

"Can I talk to you, please?"

"Depends on what you have to say."

"Holly, there isn't much I can say. Please try to understand that none of this has anything to do with you. It's all me, and it's so complicated that I just can't tell you right now. I just can't."

"You can't tell me but you can share whatever it is with those new jock friends of yours?"

"Holly, that's, I mean, it's something that just happened and I just need you to understand–"

"You know what, Elizabeth? I *don't* understand and I don't really *want* to understand, okay? So just stow it. Maybe you can snow your new friends, even the rest of the school but I *know* something's up with you that ain't kosher. All this crap with losin' weight, and your eyes, and the strange little fact that you are now as tall as I am? Well, crap it is and I just don't give a damn!" Holly slammed her locker door shut, spun the combination lock, and turned away.

Elizabeth started to say something but Holly turned around again to have the last word: "Oh, by the way, you look really swell in your mama's clothes." With the last dart thrown, Holly stomped away down the corridor. When Holly turned the corner and was out of sight, Elizabeth didn't know whether to be upset or relieved. She knew the answer when she started crying.

18

While Elizabeth was forcing herself to deal with Holly, Amy Shestack was thinking hard how not to sound like a frightened kid talking to her father. One of the problems with having a cop for a dad, especially one that was a detective, was that lying had to be done on a whole different plane–ordinary lies were out of the question. Amy had learned a long time ago that her dad could spot a lie from her with depressing ease. He could tell when she was lying to her mother in the kitchen while he was in the living room watching television. That ability mystified her no end. The irony here was that she didn't want to lie; she just didn't think the truth was believable, or at least believable to someone as logical as her dad. Her dad always said that the hardest lie to catch was the one that was closest to the truth. Bearing that in mind she continued the conversation they had started last night when her mom and dad had returned home.

"Daddy, there really isn't anything you can do, is there?"

"Sorry, Kitten. Not much, anyway. Just because you think someone was watching you last night isn't the strongest grounds for a police investigation, especially from the distance you claim the person was standing."

"Woman, Daddy, not person. I'm sure of it. She was looking here at the house, and at me."

"Amy, maybe it was just a neighbor out for a walk. Or maybe it was someone who isn't allowed to smoke in the house. Like me!" laughed Daniel Shestack.

"What if it was a burglar casing the place?"

"Amy, out of all the houses in the neighborhood why would a burglar go after the one with an unmarked unit in the driveway? Come on, kiddo, it isn't logical."

"Speaking of logic, Daddy, your car wasn't here last night."

"Amy, neither was your Peeping Tom when I went looking for him last night."

"She left, Daddy, when you pulled up!"

"Amy, without evidence to the contrary I just can't put out an APB that says *Be on the lookout for a woman who smokes.*"

"Daddy, you're not being fair!"

"No, Sweetpea, unfortunately I'm being very fair in evaluating the situation and the evidence." He thought for a moment or two. "If it upsets you that much maybe I can get Dispatch to roll a unit through the neighborhood once or twice during the night. Will that help?"

"Yes, Daddy. Thanks. You're the best cop on the block!"

"Of course I am, considering I'm the *only* cop on the block. Now, get yourself to school. I've got to run. My workload just got doubled. Baltimore Metro called us requesting help and the Captain volunteered my services on the Predator murders."

"The what?"

"Predator murders. It's the name the Baltimore Sun has given to the serial killings in the city."

"I don't remember anything about a serial killer."

"That's because Metro did their best not to alert the press that the murders were connected. But naturally the news leaked, and Bill Jordan from the Sun coined the phrase."

"You're not going to be going after this guy, are you Daddy?"

"No, Princess, you know my job: look for evidence, interview people, arrest jaywalkers. Nothing as glamorous as catching killers."

"As if! Well, please be careful anyway. Good cops on this block are hard to find."

"Go to school! Learn something besides how to be a smartass!" laughed Amy's father.

"Love you. Bye." A flash of skirt and Amy was out the door.

Once again Daniel Shestack wondered how he deserved such a wonderful daughter. It must be her mother's influence. He cleaned up the small array of breakfast dishes and poured a last half-cup of coffee before heading downtown. He was pushed for time, but something just wasn't adding up. Like most detectives, answers just didn't pop into his head. They had to percolate like the coffee he was drinking. Amy was as levelheaded a kid—or adult, for that matter—as he knew. She was never one for flights of fancy, imaginary friends, or the like. This trait was undoubtedly his influence. Amy didn't scare easy, either. Very early on, seeing that she really was a bit of a smartass, he had made her take self-defense classes. At first she had resisted, but gradually embraced the discipline wholeheartedly, and surpassed his initial wishes of just being able to hit and run. To be sure, her size was limiting, but unless the attacker was extremely big and well trained, he wouldn't bet against her in a fight. On the sly some of the instructors at work gave her help in edged-weapon fighting and the PR-24 baton. Officially he didn't know anything about it. Unofficially he was proud as hell. Of course, Sarah thought enough was enough, and that her daughter should spend more time on dates than wristlocks, which meant that he would not be the one to tell his wife their daughter was playing with knives.

All this being said, why was Amy so worked up over someone looking at the house? The perp couldn't see in; Amy said as much. All the doors and windows were locked. The house had a first-rate alarm system with a panic button, and Amy could dial 911 as easily as calling one of her friends. So why the big deal?

Daniel Shestack didn't like mysteries or pieces that didn't fit. Finally the piece that didn't fit came into better focus. He trooped upstairs to his daughter's bedroom. Usually off limits to male personnel—a female thing, Daniel felt this to be extant circumstances. He trusted his daughter and rarely invaded her privacy. He knew his policy was at odds with what other parents thought, but until Amy gave him probable cause, he would not violate her trust. Besides, he wasn't snooping. He just wanted to look out her window. As soon as he looked out his suspicions were confirmed. At this angle and distance, seeing someone by the trees was unlikely. Add to that the lack of available light and he could not see how Amy was so sure it was a woman under the pine trees.

Daniel Shestack thought on that for a minute, but for the life of him could think of no reasonable explanation. On the flip side of the argument, he could not think of any reason why Amy would lie to him about seeing someone. It was a puzzle that he did not need at the precise moment when he was due in the City for a briefing on the Predator case. Yet it took him a scant second to err on the side of caution.

Yelling goodbye to Sarah, who was in the shower, and kissing his mother goodbye, Daniel locked up behind himself and got in his car, but instead of heading to the station he detoured around the block and parked. Keeping to the pavements, he made his way to the line of pine trees, and to the place that Amy had pointed out. Being careful where he placed his feet, he came up even to the row of trees. Scanning the area with twenty-plus years of practice, Daniel had no trouble spotting an area of earth that had been disturbed by footprints. Easing into the area, he surveyed the scene. *One person, narrow running shoes. Off to the side was the imprint of a knee in the disturbed soil. Why was the soil disturbed?* Taking his pen, Daniel turned over pieces of turf until he found something that made him frown and smile at the same time. Buried under the soil were the remains of half a dozen cigarettes, all Newports. *So much for his theory of a neighbor out for a smoke. Casual smokers didn't bury their butts, nor did they stand in the same place long enough to consume six cigarettes.* Pinioning one of the butts with his pen, he removed one of the ever-present plastic bags from his jacket and dropped the butt into it and sealed the top. His smile overtook his frown when he noticed the faint traces of lip-gloss on the butt. Daniel didn't know how Amy knew, but knew she did. The *how* of it was unimportant at this point. What *was* important to him was that someone, a woman, was watching his house, and his daughter. And Detective Daniel Shestack was going to do something about it.

19

Vice-principal Barrett Jackson Sawyer was at school early this cold Thursday morning, and for good reason. Many times in the past he had experienced the feeling of riding an out-of-control roller coaster, or more to his mind, careening down the tracks in a mine car like Indiana Jones in the movie *Temple of Doom*. In roller coasters you had a reasonable expectation of stopping safely. With Indy you never knew what would happen, and that feeling was on him now. The car was speeding up, people were chasing them, and time was running out.

Sawyer had started his day by touring The Poe's hot spots, mainly the cafeteria and the industrial arts buildings. Everything seemed quiet. There was the usual necking and illicit cigarette smoking, but Bear tended to overlook the petty rules in favor of the majors like drugs and weapons. Students hid their cigarettes and stopped kissing when he hove into sight. To not do so would force him to act on the violation. But as long as they shut it down when he came into view he didn't pursue the issue, allowing the almost-adults a measure of defiance, but at the same time reining them in. It was a balancing act, and Bear knew he was good at it. In return for not being a martinet, he gave himself more maneuvering room, and the freedom to patrol the school without being unduly feared.

Halfway through his inspection tour his step faltered slightly, and he searched without. *It was subtle, but it was there. His thoughts had been else-where, and he might have been slow to pick it up. How long had it been there before it reached his conscience thoughts? A minute? Ten? Then as quickly as he sensed it the sensation was gone. Damn! Someone would get killed over this if it continued. They could only do so much. Kids!* Bear stomped back to his office, students scattering before him like quail from a fox.

Back in his office, Bear used his credit card to make a long distance call to Northern Ireland. The conversation with Dr. Rodney Broadbent was short, sweet, and spoken in an archaic form of Gaelic. Anyone overhearing what was said would have a time translating everything but the words *Amy Shestack* and *LaTisha Wood*. After ringing off Sawyer ground out some administrative paperwork. *Having two jobs was very time-consuming, and he had found that he really enjoyed the teaching environment. In all likelihood he would be forced to resign in two years. Sooner if things blew up here, which was an even-money bet. He could always get other employment. He had worked in just about every job category there was, except politics and religion. When he thought about some of the jobs that he had in the past . . . hell, some of them he couldn't even remember. He remembered that once he worked as a farrier, specializing in draft horses. The two–thousand-pound Belgians and Percherons dwarfed even his big frame. That was so long ago.* I'm getting tired of all this. Sooner or later I'll slip up, and it'll be fatal. *Look at the mess he had made of taking out Spratt and Daws. Two sure removals that had come back to haunt them. Hawk had put paid to Spratt, true, but he shouldn't have had to. If the job had been done correctly the first time there would have been no Spratt to worry about. And The Crow!* How in the name of God can you survive being pitched off the fourth floor of a building? Was it possible that the opposition was gaining strength? Or was the Ladder Society becoming a paper tiger? Enough of this. What is, is. Control that over which you have dominion, and leave the rest to Fate. Fate and The Jack. *Thinking of all this reminded Sawyer why he was so tense. He picked up the phone and punched in Hawkin's extension. It rang four times before Hawk answered.*

"Good morrow, Mr. Sawyer."

"How did you know it was me?"

"Who else would call me this early in the morning, I ask you? Besides, I felt it too, and knew you would be calling."

"Hawk, what the hell are we going to have to do to her? Handcuff and gag her?"

"If you think that would work, be my guest. Just give me time to leave town first!" laughed Hawk.

"Not funny, McGee. If she continues like this The Poe will look like Spook Central, with fireworks coming out of every window!"

"When all the powers of the Fen are laid upon a yearling you canna expect the restraint of an adult, Bear. Adjoin that with the Dodger's line and I'm surprised the Little One hasn't barbecued half the student body."

"How can you be so flippant about this? If anyone was within three miles of here they would have felt the tremor!"

"They would have, old Bear, if I hadn't shielded The Poe against such a thing first off this morning."

"You right bastard you! Why didn't you say so in the first place?"

"What, and miss all this? Think how much better your day will go now that your adrenal gland is up and running?" laughed Hawk.

"Jack Hawkins, one of these days you'll find your pants on fire, and it won't be an illusion, either!"

"I look forward to it. In the meantime, during lunch I will talk to Elizabeth about restraint, if it makes you rest easy. Did you get through to Research?"

"Yes, and no. What do they do over there? I'll be lucky to have anything before tonight. They said they'd divert resources to the questions, but both issues are problematic at best."

"What do you mean *problematic*?" asked Hawk.

"Slave traffic issues for Ms. Wood, lack of records, name changes after the civil war. World War II of course for the other."

"Okay, I see the problems. But call back at noon and check up. If they haven't the manpower tell them to pull people from Britain if they have to, *but to get it done*. No excuses. They don't want me to call them."

"Aye, I think they are well aware of who's doing the asking."

"Good. Sometimes I fear our researchers believe that information retrieval has no time constraints. Perhaps a tour in the field would rejuvenate their spirit of exigency?"

"Don't make me laugh! Can you even imagine our Nocknagle outside, let alone doing fieldwork? No, render unto Nocknagle that which is his, and leave the fieldwork to them what can still see their feet past their belly!" Now Bear was laughing, too.

"Aye, maybe you're right. If we don't talk later, then six o'clock this evening at Wolf's place."

"Until later, Mr. Hawkins."

20

Around 8:15 AM Mary Feye was sitting behind her desk at work, going over a proposal from an outside contractor. She was deep in thought when she felt what Sawyer and Hawk had also kenned. But to her it was more internal that external. Never mind that The Hawk had installed a shield over The Poe: spoken words from him would not block what was directly felt emanating from her daughter. Mary Feye's office was six miles from the school, yet she knew exactly what had happened, and for how long. The bond between mother and daughter that had been restrained for so long was now unrestricted. Soon each would feel what the other would, in real time. This could prove to be a curse or a blessing. *We will need to work on privacy issues, thought Mary Feye.*

Right now she hoped her daughter would get things under control. This last issue was of little importance. Mary Feye could sense the shielding laid over the school. Unless there was an AntiJack inside the school itself her daughter was safe. The Ladder Society was taking no unnecessary chances, unless laying the shield was a chance in and of itself. The risk must be minimal if they were using it. They seemed to be on top of everything, especially the ever so mysterious Mr. Hawkins. What was it about him that just irritated the hell out of her yet excited her at the same time? She could excuse the attraction if she could blame it on the magnetism of power, which obviously Jack Hawkins had in spades. But truth be told, her own abilities were not that shabby, and seemed to be increasing by the hour. You would think the more power she had, the less attractive his power would become. So it had to be something else. It certainly wasn't his appearance; a sixty-year-old gray-haired janitor with bad eyesight wasn't the demographic she was shooting for. So maybe it was his smile? Or was it his self-confidence? That attracted her, yes. What intrigued her was his knowing something that she didn't, or couldn't, know. What that was she had not the slightest clue. What she did know was this: Attracted or not, she and Elizabeth would not be played as pawns in this game; if queens they be then as queens they would move upon the board.

Deciding not to leave everything in the hands of the Ladder Society, Mary Feye worked her keyboard and tapped into the Web. She did not waste time searching for the Ladder Society–Elizabeth had already confirmed the lack of information. Instead she called up *Jack the Ripper*. Momentarily she was rewarded with thousands of references, far too many to research each one individually. She decided to work the headings on the priority list. The first three were busts: one was a song, one referenced a book, and the third had something to do with the coroner findings on one of the murders. On her fourth try she struck gold when she accessed an online crime library with specifics on the Ripper. The site was well laid out, with individual chapters detailing the events in the case. She only had to read the introduction to be sickened. Since each facet of the case was finely detailed she began copying each chapter on the site. Burning copies took time, so she tried to do her job work in-between running the copy stream. It took a supreme effort of will not to read each chapter as it spilled into the tray. No matter how hard she concentrated, her eyes returned again and again to the pages stacking up in the printer tray. Mary Feye finally gave up and devoted her full attention to getting the copies she needed. When all the information was printed out she sorted the copies into piles, and inserted each of the five bundles into its own manila envelope, and sealed them all. She jammed all five copies into her briefcase. Only then was she able to get back to earning a living. *Out of sight, out of mind, so the saying went. Fat chance. She didn't believe this particular piece of information was going to leave her mind for a long, long, time.*

21

English Composition class was almost as tedious as the instructor who taught it. Mr. Jarden validated Elizabeth's theory that just because you were published didn't mean you could, or should, teach. Mr. Jarden was didactic and pedantic at the same time so he preached and overteached at the same time, too. Elizabeth thought the school should change the name of the course from English Composition to Jarden Composition, as there seemed to be only one way to write anything: *The Jarden Way*. Getting an 'A' in the course was of little compensation. The lack of creative freedom had cancelled that out quite quickly. Now most of her time was geared to writing what Mr. Jarden wanted to see, mainly his own style aped by his pupils. Elizabeth went along with the herd, feeding Mr. Jarden's ego with his own words. She would write in her own style at home, in a journal. Right now all she wished for was the bell to ring. In this case, wishing was futile. Elizabeth and thirty-one other students were doomed to endure Mr. Jarden for another twenty-six minutes.

* * *

While Elizabeth was suffering through *Jarden Composition,* Vice-principal Sawyer was hip-high in school paperwork. It wasn't until Mrs. Crisp informed him that Mrs. Yoder was in the main office that he remembered the meeting he had scheduled. Bear hadn't really planned for this because they had learned all they needed to know yesterday. Still, it wouldn't hurt to investigate further.

Sawyer picked up the phone: "Tell Mrs. Yoder I will be out to her directly."

"Right."

Sawyer got up, stretched, and did his best to neaten up his desk. He put on his suit jacket and started for the outer office. Bear made it a point to first meet parents outside his office. It showed respect, deserving or not. Having never met either of Harold Yoder's parents he was in the dark as to what he would encounter in the main office. Bear was pleasantly surprised to see a small, neat woman sitting primly on one of the uncomfortable chairs in the lobby.

"Mrs. Yoder? I'm Jackson Sawyer". Sorry to keep you waiting."

Margaret Yoder stood and nodded hello. "I haven't been here long, Mr. Sawyer."

"Good. Would you care to come back to my office? Mrs. Crisp, would you please send for Harold? This way, Mrs. Yoder."

Once in his office Bear sat beside Mrs. Yoder on the old couch. "Mrs. Yoder, do you know why I asked Harold to have you or Mr. Yoder meet me here this morning?"

"Not exactly, Mr. Sawyer, but I can guess that it is not going to make my day, no matter what it is. And there is no Mr. Yoder. There was, once, but we haven't seen him for three months."

"I'm sorry."

"Please, don't be. We certainly aren't. Harold's father was consistent in his drinking; he was quite good at it, and it made him very angry at life. Since we were available, well, we made a convenient . . . target. He's gone now, and our lives go on." Harold Yoder's mother said all of this without drama or pity for herself or her son.

"Your husband is dead?"

"No, just gone. I convinced him that it would be better for all concerned if he just left me and Harold alone."

"Convinced him?" Sawyer thought it a curious use of the word.

"Harry never respected the police or my restraining order, Mr. Sawyer. But he did respect my kitchen knife."

"I see." This information set Bear back for a moment and he was forced to rearrange his game plan. What good was it to save a world if you did not try to save the individuals on it?

"Harold's in some kind of trouble, isn't he?" Mrs. Yoder phrased it more as a statement than a question.

"A little, Mrs. Yoder. Until yesterday I didn't know his name, which is a good thing in this job." Bear smiled. "There was an incident here at school and at the mall. Both are connected to each other, and two other students are involved. Would you know a boy by the name of William Parker?"

"No, sorry."

"How about Albert Margolin?"

"That name I am familiar with. Harold knows him. I met him once. He seemed nice enough."

"Yes, I agree. He seems very much like Harold. The other boy, Billy Parker, is the fly in the ointment. I've had him before me a time or two, and he is working his way through juvenile delinquency towards real criminal behavior. My fear is that Mr. Parker will impart his felonious tendencies to Albert and your son. Mrs. Yoder, would you mind giving me some insight into Harold's character?"

"I'll give it a try. He's withdrawn into himself these last three years. He doesn't like to be touched. Pulls away sometimes if I try to hug him. Average grades. No girlfriend that I know of. Works hard at home when it comes to chores."

"Does he scare easily?"

"Yes, and no. He had defiance beat out of him long ago. He fears things, yes, but certainly not physical pain. Funny . . . he doesn't fear his father anymore. Just his memory. That's rather sad for someone only fourteen years old, isn't it?"

"Yes, yes it is." Just then Mrs. Crisp called to inform Sawyer that Harold Yoder had arrived. "Thanks. I'll buzz when I want him."

Sawyer turned back to Harold's mother. "Mrs. Yoder, there are some things I need to know from Harold concerning the incident that took place." Here Bear related the story of how Elizabeth had been accosted. "Harold did not play that great a part, but he did participate. There are certain pieces of information that I need to help me trace this so-called reporter. I think Harold may have additional clues that he was reluctant to tell me earlier. I do not want to unduly frighten him, but if he has information that could help me I would be grateful. I would like your assistance."

Mrs. Yoder sat silently on the sofa, head down, hands together. Finally she raised her eyes to Sawyer's and spoke: "You do what you think is best. If you go somewhere I don't think you should, I'll tell you. Mr. Sawyer, Harold is a good boy at heart."

Sawyer picked up the phone and dialed. "I believe you, Mrs. Yoder. Let's see if your son feels the same way." Sawyer jabbed at the intercom button: "Send him in, Mrs. Crisp."

22

The bell finally declared Jarden Composition over and done with, and Elizabeth fled the room with relief. American History was next, and she was excited. Today they would start giving their oral *What If* presentations. Elizabeth couldn't remember all the questions, but some of them had great potential to be funny. Elizabeth didn't have to worry about her paper: she was in Group Two, and only Group One would be reading today. There wasn't time for everyone to read his or her *What If* in just a single class period. Elizabeth could tell that she wasn't the only one looking forward to the class by how quickly everyone reached their seats. Mrs. Hurd had already closed the door and checked the role before second bell even rang.

"Okay, class, for those of you who may have forgotten, today we start listening to the *What If*s!

As planned, Group One will give their papers today. We will determine in what order the students in Group One will give those papers by way of my magic hat." Mrs. Hurd reached under her desk and produced an absolutely hideous hat. Had the fruit on it been real, it could have fed a family of four.

"Samantha, would you draw the first victim's name?"

Samantha got up from her desk and did as instructed, and Gail Sonders was the unlucky winner. Gail was a rather tall–for a girl—a sturdy girl who looked like someone you'd see advertising a stick of butter: big smile, big chest, blonde hair. All that was missing were the pigtails. She got up nervously from her seat and stood behind the podium, cleared her throat, and began:

"Uh, my *What If* is *What if Eleanor Roosevelt, wife of President Franklin Delano Roosevelt, had died just after her husband had been reelected in 1940?*
"Eleanor Roosevelt was born in . . ."

Elizabeth listened with only half an ear to what Gail was saying, as she had actually read about Eleanor and Franklin in *No Ordinary Time,* Doris Kearns Goodwin's Pulitzer Prize-winning book. Elizabeth tuned back in when Gail got into the repercussions of Eleanor's death.

"With Eleanor dead, the President lost not only his best eyes and ears as to what was happening in America, but a friend he could rely on. But even more importantly, the President of the United States, and the country, lost their social conscience." Gail paused for breath.

"Many people, then and today, saw Eleanor as a gangly, big-toothed woman who traveled too much, did too much, and most of all *talked* too much. Many felt that she should stay at home in the White House taking care of her husband, especially since he was in a wheelchair because of polio. She did travel a lot, and she worked almost every day, and she talked all the time. But she rarely spoke about trivial matters. In fact, she was not good at all with what was called at the time *Cocktail Talk*. Eleanor Roosevelt was a New Dealer, a social changer who was already in the highest level of society. She talked with poets and writers and rulers of countries, and royalty, yet she spent most of her time trying to help those people who needed real help and social change. Her husband was trying to save the world for democracy, and he was focused on doing that with things like making guns and tanks and airplanes. When she died the United States had not yet been attacked and was not at war. But President Roosevelt was trying to save Britain by sending military hardware and food to the United Kingdom. His mind was not on social problems at home. On the seventh of December 1941, the Japanese attacked Pearl Harbor, our naval base in Hawaii, and destroyed or damaged most of our pacific fleet.

Now the United States was at war, and all of the President's energy was focused on winning the war in Europe, and then in the Pacific.

"While it was important to win the war, Eleanor was not around to remind her husband that you needed to win the peace, too, and what good was there in winning if Americans got stepped on in the process and everything was the same as before the war?

"Without Mrs. Roosevelt to advance the idea of allowing American Negroes to serve in parts of the service restricted to whites, many black Americans chose to sit out the war rather than fight for a country that did not respect their abilities. Because she wasn't there to help get Blacks into the war factories, the white owners kept them out, or hired them to do menial tasks at low wages. Black workers boycotted, and wildcat strikes were commonplace. Production slowed as black workers sabotaged machines.

"Without Eleanor Roosevelt as a leader and symbol, American women did not go into the war factories in the vast numbers they would have, and production of vital war equipment was held up because of lack of workers. It would be an extra year before production caught up with demand.

"Because of the slowed production, supplies did not reach Russia, and Moscow fell to the Germans, and an additional four million Russian civilians died. The war was won by the Allies, but it took another year and a half, and cost America alone another 300,000 soldiers killed or wounded in battle.

"Because she was not there to constantly remind the President about the people of America, the people on the Home Front, at the end of the war Blacks were still illiterate and poor, not having gotten training in the factories. The industrial cities of the North received no great numbers of southern Blacks, so most of the Black population remained in the Deep South. Females were not recognized as equals in the workplace because they were not accepted in the war plants. Women's Rights were delayed by decades.

"Without Eleanor's voice, Franklin and America stood fast by countries with colonial empires and championed few emerging nations. It would take race riots in the late 1960s for any integration to even start, and for the armed services to admit Blacks in all fields.

"In short, the Allies won, the Second World War was over, the Earth was six years older. Literally tens of millions of people had died, but nothing had changed. The rich were richer, the poor poorer, minorities still underpaid and mistreated, and Third World countries still ruled by the nations that had controlled them before the war.

"Eleanor Roosevelt complemented her husband and his Presidency; without her he was just another man who ran a country when it was at war. Eleanor made him special." Finishing her report, Gail looked expectantly at Mrs. Hurd.

"Thank you, Gail. Very, very well done. Sometimes it's hard to see that one person can make such a dramatic difference in the world. Admittedly, Eleanor Roosevelt was the First Lady, and had built-in influence. But other First Ladies had the chance to change history, and opted not to. Gail, that was a great report. Now, would you be so kind as to draw the next name for us?"

Gail left the podium with relief, walked over to the infamous hat, and drew the next name and called it out: "Dave Alston."

23

As Detective Daniel Shestack drove to his meeting in Baltimore he received a radio call from Dispatch informing him that the meeting had been postponed. He was to reroute to an address off Charles Street, and to see a Lieutenant Barry Cohen at that address. Daniel asked for more information but dispatch declined to elaborate on a clear-air channel. That alone told Daniel more than he needed, or wanted, to know. Whatever he was driving to was being kept quiet, and there was really only one thing that involved him in the city. He was headed to the scene of another possible Predator killing.

Daniel had trouble reaching his destination because of rush-hour traffic. He made use of his grill lights, but not the siren. The streets were so clogged with vehicles that no one could get out of his way even if they were predisposed to do so, and many jaded commuters were not. Traffic became more congested as he neared the address he was given. As he approached the scene he saw that one side street was taped off, and one lane of Charles was also blocked. Parking would be a problem; it looked like half the City's marked units were there, and a good many *plain jane* units as well. Daniel was forced to drive past the mayhem and park a block away and walk back to the cordoned-off area. He stood on the periphery of the crowd and studied the onlookers. It was surprising how many perpetrators of crimes just had to admire their handiwork. Daniel scrutinized the crowd, looking for anyone that fit the standard profile of a serial killer. Nothing matched. With the exception of a few street people, most of the rubberneckers were *suits* on their way to work, many with briefcases and not a few talking on cell phones, passing on the gory news to their friends and family. He had not expected to spot the Predator in the crowd; life was never that easy. But Daniel knew that if you didn't look, you'd never see.

As Daniel headed toward the police tape he noticed a man of medium height watching him intently. The man pushed off from the wall he was leaning against and slowly, but indirectly, headed for Daniel. When Daniel finally made his way to the front of the crowd the man was beside him.

"Gruesome stuff, huh?" offered the man.

"I wouldn't know. I just got here."

"You seem pretty interested in what's goin' on. How come?"

Daniel smiled: "Same reason as you. I'm on the job." Daniel moved his jacket discretely to the side so the man could see the gold shield on his belt.

"Shit. Who're you?"

"Daniel Shestack. I've been seconded here. Who has the scene?"

"Bill Watkins has this one, but Cohen's in charge overall. It's him you'll wanna see. My name's Bonner by the way. Ed." The two cops shook hands. Bonner lifted the yellow tape for Daniel and the two walked down the closed side street. Bonner called to a uniform coming toward them: "Where's the Lou, Jimmy?"

"Last I saw him he was in the lab truck, Eddie."

"Thanks, Jimmy. This way, Danny. The crime lab is parked in the alley to the right."

The portable forensic lab was sitting in the alley with its rear doors open. Plainclothes detectives, technicians, and uniformed officers were every-where–coming, going, and just standing around. Beside the big truck sat an ambulance with two bored attendants leaning against it. Ed Bonner singled out a small man in street clothes. "Hey, Lou, got somebody to see you."

Lieutenant Barry Cohen turned around and faced the two men. He was short, overweight by twenty pounds, and smoking a cigar. He needed a shave, and looked like he had slept in his clothes. His face was as rumpled as his suit.

"Who the hell are you?"

"Name's Daniel Shestack. I'm the player to be named later."

"You're Ahern's man, right? Good. Ahern says you have your shit together. You better have. Any experience in this area? Don't imagine you get much of this *Silence of the Lambs* crap where you live."

"True enough. But I worked homicide in New York City before moving to Maryland. Captain Ahern told me you could put two and two together and get four most of the time. Said if you couldn't then something was seriously wrong. He thought maybe I could help."

"What'd that bastard mean by most of the time? Ah hell, he's right. That's why I called Tim in the first place. Welcome aboard, Daniel. You met Ed, right? We call him *Steady Eddie*. Ed's as slow as an Oriole pitcher's fastball, but he's a lot more accurate and he never gives up. Me, I just yell and kick stuff over until I find something slimy underneath. What about you?"

Daniel had to think a moment on that. "I guess I'm a stewer. I throw everything into the pot and let it simmer for a while. Sooner or later it makes soup."

"So we got slow, medium, and fast. Christ, we sound like the goddamn Three Bears. Come on.

I'll show you our Goldilocks . . . or at least what's left of her."

Daniel and Ed followed in Cohen's wake, staying upwind of his cigar smoke. They came up to another line of tape, and Cohen stopped. The scene beyond was being illuminated by flashes of light. "Pasco should be done with the stills in a minute or two. She already has the video. You want a rundown, or you wanna look at the scene first?"

"Give me what you got, Lou. But nothing about the body, okay?"

"Gotcha." Cohen pulled out a spiral notebook and referred to his notes: "At 6:23 this morning Central Dispatch got a 911 from a Harvey DiAngelo. He works for the company whose loading dock that is. Said he comes in from the street entrance, cancels the alarm and then walks back to the receiving dock and runs up the overhead door like always. Then he sees something in the dock area up against the wall. Figures it to be some homeless guy but his legs is sticking out and DiAngelo thinks maybe a delivery truck'll run over him so's he yells at the guy. No response, so he goes down to wake the bum up and discovers it ain't no bum but a girl. DiAngelo thinks maybe he can help so's he turns her over and her head just about falls off. He freaks out, blows his lunch, and comes back inside and calls us. Dispatch sends two units in, the Uniforms take one look and cordon off the area and call for backup. That's about it."

"Where's DiAngelo now?"

"We got him sequestered in one of the offices inside. A uniform is with him."

"Was there any blood on him?"

"Yeah, stupid bastard knelt in it, and got it all over his hands when he turned the body over."

"Did you run him yet?"

"Eddie did. Nothing but a *drunk and disorderly* five years ago."

"Have you had time to interview him?"

"Not yet. He ain't going anywhere. I wanted to get this mess cleaned up first." Cohen nodded at the body fifty feet away. By this time the police photographer had finished her work, and was back-tracking out of the crime scene.

"Lou, with your permission? Daniel started putting on a pair of disposable gloves.

"Go for it." Cohen relit his cigar and nodded to the cop standing guard to let Daniel enter the cordoned-off area. Daniel showed the officer his ID so he could enter it into the log and ducked under the tape. As soon as Daniel Shestack entered the crime scene he relaxed, allowing the adrenaline and tension to flow outward. Daniel was the only person within the barricaded area, or at least the only person still alive. The city sounds became muted as he slowly approached the body stretched out on the concrete. From twenty-five feet away he knelt, and did a slow three hundred and sixty degree turn, seeing nothing at ground level that felt out of place. There were approximately two dozen yellow markers on the ground, each one denoting an object of possible interest: a cigarette butt, an old rag, a piece of paper. Probably all just street trash, but it would be collected and examined anyway. Daniel stood up and did another survey at eye level, then another three-sixty looking up. Satisfied, he looked back to Cohen. The lieutenant had been joined by the two ambulance attendants, still looking bored to death. It was not the best figure of speech considering the circumstances. Daniel made hand motions to Cohen indicating he would like to move the body. Cohen nodded.

There was the usual path laid out to the body, a lane already cleared of any possible evidence, and Daniel used it. He stopped within five feet of the body and took in the whole scene at once. For him, a crime scene was like diving into a cold lake; better to do it all at once rather than piecemeal. What he saw was better left to slasher movies. The victim was a Caucasian female, brunette, probably in her early or mid twenties. Daniel guessed her height to be somewhere around 5'6 to 5'10', weight proportional. There did not seem to be anything of interest at the distance he was at, so he started to move closer. He had only taken one step when he stepped back, reached into his jacket and removed a small jar of mentholated petroleum jelly, and daubed some under his nose. He was acclimated to the strong smells of death, and coped well. But Daniel Shestack had one weak spot when it came to odors, and that was vomit. He noticed DiAngelo's regurgitated breakfast by the body, and had no wish to add his own. Inhaling the pungent jelly with each breath helped kill the smell. Moving in close to the body, Daniel now experienced the feeling of intimacy that overcame him whenever he examined a victim of violent crime. He could not really put the feeling into words. It was a calling out, as if all the answers were right there in front of him and all he had to do was see them. The victim always seemed frustrated at Daniel's inability to understand, and of their own impotence. All this communicated itself to Daniel, and if he listened hard enough sometimes the victim could give him the insight he needed.

Daniel first noticed that the body had indeed been moved, presumably by DiAngelo. Evidently the body was originally face-first on the concrete, and DiAngelo had rolled the girl onto her left side. She was in that position now, almost parallel to the wall. Daniel looked again, and realized he was wrong. The girl had originally been sitting up against the wall. She must have toppled over at some point and landed cheek down. Daniel checked the back of the girl's fleece jacket and found white flecks of mortar embedded in the fibers. Leaning over her, he saw fibers that matched her coat stuck to the wall. *That meant she had been propped up in a sitting position. Whoever killed her wanted her to be found sitting up. That was interesting.*

Avoiding what little blood was on the concrete, Daniel examined the girl more closely. He gently moved her head, and saw the girl's throat had been cut deeply, clear back to the vertebrae. It looked to been made by a fairly long blade, and extremely sharp if he was any judge. The girl was bundled up for the cold weather, and her fleece jacket and sweatshirt underneath were gummy with blood. He checked her hands but could see no outward sign of struggle, although there was a slight red line around her right wrist. Daniel examined her jawline and chin, and thought he could discern some bruising. Lifting the girl up, he looked for blood underneath her body. Little evidence of blood showed on the pavement. Daniel gently placed the woman's body back on the ground. She was wearing pants, not a skirt, and Nikes, one of which was missing a shoestring. Daniel was mystified by the lack of blood on the ground. Could it all have been soaked up by her clothing? He unzipped her coat and felt her sweatshirt. It was soggy. There was also a vertical slit down the right side. It was a new cut with clean edges. Daniel stood up and motioned for Cohen to come in.

"What's up?"

"Lou, anyone go over the body yet?"

"Nope. Just a cursory look-see by me. Even the beat cops didn't touch her. Knew she was dead from a distance. Why?"

"See this cut here? It's fresh."

"Yeah, very. Our perp could have done that. But why? Her jacket ain't cut."

"My guess is he unzipped this fleece thing first."

"Again, why? Unless he wanted to cover up the cut."

"I agree. I don't want to tell you how to run your show, Lou, but I think you might want to get her bagged and removed to the M.E. before removing any of her clothes here in the middle of the alley."

Cohen looked at Daniel: "We're not gonna like what we see, are we?"

"Let's get the girl out of here. Is she ready to go?"

"I'll get Eddie to bag her hands, and then those two ambulance morons can take her in. I think I'll have Eddie go with the body just in case."

"Good thinking, Lou."

The two detectives stood aside as Eddie affixed plastic bags over the girl's hands and then watched as the girl was placed in a black body bag, put on a gurney and wheeled out of the loading dock.

"Eddie, I want you to ride with the body. Nobody opens the bag 'til I get there, understood?"

"Got it."

"Get going, and make sure to tell those idiot attendants to keep off the radio."

Eddie headed after the gurney, leaving Cohen and Daniel still standing in the middle of the crime scene. Barry Cohen relit what was left of his cigar and just stared at the small puddle of congealed blood, the only thing left to mark the passing of a human soul. "Well, shit. You want to talk or go see DiAngelo?"

"Let's talk to him first. Then let's compare notes."

"Fine. In here." Cohen led the way into the building and opened another door that took them to an unused office. Harvey DiAngelo was sitting on the desk while a uniformed policeman sat in a chair reading an old People magazine. Cohen jerked his head half an inch and the officer got up and left the room.

"Mr. DiAngelo, I'm Lieutenant Cohen. This here's Detective Shestack. We just got a few questions, then you can go with the officer outside. He'll get a written statement, you sign it, and that's it. Okay?" Cohen made it sound like a twenty-minute exercise. Daniel knew better. DiAngelo would be lucky if he cleared the station before lunchtime.

"Ah, yeah, sure. I mean, what choice I got?"

"That's the spirit, Mr. DiAngelo. Now, let's start at the beginning . . ."

Forty minutes of questioning later and the two detectives knew more about Harvey DiAngelo and what he did that day than they could ever wish to know. Unfortunately, DiAngelo had done nothing but find the body and contaminate the crime scene. Both detectives were positive that Harvey had nothing to do with the killing. Other than having his fingerprints taken just to be on the safe side, Harvey was pretty much eliminated as a suspect. Daniel and Cohen stepped back out onto the loading dock, where Cohen fired up another cigar. Through the cigar smoke both men continued to look at the vacated crime scene.

"Pretty quiet," said Daniel.

"Yeah, they still got the street blocked off. Soon as they lift the barriers the place will be full of people. Hell, three days from now somebody'll be running tours through here for the tourists."

"Barry, she was posed, you know that." It was more statement than question.

"Yeah, I know. She fell over before we could find her sitting up. By the looks of things she was killed from behind, slashed from her left to her right, blade maybe six inches or so?"

"I agree, Lou. Held her chin with his left hand and cut with his right. From the angle of the cut he either stood on a box or he was taller than she was. Did you notice the lack of blood? I'm guessing she was unconscious when he cut her, and held something up to her neck to catch the flow. I didn't see any spatters, did you?"

"Just one or two little ones. Nothing significant. I sure as hell wish Citizen DiAngelo hadn't touched the body."

"If wishes were fishes, Lou. Either way, I'm sure she was propped up and put on display. I'd bet her legs were spread, too."

"Daniel, you been here before, ain't you? Is that why Timmy gave me you?"

"Tim respects your work. He'd have sent me anyway. It's just I've had experience with this sort of thing, especially ones with sexual overtones."

"Better you than me, buddy. One murder, one killer is just fine by me."

"Me too. That's why I left the Big Apple. Say, how many people you have working the neighborhood, knocking on doors?"

"Twenty, maybe twenty-two people."

"Unless you already thought of it, you might see who has access to the roof across the street. See the little shed up there? I think it might be a pigeon coop. Maybe someone was up there and saw something."

"Shit. Good eyes, Daniel. I'll make sure someone checks. You ready to go to the Medical Examiner?"

"Ready, but I'm not looking forward to it." They started down the dock stairs just as the sun cleared the building across the street. When it did the light reflected off of something in front of them.

"What the hell is that? Daniel, you got tweezers on you?" Daniel rummaged in his jacket and came up with a pair. "Get me a bag ready, willya?

"Thanks." Cohen reached down into the remains of Harvey DiAngelo's breakfast. Pushing away bits of bacon and partially digested toast, he retrieved a black, many-pointed object.

"What do you make of that?" asked Daniel.

Cohen held the object up to the morning sunlight. "Well, Dan, looks to me like it's a toy. A toy jack."

24

Vice-principal Jackson Sawyer was already standing when Harold Yoder entered his office. Towering over his desk, Bear motioned for Harold to have a seat on the couch beside his mother. "Harold, this is a continuation of the discussion we had yesterday. I have had a talk with your mother, and she is of the opinion that you are worthy of salvation. What do you think about that?"

Poor Harold didn't know what to think. "Well, uh, I don't know. It seems like everything I do is wrong."

"Well Harold, let's try to do something right then. Let's start with how you met this reporter. Just tell me how it happened."

Harold started talking without raising his head: "Okay, we were just hanging at the arcade as usual and we saw this guy playing the air hockey game, and he kept winning, so we went over to watch.

Next thing I know we're all over at the Food Court, talking and stuff. Then the guy tells us as how he's a reporter, and doing this article on all the weird and strange things that seem to happen around Halloween. Well, he says since there are other guys doing stories like his that he was gonna narrow it down to just the spooky stuff that occurred in high schools. Then he says can one of us help keep an eye out for him at Poe 'cause he can't be everywhere at once. He had most of the other schools covered, even the Catholic schools like DeMatha. Well, nobody else volunteered so I said yeah, I'd do it. He says fine, and then he tells me it's worth twenty bucks to him if I bring him something he can use. Soon as he mentions money all the other guys wanna help too, so he says okay, anybody that gets him a story gets paid. And that was it."

"Harold, since when do you just do anything a perfect stranger says, or accept money from them? You know better," said Mrs. Yoder.

"Yeah, I know Ma, but the guy was cool, and he made the whole thing seem fun, like being an investigative reporter on 20/20 or something. And I was the coolest, because I said yes before he even mentioned the money."

"Harold, did this guy give a name?"

"Yessir, he said everyone just called him Rat."

"Harold, how long ago was this?"

"I don't remember exactly, but if must have been three, maybe four weeks ago. It was the weekend they had the new cars inside the mall."

"When you went back to the arcade, who did you leave your phone number with?" asked Sawyer.

"Rat just said to leave it at the register, so I gave it to the guy behind the counter and said it was for Rat. He seemed to know what was up 'cause he just took it and stuck it in the cash register."

"Do you remember the clerk?"

"Oh yeah, it was Marco. He's outta school, goes to college part time. Long black hair. He usually has it tied back. About six feet tall, maybe taller. Pockmarked face; you know, acne."

"Okay, then he called you back, and you said you saw some odd things occurring, correct?" Sawyer prompted his student.

"Right, then he says I should be sure 'cause he gets a lot of calls and most of them are bogus. That's when Billy and Albert and me started trying to make something happen." Harold was too ashamed to keep his eyes up.

"So then you harassed Elizabeth, twice, and nothing happened. So you just let it go?" Sawyer got up from his chair and sat casually on the corner of his desk. Harold didn't answer.

"Harold, Mr. Sawyer asked you a question. This is neither the time nor the place to hold back, son.

Please answer Mr. Sawyer." Mrs. Yoder was looking hard at her son but he failed to meet her eyes.

"No, that wasn't it . . . I met him again last night. I called the arcade and told Marco I needed to see Rat. He put me on hold, then came back on and told me that he was told that Rat would be at the 7-Eleven at 6:30 that night."

"Oh Harold, you didn't!" said Mrs. Yoder.

"Please go on, Harold," said Sawyer.

"I met him there at the 7-Eleven, and we talked about what I had heard. Most of it was just gossip, but it was all over The Poe, and somebody would have told him."

"What did he ask you about, Harold," queried Sawyer.

"Funny stuff, like was it a girl, how old was she, what color was her eyes, her hair, stuff like that. That's when I decided everything wasn't like he said it was 'cause he's asking all these questions like he's some kinda pervert. I told him what he wanted to know and then I just tried to leave, but he grabs my hand and jams a twenty-dollar bill in it and tells me I earned it, and laughs. That's when I got outta there." Harold's eyes never left the floor.

"Harold, did you tell him about our talk?"

"Nossir, it never came up."

"Harold, why did you go back last night?" asked Mrs. Yoder.

"I don't know, Ma. It was like I had to or somethin'."

Sawyer got down on his haunches so that he was eye to eye with Harold: "Harold, do you still have the money Rat gave you?"

"Yessir, right here." Harold dug around in his pocket and came up with a twenty-dollar bill. "This is it." Harold handed it to Sawyer. Sawyer could actually feel the intent of the tainted money.

Reaching into his wallet Sawyer pulled out a twenty and gave it to Harold. "Go ahead, Harold. Take it. I think this one is a little cleaner than the one you gave me. I find little fault in being paid for a news tip, Harold. What I don't condone is scaring people. I think your Mr. Rat gave you some of your own medicine. My advice to you would be to steer clear of this Rat. I don't know what he is up to but he doesn't act like a real reporter. I would also stay away from Mr. Parker. He can only lead you to trouble. As to your involvement with Ms. Feye, to make up for that . . . I would like you to do ten good things around the house for your mother. Is that a deal, Harold?"

"Sure, I mean, yes sir. Anything!"

"Then go back to class, Harold. Have Mrs. Crisp give you a pass."

"Thank you, Mr. Sawyer. Thanks, Ma."

"I'll see you tonight, Harold." After Harold left Bear sat back on the couch. "I think you're right.

He is a good kid. Right now he's at the age where he needs direction. He doesn't have much in the way of male role models, does he?"

"No. My brother, sometimes, but he lives in Chicago."

"If you can't find a male for him to look up to, then try giving him more responsibility. I find that can help sometimes by letting the child look up to itself. And monitor his friends closely."

"Thank you. Just . . . well, thank you."

Bear and Mrs. Yoder stood. Sawyer reached over and retrieved a business card from his desk. "Take this. It has my cell number on it. If you should need help with Harold, or if by some chance Mr. Yoder should reappear . . .? Bear let the sentence die out.

"Thank you. I hope it never comes to that. But it's nice to know I have someone to call. I really have to go. I can't afford to miss too much work."

"I understand." Bear walked her to the main lobby doors. "Take care of Harold . . . and yourself."

"Goodbye."

Bear watched the small woman walk off into the fall wind, again amazed how anyone, man or woman, could find the day-to-day courage to raise a child alone.

25

Lieutenant Barry Cohen and Detective Daniel Shestack made the trip to the medical examiner's facility in Daniel's car. Before leaving the crime scene Cohen detailed someone to take Ed Bonner's unmarked unit to where they were going. Cohen wanted to use the driving time to talk with Daniel.

"Barry, did you get any ID on the girl?"

"Nothing so far. Door to door guys got a description to use, and I got someone searching Missing Persons, but that will be a dry hole. She's only been dead since dawn. My guess is maybe a runaway. She didn't look hard enough to be a hooker."

"I don't know. Hookers seem to be getting younger all the time. Clothes didn't look like something a streetwalker would wear, more like someone taking a walk."

"Yeah, I saw the Nikes. Maybe she was walkin' her dog and she got jumped."

Daniel thought about that. "Damn, Lou, I think you hit something there. Did you notice that red mark around her right wrist? I couldn't put my finger on it. I thought maybe she had been wearing a watch. The more I think about it, I bet it was from a leash wrapped around her wrist."

"I like it." Cohen pulled out his cell phone and called into Dispatch, having them relay to the men and women going door to door to ask about a woman who walked her dog late at night or early in the morning.

"This'll really help if we can ID the girl fast. None of the other victims had identification on them either, and we lost time just finding out who they were."

"Barry, this is number four, right?"

"I wish. More like eight. We had a couple of others that weren't exactly like this and the press never connected them. We didn't either, officially. But there are a number of similarities in each case. Two of the cases aren't in my jurisdiction, so that threw off the local papers. There was another one up by Philly that a friend told me about, too. Adding the ones here and you get eight."

"Where were the other two similar ones?"

"Let's see . . . one was in Cecil County, and the other up near Aberdeen."

"Have you tried NYPD to see if they have anything similar? Or maybe Wilmington, Delaware or thereabouts? There's a chance our boy is migrating south along I-95. Maybe he left a trail behind him."

"Possible. I know people in Wilmington. You still got friends in high places in New York? Hey, here's our turn. Make a left."

"Yeah, I think I can get what we need. You know, the Fibbies should have a profile on this guy if he left a blood trail. Maybe we should go Interstate on this and see what they have on file."

"I'm not that keen on a bunch of Feds walking all over my case, Daniel. But if it hooks up to anything out of state, then I think I gotta call them in. Turn left there at the mailbox, then head around back." Daniel complied and circled the building.

"Park over by the steps. That's the rear entrance." Daniel and Cohen walked up to the steps of the building and rang a bell, and momentarily the door was buzzed open. Daniel followed Cohen through a maze of halls until they reached the autopsy room. Their Jane Doe was on one of the tables, still encased in the body bag. Ed Bonner was sitting in a chair talking to the M.E.

"Hey, Lou, Danny. Doc here's ready to go if you are."

"Hey Eddie, Doc. Doctor Patel, this here's Daniel Shestack."

"Most pleased to meet you, I'm sure," said Patel. "I am most ready to start. Will you be assisting, Lieutenant?"

"Yeah, Doc. Let me suit up. Daniel, you wanna help?" Both men put on spare gowns, masks, shields and gloves. Doctor Patel positioned himself at the side of the table, with the two detectives on the opposite side of the table. Patel turned on the recorder and tapped the microphone to insure it was receiving, and entered all the pertinent data needed to proceed. Patel instructed the officers to unzip the bag. Carefully the body of the young girl was removed, and the body bag given to Bonner.

"Eddie, take this somewhere and clean it out. Make sure we didn't miss anything."

"Got it, boss."

Patel gave an overview of the body, and then had the men remove the fleece jacket. Now that the fleece jacket was off they were able to slip the sweatshirt off the body. The sweatshirt was now becoming stiff with dried blood. When they finally removed it they were able to see what was underneath, and it wasn't pretty. They were shocked to see that the section of the girl's chest that held her left breast was missing, breast and all. There was a neat incision in her chest that had been sewn back up with what looked to be a shoestring. Patel untied the binding, and spread opened the incision.

"Gentlemen, it seems the heart is missing," said Patel.

* * *

The rest of the autopsy was straightforward and revealed little they did not already know. Doctor Patel confirmed that the recent rub mark on the wrist was consistent with what a leash could make. His preliminary guess as to time of death was around 5:00 AM. The cause of death was the knife cut to the throat; the chest incision was postmortem. The body was in excellent physical shape, and Patel opined that she was a runner or jogger. After the four men conferred it was speculated that all things indicated that some amount of blood was missing, strengthening Daniel's premise that a towel or similar object was held over the girl's throat when it was cut. If so, the towel was out there somewhere. Cohen thanked Patel and the three detectives headed outside for some fresh air.

"Jesus, how does Patel do that every day?" asked Bonner.

"Same way we do, Eddie. Same way we do. Lots of practice and bad dreams. Let me recap this thing. Tell me what I'm missing: White male, six feet tall or better, and right-handed. Probably not a bum 'cause I don't think this girl would have stopped to have a conversation with him if he was. So figure he looks okay, no Frankenstein, and dresses like he changes clothes every day. Patel says the stitches made with the shoelace were probably quickly done, but neat. The removal of the heart was done by someone with knowledge of human anatomy, and it was done by someone with either a lot of practice or learning. So that makes the guy a butcher rather than a baker. Or a paramedic, or EMT, or doctor, or veterinarian, or someone who spends a lot of time on the Internet. The body was not sexually molested, if you discount the missing breast. The Perp may or may not know when DiAngelo opens up. He's either lucky or careful enough that he checked out the street and alley beforehand. I bet he's both, but he's neat, so I go for careful. I think he knew his kill zone. So maybe he's been there before, and if he was, maybe someone saw him. The victim is white, five feet, nine inches tall, and weighed about a hundred twenty-five pounds. Athletic, and a brunette. Good dental work, clean, uncallused hands. I'm saying inside work, middle class background. Fact is, the more I look at this the more I think she wasn't a streetwalker. Now you guys." Cohen fired up another cigar.

Ed Bonner spoke first: "I like it. I think we should have some bodies check the dumpsters again in that area. I'd look for a plastic bag that would hold a towel. Hell, he may have gotten spooked and thrown his trophy away too. If we go with him being neat, then we gotta think plastic."

Daniel, the *stewer*, spoke last: "Ed, I agree with the towel, but not the heart. This guy went to a lot of trouble to cut this girl's heart out, and then sew up the cut. It had to be premeditated, or at least comtemplated. He would have needed something other than a knife to work the laces through the skin so maybe he brought something with him like an awl or ice pick. So he wanted the heart bad. I don't think anything would make him pitch it away after all that effort. Maybe he'd pitch the towel, but I bet he used it to carry the heart and breast, or wrapped them in it. Something we might do is check the city dog pound if you have one, and the local humane societies or SPCA. Maybe check with The Sun and flag anybody putting a dog in the Lost and Found classified. Have them ask the caller if the dog was trailing a leash."

"Hey, why not put an ad in ourselves? You know, 'Dog lost vicinity of such and such, wearing collar and leash. Reward offered.'"

"Eddie, I like it. Find someone at The Sun and get it in tonight's edition. Do that first. Then hit the animal shelters and talk to the managers or directors or whoever's in charge. Make sure this doesn't fall through the cracks. Call Dispatch, and have them tell everyone to ask about women who walk their dogs at that hour, or someone who runs with a dog. Oh, and have them recheck the dumpsters, too."

'Got it, Lou. See you later, Danny boy." Cohen flipped Ed the keys to his car and Bonner marched down the stairs and was gone.

"Daniel, let's get outta here. I hate this place." As they walked to Daniel's car Cohen's cell phone rang. Cohen listened for a bit, then rang off. "Bit of a break, there. We have a possible eyewitness from across the alley. Head back to the scene. And light the roof." As they retraced their route Cohen yelled to Daniel over the wail of the siren: "You were wrong about that pigeon coop up on the roof, Daniel!" Cohen smiled: "It wasn't for pigeons. It was for chickens!"

26

While the two detectives were speeding back to the crime scene, the man they were looking for was just returning home to his townhouse. He was dead tired–exhausted really. He unlocked the back door to his residence and dropped the bundle he was carrying onto the kitchen counter. He needed a shower.

Thirty minutes later he felt alive again, and ready to face the day. As he dressed he remembered the items he had left in the kitchen. Walking back downstairs, he reentered his kitchen and unwrapped his acquisitions. Jack carefully separated the items, putting each in its own separate freezer bag, which he carefully dated and labeled.

Neatness counts, thought the man, still a bit high on adrenaline. In a detached way he studied and admired the two objects in front of him. Taking his marker, he

204 t connor michael

wrote: I Lost My Heart at the Inner Harbor *on the bags, and then took them to the basement, carefully placing them in the freezer alongside similar bags. He smiled at some of the names on the bags:* "Boston Pops, A Horse named Phil(ly), Any Port(land) in a Storm, I Love NYC (parts of it, anyway). *Okay, so it wasn't exactly art, or poetry. Hell, Baltimore wasn't San Francisco by a long shot. But he liked the symmetry. It was all so . . . neat. The whole concept made him laugh out loud. He was the tidiest, most precise person he knew. For the life of him he never understood why they insisted on calling him The* Ripper.

27

Ed Bonner already knew his life had gone to the dogs. Now his body was following. Normally he would just use the phone, but the Maryland SPCA wasn't that far away so he decided to make it a personal call. Bonner took his exit off of Interstate 83, made an illegal U-turn and drove up the hill and parked his car in the visitor lot. As nice as this place was he still hated it. Bonner felt happier among the stiffs in the morgue. There was nothing he could do for them. But the animals here were another story. Ed Bonner liked to think of himself as a hardboiled cop. Going misty-eyed over some stupid dog in a cage did not go well with the image he had of himself. Not for the first time did he wonder why he had such compassion for caged animals, yet retained little or no pity for the humans he had incarcerated in a lifetime of law enforcement. Philosophy was not Ed Bonner's strong suit and he knew it. He just accepted life as it was and moved on.

Bonner walked up the ramp to the main office and entered. The place was bright and cheerful for a prison, the antithesis of a human jail. A counter attendant waited on him in turn, and Bonner showed his badge and asked to speak to whomever was in charge. Less than a minute later a woman in her thirties named Patti Morgan introduced herself and ushered him past the gate and into a small, cluttered office. Bonner closed the door behind him.

"Detective Bonner, what can we do for you? Are you looking to adopt a dog?" She smiled.

"What I need is some information, and some help. It involves a case we are working on, a felony case. I'm following a possible lead and that brought me here."

"Go ahead. I'll help if I'm able."

"Okay, well, let's say that I live in Baltimore City, downtown. I'm walking my dog, and he sees a cat, and runs away and I can't find him. How do I get my dog back?"

"Was your dog wearing a collar with a dog license or rabies tag on it?"

"I don't know."

"Okay . . . what kind of dog was it?"

Bonner was beginning to feel slightly foolish. "I don't know that either."

"Then I guess you don't know the temperament of your dog, either?" Bonner just shook his head.

"But it was a dog, right?"

"Probably." Bonner wasn't used to not having the answers.

"You aren't making it easy for Skippy to get back home, are you?" Patti was smiling at Bonner in amusement. "Okay, let's start from the beginning and work up. If Skippy has no tattoos, no microchip, no license, no rabies tag, no collar, then he's loose in the city with no way to get back home except by personal navigation. If Skippy has lived here for a time and has a regular routine he should know where he lives. There is a chance you could go home and find Skippy waiting on your doorstep, wondering where *you* got to. Dogs do not have a good sense of time. Most studies show that an hour means much the same to them as a day or a year. What negates Skippy finding his way home are cars, trucks, and busses. If Skippy gets hit by a vehicle and is killed, a hit and run so to speak, someone usually calls the city and the carcass is picked up. If there is no ID then a report is rarely made, and the animal disappears. If the dog is injured, then we or another animal agency might be called. The animal would be picked up and transported to a veterinary hospital for care, or taken to their own facility depending on the injury, whether they had a veterinarian on staff, et cetera, et cetera. Or, a private citizen could take the animal to their vet and have it looked at. You are more likely to have an animal-loving citizen pick up a sweet-tempered beagle than a big, mean, hurting dog. But either way, your choices are to look for newly admitted HBCs–that's Hit By Car–or check your back porch.

"Now, let's say Skippy didn't catch the cat, is disoriented, and can't find his way home without a roadmap. If he is a good-looking animal, people-friendly, and healthy, he may be picked up by one of three classes of people. The first type would keep the dog, thinking that a nice dog like this would be good for the kids. Skippy gets a new home and you or I never see him again. The second type is a concerned citizen who finds Skippy and decides to keep him while checking the newspaper *Lost and Found* ads, maybe even placing one themselves, describing Skippy. They may or may not call local animal control, or a humane society, and have them put Skippy on their *Found* list. They may or may not put up a poster, or post a note on the Walmart bulletin board. Either way, Skippy stays out of sight. The third type would get Skippy off the street and call an agency to have him picked up." Patti thought for a moment.

"There is a fourth type. Skippy could be picked up by a freelancer buncher, and removed from the area and sold to a research lab."

"Buncher?"

"It's someone who gathers animals together for sale to a third party, especially to someone that will pay good money for animals without a paper trail." Bonner had been taking notes as Patti talked. He reread what he had, then spoke: "Okay, so let's say Skippy gets lucky and the third type of person picks him up. How does that work?"

"That would depend on which agency picked Skippy up. If the Humane Officer or Animal Control Officer is radio dispatched, he or she might call in and have the office staff check the missing dog list. If Skippy matches up to a listing, then the officer may just take the animal directly to the owner's home, or have Dispatch call the owner. As crowded as most facilities are, rehoming the animal without bringing it in to a shelter is beneficial to everyone."

"Let's say that no one has filed a missing dog report that matches Skippy's description. What then?"

"The animal is processed in, checked for tattoos and microchips, then put in isolation for a time until it's health status is evaluated. Then Skippy would go into the general population."

"How long would he stay there?"

"At the very least any agency would hold the animal a minimum of three days, probably more if it had a nice temperament, they weren't overcrowded, or it was a type or breed that had a good chance of adoption."

"Such as . . .?"

"Like a young dog about one to two years old, under thirty pounds, maybe a shorthair. You want the Kiss of Death statistics? It's older dogs, big dogs, and long-haired dogs. Or a combination of the three. There are exceptions such as a Golden Retriever or Labrador, or junkyard dogs like Pitts and Rotties, but as a rule the average person with a family wants a dog that's safe, easy to manage, friendly, and won't eat their children."

"Okay, then let's say I want to do everything I can to make sure I get Skippy back. Where do I start, realizing that Skippy may or may not be wearing his collar?"

"First thing would be to scour the neighborhood where you lost him. Make sure someone is at the house if he does come home. I'd call every agency in the area and put in some kind of lost dog report. Use whatever information you have such as when you lost Skippy and where. If you don't know if he had a collar say he could have. Don't have someone rule Skippy out because you say no collar and he comes in with one. That happens all the time. Someone catches the animal, puts a collar on it, then the dog gets loose from *them*. Really, time and place are most important. The sex of the dog would be nice, too."

Patti thought some more: "Try putting up reward signs for a dog lost in such and such an area. Call the radio stations. Some of them will broadcast the information for you. Try a Hip Hop station if Skippy got lost in a Black section of town, or Country Western if you lost him out on farmland somewhere, that sort of thing. Last, I'd keep checking back with the shelters. Visit every day. Dogs get misidentified all the time."

"Jesus."

"Yeah, well, I say that about a hundred times a day. Put a license and rabies tag on a dog and I can have him home before you even knew he got out of your back yard."

"Patti, thanks for the information. If I wanted to put in a lost dog report, who would I see?"

"Just give it to me and I'll see it gets filed." Bonner gave Patti the address of the warehouse and the time the dog was lost. "The dog probably has or had a collar, and there is a chance that it was trailing a leash. That's all I can give you."

"We've had success with less. We haven't had any intakes yet today so I know Skippy hasn't been brought here. I'll get this up front for you."

"Thanks. You've been a help."

"I guess asking you what was going on would be out of the question?"

"No, Patti, you can ask. I just can't answer–yet. But if this lead helps us I'll let you know about *Skippy*. Deal?"

"Deal. Be careful."

"It's my middle name." Bonner fielded his way past the office workers and headed back to his vehicle. On the ride back into the city Bonner realized that he had not needed to go into the kennel area where they kept the dogs. And for that he was very grateful.

28

Even with lights and siren it took Daniel and Cohen fifteen minutes to make the journey down to Charles Street. The cross street had been opened up, finally allowing traffic to flow. However, the alley itself was still cordoned off. This time Daniel was able to park near the entrance. A uniformed officer was waiting for them as they approached the barricade. "Hey, Lieutenant, Jones and Barkowitz are waitin' for ya. We got the back door propped open. Go on up. It's on the fourth floor, number four-oh-five."

Cohen said thanks and the pair of detectives crossed the alley to the apartment building's rear door, entered, and started climbing. By the time they hit the fourth floor landing Cohen was a whipped dog. "Jesus, Mary, and Joseph, you'd think elevators had never been invented." The overweight detective was wheezing badly, although he wasn't concerned enough to put out his cigar.

"Too many Big Macs, no sleep, and that Garcia y Vega sticking out of your mouth probably have nothing to do with it," Daniel said, making sure he was upwind of the smoke and far enough away not to be hit.

"No shit, Sherlock. For your information, I prefer Whoppers. Jesus, do I hate stairs. Is it me or does this place stink?"

"Even your ratty cigar can't cover it, Barry. Somebody's been using the stairwell as a urinal. At least no one's puked here lately."

"Yeah, well, it's early yet. Let's go talk to this guy. Maybe his apartment smells better." They walked down the hall and found the door for apartment 405 and knocked. A plainclothes cop immediately opened the door. Another cop was inside, talking on his cell phone. He waved and continued talking.

"Daniel, this here's Leron Jones. Jonesy, Daniel. The other one's Jim Barkowitz". Cohen turned to Jones: "Where's the witness?"

Jonesy pointed: "He's in the kitchen cookin' sumpthin' you don't even wanna know."

By now Barkowitz had finished his call and he joined the other three men. Cohen made the introductions: "Daniel Shestack, Jim Barkowitz. We call him *Dog* for obvious reasons. Okay, Dog, what ya got?"

"We worked our way up the stairs. Most of the residents are at work. We concentrated on the units to the rear what faced the alley. We was halfway done when we got the word about the shed up on the roof so's we asked who belonged to it and the occupant of 307 told us it was the Mexican up on the next floor. We finished the third floor and went up a flight and hit 405 first. We like to beat the door down wakin' the guy up. He works the swing shift for a janitor service that cleans offices after five o'clock. Anyway, we asks him did he have access to the shed on the roof and he sorta hems and haws and starts shifting around so we asks him did he see anything and then he gets all quiet on us. So's I got a call into you and had Jonesy hunt up the manager to get a key to the roof door. Jonesy went topside to take a look whilst I stayed down here with Ricky Ricardo."

"He say anything? Did he ask for an attorney?" questioned Cohen.

"Nah, just started cookin'. But his English ain't so good."

"Yeah, like yours is. Jonesy, you still got the key?"

"No need, Lou. The roof isn't locked up. There's just a bar on the inside to keep someone from coming in from off the roof."

"You got permission from the Super?" asked Cohen. Jonesy nodded. "Okay, Jonesy, you stay here. Dog, come on up with us." The three detectives tracked down the hall to another set of stairs and climbed another flight, which stopped at a steel door with a piece of 2x4 across it. Dog removed the beam, opened the door, and the trio emerged onto the tarred roof.

The building they were standing on was narrow but long, extending from the street to the alley. It was close enough to its neighbors that a good broad jumper could have gone from one to the other with little effort. The roof was barren save for an old Weber grill, a couple of rusty lawn chairs and the shed Daniel had spotted from the ground.

The three walked over to the shed and looked in through the slats. The inside was fenced off into four sections. Each section contained chickens. One section had what appeared to be hens, which were gang-penned. The other three areas were divided up and reserved for cocks. One of the sections held one white bird, one section held a coal black one; the last stall held a multicolored bird.

"Whaddaya make of that, Dog?" asked Cohen.

"Not sure. A breeder, maybe?" answered Dog. "Maybe the guy just likes huevos for breakfast, si?"

"I don't know either. But somebody's put out fresh water, and they got food. Someone was up here not too long ago." Cohen and the other two men walked over to the edge of the roof and looked down.

"Well, Daniel, you're right. It someone was up here and maybe heard something and came over to look, they could see right down into the loading dock," said Cohen.

"Care to have a talk with Mister 405, Detective Cohen?"

"That is an excellent idea, Detective Shestack. Coming, Detective Barkowitz?"

29

David Alston shuffled his way to the podium and made as big a deal of arranging his papers as he could get away with. Mrs. Hurd just waited him out. Elizabeth would just as soon *tune* him out. David was never prepared, always talked during class, and believed studying history was a waste of time. She could not remember what his topic was. She didn't have to wait long to find out.

"Fellow students, my topic of discussion is *What if Leslie Howard and Hedy Lamarr were never born?* Well, I can tell you that their children would really be upset! No, really, see, these were movie stars back in the 1930s and 1940s, sorta like Tom Cruise and Julia Roberts. They were a big deal back then, maybe even bigger than Cruise and Roberts 'cause television hadn't been invented back then so they had no TV stars like the actors on *Friends* and *Sex and the*

City. Well, back in those days there was the Great Depression. It was called that because everyone was depressed because nobody had jobs and people were jumping out of skyscrapers, ha ha. Anyways, these movie stars were like idols or gods, and the people . . ."

At this point Elizabeth did tune out. What did David do, look up the names in the dictionary and that was it? She slid her eyes over to Mrs. Hurd to see how she was taking this in. It was hard to tell but Elizabeth thought Mrs. Hurd had a cross between a smile and a grimace on her face. Elizabeth knew that David was going to miss the target completely. She didn't know a lot about Leslie Howard. She could not recall having read much, and what she had learned seemed to be cloaked in secrecy by the British government. She did know he was supposed to have died on a secret missing during the war. That would have been challenging to research. As for Hedy Lamarr, she wasn't just a screen idol. She had worked with someone developing a system to keep torpedoes from being electronically jammed. Her theory was really the basis for cell phone transmissions today. That was one of those trivia things that came up all the time. David must have just thrown his paper together to have missed that bit of knowledge. As his talk hiccupped along Elizabeth turned her attention back to Mrs. Hurd. Last night's meeting had raised some questions about her history teacher. Now was as good a time as any to address those issues.

Without being obvious, Elizabeth swiveled her chair to a better angle where she could look at her teacher without twisting her neck so much. To the untrained eye Mrs. Hurd seemed totally engrossed in the manure David was spreading. Elizabeth knew better. Relaxing in her chair, Elizabeth unfocused ever so slightly, surveying the room. Slowly, words seem to float up from her classmates, their thoughts really. Some kids were actually listening to David. That surprised her. Others were going over their own reports, one boy had a headache, and not a few of the girls were thinking about boys, and vice versa. Elizabeth slowly swung her thoughts to Mrs. Hurd. At first she could divine nothing, then she started picking up her thoughts. Poor David! Mrs. Hurd already had him down for a 'D'. Her teacher was thinking about three or four things at once. Elizabeth caught a thought about a faculty meeting, something about dry-cleaning, and then something about a paper wall. The paper turned to cardboard, then brick, and finally to steel. She could see a door in the wall, which opened as she watched. An image of Mrs. Hurd stood in the doorway, smiled, and said: *Hello, Aubrey. Shouldn't you be listening to David?*

Elizabeth was so startled that her thoughts collapsed around her like a house of cards in a hurricane. She could feel the blush moving up her neck. When she managed to finally chance a look at Mrs. Hurd, her teacher was calming listening to David finish reading his paper. When he completed his report she thanked him for a most *enlightening* piece of work. David didn't even have the good sense to know he'd been busted. Instead he just grinned and sat down. Mrs. Hurd had the next name drawn from the hat, and they worked their way to the end of the period. When class ended Mrs. Hurd never said a word.

30

While Elizabeth was being ever so gently advised to stay out of other people's minds, Ed Bonner was still on dog detail. Having learned long ago that telephones were faster than shoe leather, he worked the Yellow Pages, talking to every veterinarian's office that was listed for the immediate area. He skipped the suburbs and the obvious high-end places. People with money didn't frequent that section of town. He called every shelter with a number listed in the book, filing a lost dog report at each one. He had to identify himself as a cop before two places would even take the information. He couldn't blame them. What kind of pet owner couldn't give a breed, a color, or the sex of their own dog? He persisted, making sure that if any information came in that someone would call and talk to him directly. At the rate he was going they would ID the body long before he ever found the dog–if the damn dog even existed! Trouble was, he agreed with Shestack. It felt right.

Bonner finished up his calls and went out to grab a sandwich. After lunch he was supposed to get back with Patel and see if the medical examiner could add anything that would help. In the meantime Bonner headed for a corner vendor. For some crazy reason he felt like having a hot dog for lunch.

* * *

Daniel, Cohen and Detective Jones joined Dog in Apartment 405. The small set of rooms reeked of something that had been fried to death. Dog got up from the couch and retrieved the occupant from the kitchen and the five of them gathered in the tiny living room. Cohen nodded for Jones to take the lead.

Jones introduced the newcomers, and then addressed their potential witness: "This here is Hector Arturo Vaca. Mr. Vaca, would you tell us what you saw this morning?"

Vaca looked irritated. "Wha chu wan with me? I already tell you erthin' I know!"

"Please, Mr. Vaca. You told Detective Jones and myself. The other detectives haven't heard your story. I would really appreciate it if you would repeat it for them." Jonesy voice was as sweet as maple syrup.

"Hokay, hokay, but chu makin' a beeg mistake. I din do noathin."

"No one said you did, Mr. Vaca. Please tell us again."

"I hear a *ruido*, in the alley. I loo' an' see an hombre. He walk away. Das it."

Jonesy looked at Cohen and rolled his eyes. He was going to have to do this step by step. If he waited for Hector they would still be here come tomorrow morning. "Mr. Vaca, you have a job, correct? What time do you get home from work?"

"Si, I work teel dos, maybe tres in the morning."

"What time did you return here last night, or rather this morning?"

"Abou hal' pas tres, maybe later."

"Okay, so you got here around 3:30, 3:45? Good. Now, did you go to sleep, watch television, what?" Vaca shifted slightly in his beat up Barkolounger. "I was no sleep, si? I read the periodico, the paper."

"Then did you go to sleep?"

"No, then I go arriba–upstairs–tejado"

"And why did you go up on the tejado, Mr. Vaca?"

"Gallina–comida–chew know–to fees the chicons."

"Okay, so you went up to feed the chickens on the roof. Can you remember what time it was, Mr. Vaca?"

"Si, it was cinco–five o'clok."

"And is that when you heard the noise?"

"Si, si. From the alley. Silbar–a whistle person."

Jonesy turned to his companions: "He means he heard a man whistling down in the alley."

"What else, Mr. Vaca?"

"Ladrido. Mucho times"

"So you heard someone whistling, and then you heard a dog barking, si?" Vaca nodded. "What then, Mr. Vaca?"

"I look abajo–down. I see a mujer, a hombre. The mujer has a perro."

"Then?"

"Nada. I come back away from the edge. I feed the chicons. Then dentro. Inside."

"Did you hear or see anything else, Mr. Vaca?"

"No, nada."

Jonesy turned to the other detectives. "Basically, Hector here goes topside to feed the birds, hears someone whistling, goes over to the edge of the roof and sees a man talking to a woman with a dog. He evidently ain't the curious type so's he takes care of the birdies, then comes back in. I tried to get a description of the man but Hector says it's dark, and he's four floors up in the air, the angle's bad, et cetera. Hector isn't too keen on being involved."

Cohen stood up and faced Vaca. "Mr. Vaca, you do know that a young woman, probably the woman you saw this morning, was killed right across the alley? Can you understand what I'm telling you?"

"Si, senor."

"There wouldn't be any reason why you wouldn't want to help us, would there?"

"Que?"

"Never mind. Mr. Vaca, what was the man wearing? Did you see that?"

"No, nada senor."

"Mr. Vaca, is that everything you can remember?"

"Si. It es everythin'."

Cohen looked at the other detectives knowingly. This witness saw something but was afraid to spill the beans. "Okay, then. Thank you for your cooperation. Daniel, you got anything for Mr. Vaca?"

Daniel Shestack stood up and faced Hector: "Si, teniente. Senor Vaca, where are you from?"

"Por que? Thees is America. Why you care? I doan do nada. Leaf me alon!"

When Daniel replied it was not in English: "Afedzu too ko mo okonri."

Vaca's jaw opened in astonishment. "Madre Dios!" Vaca crossed himself. Jones and Cohen were equally surprised.

"Where, Senor Vaca? Haiti? Or Cuba?" repeated Daniel.

"Si, si, Cuba."

"Are the chickens why you are afraid to talk to us?"

"Si, agente. Mis cliente es muy peligroso. Comprende?"

"Santaria unica?"

"No, rito satanico tambien."

"Comprender. Senor Vaca, the chickens . . . eso no tiene interes. Understand? We just want to know about el hombre de la calle. Can you please remember what he was wearing?"

"Si, si. Gorra de beisbol y chaqueta de Orioles." Jonesy translated: "Oriole jacket and baseball cap, Lou."

"Mr. Vaca, do you know what kind of dog, *perro*, it was?"

"Si. Tipo de perdiquero. Estoy seguro!"

"Lou, he's positive it was a golden retriever," said Jonesy.

"Dog, see if you can get Bonner on the phone and have him follow this up. Call Central with the description of the man, too. Considering this year's win-loss record, this might be the only person in the city wearing an Oriole jacket." Dog was already working the keypad on his phone as he exited the apartment.

"Mr. Vaca, is that everything you can remember?" asked Cohen.

"Si. Todo. It es everythin'."

Daniel went over to Cohen; "Give me one of your cards, Barry." Daniel took the business card and handed it to Hector. Vaca read the name. "Cohen?"

"Si, Hector. Cohen is *Lukumi*." Daniel waved at all of them. "Todo. If you ever need help, you call. Comprende?"

"Si, agente. Gracias."

"Da nada." The three detectives had already started out the door when another question came to Daniel's mind which caused him to turn around: "Hector, un momento. Did you recognize the song?"

"Que?"

"El cancion. The whistle song?"

"Oh, si, si! Mi favorito! Esta en mi cabeza! Mack el cuchillo!"

Daniel laughed out loud. "Muy gracias, Senor Vaca."

"Via con Dios, Senor Shestack," said Hector.

Daniel replied again in the language that was neither English nor Spanish: "Ki olorun ki ofu li emmi gigun." He smiled and shut the door behind him.

* * *

Barry Cohen waited until they navigated the four flights of stairs and hit the street before lighting up a cigar. After replacing the clean air in his lungs with smoke, he turned to Daniel: "Now, Detective Shestack, if I may be so bold: What the hell was all that? It's bad enough I need a translator for Gomez up there, but now I need one to understand you, too? That sure as hell wasn't Yiddish you two were talkin'!"

"Yeah," said Jonesy, "and it ain't no Spanish dialect I know, either."

Daniel laughed. "Actually, it's Yoruba. It's of Nigerian origin."

"And I guess you and Hector vacationed there?" snorted Cohen.

"Can't say I've ever been to African at all, let alone Nigeria. The chickens up on the roof sort of clued me in. They were separated, and it wasn't set up with nesting material. Made me wonder why would you want to keep them? Just to eat? Hell, you can go to KFC and get a four-piece dinner for less than it takes to feed and care for live ones. Did you notice that there were roosters of solid color on the one side? That helped too."

"Helped what?" Jonesy was baffled.

"Look, raising chickens in the city is not your average hobby, right? If you aren't getting eggs and you aren't eating the birds, where is the market? I recognized Hector's accent as probably Cuban—the way he clips off the end of his words is a dead giveaway. When he understood what I said to him I thought at least most of his birds were going to Santaria."

"What did you say to him?" asked Cohen.

"Oh, when he started off huffy I repeated a Yoruba saying that roughly translated means *frowning and fierceness prove not manliness.* That got his attention. Once he knew I knew, he loosened up. He wasn't talking because his customers aren't exactly the law and order type. He thought we might be trying to track down his buyers."

"Excuse my ignorance, but who the hell is this '*Santy Rea*' person," huffed Cohen.

Daniel explained: "Santaria, Barry. Long story short, it's not a person but a religion that came from African with the slaves. It spread in the New World, especially in Haiti and Cuba, then made its way Stateside. It's a combination, or bastardization, of African tribal worship and Catholicism. The slaves used the names of Saints to hide their own religion from the white folks. Now the two religions are intertwined. One of the aspects of Santaria is blood sacrifice. Chickens are usually the stars of the show. Before you say it, no, you can't put a bucket of the Colonel's Extra Crispy on the altar. Senor Vaca was raising the chickens for religious ceremonies."

"Well, what about the other stuff you talked about?" asked Jonesy.

"First off, you noticed the solid color black and white roosters upstairs? That is another kettle of fish, or chicken. You see, Hector is scared of the people that buy those cocks from him. He believes them to be very dangerous people. I tend to agree with his opinion. Evidently he sells to a satanic cult of some sort that uses his birds in Black Mass ceremonies. When all this is over you might go visit Hector again. He may give you a lead. I gave him your card. At the very least he may need your help sometime and you can Quid Pro Quo him."

"Yeah, well, bustin' goofballs wearing horns and screwin' like goats ain't that high on the District Attorney's hit list," said Cohen.

"True enough. Santaria sacrifice is even harder to prosecute. It's been tried but the results are always murky. No DA will to go to court over a chicken. But cult sacrifice can be worth the effort. Traditionally these people are involved in other illegal activities: Money laundering, drugs, prostitution, animal-napping, weapon violations. They're very secretive and extremely paranoid. You have to be very good or very lucky to catch them in the act. And just for the record, The Church of Satan is recognized by the government as a legitimate religious organization."

"Get outta here! No way!" said Jonesy.

Daniel laughed. "Too true. Remember that little *Freedom of Religion* thing in the Constitution? You're at liberty to worship anything or anyone you want to. Hell, you can pray to a paper bag if you want to."

Cohen just snorted. "Okay, I'll file Vaca away for future reference. Anything else?"

Before Daniel could answer Dog rejoined the group. "Goddamn Eddie musta let his battery go down. Dispatch says he's at lunch. Sorry, Lou."

"No problem. He never takes more'n half an hour. Try back in ten minutes. Daniel, you was saying?"

"Yeah, as I was leaving I thought to ask him if he recognized the song the perp was whistling, and damn if he didn't. The guy was whistling *Mack the*

Knife. It isn't much, but who knows? Maybe it's his theme song."

"Maybe, but I ain't telling the papers to advise the residents of Baltimore to avoid anyone singin' *Mack the Knife*. Jesus! I'd be laughed outta the city."

Dog had a thought: "Lou, what if someone heard that song on a previous murder? It could help tie things together."

"Yeah, maybe. I like it. Dog, get on the horn and start calling all the jurisdictions that had a similar murder case. Have them query whoever headed the investigation. Maybe we get a hit, maybe not. It's worth a try."

"Got it, Lou." Dog headed for his vehicle. Cohen yelled after him: "Don't forget to call Steady Eddie!"

Cohen turned back to Jonesy: "I want you to check in with every door-pounder we got working the street. Update them on the type of dog we're interested in. Find out how far and how wide they checked already and get back to me by phone."

"I'm on it."

Cohen turned to Daniel: "Let's you and me take a ride."

As Daniel unlocked the car doors Cohen leaned over the roof and looked at Daniel. Before Daniel got in Cohen asked him a question: "What was it you said to our boy Hector as we were leavin'? You know, that *emmy guyun* stuff?"

"Actually, I asked God to bless him with a long life."

31

Jack pulled a beer out of the refrigerator and took it into the living room. As he sat in the recliner he spilled some of the liquid on the carpet. Not that he cared–he was renting month to month. He rubbed the foam into the weave. *Neatness counts.* Jack picked up the remote, aimed it at the Rent America television and switched to channel five. He had to suffer through twenty minutes of Judge Judy before a newsbreak came on. The scene behind the black woman reporter was breathtaking: Taped off streets, cops, flashing lights, and a superb audience. It was quite a spectacle. *A veritable three-ring circus with yours truly as the Ringmaster. Please! Save your applause for later. Thank you so much. Oh, and the PIO was delicious! She was sincere, and sad, and upbeat and it took her two minutes to say absolutely nothing. Public Information Officer my foot. She had no information to give to the public. She was probably a communications major in college. To call her an officer was the height of conceit. Dollars to donuts her looks got her the job. What was the world coming to if professionals weren't hired for professional jobs? I do my work in a professional manner so is it too much to expect the same in return?*

The talking head from Channel Five News finished her live report and returned the show back to the newsroom. As she tuned out Jack turned off the set. He was content now to just relax, reflect, and revel in his work. Not without pride he considered it one of his best pieces. As he was want to do he replayed the events of the early morning hours. The beer was hitting him hard–he knew he was slightly dehydrated which caused everything to be fuzzy around the edges. He liked it that way.

Jack had located this morning's actress a week ago. Like clockwork, Ms. Dana Lieter ran early in the morning before heading for work at Johns Hopkins. She wasn't bad looking in a I'm-healthy-and-you're-not kind of way. He didn't think she drank or smoked. *She probably railed against the use of either, just like his mother. Yep, healthy as a horse and could outrun one, too. Jack had bided his time, checking her routine, waiting for the right phase of the moon. He was very patient, he was, and loved it when a plan came together like this one.*

He replayed the events in his mind, enjoying it almost as much as he did when he was doing it.

Dana came into the alley within five minutes of what he had scheduled. As soon as he saw her he started walking and whistling. When she was close enough to see him what she saw was a poor, distraught dog owner holding a leash, whistling for his lost dog. As usual she was accompanied by her dog, a large size yellow Labrador Retriever. She slowed as she reached him, and continued to jog in place, the dog panting at her side. Jack would have done her right there but he sensed someone on the roof behind him. Instead he talked to Dana, asking her if she had seen his dog. When he could no longer feel the intruder on the roof he dropped the leash, grabbed the girl and pressure-pointed her carotid artery until she passed out. He picked her up bodily and placed her in the loading dock alley. Of course by now the damn dog was going nuts, pulling on the leash and trying to escape. Jack thought the animal totally gutless until it turned on him. He was barely able to get the knife up in time as the animal lunged for his throat. As it was he only managed to cut the dog's leg. When it came down the leash loop came off the girl's wrist and the dog limped away as fast as three legs would carry it. Jack wanted to follow but knew his time was too limited for personal vendettas. He undid his jacket and pulled out a thick cotton towel, put

236 t connor michael

it to the girl's neck and slit her from ear to ear. He enjoyed the delightful sound of her gurgling blood that was counterpointed by the rapid thump of his heart. *Dana had such a small part in this drama but hey, dying on stage took a lot out of you. It was very draining. Ha! If Jack kept this up he could turn this into a comedy.* Jack had waited until the blood stopped pulsing, then placed the towel in a trash bag he pulled from his coat pocket. *Neatness counts!* It was only the work of minutes for him to do what still had to be done. Jack removed what had to be removed, straightened up his work, and then positioned Dana up against the wall, legs spread as wide as possible. He placed the toy in her mouth like the others, all the while singing *candy-coated popcorn peanuts and a prize . . . that's what you get with Crackerjacks!* The last thing he did was remove the jogging pouch from around her waist. He opened the zippered compartment, finding her driver's license and enough money for breakfast. *Thanks! Moving to the end of the loading dock he surveyed the stage: Perfect! He checked his watch: Eleven minutes start to finish. Not bad. Wouldn't it be a great encore if he found the dog on his way out? Nevertheless he was content as he whistled his way down the alley . . . ya know when that shark bites, with his teeth babe, scarlet billows start to spread . . .!*

Lordy what great theater. Too bad for Dana that she would miss the next performance. No matter—he had her understudy already picked out. One more recital and normally he would take his show on the road. The Bobbies got smarter as the years passed. But so did he. He was just one poor actor on the Stage of Life. But the number of cops were legion. He really should be making plans but something held him here. He wasn't worried—yet. If some force willed his performance to be held over then so be it. Who was he to deny them the pleasure of seeing an artiste at work?

32

Steady Eddie Bonner hadn't let his cell phone battery run down. What he had done was inadvertently shut down his phone when he dropped it rummaging for change to pay for his hot dog. It wasn't until he returned to the station and was besieged by messages that he checked his phone and saw that it wasn't on. Before he could return any of the messages Barkowitz called again and relayed the message about the golden retriever. Bonner just took the new information and started recalling all the places he had called that morning. *Why was it that none of the detectives on television ever had to do this kind of mind-numbing, repetitious work?*

Bonner just plodded along, trying not to irritate staff members as he amended the lost dog report he had filed earlier. He was on his sixth veterinarian when he hit paydirt. It was an animal hospital, and no, they didn't have a golden retriever but a woman had brought in a yellow Labrador around the time the day shift started. The dog had a gash on its hind leg and the on-duty veterinarian had sewn the dog up before all the daytime office staff arrived. Did the gentleman wish to see the dog? *Yes, thank you, the gentleman would.* Bonner was out the door before the girl on the phone could ask him his name.

It took Bonner exactly fourteen minutes to reach the animal hospital. The office was closed except for emergencies but Bonner figured this qualified so he knocked on the door until a bright young thing in a smock decorated with frogs let him in. Bonner showed her his shield and asked for the office manager or the equivalent. She took him to a back office and introduced him to the staff manager, Ginger Rhodes.

"Mrs. Rhodes, one of your people told me you took in a dog early this morning? One with a cut leg?"

"Yes we did. A very nice yellow Lab. I believe Debbie processed the animal in and Doctor Engstrom did the surgery. Is the animal yours?"

"No. In fact it may not be the animal I'm looking for. Are Debbie and the veterinarian here now?"

"Oh yes, but the Doctor is in surgery at the moment. You could talk to Debbie now if you want to."

"Please, and could she bring in any paperwork for the animal? Thanks." It took Mrs. Rhodes little time to get Debbie into her office.

"Debbie, this is Detective Bonner. He would like to ask you about the yellow Lab we took in this morning."

"Okay, sure. Whatcha want to know?"

"First, who brought the animal in?"

"Some lady. She's not a client of ours. She was driving by and saw the dog in the middle of the street so she stopped. She muscled the dog into her car and brought him here."

"Why here?"

"She said it's on her way to work. She said she sees the sign every day so she headed here. Her vet is way the hell and gone in Howard County."

"Did she say where she found the dog?"

"Yeah, somewhere off Calvert, I think." Bonner knew Calvert Street paralleled Charles Street.

"About what time did she bring the dog in?"

"I'd say about seven, seven-thirty."

"Did you get the woman's name?"

"Sure. It's all in the file–name, address, phone number." Bonner thanked the staffer, and then looked to Mrs. Rhodes: "May I look at the dog?"

"Of course. Come on back this way." Mrs. Rhodes led Bonner through two sets of swinging doors, and stopped at a room with subdued lighting. "This is our recovery room. The dog you want is in the bottom cage on the left." Bonner knelt in front of the cage. Inside was a big, tawny animal, his rear left leg bandaged from paw to hip. The dog raised his head but did not get up.

"He's still a little groggy from surgery. Another couple of hours and he'll be awake and alert."

Bonner studied the animal. "Hypothetical question: From a distance could you mistake this for a golden retriever?"

"Yes, if you were far enough away, I guess. They're about the same size and color. Big difference is that Labs are short-haired and golden retrievers have long coats."

Bonner rubbed the dog's head through the mesh of the cage. "Nice animal. This dog is certainly not a stray?"

"Probably not. His coat was fairly clean except for the blood, and he's well fed. I'd guess he got out of somebody's yard and was hit by a car."

Bonner stood up. "Mrs. Rhodes, I really need to talk with the attending vet. Time is important. Can you try and get me to him?"

"Let me go into surgery and see what he's working on. If it's something minor he'll probably talk to you as he works. Give me a minute."

Bonner had to wait four but it was worth it. Mrs. Rhodes came out of the surgery with the vet in tow. After introducing the two men she excused herself and returned to her office.

"Doctor Engstrom, I'm interested in the yellow Labrador that you stitched up this morning. Can you tell me anything about it?"

"What do you want to know? Someone found the animal on the street and brought it in because it was injured and bleeding. Debbie inducted the dog while I prepped. We rushed the animal in, knocked it down and sutured the inside of the left rear leg. The animal came out of the anesthesia without any problems. We have an IV tube in and it should recover without any adverse effects, although it has lost a lot of blood. That's about it."

"What about the wound? Was there any indication how it happened?"

"Something sharp tore the skin and leg muscle, not something jagged. The cut is clean–no rough edges. It could have been made by a sharp piece of metal under a car or truck. Is there anything else, detective? I've been backed up ever since I got in. I've got a fourth-year vet school student closing for me and I need to get back in there."

"Sure, Doc. Thanks." Doctor Engstom hustled back into the operating room, leaving Bonner to find his way to Mrs. Rhodes office. He stuck his head in the office and thanked Mrs. Rhodes for her help, and asked her one last question: Did the dog have any identification on it? Mrs. Rhodes still had the file, and according to the information listed it had no identifiers. They had scanned it for a microchip too, but there wasn't one. Bonner got the information on the Good Samaritan from Mrs. Rhodes, thanked her again, and left the facility.

Bonner was in his vehicle placing a call to the woman who picked up the dog when a young woman in a lab coat ran up to his car. Bonner rolled down the window and she handed him a collar and a leash. "Doctor Engstrom said you might want to see this. The big Lab was wearing it when it came in. Doctor Engstrom said he went out to the car and carried the dog directly to surgery. He's been really busy and forgot to give it to the front desk. Will this help you find the owner?"

Bonner fingered the rabies tag attached to the collar. "You have no idea."

33

For once Elizabeth was happy to be going to gym class. She really needed to talk to LaTisha and Amy. She hadn't reached the point where she could talk about the dreams; that had to wait. Still, she knew some explanations were in order, especially since her two new friends would undoubtedly notice the difference in her appearance. Elizabeth hustled to the locker room and made a beeline to one of the rest rooms. Quickly she undressed and put on her gym clothes, pulling a set of sweats overtop her suit to cover her arms and legs. Thankfully this was not too abnormal. The gym was notoriously drafty and cold this time of year and many of the girls layered up. By the time she was done the locker room was full. Elizabeth pushed out of the stall and searched out her friends. Both girls were at their lockers dressing and whispering at the same time. When

Elizabeth reached them they looked up and both started talking to her at the same time.

"Whoa, Nellie! One at a time. Hello to you too!" she laughed.

Amy put her hand over LaTisha's mouth and started talking while LaTisha mumbled vile things into Amy's palm. "Elizabeth, you are not going to believe what happened last night! It was absolutely weird! Ouch!" LaTisha had managed to bite Amy's finger.

"Yeah girl, it was something to see!" said LaTisha as she whacked Amy with her sneaker.

"What are–will you two stop it?" LaTisha now had Amy in a headlock. "I can't believe you two are seniors!" laughed Elizabeth.

"What did you see? What happened? Amy–you talk first." ordered Elizabeth.

"Wait. Not here. There are way too many ears. Wait'll class starts."

The class was half over before the three girls found a time and a place where they could talk without being seen or overheard. As Elizabeth listened Amy recounted the story of the previous night. She started with the feeling of being watched and ended with her dropping the jack on the floor. When Amy finished talking LaTisha explained what had happened on her end. Through the whole narrative Elizabeth was silent. *This was unexpected. The problem was how to explain it, or indeed, if it needed explaining at all.*

This might be something that her two friends just had to take on faith.

Elizabeth arranged her thoughts and spoke: "I like the *transmitter* idea. If we can summon one another using the jacks, then why can't there be other frequencies to do other things? Obviously Amy's jack has the added ability of infrared vision, plus being able to relay the signal to LaTisha's jack. It's like cable coming into the house to one TV, and then the signal goes to another television in the bedroom. I bet if you had called me I could have seen the same thing. We'll have to try that sometime. Right now I think we should be more worried about who was watching Amy."

"I agree," said Amy. "Strange as all that was, the woman I saw didn't seem mean or to be a threat. But why was she watching my house?"

Elizabeth felt she had to illuminate her friends if only to protect them. "Uh, I'm not one hundred percent sure but it probably has something to do with me. No, be still, 'Tish. Right now I'm caught up in things that I can't really explain to you. Heck, I can't explain most of it to myself. I think that both of you could be in danger just by being my friends. I think the jacks are a way to counteract the danger. That's my guess, anyway. I don't want either of you to get hurt because of me. On the other hand I'm feeling really selfish because I don't want to lose my friends."

LaTisha interrupted: "So what you're saying is that we'd be stupid to stay up with you because we could get hurt, right?" Elizabeth nodded. LaTisha looked at Amy, who shook her head. "Girl, nobody ever accused us of being stupid." Elizabeth looked crestfallen. "That is, until now. We're in whether you like it or not."

"Elizabeth, whatever it is, we'll help if we can. Honest. Besides, I got my dad checking on the Peeping Tom. Daddy'll make sure I'm okay. And nobody's bothered 'Tish. If things get too hot we can always bail, okay?"

Elizabeth choked up. "Okay . . . and thanks."

"Now, group hug!" said Amy.

"Group hug my ass," laughed LaTisha as she grabbed Amy's head and gave her a Dutch rub.

"Enough already!" Elizabeth could hardly see through her tears of joy and laughter. "On to business, you idiots! One thing we have to do is make sure we are never without our jacks. Neither one of you had yours on last night. We need to go to a jeweler or something and get them mounted on chains. I think it is really important that we wear them all the time. And I mean all the time—even in the shower. Deal?" Both Amy and LaTisha nodded assent.

"What about today after school? Can you guys go to the mall, or do you have practice?"

LaTisha laughed. "Carlin has a doctor's appointment so she cancelled practice. I can't imagine what the appointment is for. Maybe a head injury?"

"You are so bad, 'Tish! She's right, though. Carlin called practice so we can go. What about you?" asked Amy.

"Definitely. I have to go and get clothes, too. Look at this!" Elizabeth pulled out her mother's credit card. "Mom figured it was cheaper to buy me new stuff than to loan me her clothes."

Amy grabbed for the card but Elizabeth pulled it out of reach before she could snag it and said: "Nice try. Today I feel absolutely *affluent*!"

LaTisha snorted. "Did you say affluent or afflicted?"

"A little of both, perhaps. So, should we meet out front after school?" asked Elizabeth.

"Better just to meet at my car. Why stand around where everyone can see us?" said LaTisha.

"Good thinking. Hey, there's Coach. We better get back. 'Tish, you go first. Elizabeth and I can sneak in from the other side." LaTisha angled off to the game area while Elizabeth and Amy walked the long way around. "Say, Elizabeth, I've been meaning to ask. Did you go to a tanning salon last night? Your face is all red."

Red-what an apropos word to use! "If anyone asks the answer is yes. Say I fell asleep under a tanning lamp at home, okay?"

"Sure. No problem. Are you going to tell me the real reason or keep me in the dark? I'm not a very good mushroom, Lizzie. You can keep me in the dark and feed me crap but don't think for a minute those sweats fool me. It may cover what I'm guessing is a full body tan but it can't hide the fact that you're taller than you were yesterday."

"Jesus, Amy, how can you tell?"

"Come on—Ray Charles could tell. Anyway, you think my dad read me *The Princess and the Pea* as a bedtime story? No, what I got was *Everything You Wanted To Know About Being A Detective But Were Afraid To Ask.* Daddy taught me to pay attention. Look at you: Your legs are longer. Our stride was about the same yesterday. Now I have to stretch to keep up. 'Tish noticed, too. She just didn't say anything. And look at your hands." Amy took Elizabeth's hands in hers and turned them palm-up. "Where did the soft skin go? How do you get calluses in twenty-four hours?" Amy grabbed Elizabeth's arm before Elizabeth could react. Involuntarily her biceps tightened. "Where was this yesterday? You been eating nothing but spinach, Popeye? Look, Lizzie, I'm your friend. So's 'Tish. But you're gonna have to come clean sooner or later, you know?"

"I know, I know. But Amy, I'm afraid that if I do you guys could get hurt, and I just couldn't handle that."

"Lizzie, did it ever occur to you that we could get hurt because you *didn't* tell us?"

Elizabeth started to answer but stopped. There was great truth in that statement. Although Jack had counseled her not to say anything she could indeed do as much or more harm by keeping silent. Elizabeth reckoned that Jack's primary objective was to protect her from coming to harm. The safety of her friends was secondary. For her it was the other way around. She was better equipped for whatever was to happen than either of her friends. Friends stood by friends. She decided.

"Amy, you're right. After school I'll do my best to fill you in. But I'm warning you: If you two laugh at me I'm gonna beat the crap out of both of you!" Elizabeth smiled to belie the truth in the statement.

Amy looked into Elizabeth's eyes but did not laugh. "You know what? I think you could do it."

34

Mary Feye held out until just before lunch. By then the manila envelope that was screaming in her briefcase couldn't be ignored. She made a couple of calls, shifted a staff meeting, and took an early lunch. Mary pulled out one of the envelopes, grabbed her purse and hurried to a delicatessen a block away. She picked up a ready-made chef's salad and snatched a diet Coke from a cooler. After paying she found a booth in the back, opened the envelope and started reading. Although most sources were inconclusive as to how many deaths could be attributed to the Ripper, the physical accounts of the murders were well documented. Mary Feye started with the first killing and worked her way up the chronological ladder of death.

The first murder occurred on August 31st, 1888 in London's Whitechapel district, which was east of London proper. The woman's name was Mary Ann Nichols, or Polly as she was known by the locals. Polly was a confirmed alcoholic and part-time prostitute. She had been found around four in the morning, nearly decapitated by a knife cut to the throat. Polly was lying on her back with her skirts hitched up around her waist. Later it was revealed that her abdomen had been slashed and mutilated.

Before Polly's murder, two other women had been attacked in the same area, one on August 6th and the other woman months before in April. The August victim, Martha Tabram, had been repeatedly stabbed on *body, neck, and private parts with a knife or dagger.* No person of authority was willing to positively connect the two August killings, and certainly not all three. That meant little to the residents of Whitechapel. Connected or not, people were dying.

Just over a week later another woman was found murdered. A forty-seven-year-old prostitute named Annie Chapman, she too was killed in the early morning hours. Although the murder was in a different police jurisdiction—Spitalfields–it shared the gruesomeness of the other two murders. Chapman's body was also on its back, again with the skirts up around the waist. This time internal organs were lifted out of the body, some of which were never recovered. The skill in which this was done was of a level that made the police surgeon believe the killer had great anatomical knowledge. There were no false cuts. All the incisions were just where they were needed. All the abdominal wounds were post-mortem–Annie Chapman's death was the result of a massive cut to the throat. No one had heard an outcry, suggesting to authorities that she had been strangled into unconsciousness first, and then had her throat slashed. No viable clues were found at the scene. A woman on her way to the market saw Dark Annie–her street name–and a man talking in the spot where the body was later found. Unfortunately, the man's back was toward the witness and she was unable to give anything useable in the way of a description. Three ugly murders had occurred in the space of thirty-three days and the authorities were still baffled.

Mary Feye sat back and sipped at her Coke. She had lost interest in her salad after the first paragraph. She tried to imagine what Victorian England's East End was like at the time of the Ripper. She could envision poor lighting, narrow streets, and a police force trying to solve crimes that would tax the abilities of 21st century cops. Mary didn't know if the Ripper was very careful, very lucky, or eluded police because of poor forensic science. Not that it mattered much to Dark Annie. She was as dead as she ever would be and nothing Mary did could change that. However, she might be able to find something in all this to help Elizabeth. She pulled the next chapter to her and started reading.

Twenty-two days after Dark Annie's death Whitechapel was stunned by not one but two murders on the same date, the night of September 30th. The first woman found was Elizabeth Stride, a 45-year-old seamstress/cleaning woman and possible part-time prostitute. Once again the victim was killed by a knife slash to the throat. This woman, however, was not mutilated, possibly due to time constraints placed upon the killer by outside forces.

Less than a quarter mile away and forty-five minutes later another woman's body was found in a place called Mitre Square. Her name was Catharine or *Kate* Eddowes. She was forty-six years old. Kate's throat was slashed like the others, from left to right, and was the cause of her death. Unlike *Long Liz* Stride, Kate had been horribly mutilated—In fact, she had been gutted. Her chest cavity was laid open from *breast bone to pubes*, the intestines were pulled out, and a kidney and part of her womb removed and never found. Kate's face was also mutilated. Her eyelids were slashed and the tip of her nose cut off. Kate Eddowes body had been literally wreaked almost beyond recognition. A point could be made that the destruction done to her body compensated for the lack of violence attendant upon the person of Elizabeth Stride.

This last death brought the total to five murders. Mary Feye had one more victim profile to read, that of Mary Kelly. The tall-for-the-time five feet, seven inch Kelly was found dead in her lodging on November 9th, murdered. Maybe because the killer had extra time or felt more secure behind walls was the reason Kelly was the poster child for Serial Killer Mutilation. Once again, death was caused by a knife to the throat. The physician doing the autopsy literally needed pages to describe the way Kelly's body had been destroyed. The face was a mass of cuts and slashes. The abdominal cavity had been emptied and the contents ceremoniously arranged around the body. Large flaps of skin had been peeled from her thighs and other areas. Mary Kelly's heart was missing and was never found.

Mary Feye dropped the last profile on the table. There had been a long space of time between the double murder and Mary Kelly's death, about forty days. Official opinion veered towards the increased police presence on the streets and people staying in at night as the reason for the quiet period of time. Mary Feye agreed with the theory—this guy was no fool, no matter how high his blood lust. Six women dead—and this was just the known dead. How many could have ended up in the Thames without every being found?. Mary thought the Ripper was an opportunist rather than someone on a schedule. She was certainly no criminal psychologist but she intuitively felt that the Ripper just loved his work and it didn't matter when he worked as long as the work got done. He was like a farmer plowing a field—what didn't get plowed today because of rain he would get to tomorrow. If the Ripper had no schedule then he became much harder to apprehend. Worse yet, if he was this smart, then couldn't he change his modus operandi? That flew in the face of serial killer profiles but then this guy was never caught. Could he be the exception that proved the rule?

Mary skimmed the remaining information she had copied looking for clues. Even though the police had never caught the Ripper they were not without suspects. Mary reviewed the list of possibles: Montague Druitt, Aaron Kosminsky, Michael Ostrog, George Chapman, Francis Tumblety, and Prince Albert Victor Christian Edward were just a few of the people that qualified as suspects. She tended to agree with what was known about George Chapman, whose real name was Severin Antoniovich Klosowski. He had surgical skill, opportunity, was single at the time of the murders, and at a later date he was convicted of murder. What struck Mary was the documented fact that Chapman returned to America–New Jersey–in March of 1891 and in April of the year a woman named Carrie Brown was strangled and mutilated in Jersey City. The woman was maimed in much the same way as the victims in England. *Was Chapman continuing his habits in the United States?* No clues remain but the timing was right, and the technique used to kill Carrie Brown linked Chapman to the crime. Interestingly enough,

Chapman was hanged in 1903, having finally been caught for poisoning his three wives with antimony.

Here Mary Feye stopped. Before she had read the biography of Chapman she had felt that the Ripper was smart enough not to follow established patterns of behavior for too long a period. *Was he capable of switching from knife to poison if it pleased him? With the whole world at his feet could he not indulge in experimentation?* Mary realized this was rampant speculation on her part. Still, if Chapman was the original Ripper, then she had some insight, however slight, into what the man was capable of.

Just reading about this psychopath had disturbed Mary no end. *Was she really willing to serve up her daughter to this walking slice of Evil? Tonight the Ladder Society in general, and Mr. Jack Hawkins in particular, better be prepared to answer a whole basket of questions.* When Mary Feye left the deli her mind was still on the Ripper. She never saw or felt the person who followed her.

35

Barry Cohen directed Daniel Shestack to a diner west of Charles Street. It wasn't a cop joint—just a hangout for locals who liked good food at a decent price. Cohen headed for a back booth where both detectives tried to take the bench facing the door. Neither one wanted his back to the entrance. Daniel won and Cohen grumbled. They ordered lunch and waited for their waitress to leave before talking.

"Daniel, before it slips my mind—wherever did you learn Nigerian or Aruba or whatever you were speakin' to Vaca?"

Daniel smiled. "Bi a Lagbara Dze O NiIya, Ki Ofi Erin Si I."

"What the hell does that mean?"

"It means *If a great man should wrong you, smile!* It's Yoruba, not Aruba, and with that last phrase you have now heard my entire knowledge of the language. I just picked up some stuff working with cases in the City. I never thought I'd ever have the need to use them down here."

"Well, it certainly opened up Vaca like a can a tuna. Thanks. Any more hidden talents I should know about?"

"I know all the words to *The Ballad of Davy Crocket* if you think that might come in handy. Did you know it has twenty verses?"

Barry laughed. "I doubt that we'll need the info but thanks for the heads up. Listen, in case I forget to tell you, and I probably will, thanks for helping us out with this. I gotta think you moved here to get away from this kinda crap."

"Yeah, well, it never ends, does it? No matter where you go you'll find trouble. Fact is, my daughter Amy is about the age of some of the victims. Somebody's parents are inconsolable because this guy's out there. I don't want it to be me doing the grieving."

"Yeah. Here, I wanna show you something." Cohen pulled an envelope out of his jacket and removed some 35mm prints. "Take a look at these." Barry spread three photographs on the table.

Daniel studied the three prints. Two were morgue photos, the third a crime scene. The object centered in each picture was the same. "Who?" asked Daniel.

"Last three victims, not counting today's which makes four."

"They're all the same except for color?"

"If you mean identical, then no. But are they the same size, weight and design? Yes. The blue jack we found near the first body under some debris. As you can tell, the green and red jacks were found during the autopsy. They were our second and third victims. Today's black one makes a total of four. My guess is they all came from the same set."

"Think it might be a calling card? A signature?" asked Daniel.

"Sure ain't coincidence. He's a brazen bastard. Either that or he thinks we're so stupid we can't connect the murders without his help."

"As if his M.O. wasn't definitive enough. Jesus, this is one cocky son of a bitch. Who knows about this?"

"Including you? Just six people. Me, Jonesy, Dog, Eddie and Patel. I kept it tight. My boys won't talk and Patel's like a mummy when it comes to stuff like this."

"You got any theories about the jacks?" asked Daniel.

"Yeah, lots of 'em. Thought about *jack-of-all-trades* but that made no sense whatsoever. Then Dog thought maybe the colors had some significance but I don't see that going anywhere. Maybe he's trying to tell us he's toying with us. Patel thought it might be some sort of religious symbolism. Or he could just be laughin' at us saying we're a buncha *jack* asses. Tell ya the truth I just don't know."

"What about *jack be nimble*? That's another way of saying we're stupid. Then again, a guy with an over-inflated ego may just be telling us his name. Did you run local offenders with the name Jack?"

"Yeah, I'm way ahead of you there. No joy. Doesn't mean his name isn't Jack–just that we got no one listed."

"Barry, do you think all the jacks were placed inside the bodies?"

"Yeah I do. It stands to reason. I think we were sloppy on the first murder and somehow dumped the jack outta the body. Today I think the jack was in the girl's mouth and it came out when she fell over."

"Barry, did you think to have Dog ask about jacks when he called about the Mack the Knife song?"

"No, goddammit, I didn't. Let me see if I can reach him." Barry called Barkowitz just as their lunch arrived. Thankfully Dog had only reached one agency. Better yet the lead man on that case was out. Barry instructed Dog to ask about the jacks, and then hung up. "Sloppy, sloppy, sloppy. I should have done that long ago."

"Take it easy, Barry. You were protecting evidence. Trying to keep that secret obscured the obvious."

"Thanks Daniel. I appreciate the words but we both know it was a screw-up."

"It's only a screw-up if it's relevant to catching the guy, Lou. Otherwise it's just a lead that went nowhere."

"Jesus! Did you go to school to learn how to make people feel good?"

"No—it's a God-given talent." Both detectives laughed and started attacking their meals.

* * *

While Detectives Cohen and Shestack were eating, Ed Bonner was calling Patti at the Maryland SPCA. She was out of the building when he called but she rang him back within ten minutes. "Detective Bonner? What's up?"

"Patti, earlier you said that if you had a rabies tag you could locate the owner, right?"

"Absolutely."

"Okay then. I got a tag number for you." Bonner read her the tag and year number from the metal plate. "How long will it take?"

"Call me back in ten minutes." She hung up.

Eight minutes later Bonner was back on hold. Patti came on the line without preamble: "Got a pen? The tag belongs on a neutered male yellow-tan Labrador and is registered to a Dana Lieter." She gave Eddie a street address not ten blocks from the murder scene.

"Thanks Patti. I can't talk now but I promise to call later and let you know. Thanks again." Eddie rang off before Patti could say goodbye or good luck.

Eddie immediately called Lieutenant Cohen, catching him eating a late lunch with Daniel Shestack. Cohen instructed Bonner to get hold of Jonesy and Dog by phone and have them go to the address. Daniel and Cohen would meet them there. Eddie was able to reach both Jones and Barkowitz on the first try. He relayed Cohen's message, cluing them in to what he had found. Both of them would be at Lieter's address inside of twenty minutes.

36

Elizabeth was able to remain in the gym without any problem. She had told Amy and LaTisha whom she was going to see. They both were curious but held their questions for later. Since Holly was not going to be looking for Elizabeth's company at lunch she was free to head directly to The Hawk's enclave. Elizabeth knocked on the door and entered. She knew Hawk was inside. What she didn't know was that he had company. She walked down the corridor to where Hawkins sat.

"Welcome, Elizabeth. I would like you to meet KatyJay. KatyJay, Elizabeth. KatyJay is with the LS, Elizabeth. She has something to tell you."

"Milady, I am honored to finally meet you in person."

"Uh, me too, I guess," answered Elizabeth, confused.

"I'm sorry, but you have been such a big part of my life that I feel like we are old friends. I have been assigned to you, off and on, for the last five years. Recently I have been on other duty. Yesterday I was recalled and assigned to watch your friend, Amy Shestack."

"You're a Watcher?" asked Elizabeth.

"Yes, among other duties. At the moment I am charged to protect Amy from harm."

Elizabeth thought about that for a second or two. "Where were you last night?"

KatyJay looked to Hawk, who nodded. "I was watching Amy's house."

Elizabeth laughed out loud. "Oh God, that is so funny! You scared the pee out of Amy! She saw you, you know?"

"Ah, yes, I'm aware that she was able to get a glimpse of me."

"She told me she could pick you out of a lineup!"

KatyJay looked totally embarrassed. Hawk interceded on her behalf: "Milady, it was unexpected and certainly no fault of KatyJay's that she was found out. KatyJay's focus was more on the outside of the house than the inside."

"I'm sorry, KatyJay. But it is funny. You're lucky Amy's dad didn't catch you. He's a cop." Elizabeth looked at the Watcher a little more closely. "Say, I recognize you. Didn't you graduate last year? Wait—you worked at the Dairy Queen, too, didn't you?"

KatyJay smiled. "Yes, Milady. I worked in the county library too, and the Sheetz convenience store a block from your house. Like I said, I've been around for the last five years."

"Just watching me?"

"More like watching the people around you, but yes."

"Wow, have you ever been bored! I'm really sorry you had to watch me, or guard me, or whatever."

"Not at all, Milady. I fought for the assignment. Now I am detailed to other work for the time being. Mr. Hawkins has rewarded me with this meeting, even though he denies it."

"It was well-earned at any rate, KatyJay. Now Milady, to ease her work, do you know where Ms. Wood will be later today? KatyJay has drawn the task of watching her for a time."

"There's no volleyball practice after school so the three of us are going to the mall. After that I don't know," said Elizabeth.

"That will help. KJ, take it easy until after school, then pick them up after last bell. Call Wolf later if need be. Now, get out of here and rest."

"Goodbye, Elizabeth. I will see you again, although you may not see me! Adieu."

"G'bye, KatyJay. Thanks again!" KJ disappeared as if she had never been in the room. "She's very nice."

"She is one of our best. For the record, she was our first choice as your Watcher. She's rather proud of you, I think. Are you hungry?"

"Yes!"

"Then let's eat and talk." Hawkins spread out their regular fare and then continued their conversation. "I wanted you to meet a Watcher so that you would be familiar with who and what they are. They are just people doing the best they can in a difficult situation. Quite honestly, 99% of the job is mind-numbing boredom. All the jobs, not just watching you. They are not undetectable, as you have just learned. That is what I need to make clear. Helpful they are, but infallible they are not. Do not become complacent simply because a KatyJay is watching your back, okay? Rely on your own resources first." Hawk took a swig of orange juice.

"We have placed Watchers on your mother, on Ms. Wood, on Ms. Shestack, and of course, you. Last night I decided not to divulge that information but by light of day I see that was a poor decision. My original reasoning was that you would give your Watchers away by looking for them. Now I believe that you would sense them, and give them away in that manner. Do not look for your Watchers. They will be there, or they will not. I believe you now have the resources to ken whether someone following you has Evil intent, yes?"

Elizabeth had to swallow before answering. "Yes sir, I believe so. That brings up something else I need to talk about. Two things, really. My friend Holly . . . I had to . . . we . . . she would never understand all this."

"So you told her a lie instead?"

"Oh no, that's the problem! I can't lie to Holly. She would know. But if I told her the truth it would be all over school in an hour. I couldn't lie and she can't keep a secret. There was no compromise position; It's a *Catch 22*. She won't speak to me now because I won't tell her what's going on. Mr. Hawkins, Holly is my best friend. Or was . . ." Elizabeth was near tears.

"Life is full of hard decisions, Aubrey. When you lead you are tasked to make them all the time. Ms. Draper has been your companion for a number of years and I will not disparage that relationship. Yet some relationships, like your clothes, you outgrow. You just don't fit them anymore. Sometimes the clothes are out of style; sometimes they are just too small. Decide which is the case for you and act accordingly." Hawk paused. "I might add that some clothes can be altered to fit.

"Think on this: What would happen if you told Ms. Draper certain things and word of those things reached the wrong ears? It is not conceivable that some very unsavory people could subject Ms.

Draper to interrogation? You could, by severing your relationship with Ms. Draper, quite literally save her life."

Elizabeth looked up. "I never looked at it that way. I guess I wasn't thinking."

"No, Aubrey, you were thinking with your heart. Here indeed is a paradox where what is good for one is good for the many. Only *you* feel the pain. That is part of being who and what you are."

"It doesn't make it any easier," sniffed Elizabeth.

"Responsibility is rarely easy, Milady. If it were everyone would want it. In truth, you had no real choice in this matter. This is a classic case of being between a rock and a hard place. You did what needed to be done. Buckle up and move on."

Elizabeth wiped her eyes and blew her nose. "Okay, I understand. But it still sucks. I talked to LaTisha and Amy last period. I've decided to clue them in on what's happening." Elizabeth waited for Hawk's response. Of course, he just sat there.

"What I mean is, they're not stupid, and what with the jacks, and my appearance, well, I can't just ignore the situation."

"What is it you wish to tell them?"

Elizabeth paused. "I hadn't gotten that far. I told Amy that I would explain after school. We're going to the mall together to get chains for the jacks you gave us."

"I see. Are you looking for direction on this or merely informing me of your decision?" Hawkins look was intent.

"I'm . . . no, wait. Yes, I'm telling you that I'm telling them. But could you help me with what I should tell them? Please?" Elizabeth was in like a lion and out like a lamb on that question.

Hawkins laughed. "Very well, Milady. If you have trust in these two then tell them what you feel they should know. I personally do not know much about Ms. Wood and little enough about the other. Our Mr. Sawyer is checking them out just to be sure. In the meantime I believe that they can be entrusted with some of our secrets. They have assimilated the jacks they were given. I am sure they are capable of handling more of the same. If I were in your shoes I might spare them some of the more grisly details and just stick to a broad outline. Do you think that will assuage their concerns, and yours?"

"Yes . . . I think so. Amy told me today that by not telling her what was going on that I could endanger her. Do you think she's right?"

"That is very possible. Lately my focus has been very narrow. I may be doing a disservice to you and your friends by holding on too closely. Your friends are wise for their years. Say that which is in your heart and let me take care of the rest."

"Thank you, Mr. Hawkins. I feel a whole lot better."

Hawkins cleared the table and put away the uneaten food. "Now, Milady, our time is short. How was your last night's *visit*? I can see that you have spent a day or two in the sun." Hawkins couldn't keep his smile from escaping.

"Oh yes, the sun. You don't know how many times I cussed you out when I was with Billy! Do you know I didn't have a decent shower the whole time I was there? And what about the snake for God's sake! What if it had bitten me! Where would you be now! I . . . I . . ." Elizabeth had to stop because Hawkins couldn't hear what she was saying. He was laughing too hard.

"I'm sorry, Little One," he laughed, "Was it all that bad?"

"Mr. Hawkins, it's, it's not funny, dammit! I'm never gonna get all the sand out of–" She couldn't finish her statement. It *was* funny. "Okay, okay, ha ha for you. Billy worked my butt off. Literally! You knew he would, too. At least you could have warned me."

"What, and miss this? No, Aubrey, not a chance. Seriously, it was best that you go in the first time with no preconceived notions. You did learn a thing or two from Billy I hope?"

"Yes I did. And before you ask, yes, it was worth the effort. Billy said to tell you that I was now someone *to ride the river with*, whatever that means. And that you were to come for a visit."

"Good, very good. First bell is about to ring. You had better get to class. You and your mother should plan to be at the *Jack-in-the-Box* around six-thirty, okay? Don't bother eating–we'll have something there. We can talk about your other adventure then. Now git before Mr. Sawyer gives you detention for being late for class!"

Elizabeth hurried out of the storage room and up the ramp toward Chemistry class. She was almost in her seat before her own words struck her. Whatever had Billy meant by having her ask Jack Hawkins to *visit* him?

* * *

In another part of the school Jackson Barrett Sawyer was doing his best to understand what was being said on the other end of his telephone. *Satellite technology be damned! One little sunspot and you might as well be using two cans and a piece of string.* In the end he gave it up as a lost cause. He caught the gist of it anyway. Basically, so far Rodney had zip. He said they would keep on it all night if need be. For his sake Sawyer hoped he would find the necessary information. He wouldn't want to be Rodney Broadbent if Hawk went into the meeting tonight empty-handed.

Sawyer guessed that the information concerning Amy and LaTisha was not of critical importance.

He also knew that Hawk was a detail man, never wanting any puzzle to have missing pieces. That was what made him so good at his work. He was able to not only keep all the balls in the air but know where each ball was, when it would come down, and what color it was. Sawyer could never have laid a shield over the *Jack-in-the-Box*, block the power generated by The Mare, cover his own identity and physical appearance and do it all under the weight of *The Curse*. Sawyer lacked the talent. What he could do was juggle three heavy medicine balls at one time, something that required great strength but not nearly as much concentration. Sawyer sighed. *To each his own.*

The Bear stopped staring at the telephone. *If wishes were fishes he'd have an aquarium. Shifting his bulk around Bear surveyed the disaster area he called a desk. He was hip-high in paperwork again. If he started on it right now he would still have time to visit the Mystic Arcade before tonight's get-together. He wanted to have a conversation with the clerk Harold Yoder had described. Yes, a nice little talk . . . up close and personal.*

* * *

While Vice-principal Jackson Barrett Sawyer was plowing through his snowdrifts of bureaucratic nonessentials Elizabeth was doing her level best to evaporate. She would have welcomed a snowdrift to hide under. As it was, her last three classes seemed interminable. Sitting here in math class after the equivalent of months out-of-doors doing physical labor was torture. Her internal modem was moving at a far quicker pace than the clocks mounted on the walls of her classrooms. As miserable as the time differential seemed to her, the personal aspects of the afternoon were even more distressing. It went without saying that Holly was still not talking to her. *Heck, she was being totally ignored by Holly.* This was especially painful because for Elizabeth months had passed, not hours. Holly would have been the first person she turned to if things weren't the way they were. Now she had lost that outlet. In many ways Elizabeth was an adult but in this arena she recognized that she was still a fifteen-year-old girl. Losing your best friend wasn't easy even if you knew it wasn't your own fault. Besides, Elizabeth didn't have that many friends to lose. Thinking of Holly made her conscious of the fact that Philip was sitting directly behind her. During journalism class they had both been busy. The school paper was due out soon and that always rushed things. They didn't really talk except to say hello, and for Elizabeth even that was strained. Busy as they had been, Philip had still managed to look her way. Elizabeth could feel him watching even when she couldn't see him. She imagined she could sense him questioning his own eyes, wanting to ask questions but afraid to. Now here he was, three feet behind her. *What would she say if he started asking questions after class? Was this to be another lost cause, like Holly? When in doubt, procrastinate! She would take her time leaving and hope Philip had to hurry to catch the school bus home.*

After forty-five minutes of infinity Mrs. Wicks assigned homework. The final bell punctuated her admonition to pay attention to details in problem six. Elizabeth would remember those words later and wish she had paid attention to the details of getting out of her chair. She dawdled as long as she could, taking an inordinate amount of time to arrange her schoolbooks. Philip still hadn't left but she couldn't stall any longer. Everyone else had already departed when she rose from her desk. Unfortunately she managed to catch her calf on a metal burr as she stood. The sharp metal penetrated the fabric of her slacks–*oh great, Mom's slacks!*–slicing her skin. It was superficial but of course it bled quickly. Before she could flee the room the blood had seeped through the cloth.

"Elizabeth! You cut yourself–look!" exclaimed Philip. "Here, let me grab a paper towel." Before Elizabeth could protest or stop him Philip was gone, heading to the roll of towels Mrs. Wicks kept on hand to wipe down the eraser board. He was back in seconds.

"This will help. Pull up the leg of your pants and we can use this to stop the bleeding." Without a brain cell in attendance, Elizabeth did as instructed. It was not the best decision she made that day. As Elizabeth lifted the fabric off her calf Philip applied the paper towel to the gash. It wasn't deep but the cut capillaries were pumping for all they were worth. Philip kept the pressure on until the paper towel was soaked at the point of contact, then he quickly swapped it for a fresh one. It wasn't until he had stanched the flow that trouble arrived.

"There. I think we got it." Philip gently pulled the paper towel away from the cut, leaving a little of the paper stuck to Elizabeth's skin. "I think it stopped . . . bleeding . . ." Elizabeth watched in stupid fascination as Philip just let the sentence peter out as he just stared at her leg. Now that the excitement was over Philip wasn't distracted. She watched as his eyes rose up to meet hers, a million questions bubbling inside them. Elizabeth quickly slid her slacks back down her leg.

"Elizabeth . . . I . . . uhh . . ." Poor Philip looked like a clown with his mouth hanging open, unable to articulate what he wanted to say. As quickly as Philip's wits left him, Elizabeth's returned to her.

"Thanks a lot, Philip. You were great. Sorry I can't stay and talk but I'm meeting Amy Shestack and LaTisha Wood. They found out I've been jogging after school and on weekends so we're gonna run together starting this afternoon, then go to the mall. I want them to try the tanning beds I've been using over at *Sunset Boulevard*. Thanks again, Philip. See ya tomorrow!" She snatched up her bookbag and literally ran out of the classroom, leaving Philip behind, still on his knees as if praying to someone, *anyone*, to answer the questions stacked up in his mind.

* * *

Elizabeth had lost precious time dealing with Philip. She was now force-marching her way to the student parking lot to meet her friends. As she feared, the two girls were already waiting in the car. Elizabeth pulled open a rear door and climbed in. One good thing about her time in the *Otherlands*: She wasn't the least bit winded.

"Sorry, sorry, sorry. I caught my leg on my desk."

Amy turned around. "Let me see–ugh–you can kiss those pants goodbye. Hey, is that blood?" At the mention of blood LaTisha turned around too.

"It's just a scratch, really. It just bled a lot. Philip Gartner got some paper towels and stopped the bleeding. That's what took me so long."

LaTisha looked at Amy, then at Elizabeth. "Oh, okay, we understand."

Elizabeth was confused. "Understand what?"

"How you could lose track of time with Philip's hand up your leg."

Elizabeth blushed from stem to stern. "It wasn't like that! He sits behind me last period and when I cut myself on my desk he . . . oh, you two are just too funny!"

When LaTisha finally got control of herself she started the car and headed for the mall. As they drove Amy initiated the conversation: "Since you were late 'Tish and I had a little time to talk and we sort of came to a conclusion or two."

LaTisha took over: "You see, we both kinda figured some stuff out, and we can guess at other stuff, but it all comes back to you and the janitor." She paused as she made a right turn. "We notice things, some of it because we're looking for it, some 'cause of what happened last night. And we feel that, I mean, we want you to feel, I mean—"

Amy broke in: "Elizabeth, what 'Tish is trying to say is that maybe I pressured you into this, and maybe I shouldn't have, so we figured that if you don't want to say anything it'd be okay with us."

Elizabeth looked at her two friends, one eye to eye and the other by way of the rear view mirror. *She had her* out *if she wanted it. But she didn't want it, especially since she no longer had Holly to lean on. In all fairness, she owed them both a great deal. Was it only a week ago that we became friends? Elizabeth made her decision.*

"Okay, here's the real deal, straight up four-one-one. Please believe me when I say I can't tell you everything. Just believe that what I do tell you is the truth. Amy, LaTisha, you can't tell anyone. I mean it. Not a soul. Not even your parents. LaTisha, not even Shelby. If we can't agree on that then I just can't say anything. It's just too important, okay?" Both Amy and LaTisha nodded.

"Not good enough. I need to hear it from you both. This is very serious, more serious than the time on the ramp with the jacks."

To their credit neither girl hesitated. Their *yeses* were simultaneous. "Okay, LaTisha, would you turn up the radio a little louder? Thanks. Now pull into the strip mall on the right and park around back. Let the motor run." Elizabeth's friends were mystified but LaTisha did as she was instructed. "Good. This is your first lesson in Paranoia 101. We use the music and engine to mask our conversation. It won't stop a determined listener but it makes things harder. Now, each of us takes a quadrant and watches it. I'll cover the front, Amy the left and 'Tish the right side of the car. If you see anyone stop talking immediately, okay? Look, I know this seems like a scene from a bad spy movie but it isn't a movie and the danger is very real." Elizabeth made sure both of her friends were paying attention. She thought for a moment how to start off and it came to her quickly. Her friends were like her–young, intelligent and flexible. Better to whack them over the head with a brick first and see what damage it caused rather than constructing the story one brick at a time.

"Okay, guys, a question: Except for today in gym, when was the last time you saw me?"

LaTisha answered: "Yesterday, of course. Right, Amy?" Amy nodded.

"What if I was to tell you that until today I hadn't seen either of you in over nine months?"

"Nine months? I'd say that you needed a new watch. Either that or you were pregnant and went away to have the baby and left an android here in your place," answered Amy.

"That makes zero sense as usual, Amy. If we assume that Elizabeth is telling the truth then logic dictates that time is distorted in some way, either for her or for us. Elizabeth?"

"Yes. You remember last week when you two saved me from being shoved into the gym naked? Look here." Elizabeth stripped off her long-sleeved sweater and threw her friends into the deep end of the pool.

LaTisha and Amy could only stare at Elizabeth's upper body. She was wearing a sleeveless blouse so the view was unobstructed. The look on her friends' faces was priceless. She had certainly missed a Kodak Moment. Amy broke the silence: "LaTisha! Shut your mouth. You're catching flies!"

LaTisha ignored Amy's comments as usual. "That didn't happen in a week. Hell girl, you couldn't get that tan in just a week, let alone that body. Your skin looks red. You didn't get radiation poisoning, did you?"

"Is it really yours?" asked Amy.

Elizabeth beamed. "Yep, all mine, and it goes all the way to the floor. I weigh one hundred and seventeen pounds, I'm taller, and I have less than 1% body fat. No radiation unless you count endless hours in the Arizona sun. That was my problem with Philip. He saw my leg when I cut it. I ran out before he could ask questions but you know he has to be wondering. I made up a lie about how I had been running at night, and that we were running this afternoon, then going to the tanning place at the mall. It was all I could think of at the time." Elizabeth thought about what she would say next.

"Here's the short version: You can ask questions after. My daddy and my mom are both descended from a long line of special people. Each one's family was different. When they had me I inherited both their abilities. Sort of like if the World's two greatest athletes had a kid and the kid turned out to be the absolute best athlete ever. That kid would be me. Stop laughing. It's true. I can do things that a normal person can't. LaTisha, you were the first person to notice. Remember when I hit Carlin with the volleyball? That was no accident. Give me a hundred tries and I could hit her every time. But that is just the tip of the iceberg. I don't understand everything that's going on but I'm in the middle of trouble. So are you if you hang with me. Sort of guilt by association. I think I'm rambling. Sorry. Let me try again. Think of basic Good and Evil. My ancestors have been fighting Evil for centuries. I'm just the latest member of the family to get involved. There is real Evil, it's here, and I think it's looking for me." Elizabeth let that sink in.

"Okay, here's the really weird stuff: I have a way to travel to places in time." Both girls just looked at Elizabeth. "Right. See this tan? I got it in Arizona last night. I was there for over half a year. Don't look at me like that! It's true. The people that I'm with sent me there to toughen me up and to be skilled in martial arts."

Amy's interest went up another notch. "Karate? Now you're saying you know some type of oriental combat? How much?"

"I'm not sure but Billy said it was the equivalent of studying for five years."

"You learned in one night what it's taken me years? Come on! That's not fair! You're not just saying that, are you?"

"You don't understand, Amy. It took me one night of *Here* time. In Arizona I spent the longest six months of my life. We worked every day for ten or twelve hours. Amy, I earned these muscles!"

LaTisha cut in: "Girl, you're saying you could whup Amy's butt in a fight? This I'd like to see!"

Amy started to say something but Elizabeth stopped her: "'Tish, that's not the point. I was taught this because the Society was afraid for me. They needed me to be able to protect myself."

"What Society? And protect you from what?" asked Amy.

"The Ladder Society. They are the guys with the white hats. They're also called the *Jacks*. My father was Clan leader of the Jacks before he was killed by the *AntiJacks*. The AntiJacks are the bad guys. And I might also need protection from the serial killer the papers are writing about. You know, The Predator."

"Girl, you're trippin'. What does a sophomore in the suburbs have to do with a serial killer in Baltimore? I don't see the connection," asked LaTisha.

"I didn't either. But this killer isn't from here."

"So, what, like he's from Boston?" said Amy.

"Nooo, actually he's from London. He used to live there. In 1888."

"You mean 1988, right?" asked Amy.

"No, Amy. I meant 1888. Somehow, someway, Baltimore's Predator is London's Jack the Ripper." This revelation was greeted by an unaccustomed total silence. Even Amy found it hard to vocalize what she was thinking.

Finally LaTisha spoke: "Right. Now pull my other leg so they'll be even again. You mean the real Jack the Ripper? The guy that killed all those women in England? I bet I've seen five movies about it. Johnny Depp was just in one. The guy is all over the place. He's like a cult figure, or a cartoon character. Maybe this Predator is like a copycat killer. I mean, how do you explain the time difference? I mean, he'd have to be what, a hundred and thirty years old by now. That doesn't make sense to me. He'd have to be immortal."

Amy added her two cents: "Come on. How are we expected to believe in a story like this? He's like this big legend or myth, like Paul Bunyan, and now he's not only real but somehow made it into our time? This is too much like a story from our school's namesake, Edgar Allan Poe."

"LaTisha, Amy, I just don't know. I'm just telling you what they told me. They're all intelligent adults and they believe it like it was gospel. I don't know any of the details. Tonight my mom and I are meeting again with Mr. Hawkins. Maybe he'll have the answers. Until then I guess we have to take all this on faith."

"I knew that janitor was something other than what he seemed. Who is he for real?" asked LaTisha.

"He's a member of the Ladder Society. He knew my dad before he was killed. Now he sort of . . . well, he's been watching over me even since before I was born. Sorta like a guardian angel." Elizabeth blushed.

"Why you?" asked Amy.

"It's like I said before: They think I'm a special tool or weapon to use against the AntiJacks. I think they had to wait until I was older before they used me because I couldn't access what I was born with. My mom thinks they are very good at using people."

"Like Amy and me?" asked LaTisha.

Elizabeth paused, surprised at LaTisha's quick perception. "Yes. I wouldn't put it past them. I sorta asked that same question. Jack basically said that you two came aboard of your own free will. But I think he is secretly glad that you did. He seems to know a lot about you both. He's very strange in a cool sort of way but I don't think he would have given me the jacks if he didn't already trust you. How he knows anything is always a mystery to me."

"Whadda you mean he knows a lot about us?" queried Amy.

"I don't know. But I bet that if I asked him your bra size he'd know the answer."

Amy flushed. "Get out of here!"

"As if anyone would want to know that," deadpanned LaTisha.

"Serious! Amy, 'Tish, you have to stop thinking inside the box. I have trouble coming to grips with this all the time, but it's real. If we took penicillin back to the Middle Ages would it be magic or science? Would we be knighted or burned at the stake? All I'm saying is that until somebody proves them wrong, the Ladder Society can do what they claim. For what it's worth, it *feels* right. I'm in this thing because I was born into it. You guys volunteered."

There was a long silence before anyone spoke. "Okay," said Amy, "then where do we go from here?"

LaTisha answered that: "To the mall, of course!" Everyone laughed and that eased the tension.

"LaTisha's right. Let's get going. We can talk on the way. First things first, though. You guys have to back me up on the running and tanning thing, okay?"

LaTisha snorted. "Now how am I supposed to get anyone to believe that I was using a tanning bed?"

Elizabeth blushed. "Oops! I didn't think that one through, did I? Okay, then just say you come along to laugh at Amy for trying to look like you."

"That sounds about right," laughed LaTisha. "Besides, nobody would dare ask anyway."

"Back to business," said Elizabeth. "Where was I? Oh, the second thing you both need to do is be more alert. Don't either of you go anywhere alone. Stay out of dark places. Lock up at home. Lock the car doors when you're driving. Stuff like that. If you get in trouble I think Mr. Hawkins will do his best to get you out of it. But I also think he would forfeit you if it meant saving me. I mean that with all my heart. The Ladder Society has an acute case of tunnel vision. Their whole lives are dedicated to combating Evil. If by sacrificing Amy they could have killed Adolf Hitler I'm sure they would have done it without a second thought."

Amy answered that in a soft voice: "I'd do that willingly."

Elizabeth looked at her friend and suddenly saw her not just as Amy but also as a Jew. That thought revived another. "Amy, I'm positive you would too. Speaking of the late, unlamented Adolf, Mr. Hawkins said I was to talk to you about the Jewish people in World War II. He pretty much said you could give me a personal viewpoint. Do you know what he was talking about?"

"I . . . think so. Not me, though. He probably meant my uncle. He was—wait a minute! How would he know about my Uncle Ephraim?"

"Amy—get outta the box," laughed LaTisha. "Elizabeth already said he knows all about us! You know, *powers and abilities far beyond those of mortal men!*"

"Yeah, well, excuse me if it creeps me out, okay? You didn't have someone watching you last night!" Amy snorted with indignation.

"Uh, Amy, by the way . . . I sorta know who was watching you last night. It was a Watcher, sort of a bodyguard Mr. Hawkins sent over to your house to protect you, uh, just in case."

Amy sputtered. "You mean I was being scoped out by the good guys and not some pervert?"

"Yeah, actually, I met her today. Her name is KatyJay. She's very nice."

LaTisha laughed: "And you almost called the police!"

"S'not funny, 'Tish. With a capital Not."

LaTisha chilled immediately. She knew how far she could go. "Sorry."

"Look guys, for what it's worth we all have personal shadows watching over us. Unless there is a need we'll never know they are there. They aren't really watching us. They're looking for people who might be following us. Just let it be, okay?"

"Are they watching us now?" asked Amy.

"I would bet on it. See that gray car about six cars back? It's been following us ever since we left The Poe."

"Elizabeth, how the hell do you know that?" asked LaTisha.

"It's more of my training. I don't want to get into that right now but I learned a few things about trailing a suspect. In that car is a Watcher detailed to one of us. Anyway, back to Mr. Hitler. Amy, what about your uncle?"

"Well, I don't know all the details but Uncle Ephraim survived the war. He really doesn't talk about it much but if he'll talk to you, you'll get more than you want to know."

"What do you mean?" asked LaTisha.

"Uncle Ephraim was an inmate at Treblinka." There was a stunned silence in the car that even the outside noise could not penetrate.

"Oh my God, Amy. Really? How did it happen? How did he survive?" asked Elizabeth.

"I can't really answer that. Besides, you should ask Uncle Ephraim that yourself. It has more meaning when he tells it."

Elizabeth asked: "Does your uncle live near here?"

"He lives here in town. He works at the mall. We can go visit if you want to. I don't know if he will want to talk to you. Just be prepared if he feels like talking. What little I've heard isn't pretty."

"Where does he work?" asked Elizabeth.

"Village Optometry. He owns it."

Elizabeth couldn't believe it. "Your uncle is Doctor Sauble?"

"Great-uncle really, but yeah. Why? Do you know him?"

Elizabeth smiled: "It's a small, small world."

37

It took twenty-five minutes for all the players to assemble at the address of the woman identified by Ed Bonner as Dana Lieter. The structure was a small, six-unit apartment building in an area undergoing urban renewal. Since they had no keys Jonesy rousted the building manager who lived in the rear basement apartment. He escorted them to apartment 3A on the second floor. Jonesy asked Maury the manager to unlock the door and come inside with him. The others stayed outside. Jonesy had Maury stand by the doorway until he found a picture of the girl. He brought it to Maury, who identified the girl as the tenant of 3A, Dana Lieter. Jonesy thanked the man and asked him to go back downstairs with Detective Barkowitz.

When the super and Dog were gone Jonesy nodded to the other detectives. "It's her, Lieutenant.

This picture's even got the dog in it." Jonesy handed the framed photograph to Cohen. The photo had the two of them together in an obviously posed setting. Dana Lieter looked a great deal better in the picture than she did now in death. He handed the photo to Daniel who stared at the image for a long time. Unhappily her picture and her corpse had little to say.

"Okay," said Cohen, "let's get busy. Eddie, make the call and get the techies up here. Everybody glove up. You know what to look for; letters, address books, computer stuff, a diary. Jones, check the phone for messages. Try not to disturb anything. Look, I think we all know that this is a dry hole. Nothing connects the other victims so I wouldn't bet my pension on this one but let's do it anyway. And do it by the numbers. We'll need to find next of kin info so public affairs can notify 'em. Get me a name."

The men spread out and carefully went through the apartment. There was no answering machine, hence no messages. There was no diary, no day-planner, and no scheduled meetings with strangers. Cohen found the girl's pocket book on the dining room table. A wallet was inside but the clear pocket intended for her driver's license was empty, leading Cohen to believe she had carried it with her even though it was not found at the scene. Also found in the purse was an address book. Cohen flipped through it quickly, stopping at M. Under that listing was written *Mom and Dad* along with the corresponding address and telephone numbers. This was one call Barry Cohen was more than happy to pass on to the higher-ups.

Within half an hour reinforcements had arrived and it was getting crowded in the small one-bedroom apartment. Cohen pulled his crew out and handed over the address book to the newly arrived staff officer. With that out of the way he detailed his crew to checking with the neighboring tenants. When they reconvened it was five o'clock in the evening.

"Barkowitz, what'd the Super have to say?" asked Cohen.

"His name's Maury Epstein. Lived here for years, got a wife, no kids that live with them. Pretty much confirms what we suspected: Lieter was a day-shift nurse at Johns Hopkins, maternity he thinks, he ain't sure. Anyway, she gets up real early 'cause she's a health nut an' likes to run. Says she runs real early in the morning because her shift starts early an' she always takes the dog with her. Epstein says she killed two birds with one stone; she got her exercise and so did the dog. He says the dog's why she lived here. The building allows pets which most places don't do around here. She runs regular, leaves the apartment around four-thirty, four forty-five and gets back around five forty-five or so. She don't run that early on weekends. Epstein says she's a nice one, no parties, no drugs, just her and the dog. She been here two years and he only ever saw one, maybe two guys come by for her, none recent."

"Dog, does Epstein know the score?" asked Daniel.

"Yeah, he ain't much to look at but he's pretty sharp. He says at his age he don't sleep so good so he hears what goes on. He didn't remember hearing Lieter and the dog come back this morning. His wife had the TV on later and he saw the news bulletin. He and his old lady were thinking about calling us but they was waiting to see if she showed up after work. More than that I think they was afraid it was her and didn't want to know for sure. I got the feeling they liked her a lot." Barkowitz looked down at his shoes. "You wanna know the real pisser? Epstein's wife asked her why she wasn't afraid to run when it was still dark out and she tells her she don't worry 'cause the dog would protect her."

"How many times you hear that story from someone that's been robbed or mugged?" asked Jonesy.

"Too many. Way too many. Somehow this guy was smart enough to disable the mutt and then take his time with the victim. I don't know. Let's move on. Jonesy, you and Dog check with the guys inside an' see where they are with getting aholdt of her parents. If they've made contact then head over to Hopkins and catch the swing shift people. It's too late for the day crew so do that first thing tomorrow. Eddie, you wanna talk to the parents and see if they know of any boyfriends? That's for tomorrow. Give them tonight." Cohen sighed. "Unless anyone can think of something I missed then let's call it a day."

Barkowitz, Bonner, and Jones made their way down the stairwell without any conversation. Cohen went back to Lieter's apartment for a final check with the remaining technicians while Daniel waited outside. During the interim Daniel had time to mull over the new information garnered from the Dana Lieter's apartment. Although hardly illuminating the case there was something that niggled at the back of his mind—something someone had said. Daniel let his thoughts swish together inside his brain for a minute or two until two ideas collided and gave him the answer. Cohen reappeared and the pair started back down the stairs. "Christ, I might as well own a Stairmaster what with all the floors we've gone up and down today," grunted Cohen as he tried lighting a cigar as they descended the staircase. When they hit the street it was almost dark.

"Daniel, I've had it for today. Let's bag it and start again in the morning. I'm too old for this crap. You wanna take me to my car or you want I should get a unit to drive me?"

"I'm in no hurry. I'll drop you off," said Daniel.

"Thanks, and if I fall asleep it ain't because of the company, okay?"

Daniel laughed as they buckled up and got underway. "You wouldn't be the first. I do have something that might keep you awake. It's just a theory."

Barry yawned. "Go ahead. I could use a good theory." Daniel Shestack started talking. Lieutenant Barry Cohen did not fall asleep.

38

Jackson Barrett Sawyer wasn't the least bit remorseful about leaving his remaining paperwork stacked on his desk like cordwood. No matter how much paper he whittled down today there would be a new supply tomorrow. For once his timing was in sync with the rest of the world; he was leaving The Poe when he needed to. He called goodnight to Mrs. Crisp and hauled out the door. Wanting no delays he put on his game face, effectively neutering any attempts at conversations by student and teacher alike. His only delay was a shoving match between two girls waiting for a bus. It took Sawyer all of seven seconds to give the girls the choice of *cease and desist* or to continue the argument in his office in the morning. They chose wisely. Sawyer was already in his car before they had managed to pick up their scattered books.

Bear checked his watch and saw that he was going to be five minutes early for his appointment. That was all for the better. He had called the Mystic Arcade earlier, finding out that Marco came on duty at four-thirty in the afternoon. If Sawyer was lucky he might catch the boy before he went inside the arcade.

Making the turn into the arcade parking lot Sawyer positioned his Ford pickup where he could survey the traffic coming and going. He had a good description of the clerk from Harold. Polopolis was six feet tall, had black hair worn in a ponytail, and an acne-scarred face. He shouldn't be hard to spot. He wasn't. Within five minutes of Bear's arrival a cold-yellow Mustang spun into the lot, backed up, and parked diagonally across two parking places. Sawyer could see that it was the boy he was seeking. Not waiting for the boy's engine and incredibly loud music system to shut down Sawyer walked the short distance to the car and knocked on the windowglass.

Marco had not seen Sawyer approach as he was still bopping to his music. The knock on his window actually startled him. When he looked up and saw Sawyer standing by his car his face blanched. Then he freaked. Before Sawyer could say a word the boy jammed the car into gear and left a trail of burning rubber in his wake. Unfortunately for all concerned he overcompensated at the entrance and the Mustang's rear fender clipped the vehicle parked on the corner. It slowed the Mustang down but did not stop it–the car slewed its way onto the main drag and disappeared.

Bear was positively dumbfounded. What was all that about? The lunatic had run over the edge of his left Wingtip, missing his toes by less than an inch. He was so intent upon the fact that his feet were still intact that he was halfway to his vehicle before he realized that it was his truck the sorry bastard had hit on the way out. When Sawyer reached his pickup he saw it now sported a dented front fender, overlaid with a coat of yellow paint from the Mustang. *Talk about adding insult to injury! The boy better have insurance and plenty of it, or else.* Bear opened up the truck and grabbed a card from the glove box and headed into the arcade.

Using the fake business card identifying him as an agent for the Internal Revenue Service, Sawyer was quickly able to scam the assistant manager–who was all of 20 years old–into giving him George *Marco* Polopolis's address and phone number. Sawyer thanked the girl and headed directly for the address given on his employment application. Bear knew the area well. It was a spread of marginal townhouses on the west side of town. Bear drove by the address at the posted speed, barely glancing at the number he wanted. There was no yellow Mustang parked in front. Sawyer turned on the next cross street and parked. He got out and walked up the alley behind the address. Sawyer was only one hundred feet down the alley when he spotted the Mustang. Retracing his steps, Bear got back into his pickup and turned around. As he went by the first time he had spotted a parking place almost directly in front of 5621, which was the number he wanted. He did not have time to call a Watcher for backup so he would have to be tricky instead. Besides, he wanted this guy for himself.

Quickly and quietly parking his pickup Sawyer went up to the front door, rang the buzzer and pounded on the door as loud as he could. Then he quickly exited the front porch, rang alongside the house and positioned himself behind a hedge near the yellow car. He didn't have to wait longer than ten seconds before the back door crashed open and Marco came barreling out, carrying a knapsack. He jumped off the back porch and hit the ground running. The next thing he hit was Jackson Barrett Sawyer.

Ever the polite citizen, Bear picked the terrified boy up—albeit by the throat—and stood him up against his car. "Hello, George. Nice to run into you again. Or rather, nice of you to run into me again. Here, let me dust you off." Sawyer patted Marco down for weapons under the guise of brushing the dirt from his clothes. "Funny, you're not so tough without your car." Marco made a half-hearted attempt to free himself from Sawyer's grip but Bear would have none of it—he just increased his pressure on the boy's windpipe until he ceased his exertions. "Now laddie, don't be aggravating my good nature. So tell me–how's the family? Cat got your tongue?" More gurgles. "Sorry boy. Holding on too tight, am I? Wouldn't want you to fall down, now would we?" Polopolis's response was a well-aimed kick to Sawyer's groin. Unfortunately for him Bear was waiting for him to make just such a move. He swiveled his hips and the blow landed on his thigh. In a relaxed motion Bear wiped the dirt from his trouser leg and just as casually returned the kick from whence it came. Only Bear's knee connected in a most tender spot. Now the only thing holding Polopolis up was Bear's hand around his throat. Lifting him bodily with his left hand Sawyer body-slammed the boy on top of his car, putting a rather large dent in the hood of the Mustang.

Sawyer patiently waited for the boy to regain the ability to breathe. In the interim he stripped the laces from Marco's sneakers and spread-eagled him on the hood, securing his wrists to the rearview mirrors. Once Polopolis was immobilized Bear retrieved the book bag the boy had been carrying and emptied it. It mainly contained personal items and CDs but in a large zipper pocket Bear found cash money. It counted out to over three thousand dollars. *Interesting*. Sawyer went through the car but found little of interest. *Was nothing easy?*

Sawyer leaned over the boy and smiled. "Well, bucko, it seems we have a problem. I need some information from you. You, on the other hand, are badly in need of some ice for your testicles. Now how do you think we can both get what we want?"

"You're crazy!"

"People have said that before, although you are hardly in a position to make an unbiased opinion. And please, don't force me to give you another attitude adjustment. I don't think your gonads could take the strain."

"What difference does it make? You're gonna kill me anyway."

"Now wherever did you get that idea?"

"A friend of mine already warned me about you."

"Really? Care to tell me who that friend is?"

"Yeah, right. Like that's gonna ha–". The boy found it impossible to finish the sentence once Bear's hand started crushing his scrotum.

"Now Georgie, what did I say about attitude adjustments? If you want to be a capon for the rest of your life then just keep giving me attitude. I'll be happy to oblige."

Polopolis' eyes returned to their sockets once Bear released the pressure. "Crow, okay? The guy called himself Crow."

"Much better, lad. What is your relationship with this *Crow* person?"

"He come into the arcade with another dude called *Rat* about six weeks ago. Said they was reporters doing a story on psychic events in high school and wanted me to keep my ears open. He said he was willing to pay for any tips and I was to contact him if I heard anything. I thought the guy was bogus but he laid two Benjamins on me. I knew he was working an angle but the money was real so I took it."

"Were you able to supply any leads?"

"Yeah, 'bout half a dozen. He never said nothing about it—just slipped me a hundred each time."

"So if all you were doing was helping out a fellow citizen why did you panic when you saw me?"

"Because Crow described you and a couple other people and said if they ever showed up I'd better bail 'cause they would kill me for the same information I was feedin' him. Especially you."

"You believed him?"

"Hell yes I did. I didn't know for sure what the dude was into but his eyes were deadass cold. He was always smiling, too, like some private joke was going on and he was the only one in on it. It came true, too." The boy could barely look at Sawyer.

Bear ignored him. "Do you know where he lives?"

"Yeah, right."

"How did you contact him?"

"He gave me a number to use. After each tip he said to forget that number and then gave me a new one. It was a cell phone for sure 'cause of all the static."

"Describe him."

"I guess he's about thirty-five or forty years old. He's kinda thin but wiry and he's got coal-black hair that he's slicked back. He liked to comb it a lot. He had a messed up jaw. He's shorter'n me, maybe weighed a hundred and seventy pounds. He has a strange way of lookin' at you–he cocks his head and stares at you with one eye. But cold eyes like I said before."

"What's the current phone number?" Polopolis was reluctant to divulge the information until Bear reached toward him. "It's in my wallet, okay! I wrote it on a business card from the arcade." Bear dug out the boy's wallet and retrieved the card. It had a bonus: All the previous numbers were listed along with the new one.

Bear asked a few more innocuous questions before he slipped in the zinger: "How much dope do you sell a week?"

Before he could stop himself Marco answered: "Maybe ten or twelve baa…" He nearly gagged on the last word when he realized what he said. "How did you know?"

"Elementary. You live in a crappy neighborhood but you drive a flash car. You go to school part-time and work a job that pays squat. Your bag has three grand in it. It's simple deductive reasoning. Plus the fact that you are a lowlife operator with no conscience or morals." Bear paused for effect. "Give me one reason why I shouldn't do the world a favor and *off* you right here and now."

Marco's eyes expanded along with his bladder. Neither was a pretty sight. All he could blubber out was: "Because you're not like me."

Sawyer looked at the boy. "How old are you?"

"Twenty-two."

"Twenty-two years on this earth and you have yet to learn a thing. What an absolute waste. Your parents must be very proud." Bear stared down the alley and thought over his options, then turned back to the boy. "You're right, Georgie. I'm not like you. If I were, you would now be stuffed in the trunk of this silly little pimpmobile. So thank your lucky stars and celebrate the differences between us. I'll tell you how this will play out. First, the cash from your book bag is forfeit. You can keep the two hundred in your wallet. Second, I'm going to untie you and let you go. And go you will. Now. Today. Start driving this banana and don't stop until you're at least five hundred miles away. I have no interest where you go as long as it's far away from here. In return for your sorry-ass excuse for a life you will do two things. You will not sell drugs and you will not even *think* about calling this Crow or Rat and telling them what happened. Can you live with that? I emphasize the word *live*. The choice is yours."

"What about my–" Bear cut him off. "No negotiations, George. It's all or nothing." Bear reinforced his position by leaning toward the boy.

"Okay! Okay! It's a deal."

"You have made a wise decision, Mr. Polopolis." Bear picked up the book bag, removed the cash, then pulled out a folding knife. He held the knife in his hand and leaned over the boy. "If you deal dope again, I'll know about it in a week. If you call Rat or Crow or anybody else here in town I'll know that even sooner. Make no mistake, Mr. Polopolis, I will come for you and when I leave I will have your testicles as a trophy. Do we understand each other?"

Polopolis could only gulp and nod. Bear reached over with his knife and cut one of the laces holding the boy's wrist, then the other. "Get out, boy, while you still can. And don't spin your tires when you leave. It disturbs the neighborhood."

Polopolis slid off the hood and shakily got behind the wheel, wet pants and all. He carefully backed into the alley and drove off without a backward glance. *Bear just watched him go. He knew that his threats would wear off in time. The boy would start feeling safe, and would ultimately return to selling dope. If dealing with the Little One wasn't taking precedence he might not have given Polopolis the option to live. This one was long past salvation. God, how Satan loved misdemeanors.*

Sawyer returned to his pickup and headed back toward city center. He felt a lump under his butt and pulled out the rubberbanded hundred-dollar bills he had removed from the book bag. Bouncing the wad of cash in his hand helped him decide what to do with it. At a stoplight he peeled off a thousand dollars and put it in his wallet. Mr. George *Marco* Polopolis didn't know it but he was about to pay the repair bill on a dented fender.

39

Elizabeth, LaTisha and Amy hustled into the mall and spent the next hour giggling over what clothes Elizabeth should buy. Out of the thirty items she tried on Elizabeth bought only enough clothes for a week. She relied heavily on her friends' opinions but still managed to tone down their picks a step or two until she found the right balance between the old Elizabeth and the new one. Mostly she picked mix and match things so that she could stretch her mom's money. When they were finished she had purchased two sweaters and skirts, five tops, one pair of jeans, two pairs of slacks and two week's worth of underwear. Elizabeth knew she would have to buy more clothes later but for now this would get her through the next week without wearing the same thing twice. *Nothing pumped up the ol' ego like new clothes!*

The three stopped off for a quick soda before heading for the jewelers. Elizabeth never realized that shopping could be so dehydrating. While they were sitting Elizabeth asked Amy to be point man in the jewelry store. "Let 'Tish and I stay outside. You take the jacks with you. You're the best at lying. Make something up but we can't leave the jacks. They have to be able to do it now, okay?"

Amy looked sideways at Elizabeth. "I don't know if that was a crack or a compliment. Therefore I shall take it as an accolade to my abilities to obfuscate."

LaTisha snorted. "Jesus, will you just get over yourself! Get in there!"

"Okay, okay. Pony up, girlfriends." LaTisha and Elizabeth handed over their own jacks. "Now watch the Master in action."

"Amy, the only action you're gonna get is a boot up your–" LaTisha's remark was terminated by Elizabeth's tugging on her elbow.

"Come on, 'Tish. Amy, meet us at your uncle's store when you're done. Let's go, 'Tish. I want to say hello to some friends of mine." Elizabeth led LaTisha to the second floor of the mall, and then to the door marked *Martha's Stamps and Coins*. Elizabeth opened the door to the expected sound of sleigh bells and they entered the shop. There was no one at the counter but presently a man appeared from the back room.

"Hello girls. What can I do for you?"

"Nothing really," answered Elizabeth, "we just came to see Big Martha."

"Sorry, she ain't here at the moment. Had to do some shopping so's she asked me to watch the place. I'm Joe, her boyfriend. Why don't you stop back in an hour or so?"

"So, is Martha D here?" asked Elizabeth.

"What, you mean here in the mall? Yeah, like I said she's shopping. Come on by later, okay?"

"Uh, okay. Thanks, Joe. Come on, 'Tisha." Elizabeth nearly dragged LaTisha out of the store. When they were around the corner she stopped. "LaTisha, something's wrong in there. I think the store is being robbed."

"How? Why?"

"Look, that Joe guy doesn't know the difference between Marthas and anyway I think Big Martha is gay. I know he's lying. I can feel it."

"What Marthas? I don't understand. If there's a problem then why don't we get the police or call security?"

"No! We do that and we're involved. I have a cunning plan."

"Oh crap. Five of the most dangerous words in the English language. All right girl, what's it to be?"

* * *

Three minutes later the two girls reentered the coin shop, only this time LaTisha was holding Elizabeth up as she limped along. Elizabeth had used a nail file to reopen the cut on her leg and slit her pant leg up the side about fifteen inches. She was banking on Joe not having seen the stain the first time they came in. As the bells rang Joe reappeared. His smile turned to annoyance as he recognized who had entered. Before he could say anything LaTisha spoke up.

"Joe, help! Alice here fell on the steps and cut her leg. It's bleeding!" All the time she was talking she advanced into the shop until she was in the middle of the open space. Without thought Joe stepped from behind the counter, probably hoping to get these kids out of the shop as fast as possible. "Let me look" was the last thing he would say. As he bent down to view the damage Elizabeth brought her *hurt* knee up and connected with his jaw, shattering it. As he staggered she laid a forearm smash to the side of his skull and he dropped unceremoniously to the carpet, unconscious. Elizabeth wasn't even breathing hard. LaTisha, however, was.

"That . . . that was awesome. You weren't kidding in the car, were you?"

"No joke, 'Tish. Here, help me get this guy off my legs." Elizabeth got clear of the body. "Tish, watch him. I'll check in back." Elizabeth hurried into the back room and found Big Martha lying on her side, unconscious. She heard a noise from behind a door and quickly opened it, ready to deal with an accomplice. Instead she was bowled over by Martha D. She barely stopped to say hello before she was at Big Martha's side, licking her face. While not the Red Cross's approved method for assisting in regaining consciousness its effectiveness was hard to fault. In short order Big Martha was sitting up.

"Oh lordy, does my head hurt! Wha–say–it's Elizabeth, right? What you doin' here, child?"

"Just returning a favor, Big Martha. What happened to you?"

"Oh, I must be gettin' old and stupid. Some guy come in here an' laid out some coins he wanted to sell. Martha D was growlin' low like but a course I didn't pay her no mind. Next thing I know he got a gun in my face. Martha D was 'bout to take him on when he said he'd kill her right off if she moved." Big Martha was crying. "I didn't care 'bout me but I couldn't let anything happen to her. I had to lock her in the bathroom. Then he made me open up my safe. I guess he done whacked me on the head soon's I done that."

Big Martha continued to hold her dog. "Long as Martha D is okay I don't care how much got took." Big Martha looked over at her safe. It was empty. In front of it were two Sears shopping bags filled with the contents of her safe. "Oh my. What happened? How come he didn't take my inventory?"

Elizabeth had to smile. "Because he's still here. No, it's okay. Think you can stand up?" Big Martha nodded. Elizabeth assisted Big Martha to her feet and helped her walk into the showroom.

"LaTisha, I'd like you to meet Big Martha. The dog's name is Martha D. Big Martha, this is my friend LaTisha. I believe you already met the gentleman on the floor." LaTisha said hello, Big Martha mumbled hello in return then just looked at Joe. She couldn't see much of him because LaTisha was sitting on him.

"Is he dead?" asked Big Martha.

"Not that I know of. He's breathing," said LaTisha.

"Girls, I'm a bit dizzy. Let me set down here for a spell."

"Big Martha, before you ask questions can we beg a favor? We really don't want to be involved with this. Do you think you can deal with this without us?" asked Elizabeth.

Big Martha thought for a moment. "Girl, git up offa that piece of trash and pull the curtains. Lock the door and turn the sign 'round." LaTisha did as she was told. "That's better. Now, 'for I go committin' a felony—is anyone else involved?" Elizabeth shook her head in the negative. "Alrighty then. Just the two of you done this?" This time the nod was positive. "Then I ain't gonna ask no more questions. I think you saved Big Martha's life today. That crackhead prob'ly a killed me when he was done. Not like he was wearing a mask. Far's I'm concerned you never been here."

"Thanks. Are you going to be okay?" asked Elizabeth.

"Oh yes, child. I got a real hard head. Just ask anybody what knows me!" Big Martha started to laugh at her own joke but it hurt too much. "Why you girls up here in the first place?"

Elizabeth answered the question: "No reason. I just wanted to say hello and I wanted LaTisha to meet you. We just sorta stumbled onto this guy."

Big Martha looked at the prostrate robber laid out on the floor. "Looks to me like you stumble pretty good. How did you know he was robbing me?"

Elizabeth grinned. "Two things. When I asked him where Martha D was he thought I was still asking about you. And he said he was your boyfriend."

Big Martha tried to blush but that hurt too. "You're right perceptive for being so young. But I said no more questions so you two git on up outta here." She looked at the man on the floor. "Big Martha will take out the trash." She got up and hugged both girls at the same time, nearly crushing them. "Big Martha and Martha D won't ever forget this kindness you done us. Whatever you need, you call us, hear? Now go on outta here."

The two girls left a misty-eyed Big Martha standing over the thief. Martha watched the two young

girls leave. *I guess there's hope for the next genera-*
tion after all, she thought. Now to business. Her first
thought was to call security and have them come
and get the man. Then she discarded that idea. The
jerk would spill his guts about the girls for sure.
Normally she would be physically able to deal with
the problem. She certainly had the size. But right
now someone was playing the *Anvil Chorus* in her
head. She wouldn't be surprised if she had a concus-
sion, never mind what she said about having a hard
head. Although thinking was positively painful she
managed to pull some related items together and
into focus. She went to her Rolodex and called a
number. It rang four times before someone answered.
"Bandy, this here's Big Martha. I need some help."

* * *

LaTisha and Elizabeth had to wait ten minutes
before Amy showed up. Amy stopped LaTisha before
she could spool up: "Don't even say it, 'Tisha. Just
be glad there are three jewelry stores here in the
mall. One place wouldn't do it and the second
didn't have anyone who *could* do it. But the third
place had a cool old guy in the back that even let
me watch. Here." Amy handed the jacks back to
LaTisha and Elizabeth. "Neat, huh? By the way, you
both owe me seven dollars and twenty-five cents."

The jeweler must have had some artisan in him because the craftsmanship was superb. He had woven silver wire around the prongs and center of the jacks, counterpointing their beauty. He had tied the two ends onto a circular ring at the top of the jack, creating a triangle of wire from the ring to the left and right sides of the jack.

"Take a look," said Amy; "I already bought a necklace for mine." Amy discretely displayed her jack to the others. The gold jack hung from her neck on a simple strand of the same metal. The wire, the jack and the necklace matched up perfectly.

"Beautiful, just beautiful," said LaTisha.

"Isn't it? 'Course there goes my allowance for the next three weeks! The chain is worth it, I think."

"Absolutely!" exclaimed Elizabeth. "Now put them away before we attract the whole mall. Amy, what did you tell the jeweler?"

"That was easy. I told him I was rushing a sorority and as a pledge I had to get three gifts for my sorority sisters. I forgot he could tell the jacks were real so I had to backpedal a little. I told him the sorority girls gave me the jacks and it was my job to return them looking like something worthy of wearing. I said I thought of earrings first but they only gave me three jacks. Anyway, he figured out how to suspend them with wire and it only took him fifteen minutes. So, anything exciting happen to you?"

LaTisha elbowed Elizabeth. "Nothin' much. We'll tell you later. Let's go inside."

As they went inside Amy noticed Elizabeth's pants. "Lizzie, your leg's bleeding again." Indeed, blood was still seeping into the cloth of her slacks.

"It opened when we went up the stairs. Maybe Doctor Sauble has some Kleenex," explained Elizabeth. No sooner had she spoken his name than Doctor Sauble came out from the exam area with a female customer. They waited until he had said goodbye and the woman had left the shop.

"Shalom, Uncle Ephraim," said Amy. The optician turned and saw his niece. "Ach, my little Amy come to visit! Vhat a surprise! And look, you brought company! LaTisha! Shalom! And vat's this? Is that Elizabeth Feye I'm looking at? Don't tell me you are running around with this horrible child Amy!"

"Uncle Ephraim!" cried Amy.

"Pay her no mind, Elizabeth. From vhen she vas a little girl, she's been yelling. You couldn't shut her up with a sock."

"Boy do we know it!" cracked LaTisha.

"Oy, is that blood I'm seeing? Sit, sit, a first aid kit I've got in the back." Doctor Sauble was back in seconds. "Okay, Elizabeth, let's see vhat is happening here. Hmmm . . . not bad. Not good either, but nothing that vill leave a scar. LaTisha, soak this gauze in the peroxide. Amy, keep pressure on the vound vhile I make a bandage. Gut! Now wipe the blood off. Gut, gut, now the peroxide. Not much bubbling I see. Amy baby, take the antiseptic und spread it on the gauze here. Nice, thank you. LaTisha, vipe one last time und I vill apply the bandage. Now ve hold pressure for a little bit, put on some tape, and good as new you are." Doctor Sauble sat back and surveyed his handiwork. "Not Albert Schweitzer, but not Doctor Who either! Laugh! It is a joke! You young people, you never understand a good yuke! Elizabeth, I don't think those pants vill ever look gut again."

"They're my mom's."

"Ach, are you in trouble! Maybe you could quick find a tailor, have him make shorts out of them? I'm joking! So, vhat is it, Amy, you are vanting today? It's not your birthday already?" He was smiling.

"Uncle Ephraim, please! You're embarrassing me!"

"It's good to be embarrassed. It keeps you humble my darling. But for you, I'm stopping. Now, vat is it you vant from your favorite uncle?"

"It's a really big favor. We'll understand if you say no."

"How can I say no vhen you don't tell me vhat I'm supposed to say no to?"

"Uncle Ephraim, Elizabeth here needs to know about the war, your war. What happened to you at, you know . . ." Amy had trouble finishing the sentence.

"Treblinka, my niece. Don't be afraid to say it. The more ve say it the less ve are likely to forget, nuh? Und vhy vould you vant to know about this place, Elizabeth, if an old man can ask?"

"Doctor Sauble, it's part of my education. A friend of mine told me to ask Amy, and she said to ask you."

"Und vhat kind of friend vould send you to a tired old eye doctor who sells pretty frames to people who haf more money than sense?"

"Actually, it was someone in our school. He's one of the janitors. His name is Mr. Hawkins."

"Ach, I see. The enigmatic Jack Hawkins."

"You know him?" asked Elizabeth. She was immediately attentive.

Yes, I have heard his name. He has been a good friend to our people although he doesn't vave a flag so you should be avare. Did anyone ever tell you about the time some little ratniks vere painting swastikas in the cemetery? Nuh? I thought not. The policemen caught them red-handed vich was easy for them—they found them naked, duct-taped to a tree, completely covered in their own paint! Vhat a sight! Later, from a friend, from a friend, from a friend ve heard your Mr. Hawkins had something to do with it. Ya, I haf heard of your Mr. Hawkins."

Elizabeth smiled. "That certainly sounds like Mr. Hawkins. I don't think he has much tolerance for that sort of thing."

"Girls, if only the vorld had more men like your Mr. Hawkins. He's a mensch." Doctor Sauble removed his glasses and cleaned them. "Amy, vould you locken the door und put the sign in the vindow, sweetie? Okay, ve outten the lights und go in the back vhere no one can bother us." He led them to his private office in the rear of the store. "Find a seat, be comfortable, und I vill talk until you get sick of me! It's vhat old men do–talk, talk, talk. Ve can't have sex anymore so ve just talk. Vhat, Amy? You think your poor old uncle doesn't know from the birds and the bees? I vas quite a catch at one time, vould you believe it? Before television came along. After that I think all people became less interesting, nuh? Ugh, look who I'm asking! Your generation vould die out without the TV. Don't get me started! Girls, I'm joking! A little, anyway. Okay, the story I'm telling, it's not so pleasant so be prepared. If you haf questions go ahead and ask, or maybe better, vait until I'm ending the story. Old men like me haf trouble staying on the tracks, nuh?"

40

Daniel's day had been long and hard but very fulfilling, if one could call looking at a corpse rewarding. He should be dog-tired. Instead Daniel was alert and at the top of his game. He had forgotten about the excitement he experienced trying to run down a criminal, especially a rapist or killer. Fact was, he left the city to get away from just that very type of work. Now he was back in the thick of things, and loving every minute of it. Intellectually he knew the *high* would wear off and he would be left with bad food, tedium, and nightmares. But right now he was enjoying the moment. As he drove toward home he reflected on the theory that he had advanced to Barry. It had taken time to bring the idea together, especially since it had nothing to do with the physical evidence they found at the victim's apartment. Ironically, it was *Dog* Barkowitz talking about dogs that put the idea in his head. According to Barry there was no thread, however thin, that connected the victims. They were of different ages, different sizes, and different ethnic groups. Some had different jobs, or lacked one. Even hair color was ruled out. *So why these particular women and not the woman next door or across the street?* Half the victims were educated, the other half street-smart. To Daniel's analytical mind that meant one hundred percent of the victims, on one level of intelligence or another, *knew* what to look for when it came to bad news. Following that premise, it therefore stood to reason that the Predator was camouflaging his intent in a novel way. *In what circumstance would a woman, at night, allow a man she did not know to approach her?* His first thought was to fake an injury, but he discarded that idea quickly. Too many people would just run for help or call out, or use a cell phone to dial emergency services. His next brainstorm was for the perp to carry a child or baby. Again, that scenario was not really viable. What respectable man would have a kid out on the streets at four o'clock in the morning? Barkowitz's comment brought him to his third and hopefully correct theory: That somehow the Predator was using a dog to get in close to the women.

The closer to home Daniel got the better the idea sounded. The first piece of evidence pointing to his idea was of course the fact that Dana Lieter was running with her dog when she was murdered. *Could she have stopped to talk to someone who also had a dog?* It fit, but not exactly. It depended on whether Dana mainly ran for the dog or for herself. If she ran for the dog, it fit tight. She wouldn't mind chatting about dogs if her main intent was to exercise the dog. On the other hand, if she were running for herself then stopping just to talk wouldn't seem likely, especially if she were into a cardiovascular workout. They could probably find for sure why she ran when they contacted her co-workers or family.

The labor-intensive part of his theory involved the other victims. The team would have to start making calls tomorrow, once again upsetting grieving family members and annoying other cops. But if they could establish that each victim either owned a dog, or were know to be dog lovers, then they would have their first insight into how the Predator lured in his prey.

As Daniel pulled into his driveway he thought of two things simultaneously. *First, what if there were reports on file about attempted assaults involving a man walking or running with a dog? He could really do nothing about that until tomorrow. The second thing he had remembered he* could *do something about. Still sitting in his car, he radioed in and kept his promise to his daughter.*

* * *

Ephraim Sauble settled back into his swivel chair, gathered his thoughts and took the girls backward in time half a century. "Vhere to start? Not at the beginning. For us it vould be too long a time. So let's start just before the var. With Amy you cannot tell, but I am a Polish Jew, vich is good and vich is also bad. Good to be a Jew, not so good to be a Jew in Poland. For years und years the Poles have hated the Jews that lived beside them. The Russians, ach, they too hated us. Geographically speaking, Poland is in a bad place. Everybody vants a piece of Poland. Und everyone vhat vants a piece does not vant the Jews that live there. So, ve get beaten, ve have pogroms, ve suffer, ve die. But ve survive! Governments come und go but ve stay. At the start of the var, Poland loses quickly, a month it takes the Germans to kill the army. Then they take Belgium, und Luxemburg, und France. Ve sit, ve vait. Then Adolf Hitler, may he still be rotting in hell, has a brainstorm: Let's invade Russia! In June of nineteen and forty-one he attacks his good friend Josef Stalin, another great humanitarian, you should pardon the joke. For us in Poland, perhaps this is good. Russia is not a friend. Our own Polish people hate us. Maybe the Germans vill be better? Who knew? You see, kinder, ve were always hoping, praying that ve could live in harmony with the gentiles." He stopped for breath.

"I vas living on a farm outside the city of Vilna helping my aunt and uncle vhen the Germans came. My mother und father und sister lived in Warsaw. I also had an older bruder who vas studying in America, Amy's Grosspa. It vas summer und I vas in Vilna to help mit the crops und the harvest. Of course ve didn't know then vat we do now. Then it all seemed so reasonable. To continue, the German soldiers collected all the Jews together und marched us down a road. Up ahead ve could see the road vas splitting, und some people vere going left und some people going right. Everyone vas valking slow so ve had plenty of time to decide vich vay to go. In the end, ve split up. My aunt und uncle vas to go to the left, und my cousin Petra und me to the right. Who knew vich vay vas salvation? To this day I don't know. In the end it vas all the same. My aunt and uncle vent to the ghetto they had made in Vilna. Seventeen blocks, mit five hundred houses for sixty thousand people. The Germans are good at math. It vorked out to six people in every room.

"My cousin and I vere told ve vere going to a work camp in Ponar, a little place about six kilometers avay. But it vasn't to vork–it vas to be killed. Ve stayed overnight in a place ve thought vas the new ghetto, but in the morning they marched us to Ponar. There vas a trench dug in the ground, and they lined five people up at a time, und shot them. The bodies just fell into the ditch, dead. Kaput.

There vas no running, no screaming. Ve could not believe vhat vas happening even to look mit our own eyes! It vas our turn, Petra und me, und ve held hands und cried und then the guns fired . . . und then nothing." The room was silent while the old man collected himself.

"It vas dark ven I awakened. I could not believe I vas not sitting with God. My face and head vas covered in blood from the bullet that creased my skull. I vas being crushed und I could not breath. You see, kinder, I vas buried under the bodies of my fellow Jews. I vas dizzy und so very thirsty. I had to tunnel my vay out from under the dead people. It vas vorse than any of your horror movies, nuh? Vhen I got out I tried looking for Petra but it vas dark und she vas buried under so many layers of people I could not find her. I vas so scared that I ran away. I never said Kaddish for her. I vill always be sorry for that, and my soul damned." Ephraim sighed once and continued.

"I vas meshuganah for a vhile. How long? Who knows? I vent back to Vilna after a time. By now all the Jews vere in the ghettos. For once they felt safe, alone mit their own people. The Germans had conditioned us, of course, making the Jews think being jammed together vas good. All it did vas make it easier to find us later. Finding my aunt and uncle vas impossible because by this time they too had been swept up in a raid. They vere never seen again. If God is merciful they are mit Petra in heaven.

"I tried to tell people that Ponar vas nothing but *Death* but the Germans had verked on them too long. Most did not vant to believe. The rest, vell, they thought it vas a test from God. Personally, I had already been tested und I did not care to try again. I sneaked out of Vilna before the next group vas selected for *Relocation,* which vas vhat they called it. I had to get to Warsaw und my family und varn them.

"The first trains to Treblinka left on the twenty-second of July, nineteen and forty-two, before I could reach Warsaw. Back then, you could sneak into the ghetto mit out too big a problem. Later, vell, it vas harder. It took me three days to find my family. The ghetto vas small but so much crowded. They had already said prayers for me, thinking me dead. Even then the stories und rumors vere not so good. Ven I told Papa his bruder vas dead I think he died then too. There vas nothing I could say to get him to leave. I vas going to go but how could I leave my mother und little sister? Finally I talked to Momma und it vas decided I vould try to escape mit Hannah. Momma vould not leave Poppa. I gathered vhat food und money I could und vaited days until the moon vas dark . . . but I waited too much. An early morning raid emptied our building. I von't tell you about the train trip ve took to Treblinka–just understand that twenty Jews died in the cattle car ve were in. In some vay I think they cheated Hitler even if the end vas the same.

"Ve vere still together vhen ve reached the station: Papa, Momma, Hannah and me. As soon as ve unloaded, Jews who vere already there started cleaning the dead out from the cars. Germans were there to give orders und Ukrainian soldiers to make sure the orders vere carried out. The first thing they did vas separate the men from the women und the kinder. They told the vomen they vas going to take a shower und see the hairdresser, vould you believe? I didn't vant Momma und Hannah to go but there vas no choice. Momma said *I love you* und took Hannah's hand . . . that vas the last I ever saw of my sister and momma alive." Ephraim blew his nose into a silk handkerchief and continued.

"The men were alone now und the Nazis had come up with a plan. It vas in four parts und it vas devised to leave the strongest und the smartest standing. They needed two hundred men to vork as slaves for them, two hundred only. First the German officer lines us up und tells us anyone mit a skill to step forward. Of course many people step up, Poppa und me included. Everyone who doesn't is marched off to die. Then the officer asks for people who understand German, vich vas stupid because ve all could speak Yiddish. Poppa held me back. He had a premonition. Some stepped forward thinking to be interpreters but—it vas a trick! Off to the showers they go. The third test vas harder. There vas maybe nine hundred of the men left. The officer says now the guards vill beat und vhip us und whoever falls down vill be killed. It vas a long fifteen minutes but at the end Poppa und I still stood, even though I vas supporting him. There vas dead all around us.

"The last trial vas the vorst. Ve vas separated into two groups. One group vas to take all the baggage und clothes left behind und stage it away from the train station so it could be separated into piles. They must run und carry many things or they vould be killed. Poppa und I vere in the second group. It vas our job to carry the bodies from the gas chamber vich they called a shower to the ditch where they vere to be buried. Ve too had to run or be killed. This vent on until dark. On one of the last trips I saw Poppa drop the body he vas carrying just before he reached the pit. He vas just kneeling there, looking down. I threw my burden into the ditch und tried to raise Poppa up before the guards came but he shook me off. I had never seen my father cry but he vas now. He looked up und told me: "Ephraim, you must live to tell of this. Do not let us die in vain. Go my son. Go! I am dead already." By now the Ukrainians had seen Poppa vas on the ground und vere coming for him. His eyes pleaded for me to leave. I got up but not before I saw the face of the body at Poppa's feet. It vas my sister Hannah." There followed a very long silence unbroken by anyone until Doctor Sauble could continue.

"So, I ran und didn't look back. I could hear them hitting him with their rifle-butts. They vould not vaste a bullet on a Jew. I knew he vas dead. I vas the only one of us left. If not for Poppa's words I too vould be dead. I swore I vould live for him, und Momma, und Hannah, und the thousands lying in that devil's pit. But staying alive vas hard work. I vas young, und resourceful, und very lucky. You vant luck? I vill tell you a story of luck: There vas a German named Kurt Franz, ve called him *Lalka* because he looked like a doll in the face, he vas so pretty. Sometimes he would sit on a pile of clothes und just shoot anyone who he thought vasn't vorking hard enough. Once I stopped to scratch a fleabite und he must have seen me. Just as he pulled the trigger a group of men ran in front of me carrying suitcases und one vas killed instantly. I started running with the rest und he never knew he missed me, or maybe he just didn't care. This Jew or that one, it meant nothing to him. So easy to die there, so hard to live."

Elizabeth ventured to ask a question: "Doctor Sauble, how did you get out of Treblinka?"

"Ach, another long story. I vas there for a long time, months, holding on to hope. But finally even that vas taken. You see, kinder, even if only one Jew vas to survive, each of us hoped *he* vould be that one. In the spring of nineteen and forty-three ve finally knew positive that there vas no hope. There never had been. A young German woman mit two sons arrived on one of the trains. The poor woman had accidentally gotten on the wrong train. She vas a gentile, the wife of a high-up Wehrmacht officer. She yelled und screamed until Llaka, who now ran the camp, came und heard the story. He just walked away. The woman vas made to strip the boys und then undress herself in the middle of the square. She vas then processed mit the rest of the Jews. Then ve knew. If they could not let one of their own leave that place, vhat chance had we?

"Soon after, another champion of the Jews came to see Treblinka, Reichsfuhrer Heinrich Himmler himself. He vas recognized immediately. A few days after his visit a horrible black smoke came from Camp Number Two. The Germans vere getting nervous about maybe not vinning the var, I think. They didn't vant to leave any traces of vhat they had done. So they vere digging up the bodies und cremating them.

"This vas the end. Ve knew it. Burn the bodies, shift the ashes, burn them again. They vould finish there, then kill us who did the dirty vork, then maybe kill the Ukrainian guards. They could not let anyone live to tell vat happened. Mit out hope ve could only die, or revolt. Ve had been dying all along so it vas decided to attack the guards und make a break for it, vich ve did. It vas the second day of August, nineteen and forty-three. It did not go exactly as planned, but vhat revolt does, I ask you? Ve were dead men anyway. Even the Nazis couldn't make us dead twice. Six hundred out of a thousand who tried made it to the voods. Ve left a lot of dead Germans behind und burned vhat vooden buildings ve could. The gas chambers vere brick zo ve could do nothing to them. Not so bad for a bunch of cowardly Jews, nuh?"

"What happened after that, Uncle Ephraim?" asked Amy quietly.

"Ach, I'm not so Jewish I couldn't pass for a Polish peasant. I bought identity papers mit gold taken from the Jews at Treblinka. Then I vorked on a farm. Vhen the Allies landed in France I started vorking my vay to the vest. Already the Cossacks in the east vere pushing the Germans vest toward Berlin. After the var I vas a DP, a Displaced Person. Vhat a name! Since I could speak Polish und German und Yiddish I vas hired at the camp I vas in to help mit the papervork. I learned English from the Americans. My papers did not say I vas Juden und I never told anyone. I vas a hard worker und after three years the friends I had made helped me get to America. My older bruder Ben took me in. I met your aunt Elise, ve married, had kids, grew old. Vhat more can a man do?"

"Doctor Sauble, have you ever been back there, to Treblinka, I mean?" asked LaTisha.

"For vhat? My family is nothing but ashes now, mixed mit that of eight hundred thousand other Jews. Vhat could I give them, or they me? Treblinka is gone, plowed under. The Nazis planted grass und flowers on the graves to disguise them. It is enough. They are in my heart vhere they vill always be safe."

"Doctor Sauble, did Treblinka produce anything? I mean, did they make shoes or hats or anything like that?" asked Elizabeth.

"Nine, Elizabeth. This vas one of the first death camps. In the famous places like Auschwitz they vould vork the men until they dropped, getting the last drop of blood from the Jews. Treblinka had only one reason to exist. It vas there to kill the Juden. Of course, they stole everything the Jews took mit them to the camp. All the shoes, vatches, jewelry, clothes, money, gems; everything. Even the gold teeth in their mouths und the hair on their heads. They had no time to get vork from the people. At one point they vere gassing fifteen thousand Jews a day. Funny I should remember now the shoes. At first they collected all the shoes vich vere then to be shipped back to the Fatherland. But they just threw them in a pile. Mit one hundred thousand shoes in a pile who vould find their mates? Ha! They had to throw them away. Later, vhen I vas there they gave you a piece of string to tie them so the pairs would stay together. German efficiency! Always improving!"

"We studied the concentration camps in school, Doctor Sauble. Our teacher talked about a gas called *Zyclon B*. Did you ever see it used?" asked LaTisha.

"Again with the German efficiency! It vas a later development. Treblinka vas the model that vas improved upon in other places. Nine, ve used carbon monoxide. The Germans built an airtight building, got the people to go in thinking it vas a shower room. They shut the door, turned on a diesel engine, und pumped the exhaust inside. In no time at all—poof! No Jews."

"Doctor Sauble, how could we, the world that is, just sit still and let all this happen?" asked Elizabeth.

"Who vould know? God maybe. Me, I don't know. Did God sacrifice six million of his people so that Israel could be born? I hope not. Vas it apathy, or fear that if you stood up, you vould be next? Did people stop caring about each other as people und saw them only as Jew, or Pole or Catholic? How do you understand a people that vould kill Jews who fought side by side mit them in the Great War, heroes mit Germany's highest honors und medals? I don't know how it happens but I think I know how it starts. It starts small, little things, und ve let it go. Then the little bad things become bigger, und bigger, until they haf a life of their own."

Elizabeth mumbled something. "Vat vas that, dear?" asked Sauble.

"Oh, I said that Satan loves misdemeanors."

"Ach, that's gut! Very gut! From there ve get felonies, ya? Amy, you should bring Elizabeth to Temple. I think she could argue Rabbi Melnik to a standstill!"

"I wouldn't be surprised, Uncle Ephraim," laughed Amy.

"Did they ever catch the Germans that ran Treblinka, like that guy Lalka?" asked LaTisha.

"Oh yes, most of the important people vere caught. Lalka vas given life in the prison, und some others too. Later they caught the commandant in Brazil, or vas it Argentina? I forget. Anyway it vas in nineteen and sixty-four I think. He vas given life imprisonment too. So, to use a phrase I hear today: *What goes around comes around*? Unfortunately it vas to come around too late for six million Jews. You know, you should go to the Capital, to Vashington, und haf a look zee at the Holocaust Museum. You vould learn und see many things that I could never tell you. I vas only in two ghettos und one camp. There vas so many camps: Auschwitz, Belzac, Solibor . . .but it vasn't just the camps vere the Jews vere dying. It vas everyvhere the death. Und the beatings und the torturing, und yes, the rapes. The Nazis made it *permissible*, you see. It became *okay* to hurt a Jew instead of just tolerated. You zee the difference?

Vonce you allow something you *condone* it by not speaking about it."

There was a difference. Elizabeth doubted if she could ever fathom the depths of suffering this man had gone through. She wondered how he had kept his sanity. Was it his faith? "Doctor Sauble, are you religious?" she asked.

"Ach, vhat a question! God only knows. Vhat about you? Vhat about LaTisha who is a Lutheran? Und Amy, the first in our little Temple to Bat Mitzvah? Vhat is this *religious* mean? It is not zo easy to answer vhen the glove is on the other foot! I vas once, long ago, I think. But now I'm not so sure. Being Juden killed most of my family, my friends und my village. Again I ask, did God kill six million of his people so that Israel could be born from the ashes? Is my sister dead because she vouldn't eat shellfish? My head hurts from thinking of it! But I vould tell the vorld I vas a Buddhist if it vould bring back my family. Vhat I say does not matter to me. Vhat I feel in my heart is the truth. Jews have had to make this choice for centuries. If they vere all like me there vould be no Jews today. So maybe I'm wrong. I still go to Temple to please my family. If it also pleases God, so be it. But the vorld has to change before you can call me religious. You know who they should build a monument too? A statue even? Reginald Denny. I vould put them all over the vorld so people could read vhat

he said: *Why can't ve all get along?* Vhat is with this
Bosnia, und Ireland, und the Middle East? You
zee, kinder, everybody thinks their God is Number
One. Look at us Jews. We call ourselves the Chosen
People. Maybe ve are und maybe ve are not. Who's
to know? But Ephraim Sauble is not telling anyone he is better than he is. You want philosophy?
Philosophy I got. Und you know who gave me this
insight? Moses? Billy Graham? Jesse Jackson? Ha!
It vas the Monkees! No, not the chimpanzees but
the singers. Many years ago there vas a television
show mit four meshugana boys running around
und playing music. There vas one song of theirs,
the title I couldn't tell you if you poked sticks in my
eyes, that vent like this: *I'm a little bit wrong, you're
a little bit right.* Vell, when the vorld starts singing
I'm a little bit wrong, you're a little bit wrong, then
I vill haf faith again.

"You see, in the Monkee boy song it says *I'm a
little bit wrong*, vich means I'm mostly *right*. Then
it says *You're a little bit right*, vich means you are
mostly *wrong*. It is like a magician mit a two-headed
coin; either vay you lose. It is a subtle difference but
an important one. The vords—all semantics. Ve could
send Rabbi Melnik to Cloudcuckooland discussing
this. Ve Jews are very big on meanings und vhat is
said. Ask three Jews vhat the meaning of sundown
is in the Torah und it vill *be* sundown before two
of them agree! See kinder vhat happens vhen you

ask an old Jew a question? He never knows vhen to begin stopping. I haf that disease vhat makes you not remember, but I can't remember the name!"

"Alzheimer's?" volunteered LaTisha.

"Gezuntheit!" laughed Sauble. "Amy, it vas a joke! Laugh!"

"Are you happy, Doctor Sauble?" asked Elizabeth.

"Again mit the questions mit no answers! Are you sure you are not Jewish, Elizabeth? By the way, before the Alzheimer's makes me forget, you've lost veight. You look very pretty. Oy, there I go again. Am I happy? You tell me. I'm alive. I haf a good vife who takes care of me, I haf lots of money because they say that's vhat ve Jews are good at, though God forbid Amy's father my nephew should try to make some instead of running around playing cops und robbers and whacking people. Here, the people make laughs at the little Jew who talks funny. But they don't break my vindows und I can mostly sleep at night. It is so much more than I deserve that I am grateful for vhat I have. But happy? I don't even think about it. To have Petra's forgiveness is the one thing that could ease the guilt I carry. But that is impossible. Ve Jews invented guilt. It's true. Look it up. A small joke, kinder, although, who knows? It may even be true.

"Now girls, I'd better be getting home. Elise will think I gotta girlfriend! Elizabeth, I hope you got vhat you needed for school. Amy, a kiss for your uncle, yah? Don't be such a stranger. LaTisha, you too! Now go and make the young boys' eyes shine like the stars when they see you. Gutentag!"

The three girls unlocked the store and let themselves out. They had not gotten beyond the Radio Shack when Elizabeth told them to wait; she had forgotten her packages. She hurried back to the shop. Luckily, Doctor Sauble hadn't locked up behind her. She went in and called softly to him but there was no answer. Fearing trouble, Elizabeth walked quietly back to the office. *What were the odds on walking in on another robbery?* She heard noises coming from the office she had just left so she eased up to the door and peeked through the hinges. There was no robber. Just the old man. He had his sleeve rolled up, staring at the numbers tattooed on his arm, and crying. Elizabeth wanted to reach out to this sad human soul but knew his grief was a private one. She would not intrude. She picked up her packages and retraced her steps, leaving the store without a sound.

* * *

It was a subdued trio of girls that made their way back to where LaTisha had parked the car. Elizabeth said nothing about her having seen Doctor Sauble crying. They were driving out of the mall parking lot before anyone really spoke.

"I've known Uncle Ephraim all my life and I never heard the whole story he just told us," said Amy. "I don't see how he manages to go on with life."

"Maybe because he was spared he feels it's his duty to go on living, especially living life as a good person?" asked LaTisha.

"I think your uncle is more of a Jew that he gives himself credit for, Amy. He and your family have suffered beyond any reasonable limits I can dream of, yet he struggles on in spite of the tragedies. I think he's proving to the world that you can kill individuals but not ideals. I wish I had his strength," said Elizabeth.

"Yeah, isn't it funny to equate immeasurable strength with such a tiny old man?" said LaTisha.

"I don't think you can use a regular yardstick to measure him with, 'Tish. But it makes me proud to be his niece. Say, isn't it just too neat that he knows our mysterious janitor, Mr. Hawkins? Does that guy get around, or what?"

LaTisha laughed. "Somehow I can't picture our old janitor catching a buncha punks and decorating them with their own spray paints."

"Maybe so, but did any of us have a clue what Amy's uncle was capable of until tonight? I just, well, I just thought he was a nice old man who had a funny way of talking. I'm ashamed that's all I saw," said Elizabeth.

"Well yeah, but I'm his niece and I really didn't have a clue, either. I knew people at Temple really respected him, and looked up to him, but I just figured it was because he was old. I guess we shouldn't judge a book by its cover, huh?"

All three girls agreed to that statement, even though Elizabeth opined that it sounded suspiciously like something her mother would say. By this time LaTisha had made her way to Elizabeth's house and pulled into the driveway. None of the three were consciously aware of the Watcher that was following them.

"Okay you guys, be careful going home, and *at* home. Don't do anything stupid. And for gosh sakes don't get separated from your token, and don't go experimenting with them! Remember how the bad guy in Lord of the Rings could sense when Frodo used the One Ring? Maybe it's the same thing. I think we should reserve them for emergencies, okay?" Both LaTisha and Amy nodded their agreement.

"I'll get with you tomorrow and let you know what went on tonight. Did I tell you I was meeting with Mr. Hawkins again? Anyway, I hope to learn more about what the heck's going on, if he'll tell me. Until tomorrow, then. Be safe!" Elizabeth gathered her gear and headed for the back door. Following Elizabeth's advice, the two girls waited until their friend was safely inside before driving off.

On the way to Amy's house LaTisha was able to recount to Amy–despite numerous interruptions–what had transpired upstairs at Big Martha's coin shop. Amy was most interested in how Elizabeth had subdued the robber, and made LaTisha retell the tale three times until she was satisfied she had the right of it. Their conversation would not end when LaTisha dropped Amy off at her house. They would still be discussing what Big Martha might have done with the robber when LaTisha's mother made her get off the telephone hours later.

41

Elizabeth had scant time to herself. Her mother would be home very soon and then they would have to leave for *The-Jack-in-the-Box*. Elizabeth took her purchases upstairs and put away her new things, leaving out one set of clothes to change into. She didn't want to go out looking like a tiger had mauled her. Her mother's slacks were totaled. She had no hope of breathing new life into them. Neither she nor her mother was especially handy at sewing. In fact one could say they were both stitching-impaired. Elizabeth would tell her mother what happened and let her decide whether to try to make shorts out of the remains or to bury them with honors.

Elizabeth stripped off her mother's borrowed clothes and threw them in the hamper, then took a quick shower without wetting her hair. She paid special attention to her leg and after cleaning it she taped on a gauze pad just in case the wound seeped. Before redressing in her new duds she sneaked a quick peek at herself in her mirror. Nothing had changed since the morning. Everything was still in place and looking good. Elizabeth had to smile. *The heck with good! Considering where my body was, I'm lookin' GREAT!* Even so, she still gave a wistful sigh when she looked at her breasts. *You'd think, being Ruler of the Elves and all, she could do something about that. Oh well, beggars can't be choosers!* She had just reassembled herself in a new skirt and top when she heard her mother's car come into the driveway. Not wanting to be the one to hold things up Elizabeth quickly fussed with her hair, brushed her teeth, and headed downstairs.

Mary Feye whirled into the kitchen like an excited tornado, greeting her daughter with a hug and a kiss. "Don't you look nice! Is this the bounty from the Credit Card God? No, no need to answer. I can see it in your face! Did you break us, or did you leave me enough money to pay the electric bill?"

"Mom, you would be very proud of me. I only spent about two hundred and fifty of your hard-earned dollars, and bought a pair of sweaters, five tops, two skirts, two pairs of slacks and a pair of jeans."

"Please tell me you also bought some underwear?" Mary Feye was smiling.

"Mom! Of course I did! Two week's worth. After that I do laundry or borrow yours again!"

"No problem, daughter of mine. I will get you your own box of detergent!" laughed Mary Feye. "Are you ready to go visit the Three Wise Men?"

"Yes, ma'am. Ready and able, sir! Et tu, Mama?"

Mary Feye grinned: "Ready with both barrels, my dear! Let us away!" With great spirit mother and daughter exited the house and climbed aboard the family chariot, that is, their three-year-old Volvo. To Elizabeth's surprise and delight, her mother handed her the reins, or rather, the ignition key.

With Elizabeth driving there was less talking than normal, as Elizabeth's attention was focused outward to the world around and in front of her. She did find time to explain the torn slacks and how they came to be in that condition. As anticipated by Elizabeth, Mary Feye opted to bid farewell to the bloodstained remains. As to her driving abilities, her mother was very forgiving in her criticism, which made Elizabeth suspect, until she remembered that because of James her driving was now above reproach. Since coming home her mother had exhibited more exuberance that she had for many a day. She wanted to ask why but decided to let sleeping dogs lie. Had she asked, her mother would have brushed off the query with a light answer. In truth, Mary Feye was hiding her feelings behind a façade of playful banter. Although not fearing the three men they were soon to meet, Mary Feye was fearful of what she would learn this night. She was not one to give credence to premonitions but she was beginning to have a bad feeling about the future. Whether that future was hers, her daughter's, or the world's, she could not fathom.

Mary Feye was brought out of her revere when Elizabeth started her parking sequence in town. She held her tongue as Elizabeth struggled to place the small car within twelve inches of the curb. After five minutes of effort Mary Feye announced that the car was close enough and for Elizabeth to shut down the vehicle. Mary Feye fed two quarters into the meter just in case and she and Elizabeth walked up the street toward Serra Alley. Neither woman noticed nor felt the plain sedan that parked half a block away.

42

Across town Daniel Shestack was just getting home to his wife, daughter and mother. It too, had been a long day for him, yet he felt strangely alive and alert. He knew the reason but actively chose to ignore it. Daniel did not care to admit, even to himself, that tracking down the scum of the earth made his day. After greeting his wife and checking in on his mother Daniel went upstairs and knocked on his daughter's bedroom door. "Amy, you got a minute?" Daniel heard the sound of the telephone handset hitting the receiver, and seconds later the door opened.

"Hi, Daddy! Home safe and sound I see. What's up?"

"Not much, Honey. Just checking in to see how you are. How are you?"

"Great. I'm just doing my homework."

"I didn't know you used the telephone to do homework nowadays," smiled Daniel.

Amy blushed. "Well, okay, I was talking to 'Tish and doing my math at the same time. We call that *multitasking*, Daddy."

"I see. In my day we called it goofing off. Did everything go well at school today? No problems, nobody following you home or anything?"

Amy had to think quickly. Obviously her father was referring to her late-night watcher. She couldn't tell him about that, at least in a way that wouldn't compromise Elizabeth. Amy decided to fudge the truth. "No, everything was fine. And about last night, Daddy, I think that was just a mistake. I was talking to some of the girls and one of them thinks Robbie Lemaster likes me. He's pretty shy, and she thinks he might have come over but was afraid to knock. It was probably him that I saw, not some robber or rapist."

"Oh, a boyfriend. I see. Do you have any interest in him?"

"Well, not really. I hardly know him. But any interest is good interest, right Daddy?" Amy looked hopeful.

"Anything you say, Sweet Pea. If you think Robbie is our stalker then I'll cancel the drivebys for tonight. No sense wasting the taxpayers' money and my guys' time, is there?"

Amy found it hard to agree without her face flushing. She was a poor liar when confronting her father.

"Okay, then. Your mother says supper is in fifteen minutes. See you downstairs." Daniel tactfully shut his daughter's door and headed downstairs to the den to read the newspaper before dinner. As Daniel skimmed the paper his thoughts returned to the discussion he just had with his daughter. He would be very pleased to meet Mr. Robbie Lemaster. He must be a rather unique teenager. Not many boys his age smoked *Newports* . . . and wore lipstick.

* * *

Jack normally felt the need to move on after a short stay in one place. Some inner sense always told him when it was time—or necessary—to hitch up the wagon and head out. But now another voice was calling him, quietly, yet insistent. Very insistent. It had something to do with what was stored in the basement. It was right on the edge of his brain . . . but he couldn't pull it out. A puzzle came to mind; bits and pieces, locking together. It worried him. It was time to head south. The Peelers were getting close. He could feel their smoky breath on the back of his neck. Yet . . . he must stay. There was one last thing he had to do—must do. He had a date tonight, or tomorrow night, oh yes, a most wonderful assignation with a certain Lady of the Evening he had met the night before. It would be child's play to trace the license number he had written down. He did not as yet know where he was taking his lovely companion. However, he did know how the date would end, oh yes indeedy. Then it would be Halloween. After that he could—and would—leave this rapidly chilling city. Savannah was still very warm this time of year. It was a fun town. So full of life . . . and blood.

43

The wards set around *The-Jack-in-the-Box* were easily twice as intense as they had been the night before. The alley was dark and misty although no rain had fallen. Mary Feye and Elizabeth pushed through the manmade elements that parted before them and sealed tightly after their passing. The door was not hidden from them and they walked directly to it and knocked. They waited but a moment or two before the sound of Wolf's wheelchair was heard on the other side of the door, and was opened to them. The warm cheery light and Wolf's smile greeted them.

"Miladies, welcome you are, and more! Twas it but a day that last we met? Please, come in outta the night air and warm yerselves. Ya be the first here save meself, but I've word of the others, and they be soon." Bandy ushered the women in as best he could without running over their feet with his wheelchair.

"Good eve to you, Mr. Bandy. I trust you are well?" said Mary Feye.

"Tis good as to be expected, what with the Curse here an' all. But I have no complaints to voice, not tha' anyone would pay attention if I did!" Wolf laughed to take the sting of truth out of his words. "And how be thee and yours, Milady?"

"As you, all things are as good as one can expect in this times," replied Mary Feye.

"And you, Aubrey de la Feye, how would you be doing this crisp October evening?"

"I'm fine, thank you." *Elizabeth felt foolish replying in just plain English. How did her mother slide right into that proper, slightly archaic speech pattern?* Elizabeth was looking at Wolf when she caught him *still* himself, then settle back in his wheelchair.

"Ladies, it has been grand up ta now. But I'm afraid we are doomed to boredom and distraction from this point onward. That which I fear most is now at my very door, and liable to break it down lest I open it. Hold now, ya Barbary ape! Make believe you learned some manners at yer mam's knee! This contraption isn't jet propelled!" With those last words flying in the air Wolf pushed his way to the front of the store and let Vice-principal Jackson Barrett Sawyer into the room.

"God, man, are you deaf as well as dumb? Would you have me beating the door 'til the bobbies come to investigate the commotion? For the life of me I can't . . ." Sawyer's voice petered out as he saw the two women standing at the end of the room. "Jaysus, Wolf," hissed Sawyer, "Why didn't you tell me they were already here!"

Wolf smiled: "If the Bear would stop bellowing mayhaps he would hear and sense that Miladies were present, eh?"

Sawyer just glared at Bandy and stalked up the aisle to where Elizabeth and her mother were standing. "Forgive me, Miladies. Had I known you had arrived before me I would have attempted to enter with less *effort*. It seems our host has warded the place so strongly that even those who are welcome have trouble entering." Sawyer eyed Bandy as he wheeled up to the group, daring him to make issue.

"Perhaps I have overdone security Miladies, but in a good cause, if you take my meaning. Please, let us retire to my quarters where we can be comfortable." Bandy led the way into the rear of the shop where he lived. "Excuse the mess, if you will. 'Tis been a busy day and I've naught had time to tidy." Here Mary Feye and Elizabeth exchanged looks–the room was neater than any room in their house. "Please, sit. May I get ye a beverage while we wait for The Hawk?"

"I'll take a diet Coke, please," said Elizabeth.

"Make that two, Mr. Bandy, if you will," said Mary Feye.

"Would ye not be sampling a bit of this wine I've set aside?" asked Bandy.

"No thank you, Mr. Bandy. This night's work demands a clear head, and I wish to retain mine."

"Well spoken, Milady," said Bear, "but *my* poor head remains muddled unless I have something to settle the muck." Saying that Bear went to the bar and fixed himself a bourbon and water. "Wolf, are you partaking?"

"Aye, but I've already a store set by here on me chair." Bandy lifted a glass from a cup holder and held the glass in salute. "Since yer already there, get the ladies their drinks, will ye?" Bear just growled and took his drink to a chair and levered himself into it. Bandy was forced to scoot over to the bar and fix the drinks he himself had offered. As Bandy poured the soda into glasses he noticed that Jack Hawkins was standing in the doorway. "Jaysus! Hawk, up to yer tricks again, I see! And how long have ya been eavesdropping on honest folk's conversation?"

"Long enough to know someone isn't paying as much attention to security as he purports to be."

"Ah, Hawk darling, ye know ye can pass any ward me poor self is able to set, so don't be doggin' me work in front of the ladies."

The Hawk smiled. "Just checking, Wolf, just checking. Miladies, good eve to you both, and to you, Vice-principal. Let me grab something from the bar and we can begin." Hawkins made his way to the bar and fixed himself a club soda with lime. He returned to the living room and found a seat. "Have we an agenda tonight, or shall we just wing it?"

Mary Feye answered: "Questions, Mr. Hawkins. Lots and lots of them. That is what is on *my* agenda. What Sir, is on yours?"

Hawk smiled. "Answers, Milady Feye. Lots and lots of them. Let me begin with a quick history lesson."

The Hawk settled in for the telling: "Let me restate the obvious as we know it to be. That there *is* such a thing as tangible Evil. Like most things, Evil comes in many shades of darkness and many forms, not just black and not just the Devil. The levels and degrees are myriad. Our main concern is that Evil as a presence in our world does exist. If left unchecked the world would in all likelihood spin out of control. But with ultimate Evil there is Good, and those who strive to block the spread of Evil. Long ago scholars deduced that without organized resistance Evil would continue to have the upper hand. We are talking Biblical times, here. A group of people formed an alliance, in essence banding together for the greater good. As I told you earlier, these people took their name from Genesis, Chapter twenty-eight, Verse twelve, the reference to the stairway that led to heaven which became known as Jacob's Ladder. Early membership varied, and then stabilized at exactly five hundred souls. Unlike many societies of the time, membership was open to all, be they black, white, brown, yellow, male, female, Druid or Jew. The only true criteria for membership was the devotion to duty and the declaring of oneself to forever stand in Evil's path. Literally and figuratively these were the messengers of God, balancing the scale of Life. Many centuries ago the agents of the society were called Jehovah's. It wasn't until much, much later that the agents of the LS were to become known as Jacobs, then later the name was modernized to *Jacks*. Two millennia ago the Jacobs were known to exist by some people outside the society. As times changed and belief systems modified the LS became less visible. Soon the Society realized that this hidden style had advantages over the more open agenda practiced earlier. Indeed, more could be done with much less fuss. The LS went totally underground. It became a secret society that shunned the spotlight at every turn. This strategy change also weeded out those who had joined for glory, for now few outside the LS would ever know what was accomplished in the name of Good. Any questions so far?"

"I have one," said Elizabeth. "If there were all these different people from different cultures, how did they decide about who was God?"

"I can answer that, Elizabeth," said Sawyer as he stood up. "God as you mean it was never mentioned. Such was the power of the first *Jacks* that they were able to agree to disagree on a Godhead. Instead they chose to fight for what each person's God stood for, namely Good with the capital G. Fact is, some gods never made the grade. To my knowledge no Aztec has ever been in the LS because human sacrifice was a main ingredient of their worship. There have been many other exclusions but you would have to ask our Professor Nocknagle for the research on that. I readily admit that I am no scholar in that area. But a *good* god that deserved worship would wish for goodness above all else, even worship. Call it sort of a divine Golden Rule if you will. Once that was established, the LS gathered many followers outside traditional religious boundaries. Does that answer your question?"

"I, I guess so. Is this another example of the good of the many versus the good of the few? It seems we are once again in an episode of Star Trek."

Sawyer smiled at the reference and continued: "Absolutely, Milady. Our progenitors put aside their *religion* so they could apply their *faith.*" Sawyer looked at Hawkins. Jack Hawkins took the cue and continued the narrative:

"Through the centuries the LS has intentionally sidestepped the mainstream of society yet stayed abreast of it, and in many ways it has been a step or two ahead. Without being burdened with a religion per se they were able to forge ahead to meet the future. The LS maintains a vast database, the core of which is illuminated manuscripts. Of course now just about everything is on computer, though many arcane texts are still consulted. It is without false pride that I say that our files are more complete than any on Earth. It is with the help of this information that we are able to keep tabs on what happens around the world. Having access to Fox News and the BBC helps too, of course." Hawkins smiled and took a swallow from his glass.

"This more or less brings us to our time now. The Ladder Society is itself hidden, yet some of its members are not. At times it has been necessary to place a *Jack* in the open. More than not that person has paid the ultimate price for their devotion."

Mary Feye interrupted: "What do you mean by that, Mr. Hawkins?" Elizabeth's mother was well tuned to anything that smacked of a sacrificial pawn.

Hawk hesitated, and then answered: "In our own time, in this country, leadership was sorely needed. We advanced one of our number in the hope that we could avert what looked like global thermonuclear war. In that endeavor we were successful, and the nineteen-sixties passed into history without nuclear destruction. But we were unable to cover every contingency, and we lost the *Jack* to a mere puppet of Evil. We were able to have the culprit captured, but before we could interrogate him the AntiJacks silenced their own killer."

Elizabeth looked at her mother and saw that her complexion had blanched. Concerned for her mother, she looked to Hawk.

"Yes, Mare, it takes some getting used to, but I see by your face that you ken the answer. John Fitzgerald Kennedy was a member of the Ladder Society."

* * *

Elizabeth was stunned. In one short minute The Hawk had turned upside down everything she thought she knew about American history. Yet it explained so much. She had to ask: "Then how? Why?"

Hawkins smiled. "It would fill a book, Aubrey. Jack Kennedy was a good man, and a good friend. He was flawed as are all God's creatures but he stood by his oath even when he knew his chances of survival were slim. Oswald was just another tool, and when he had served his purpose he was disposed of. He must have known something because the AntiJacks sacrificed another of their own to insure Oswald's silence." The Hawk waited for Elizabeth to connect the dots.

"Oh my. Ruby. *Jack* Ruby killed Lee Harvey Oswald."

"Indeed he did, Milady," said Bandy. "'Twas a mean little rat of a man, he was. Dealt with him a time or two befor' the killin', and I've forever wished I'd done him in the first I set eyes on the bastard." Bandy made as if to spit on the floor but remembered his female guests and thought better of it.

Although taken aback by this revelation Mary Feye recovered quickly, and with some heat: "Sorry I am to hear that Kennedy was killed in your service, and my condolences to you, Mr. Hawkins, if indeed you did know him. Yet this seems to me another example of your group's inability to protect its own! Did you even *bother* to try and save your man once the Cuban Missile Crisis was resolved? Or had he too served his purpose?" The peat fires of the fen blazed hard green in Mary de Feye's eyes.

The Hawk's eyes glistened and seemed to harden into granite. Then the lines around his eyes relaxed, and softly he spoke: "Meriam de Feye, no greater friend did I have than Jack Kennedy. Because of your daughter do you speak thus, and without clear thought. For that I grant forbearance. But do not test my resolve, or my duty. What is now upon us is beyond even your ability to comprehend. I have pledged my soul to protect your child, but Destiny takes its own road. If you wish to travel alone—do so! But do not shame the people here with words that mean so little and hurt so much." The Hawk's eyes never left those of Mary Feye, nor did his voice reach much above a whisper.

Elizabeth looked first to Hawk, then to her mother. Her mother's cheeks were red, from embarrassment or anger she could not tell. The answer lay in her mother's response: "For whatever reason you bring out the worst in me, Mr. Hawkins. For fifteen years I have been a mother trying to raise a daughter. Please forgive me if I continue to wish for her continued growth. I apologize for slurring the memory of your friend. May he rest in peace, as may this thing between us. Please bear in mind that I lost my husband as you lost Jack Kennedy, and grant me time to understand all that is laid before me."

"Would that I could, Milady, but while we bicker our enemies plot, and so must we. There is but one thing that must be accepted, if not understood: We, all of us, are in the end, expendable, should it be necessary. If we fail you will not care to live in the world that is to come." Hawkins stood up and slowly freshened his drink at the bar, allowing Mary Feye to digest an unpalatable future.

With his drink in hand he turned and continued his talk: "There are five hundred of us, more or less. The number has been set since just after the Great Plague in the fourteenth century. Incidentally, that was about when the LS went totally underground. Through the years we have had great successes and dismal failures. The recent world war was especially painful as we lost fifty-one of our number in the Holocaust alone. Vietnam was another pustule on the ass of mankind. The LS lost twenty-two there, and not all on the same side. So it goes. There is a flare-up and we respond. If we are quick we stop the crisis before it becomes a problem. And we are constantly mitigating. To say that we have achieved a stalemate is to be generous. Unfortunately for us things seem to be reaching a crescendo, sort of a *winner takes all* scenario. Questions?"

Elizabeth had one, or a dozen: "How do you do what you do? I mean, say you want to have a certain thing *not* happen, like a military coup?"

Hawkins looked to Sawyer for a reply. "Elizabeth, we do what has to be done. If a person is marked and documented, and removing him from the equation is warranted, then he is removed. Or her for that matter."

"Removed?" The terminology confused Elizabeth.

"Aye, lass, removed. Bear, doan sugarcoat it and make it what it isn't. Killed, terminated with extreme prejudice, iced, whacked, given a permanent nap in the sod. Aubrey, 'tis a dirty business you've fallen into, but you best be knowin' the truth of it, or it will kill ye instead. We torture, and we kill, an' we do things that make it hard to sleep at night. We're up to our elbows in blood, we are, an' twill never wash off."

"Wolf!" spoke Hawkins harshly.

"Heave away, Hawk! For once the leprechaun's right. The Little One has the right of knowing what we are. Elizabeth, what other questions?" asked Sawyer.

"Uh, well, I sorta guessed that you couldn't play by the rules and do everything you say you do. I hope no one expects me to become an assassin because I don't think I'm cut out for that. But what about the law? Is the Ladder Society above the law?"

"No," said Hawkins, "no one is above the law. But you must understand that we are responsible to an authority higher than any temporal government. When able, we abide by the law of the land. If not, we bend it or circumvent it. If all else fails then we break it. But we are responsible to ourselves and to the Society. Make no mistake; our actions are under constant review. Should we wantonly disregard the law, hurt the innocent, or cause needless pain to others then *we* are put to trial, and judged. The sentence is final, not subject to appeal, and usually fatal. No, we are not above the rule of law."

"I think both Elizabeth and I can live with that creed," said Mary Feye. "Now *I* have a question. You've explained what the Ladder Society is. Will you now explain what the AntiJacks are?"

"'Tis a rotten barrel of triple-dipped bas–" Bandy was stopped in mid-sentence by a look from both Bear and The Hawk.

"Forgive him, Lord, for he haseth a big potty mouth," said Bear.

"And I second that opinion. Wolf, let's try to keep the invective down to a dull roar if you please?" said Hawkins. Bandy complied but with ill-concealed temper.

"Notwithstanding Bandy's last remark, which would have merit at another time, the AntiJacks could best be described as a response to the Ladder Society. Its formative history is clouded and its origin obscured. For many years Evil was above board and easily seen. The better for business as it were. Delights seen are more desired than pleasures hidden. When we went underground our efficiency level increased, and that was duly noted by those that walk the dark road. Evil decided that their task force needed to disappear too. It was called in years past as the *Barak Dymdik Ky*. Literally translated it means *minions that foil the unbad*. We call them AntiJacks or AJs for simplicity's sake. We don't know their numbers but best guess puts it at about one thousand. They have no creed or ethos. Some are mere soldiers while others, like our Mr. Daws, are well placed in Evil's hierarchy. Most of these people work undercover but some do surface from time to time when Evil deems it efficacious."

"Could you, or would you, tell us the names of some of the open ones?" asked Elizabeth.

"Historically, yes. One of the more obvious is Jack Daniels. The man never knew his drink and his name were co-opted. They must have laughed themselves sick over that one. There was Thomas Jonathan Jackson, whom you might recall by his nickname *Stonewall*. Tom was actually a good man but was subtly turned in the end. He had the ability and skill to defeat the Union had he lived."

"Wasn't he accidentally shot by one of his own soldiers?" asked Elizabeth.

"Doan you believe everthin' you read in the history books, lass. There be many o' slip between reality and history," spoke Bandy. "Twas one of the Society that did the deed and put Tom Jackson in his grave. He were one o' the best an' bravest men of his time but at last call he chose to walk the wrong road. And he paid full measure, more's the pity. A righteous man, he was."

Hawkins continued: "There have been others, famous and not so famous. There was John Ketch, who died in 1696. He was an English hangman notorious for his brutality. Again, here in the New World, was the equally famous John Wilkes Booth. Currently we have one that the jury is still out on, the Reverend Jesse Louis Jackson. He has done good works but things are pointing in a direction I'd rather they did not go. One cannot preach fidelity if one does not practice it. I fear he will fall as a role model to young men of color here in

America. Reverend Jackson is flirting, not only with the opposite sex, but also with the Devil. I hope he can withstand the temptation."

Hawkins paused. "I think that gives you a good enough background to understand what the Ladder Society was, and is now. I'd like Mr. Sawyer to say a word or two now about what an individual *Jack* is. Bear?"

Jackson Sawyer heaved himself up from his easy chair and assumed his best teacher demeanor. "As Hawk has stated, there are no restrictions on who a *Jack* can be, ethnically, religiously, sexually, or whatever. They are just as apt to be an old Buddhist woman as a United States Navy Seal. Usefulness and ability are not measured by strength alone. The LS has a team of five people whose sole job is to scout the earth looking for prospective members. Our Professor Nocknagle and his research staff are also involved. Sometimes it takes decades to place a member. Other times just a day. This is the main way that agents are recruited into the Ladder Society." Bear looked for questions.

"You said the *main* way, Mr. Sawyer?" asked Mare, ever quick to spot an anomaly.

"Yes, others come to us of their own accord."

"How so, if the Society is hidden from view?"

"True enough, yet the LS is not always hidden to those that know where to look, or have a built-in homing device that leads them to us."

"I don't understand. What do you mean, Mr. Sawyer?" asked Elizabeth.

"Have you read *Animal Farm*, Elizabeth?"

"Yes, sir, of course. In junior high."

"Then you will remember this quote: *All animals are equal, but some are more equal than others.* All *Jacks* are equal in the LS, but some have abilities beyond that which we would call normal. In simplest terms, there are basically three types of *Jacks*: The first is your basic everyday person like your friend Philip. They are regular people, mundane, and unremarkable in any extra-natural way. The second is a step up from that. It is someone who has a talent, an ability so to speak, that makes them special. In earlier times they might have been deemed witches or conjurers. Today we might just say that they are able to access certain parts of the natural and metaphysical world that others are not in tune with. Many of our Watchers are in this category. With me so far? The last are the ones that form the Corps, the never-ending eternal link to our past. The Corps numbers are not set in stone; they rise and fall with the times. But the number is low, less than five per cent of the total membership of the Ladder Society."

"So," asked Mare, "what makes these *more equal than other* others more equal?"

"Physically, nothing really. It is the, the . . . Hawk, can you do better with this?"

Hawkins took over: "I'll try. Miladies, it might strain your reality here but if you can accept what you already know then you should be able to deal with this. Let me try a train analogy again. Think of Time as we perceive it as a train running on a track into infinity. This *Time Train* has passenger cars, and when you are born the train stops, you get a ticket and climb onboard. The Time Train continues on, and when the conductor punches your ticket, you die. The train stops and you get off. That part is simple. Now add the population of Earth to the train and we get over twelve billion stops and starts just to load newborns and offload the dead. Obviously the train, that is, Time, can't stop for all these people coming and going. So somewhere, the people or person who is in charge of the train decided that to keep the Time Train on schedule they need two trains; a Local Ghost Line and an Express. The Express Train keeps time on schedule, and the Local Ghost Line does the dropping and picking up. Now the Local Line is straight, veering neither left nor right. The Express, however, looks like a snake, making loops back and forth across the straight Local Line. Picture it like a Caduceus; a snake coiled around a staff. The Express Time Train never stops. It just has to go further to reach the same point as the Local Line, giving the Local Ghost Train time to pick up passengers, intersect with the Express, put the newborns on the train and take off the dead. Here, let me draw you a picture." Quickly Hawk took paper and pencil and laid out his example. "Understand so far?"

"I think I understand. The straight line is the slower train, because it has to bury the dead and pick up the newly born and hold onto them. Then when the Express crosses the Local line the Express exchanges those newborns with the newly dead. This allows the Local to drop off the dead and pick up the newborns at its own pace. But what does that have to do with *Jacks*?" asked Elizabeth.

"I'm coming to that. Bear with me. Some of the passengers get special tickets. For want of a better analogy let's call them season tickets, or maybe an eternal membership. Within certain limits they are able to ride the train forever. For the sake of argument let's call this a Blue Ticket. When certain people are born they are issued a Blue Ticket when they board the Time Train. Now, when they die their ticket is punched; *but when the Express Line crosses the Local . . . they do not board the Local.* Instead, they stay on the Express Train and immediately reenter the world as a newborn. Now here's the kicker: When they reach a certain age they are endowed with the past memories and knowledge of all their past lives." The Hawk waited for that to sink in and the inevitable firestorm of questions to follow.

The Mare was the first to speak: "Are you telling us that these particular *Jacks* are immortal?"

"Yes . . . and no. As you personally know, The Dodger was knifed and died. All people die. All *Jacks* die. Yet some are given the chance, and the burden, of returning at a later date. If Bandy were to die at the age of seventy he would return to the world as a newborn. He would live a normal life–until such time as his *jack self* was reborn, at which point his past would reveal itself. He would be like a computer that became self-aware. To be immortal would be to never die at all."

"Isn't what you just described to us called reincarnation?" asked Elizabeth.

"Not so, Milady. Reincarnation could involve ye comin' back as a beetle, or tree, if you take my meaning. An' most people what think about reincarnation say naught about rememberin' all that went before. No, this is a different bucket o' fish," said Bandy.

"But in essence," said Mare, "these people would always be reborn, and thus live forever."

Bear said something under his breath that Elizabeth and her mother failed to catch. "You said something, Mr. Sawyer?" queried The Mare.

"He said *unless your ticket gets punched,*" spoke Bandy. "Subtle as a rockslide, the man is."

Forestalling an argument Hawkins quickly spoke up: "To put it bluntly, there is one way for this system to be derailed. Simply put: If a *Jack* is killed outright, or later dies of wounds inflicted by an

AntiJack, then the Blue Ticket is forfeit, and you are removed from the train like anyone else." Hawkins spoke the words like a litany. He watched Mary de Feye closely, waiting for realization and hope to rise and fade in her eyes. "I'm sorry, Mare, but what you have surmised is true. Since your husband The Dodger was killed by an agent of the *AntiJacks*, there is no hope for his return. He is lost to us forever."

44

While Mary Feye and her daughter once again tasted the bitter fruit of loss, The Predator was busy across town. As he had known, it was indeed child's play to trace the license plate number of the car from last night. *The coppers weren't the only ones that could be detectives.* Jack stopped first at the diner where he had met the prostitute and scoped it out. No luck, but then he didn't figure she would be there. *On to Plan B.* Jack made his way in the darkness to the address listed on the car's registration, and lo and behold, the beat-up Buick LeSabre was in the driveway. The house was a brownstone similar to the place he was renting, only older and down at the heels. The area was not conducive to late-night strolls, or sitting on the porch swing, or parking your car without first setting the alarm and locking a bar across the steering wheel for good measure. In short, it was his kind of neighborhood.

Jack walked boldly up to a front window and looked in. He did not worry about being seen. All the adjacent buildings were shuttered, blinded and curtained against the terrors of the night. Jack could hear music coming from inside and voices both low and shrill. *Ahh, we have guests!* Using the preternatural senses developed over many a year he was able to discern three distinct voices downstairs. *Listening closer he thought he heard muffled sounds coming from upstairs. Probably a bedroom, yes? No doubt a lady of the house was entertaining someone privately.* Since this was obviously a party Jack saw no reason why he shouldn't be the Guest of Honor. Going round to the rear of the building he pulled out his invitation—a set of lock picks—and invited himself in.

Entering without the least sound Jack edged his way over to the door that connected the kitchen and dining room. Jack turned around and surveyed the kitchen. *Hmm . . . messy messy. They really should clean up the place. Maybe later I'll come back and neaten things up.* Jack opened the swinging door ever so slightly and peered into the next room. *Much better. But mismatched furniture! That hutch does not go with these Queen Anne chairs. And look at that beautiful dining room table. It must be ten feet long! Why, you could almost perform surgery on it. And see—it has a linen tablecloth. But something is wrong. Yes! The silk flowers in the bowl. I think we can come up with a much better centerpiece. All we have to do is try.*

Jack quietly opened the kitchen door and slipped inside the dining room. Sliding along the wall Jack was able to move close enough to the living room without being seen. With the music playing there was little chance of his being heard. When he viewed what was taking place he knew there was even less chance he would be seen. There were three people in the room—two men and a woman. Jack recognized the two men from the night before; they were his would-be muggers. The black woman he didn't know. Of all things the theme from *Bolero!* was playing on the stereo. The woman was doing an incredibly poor imitation of a stripper. By her movements Jack would bet she was either drunk or doped to the gills. As bad as the performance was she had captivated her audience. The two men sat on the sofa, mouths open, eyes watching every inept move the woman made. *That's entertainment? You poor boys must be from out of town. Are you that starved for amusement? If that dancing* thing *excites you then you're gonna love this!*

Running his hand down the wall by the door Jack found the light switch and dropped it. Since there was no ceiling light the switch was connected to the table lamp on the stand beside the couch. The lamp went out, leaving just the willowy illumination of two candles stuck on the stereo speakers.

"Yo, what's up? Hey baby, you done shook the light right outta this here lamp!" laughed the bigger of the two thugs.

"Honey," slurred the woman, "I don't need no lights to make you hot. You jus' watch my shadow, 'kay?"

The woman started up again, trying in vain to match her gyrations to the beat of the music. Mostly she just swayed in place and attempted to unzip and unbutton pieces of her clothing. It didn't matter. She would never have a more attentive audience. For that matter she would never have *any* audience after this one, for Jack was on the move.

While the two thugs were mesmerized by the woman's attempts to disrobe, Jack had followed the wall until he was around the couch and behind the men. As these were mere annoyances Jack did not waste effort. *When it was time to butcher the hogs you just have to get on with your work, didn't you?* Taking one of his *toys* backhanded in each fist and standing between and behind the two men Jack simultaneously reached across each man's throat, pressed in, then dragged the blades across their gullets with as much force as he could apply. It was more than enough.

Ah, Bolero! Gentlemen, if you could but listen you could hear your blood gushing out to the beat of the music. Bravo! Author! Author! Why, that's me! Thank you thank you thank you you're really too kind. No please, don't get up. Silly me—you can't get up! Just rest then. Sleep . . . perchance to dream. The smaller of the two had slipped sideways so Jack propped him back up and positioned his head so he could still watch the woman strip. *Wouldn't want to miss the best part of the show, now would we?*

The entire episode had taken less than thirty seconds. The sense-impaired woman was still fumbling with a stuck zipper and hadn't the faintest clue that she was now dancing for a pair of corpses. When she finally did look up she had to shake her head because now she saw three men, not two, sitting on the couch.

"Hey baby, wher' you come from?"

"Oh, I just dropped by to see my friends here. You certainly are good at what you were doing. Are you by any chance a professional dancer?"

"Baby, I be anythin' you wan' me to be. But Honey I got bills to pay so's you wanna watch you got's to pony up some cash, okay?"

"Of course, of course! I wouldn't think of depriving you of your livelihood. I think you should get everything you deserve. Now come on over here and I'll be more than happy to give it to you." If the woman had been able to see the look on Jack's face, even in her reduced state of mind, she would have run screaming in the other direction. Instead she did a clumsy stroll toward the sofa. As she approached she looked to her earlier customers who, unknown to her, had exsanguinated into the couch and carpet.

"Martel . . . Rollo, you guys fall asleep or die on me or what?" She leaned in closer to look at the man she called Rollo.

"A little bit of all three I should think," laughed Jack as he grabbed the whore by the neck. "Here, let me help you with that nasty ol' zipper." Jack took a knife from behind his back and cut out the zipper from the front of her dress. Jack started to giggle. "Oops! Did I make a mistake or what? I might have gone too deeply there. What do you think, my dear?" The prostitute was not in a position to respond. Having been gutted from sternum to belly she was too transfixed by the sight of her intestines spilling from her stomach.

"What say, Deary? No stomach for this line of work? Why of course. How stupid of me! There's your stomach on the floor! Messy, messy. You really should be more careful where you put your internal organs. Someone could slip and fall! Here, let me help you." By this time the woman had collapsed on the floor. Jack *helped* her by replacing the spilled organs. "There, isn't that better?" Jack received no reply, not that he expected one.

"Well really, don't just lie there in the middle of the room. Why not join your friends on the couch? You'd like that, wouldn't you?" Jack didn't wait for an answer to that question either. Instead he picked the hooker up and sat her between her two customers. "Symmetry, I do love symmetry. Now, you three just wait here while I go upstairs and say hello to a friend of mine. Enjoy the music–and please don't be naughty . . . keep your hands to yourself." Humming softly to the music Jack grabbed the banister and started up the stairs.

45

It was The Mare that recovered first from the remembrance of the fatal stabbing of her husband and Elizabeth's father. Although devastated by the memory she realized that she must project an image of strength to her daughter. "Mr. Hawkins, this is very disturbing. If what you have described is not immortality then it is as near as one can get. Does this *system* work the same way with Evil also?"

"It works in exactly the same manner, Milady. If you will remember the incident with Mr. Sawyer, The Crow, and the fourth story apartment house? Had Crow died from the fall he would not be here giving us problems today."

"Mr. Hawkins," asked Elizabeth, "since Jack Daws didn't die then how old is he? I mean, couldn't he be really old?"

"Absolutely, although I would venture to guess that he is not as old or as talented as he would want us to think. The records of the Ladder Society do not document an individual with his *statistics* beyond a possible three generations. Cumulatively he has probably lived longer than any normal human but I am sure there are others that are older and smarter."

"So you're saying that this Crow could have spent three lifetimes on earth, or well beyond one hundred years?" asked Mare.

"It wouldna surprise me atall, Milady. The black-hearted son of goat has been a stench in the nose o' mankind for many a year, if ye pardon my French," added Bandy.

"Wolf, enough for now," warned Hawkins. "Let us try to stay on course. Aubrey, I would like to talk a bit about you right now. You have grown into quite a handsome young lady in the last twenty-four hours. Well, at least *our* twenty-four hours! It seems the desert air was good for you. I think that you might as well cancel any appointments you might have with the dentist or Doctor Sauble. They would only question and possibly deny the truth in front of their eyes. Your teeth and vision have been corrected by your use of power. As the person you are to be realizes what it needs, it *fixes* things it finds less than optimum. Your teeth were crooked so it straightened them; your eyesight was less than perfect so it improved your vision. It is really nothing more than you channeling energy to the right place. As to your, ahh, less than perfect weight to height ratio, most of that was burned off as energy, both in your dreams and during your *exercises* of power at school. There is not much magic involved here; you run around all night in a dream and you lose weight. To gain the *oomph* that you need you pull energy from the stored fat in your body. I know this doesn't sound very sexy but the proof is in the pudding so to speak. At this time I'd guess you are very close to your optimum height and weight. Maybe an inch or two in height, maybe some more muscle weight to balance out the added elevation. Aubrey, you have become as beautiful as your mother."

Elizabeth could not have restrained the deep blush that encompassed her face had the world depended on it. On the other hand her mother was more successful; she kept the color to a minimum.

"Uh, thank you, Mr. Hawkins."

"Merely the truth o' the matter, Elizabeth. Ye canna guild the lily if you take my meaning," said Bandy.

"Although I might take exception to my own appearance, I must admit that you have become a lovely young woman, Elizabeth. I guess I've been too close to you to notice."

"I can understand that," said Hawkins, with something else hidden behind the words. "But let us move on if we can. Elizabeth, would you be kind enough to enlighten us about how your *music lessons* went last night? I assure you we all are most curious."

"Yes, that includes me too, Honey," said Elizabeth's mother.

"Well, okay. Do you want the long version or can I just sort of give you the highlights?"

Hawk answered: "I think just the highlights will do for now, Aubrey. When this time has passed us we can return to the tale and hear the details."

"Okay then, here goes: As Mr. Hawkins knows, I visited Arizona sometime in the late 1960s or early 1970s. I meet a man named Billy who was some sort of Indian Tribal Policeman who took me to his hogan, his house that is, and I spent about half a year with him."

Mary Feye interrupted: "But you were only asleep one night!"

"I know, Mom, but time isn't the same in my dreams. To you it was maybe eight hours but for me it was a pretty rough six months. You don't have to understand it, Mom. I know I don't. But take it from me it's possible. So during the time I was there Billy made me exercise and walk and run and climb all over the place. He showed me different plants and how to use them, then showed me what kinda things would kill you or make you sick. After he got me toughened up he taught me self-defense, I guess it was karate. Nothing fancy, just the basics.

Actually Billy said I was pretty good at what I knew. Anyway, he taught me a lot."

Sawyer spoke: "Was there a special lesson or lessons to be learned or did your Billy just teach you generalities?"

Elizabeth mulled that one over. "There were bunches, but I guess the one that sticks in my mind is that even if you have power over someone that doesn't give you the right to use it."

"Is that all you learned, Little Sister?" asked Hawkins.

"Oh yes, I almost forgot! Mom, there was this really cool rattler called Grandfather Snake, and he came and lay down in my lap! Can you believe it? Oh, and I got in a fight with some boys because they were throwing rocks at his grandchildren!"

"Whoa, Nellie!" interjected Elizabeth's mother, "What do you mean you had a rattlesnake in your lap?"

"I did Mom, really! And they're not slimy at all, they're, well, I can't explain it but it wasn't gross or anything. Let me explain." Here Elizabeth relayed to everyone her first meeting with Grandfather Snake, then the incident with Bernard and the other two ruffians. Bear and Wolf were duly impressed with her skill in unarmed combat, her mother incredulous and concerned about her streetfighting and playing with vipers. The Hawk, however, produced a small smile when Elizabeth told how she stopped short of maiming Bernard.

"Aubrey, like Jesus, you have returned from the desert a new person. I think I speak for the entire Ladder Society when I give you my congratulations," spoke Hawk.

"Me too, Honey. You did great. But who was this Billy? Surely not Billy the Kid? Besides, the time frame isn't right. What cowboy did you visit out West?"

"I don't know, Mom. Besides, he was an Indian, or mostly Indian. He never gave me his last name, just the first and middle: Billy Jack."

The three men laughed. It was Bandy who corrected her: "Lass, you got all of it but ye never glommed on to it! The man has no middle name that we be aware of. His full name be Billy Jack."

Elizabeth was still in the dark. Evidentially this was one song, or movie, that she had missed. But her mother was a generation older. She made the connection quickly: "*One Tin Soldier*, correct? By ABBA? No, that isn't it. Coven? Yes! It was a song by Coven. It's the only song of theirs I remember."

"Once again The Mare shows us she did not misspend her youth," laughed Sawyer. Mary Feye looked pleased in spite of herself. To cover her embarrassment she took the time and explained to her daughter who and what Billy Jack was.

"I really didn't have much time to think about who he was," said Elizabeth. "At the end of the day I was so pooped that I fell asleep as soon as my head hit the sleeping bag. Oh, and speaking of heads! Look at this!" Elizabeth removed the headgear from her bag as carefully as she had packed it. "The beret is a gift from Billy Jack. He had a friend embroider the emblem. Isn't it beautiful?" Everyone agreed, and meant it, especially her mother. "And the rattle is from Grandfather Snake."

Mary Feye was less enthusiastic about the snake rattles. Was there a rattleless snake somewhere that held a grudge? Or was that just in the dream? Thinking of that, she wondered if it was possible for Elizabeth to visit a song in her sleep, then visit another place if she fell asleep hearing another song in that dream. And so on and so on . . . She mentally shook her head. *Let's not over-think this. Start thinking logically and you would go nuts.*

It was Hawkins that was most surprised at seeing the rattles trailing from the beret. While many things were revealed to him that others could not see this came as an utter and total surprise. *Just when you think nothing can astonish you! I wonder if Billy had anything to do with this?* Hawk tuned back into the conversation just as Elizabeth told the assembly about Grandfather Snake's words: *Should you have need you but have to shake the rattles. Those of the Clan that are able will come to your aid.*

The Hawk asked to see the rattles attached to the beret. He held them gently, turning them in his slender hands. "Elizabeth, I should be very careful with these. They are from the *Before,* when man still lived *with* the earth instead of just upon it. There is a very powerful summoning spell embedded in these rattles. Use this talisman wisely . . . or not at all." Hawkins carefully returned the beret to its owner.

Elizabeth took her beret and returned it to her book bag. She had felt the power of the rattles but had no idea that they had the ability to impress members of the LS, let alone Mr. Hawkins. Later tonight she might remove the rattles from the beret and put them in a safe place. Thinking a bit, Elizabeth remembered a question she had been wanting to ask The Hawk. "Mr. Hawkins, Billy Jack told me to tell you to come visit some time. What did he mean by that?"

Before he could answer Bandy yelled out that the light dinner he had prepared was ready, and for everyone to grab a plate while the food was still hot. What with the commotion Elizabeth's question was forgotten in the shuffle . . . as it was meant to be.

46

Jack lightheartedly slipped up the front staircase to the landing at the top. He cocked his head to better hear the voices. *Ahh, let's see . . . do we pick Door Number One, Door Number Two, or Door Number Three?* Stepping lightly down the hallway Jack stopped at the second door on his right. *And the winner is Door Number Two! Now I wonder what we will find on the other side of the door? Could my little sweetmeat be doing naughty things behind closed doors? Only one way to find out. Ready or not, here I come!*

Jack slipped through the door with minimum noise and effort. Once in the room he plastered himself against the wall. The two occupants were more intent on each other than on visitors, and their failure to notice him was a fatal error. As before, Jack dealt with the man first, and quickly. Stepping swiftly to the bed Jack slit the man's throat from ear to ear, and then directed the blood flow into the face the woman beneath him. The onslaught of warm blood gushing onto her face extinguished all desire instantly. The incredible realization of what was happening short-circuited the prostitute's mind. She could do nothing but gag on the blood Jack was directing into her mouth.

"Hello, baby. Thirsty? What? Cat got your tongue? No? Okay, then may I have it?" The paralyzed, terror-stricken whore could neither speak nor move as Jack deftly inserted a narrow, razor-sharp scalpel and cut out her tongue. Thankfully, her mind had taken her to another place and she felt nothing. Jack took his trophy and placed it in his pocket.

"Well, they say talk is cheap. Now you can save even more money. Or can you talk out of the other side of your mouth?" Jack was making it up as he went but the whore just lay on the bed, eyes as wide as if she had a thyroid condition. She was beginning to irritate him.

"Now look here, missy! The night is young even if you aren't. You really must make an effort. Hello! Is anybody in there? Knock knock!" Jack punctuated his questions with a couple of sharp raps to the woman's skull. She was quite beyond response. "Okay, fine. If you don't want to play in the bedroom then we'll go someplace else. Or do you consider this your office since you work here? No matter, Dearie. Let's go downstairs and have some fun."

Dragging the man's bloody corpse across the bed Jack grabbed the woman by the wrists and pulled her to her feet. She responded as if she were sleepwalking, allowing herself to be manipulated out of the bedroom and down the stairs. She was unencumbered by clothes of any kind. Jack led her into the den. "See, your friends have been waiting for you. Very polite, your friends. Quiet as the dead." Here Jack walked the woman around to the front of the sofa so she could view what was left of the three people. "Oops! My mistake. They really are dead! Now who could have gone and done that? I bet it was the butler. What? You have no butler? Then it must have been a triple suicide, don't you agree? I said, don't you agree?" Jack was forced to move the woman's head up and down himself for a response. "Come on, Dearie, don't be such a stick in the mud. Let's go into the dining room and amuse ourselves."

Jack sat the prostitute on a dining room chair so he could go to the window and cut off some cording from the venetian blinds. Returning to the woman he levered her up onto the dining room table, using the cord to fasten her, spread-eagled, onto the tabletop. Jack was delighted. "Yes! Now that is a centerpiece! Perfect . . . except . . . it lacks color." He looked around and spotted the flowers he had removed from the center of the table. "These will do nicely." Jack took the flowers and placed them between the woman's legs, arranging them this way and that. "What one must do in the name of art," he chuckled.

For whatever reason the gods had, as Jack moved to the head of the table the streetwalker's mind returned to her. With it came realization, and acute pain. She attempted to scream but found she had lost the ability. Instead a gush of blood and spittle was discharged from her mouth. Jack noticed immediately.

"Oh no, Dearie, not now. I asked politely early on and you declined to play. Now it is too late. Sorry!" A sly look came over his face. "But you can watch." Jack left the room and returned with some duct tape he found in the kitchen. It took him but a moment to tape the poor woman's eyelids open. "Now, isn't that better? Who says you can't have fun at home?"

As Jack picked up his *toy* the woman strained at her bonds, popping tendons in her frantic efforts to escape. But no one ever escaped from Jack. It was a long, long time before her eyes ceased to see what horrors Jack was perpetrating on her body . . .

47

"Wolf, that was delicious!" exclaimed Sawyer. "However do you manage?"

"Tis easy enough. What else have I to do all day but cook for the likes of you? Not meaning you, Miladies. Do ye think this place be overrun by customers all the livelong day now?"

"Just trying to give you a compliment, you pig-headed Irish twit," mumbled Sawyer in a voice too low for Wolf to hear.

"The Vice-principal is most correct in his evaluation, Mr. Bandy. Your repast was most delicious and delectable," said Mary Feye.

"Yes, and it tasted good, too!" piped in Elizabeth.

"Yes Wolf, our thanks. Now, whilst Wolf cleans up let us return to our talks. Mare, I see you carry with you some envelopes. Are these of importance to us this night?" said The Hawk.

"Yes, they are, I think. I pulled this off the Internet today and made copies for each of us. It may be old news to the three of you but it bears upon our situation." Mary Feye handed out a manila envelope to each person, including her daughter. "What I have given you is what is know about Jack the Ripper, albeit in abbreviated form. It lists all the murders reported, when and where they happened, and also best guesses as to the identity of the killer. It is gruesome reading, gentlemen."

Everyone took ten minutes or so to read through what she had given him or her, including Bandy who stopped his cleanup. "Ugly it is to read, and uglier still to the victims. Mare, would ye be havin' a favorite as to who is the culprit?" he asked.

Mary Feye answered immediately. "That I do. I've had time to read the reports and the theories, and to me Chapman seems most likely. Also, I'm loath to state it, but I have a *sense* that he is the murderer."

"Don't sell that sense short, Mare. Odds are that if you feel it then you are right on the money. Even if you are correct, how will this help us now? He will have come back from that time with a different look to him, so a physical ID comparison won't help." stated Sawyer.

"Let me answer that," said Hawk. "If Chapman is our man we would at least know something about him and the way he thinks. He would undoubt-edly retain the same patterns of behavior, likes and dislikes, no matter how many trips he took on the Time Train."

Elizabeth ventured an opinion: "If this guy is the Ripper it might explain why he is here in the United States. It says that Chapman was Polish by birth but came to the States after the murders ended in London. So he would at least be familiar with our country, and of course speak the language. But it says that he was executed in England. What does that mean?"

Sawyer answered her: "It means that he was executed by temporal law and not by the hand of a Jack; as such he could return. This could be our man. If so, and the consensus seems to be just that, perhaps we can learn more about George Chapman in the time remaining to us."

"Why hasn't this already been done?" asked Mary Feye.

"Because," spoke Hawk, "until now the field had not been narrowed. Our resources are not limitless. We are thin on the ground in this area. Only now your sense of the man points us in the right direc-tion. Bear will put Nocknagle on this straightaway. Any help, however slight the chance, is welcome."

Mary Feye was not totally satisfied but held her peace. *For a super secret society they certainly dropped the ball too many times for her comfort.* "Mr. Hawkins, earlier you spoke of Destiny. Is this some-thing you feel to be true, or wish to be true?"

"Now that is a question. Personally, I believe in Destiny. Yet I also believe that it can be bent. Many things have we found in the old manuscripts: Prophecies, visions, mention of things not yet in the world when they were written about. It is my personal belief that our path is drawn. We need only the wisdom to follow it."

"And what draws you to this conclusion?" queried Mary Feye.

"Wolf, if you please, may I have the translation?" Wolf opened a safe beneath the counter and retrieved an envelope from its interior. He wheeled to Hawk and handed the item to him.

"Obviously this is not the original, merely a copy. The translation is not exact, but as close as Nocknagle's people can come, considering the age of the prophecy and the difference in language. Hawkins read what was written on the paper:

> *Two millennium's days will Shadow stalk*
> *No rhyme or reason to be seen;*
> *The Blackmarch deeds shall not be balked*
> *Except by Fairy eyes most keen.*
>
> *As pieces fit and smoothly groove*
> *The parts become a whole;*
> *True Evil goes upon the move*
> *And Kingdom's heads will roll.*

In Future Time should all connect
Then Evil be at Aces;
Part in part let them adjut
To sear God's angels' faces.

Take part and piece and piece and part
And gather them All Hallow's Eve;
If placed within that made of bark
Then all God's good will fall asunder.

Yet one alone stands thwart the pass
And bars the way of witch's season;
Not muscled brawn but slightly lass
Shall heal the world's torn lesions.

A Chosen Child from lines long dead
Will topple earth and tower;
From long dead lips what must be said
Can prove the mightier power.

Sired of granite, born of fen
The Chosen One shall lead them;
Form the Diamond once again
And then . . .

Here Hawkins stopped. "That's it, I'm afraid.
The manuscript was in a damaged state and the
last stanzas are missing. Again, please realize that
the wording is paraphrased as best as possible to

give us the feel of the work. The wording cannot be considered exact."

Mary Feye asked that Hawkins reread the prophecy again, which he did. "What is your take on this, Mr. Hawkins? Or any of you for that matter."

"Well, I'll give you what we think we know first. If we literally translate, then two millennia would put us in this time period, taking into account when the document was written. The lines intimate that something dreadful will occur near this time, probably on Halloween, unless something is done to stop it. Here again, the different paths of Destiny. I read it that parts of something or other will be assembled, and then *placed within that made of bark.* I'm not quite clear on that reference. But it then gives hope by saying a *Chosen One,* a *lass,* will carry the day. As to the granite and the Diamond reference we haven't the foggiest. Even so, all portents point to Aubrey as being the Chosen One. Anyone care to add anything?"

"I would just say that there are two references to the fairy folk, which ties both of you ladies into the mix. And I've always been fearful that the parts come together to make a nuclear device," said Sawyer.

"I agree with the first and would refute the last o' that: What atomic bomb would ye be puttin' in something made out o' bark?" said Bandy.

Elizabeth piped up: "What if it meant something made out of wood? Like maybe a box or something? Remember in *Raiders of the Lost Ark* the Ark of the Covenant was shipped by the Nazis in a wooden crate?"

"Possible. No way to prove or disprove that theory," said Sawyer, "but wood does make more sense to me than *bark*. And it could be a translation anomaly."

"True enough," said Hawkins, "but why would putting these so-called parts or pieces into anything, let alone a wooden crate, have significance?"

"Could the box be some sort of amplifier, or activator? Could the box itself start a chain reaction?" asked The Mare.

'Forgive me fer sayin', but it would have to be a right rum box to cause all that, if you take my meaning," said Bandy.

"If you put fruit in a container it will sometimes ripen. Or ferment," added Elizabeth. She was surprised to see all four adults staring at her.

"Out o' the mouth of babes, it tis," said Bandy.

"It was there staring us in the face all the time. To use a bad pun, we weren't thinking outside the box!" laughed Sawyer. "We had our thoughts geared to inanimate things, not organisms like bacteria. Perhaps this wooden crate is merely an incubator for whatever goes inside it. Or maybe it just concentrates these things in a special way. That has a certain logic to it, I think."

"Ah, I have one more idea? Mr. Sawyer, you mentioned an incubator. It could also hatch something, couldn't it?" asked Elizabeth. She was once again the object of four pairs of eyes.

"Are we really this dense, or are we just having a very bad day?" asked Sawyer. "More and more I think we zero in on the meaning of the prophecy. Hawk, what say you?"

"It all seems to have a running logic to it. Yet I can't see how everything fits together. The Ripper is here, now, and an obvious target for the LS. Our friend The Crow is near, sniffing around the edges and grows ever closer. Behind him I feel a greater power manipulating him, pushing him harder than he has ever been pushed. Pawns are being rushed into play, and sacrificed without a backward glance. Resources are being consumed at a tremendous rate. All this isn't conjecture: It is plain cold fact."

"Then what must be done to counteract all this? Mr. Hawkins, what *has* been done?" demanded Mary Feye.

"What has been done? More than you know and less that I can tell you now. Give me a week of evenings and I might be able to list all we have done, where we have succeeded, and where we have failed. Would it comfort you to know that fully eighty percent of the Ladder Society's resources have been marshaled to deal with this threat?" Hawk was getting testy.

"Eighty percent! That's four hundred people!" exclaimed Elizabeth.

"Exactly so, Elizabeth, not to mention many others that are aligned with us but are not members. Yet still we trail the game. If we do not find the answers we need to this riddle in two day's time I fear we shall long for better days. I still believe the Ripper kills here now to flush the LS out, and with it you, Aubrey. I think The Crow searches for you with great diligence. He fears you. Yet he fears his master even more. You can but kill him. The one behind him can do much, much worse. So Daws is motivated and literally cannot stop for anything. He must find you and eliminate you from the board. Yet how all this ties together is beyond my ken. That is why we must return you to Whitechapel so that we may learn what this Ripper is about, and get a line on him."

"How am I to do that?" asked Elizabeth.

The Hawk looked Aubrey straight in the eye: "You have to find and bring back to us his diary."

Mary Feye was on her feet while Hawk's words where still in the air. "His diary! What is my daughter to do? Just go to his house and knock on this psychopath's door and say *Please, I'm from the future and I want your diary?*" Once again Elizabeth's mother had caught fire.

"Easy, Mare," soothed Sawyer, "we know it sounds horrific but it will be easier to do than you realize. We all feel now that George Chapman is the Ripper. You have convinced us. All Aubrey has to do is go to where he lives, and using the time of death for one of his murders, enter his house when he is absent."

"I don't like it. What if the newspapers were wrong? What if history gets changed somehow? What if the bastard doesn't keep the diary in his house? What if he has a watchdog? And why do you need his diary? For that matter how do you know he *has* a diary?"

"I agree that the risk is great, Mare. But my confidence in Aubrey is ever growing. When Aubrey is sent she will be as well equipped as anyone on earth. Look how far she has come in just one week! Aubrey will prevail, Mare. I am confident of that," spoke Hawkins.

"More so than I, sir. And as usual you have answered part and left part be. Why the diary? And how are you aware of it?"

Hawkins was forced to reveal more than he wished: "Our research has led us to facts that point to a diary being extant. Nocknagle's research department has spent countless hours pouring over every manuscript, every newspaper account and every piece of recorded oral history they could access. Beyond that certain esoteric means have been used to gain insight into this mystery. Everything they have learned reinforces the idea that this document exists. We are calling it a diary for lack of a more distinct or more technical name. As to the reason why we need it, that same research shows the possibility exists that this is no ordinary diary. It could be some type of time line entry log. It may well chronicle all the lives of the Ripper. We also believe that this thing was created not just of mundane materials. Nocknagle came across a very old manuscript that refers to something like this diary, although it wasn't called a diary. The text refers to the AntiJacks, again, not by that name, and how this diary is connected to them. Nocknagle sent me this excerpt from the source he found." Hawk went to a folder he had brought with him and pulled out a note card and read from it:

Thus this learning has come unto us from many places. The Holder of Lives does exist and contains great knowledge and greater Evil. The holder is old beyond our years and a single lifetime could not compile all that is written. Jacob's Prophesy is one with, and apart to, this thing. Dire is the holder! Righteousness can not touch it. Many have sought this thing for both grim and righteous reasons. The one who gave us what we now know did not survive the journey. Many are the years before the time of the prophecy. We shall not stop the search until the holder is found and destroyed, no matter what cost. If we fail and other eyes beyond our mortal stay see this work then heed my words: If thou seeks the holder, Beware! Darius says this."

The Hawk stopped speaking. The room was deathly quiet. "So, you see the data this *holder* contains would be of immense value. I personally believe that it may contain a clue as to whether or not The Ripper is personally involved in the prophecy. Either way would be significant information."

"Well that certainly makes me feel much more comfortable!" said Mare. "Forgive me if I play Devil's Advocate, but surely the Ladder Society has a Level Five member capable of returning to London and just reading the damn thing while The Ripper is out having dinner!" Mary Feye was building another head of steam. It was Wolf who put out the fire.

"Milady, nothing is that easy, in this life or the past. Do ye think we woudda not tried that first off? We almost lost a bonnie lass in the bargain, too. She were held up in her lookin' and nearly overstayed her welcome when she visited Chapman's time."

"Then why doesn't she go back since she is familiar with all this?" demanded The Mare.

"Because she was there for a long time. She had to check out each of the suspects, not just George Chapman. The experience broke her nerve for the Otherlands. She does not wish to return, and we have no wish to force her," stated Hawkins.

"Where is she now? And why not use another Five?" asked Elizabeth.

Sawyer answered the question: "She is still with us, Elizabeth, as a valued member of the Ladder Society. She does honorable work for us and the community. As to using someone else, well, you did the math. Fives are not easy to come by. She is our only owner capable of that skill at this time"

"What does she do?" asked Elizabeth.

"Doan ask me why she would torment herself, but would ye believe she is a schoolteacher? Twere me, I think the *Otherlands* the better o' the pair o' choices," laughed Wolf.

Elizabeth happened to be looking at The Hawk when Bandy answered her. She saw him ever so slightly tap the side of his head. It caused her to react, to use her mind with this new information. It took her a mere instant of time to realize and confirm with a look to Hawk what she now knew to be true: The person they were talking about was her own history teacher, Mrs. Hurd.

48

Jack had enjoyed the evening immensely. He didn't even mind that when he left he met someone coming up the walkway to the row house he was leaving. The woman had even asked if Junie was in. Jack told her. "Yes, of course. She's having some people over for dinner. Go right on in. I'm sure she won't mind." He had whistled his way down the walk as the woman rang the bell and watched him go. Now he was home. He had taken his prize to the basement first thing. He had just finished his shower–*cleanliness, et cetera et cetera,* and headed to the kitchen for a snack–*he had worked up an appetite, yessir.* As he passed through the living room he felt, or sensed, that something wasn't right. He stopped dead in his tracks. The lights in the room were off but there was some illumination seeping under the swinging kitchen door. He slowly turned in place and came upon someone sitting in his favorite chair.

"Hello, George," said Jack Daws to the Ripper.

Jack didn't react rashly. *Rash acts got people killed and up to now he was the one that did the killing. His visitor was in shadow, a lean shadow it was, too. Sitting on his Barkolounger as if he owned it. Jack's hand longed for the feel of one of his toys. He must learn to keep one in the pocket of his bathrobe. Not the best time to learn that lesson, though. Well, curiosity killed the cat. Let's see which one of us is the pussy.*

"Do I know you, sir? If you're a thief I fear you'll find sparse pickings here."

Daws laughed. "No, I'm not here to rob you, George. Or do you prefer Severin Antoniovich? Or is it Klosowski?

Jack thought quickly. George? Antoniovich? This guy was crazy. Best to humor him until we see what the deal is. "Sorry, mister, but the name is Jack, not George, or Seven Anthony-wich either. You got me confused with someone else. Must be you got the wrong townhouse. Easy mistake. They all look alike to me." The man rose from the chair and moved forward a step. *The man was a kaffir! I don't think he liked that last remark.*

"Not to worry, Jack. They all look alike to me too. But it is you I wish to talk to. You've been very busy lately. How's the collection coming?"

Jack backed up a step. "Who are you? You a Peeler?"

Daws roared with laughter. "Me, a cop? Now *that* would be funny. No Jack, I'm a friend of yours. You just don't know me yet. Tell me, are you sleeping well lately? Having dreams, nightmares? Yes, I thought as much. I see it in your eyes. Does the landscape sometimes seem to shift on you, like you see the streets as they were years ago?"

Jack was perplexed. How did this guy know about that? "Yeah, so what?"

"Aren't you afraid these little *episodes* will interfere with your work?"

Whatever this guy knew was too much times ten. Time to say goodbye to this particular nightmare. Jack stepped back a pace or two until his back was up against the sideboard. "Look pal, why don't you go drink some more Sterno and enjoy what's left of the evening and leave me alone, okay?"

"Oh Jack, you are a real card! And please, don't reach into the drawer for one of your *friends*; I'm the best friend you have." Daws stepped forward again and this time his face was visible to Jack. One look and Jack shrank back from the sight of the disfigured jaw.

"Better, much better, boy. Now listen to me! Up until now you've done a great job. I've followed you from Boston to Baltimore and you've yet to make a slip. But tonight! Damn man, you went too far! This bit of business will be Page One news! You need to take a cold shower or something. You're out of control and I just can't have that. Whether or not you know it you have one more piece of business to conduct Friday night. I'm warning you now: Make it quick, make it sweet, and above all make it quiet! No theatrics, hear? In, out, and done. Comprendo?"

Jack had only a vague idea of what Daws was going on about. But on some level realization was alive, and revelation birthing. *He was on a mission of some sort. This black fellow was his boss of sorts. It was best not to anger the boss. Bad things happened when the boss wasn't pleased.* "Yes, get what's to be gotten and get out. Fast."

"Good boy, Jack. All will be clearer tomorrow, and bright and shiny as a new penny come All Hallow's Eve. You will remember all then. Until that time I suggest you get some sleep. You look like shit." The Crow spun on his heels and was out the door before Jack could say a word.

Jack could only stare at the doorway, wondering what had just taken place. He wished he knew more. But first things first. He opened up the center drawer in the sideboard and put a sheathed scalpel into the pocket of his terrycloth robe. As he climbed the steps to his bedroom he didn't take notice that he was singing . . . in Polish.

49

Mary Feye was furious. *Could these people not see that they were sending her daughter to almost certain death?* "If this tale was a balm for my soul you miss your mark! How in hell do you expect a fifteen-year-old girl to succeed where an obviously experienced field agent failed? Not only failed but was so traumatized by the event that she will no longer travel to the *Otherlands*? What is wrong with you?" Mary Feye stood up. "There is no one on earth that can convince me to send my only child on this, this *suicide* mission. Come on, Elizabeth. Let's go." Mary Feye gathered her things and started for the door.

The Hawk spoke to her back in a near whisper: "Stay thyself for a moment, Milady. Please. I would request you grant this last boon. Hear what is said, and if it moves you not, then go, and we will trouble you no longer."

The appeal stopped her but did not lessen her antagonism. Her green eyes smoked and bore into Hawk's, looking for a clash of will. She met nothing but a calm sea of grey; no anger, just acceptance of what was to be. "I will listen to you," she replied simply.

Instead of addressing her The Hawk spoke to Bandy without removing his eyes from Mary Feye: "Wolf–get it, please." Bandy wheeled away as Hawkins starting speaking. "Milady, it is beyond time for you to listen to me. And you have the right of it when you say that no one on earth can convince you to our need." Hawk got up as Bandy returned from his bedroom. Bandy handed him a slim package wrapped in brown paper tied with twine. It had an aged look to it. Bandy nodded to Sawyer and together they left the room.

"This was not unexpected, Milady. We, I, hoped that by force of will I could sway you. I should have known better. They say only a fool will enter the fens when the mist is upon it. So be it." Hawkins handed her the package. "If you will not listen to me then perhaps you will heed another. Aubrey, remain or come to me as you or your mother wishes. The device is on the bar, Milady." The Hawk removed himself from the room and gently closed the door.

Mary Feye held the package lightly in her right hand and stared at it. "What do you think this is, Elizabeth? A gift? A bribe?" She put the box on the coffee table and watched it as if it was alive. The package did not move. Resigning herself she picked it again but this time the box seemed to tingle in her hands. She dropped it like her hands were afire and quickly sat down, dizzy.

"Mom, are you okay?"

"Give, give me a minute, sweetie." Mary Feye took close to three of them before coming back to normal. "I can hardly believe this. Elizabeth, take the package in your hands. Please." Elizabeth did as she was asked but did not drop it. Instead she could not stand and buckled at the knees.

"Elizabeth!"

"I'm . . . okay, Mom. It just stunned me, that's all. Is it true? Really?"

"Yes, I believe so. Whatever is in this package belonged to your father. I guess I should open it."

"Should I stay here or go?" asked Elizabeth.

Mare thought a moment. "Stay, I think. I'm guessing this concerns you as much as it does me. Mary Feye picked up the small parcel, undid the twine and started unwrapping the package.

* * *

All three men at the counter in the adjoining room were silent. The Hawk was the first to break the quiet. "Damn."

"Give over," said Bear, "it was the only way and you know it."

"Aye, she be the only person that's more hard-headed than yon black rock," said Wolf, pointing at Sawyer. "Or maybe you, Hawk."

"Yes, maybe, but what will her stubbornness gain her this night? More heartache? And the Little One? Have you thought about what this will do to her?"

"A bit. But Wolf and I have some distance from the problem. That is a luxury that you deny yourself. What good will they be in the end if they can not accept this in the beginning?"

"Bear 'tis right. Curse or Blessing, they must be havin' the know of it. Intween, what say we hear about Bear's adventures with Marco Polo? Bear?"

"Not too much new to tell, really. This morning I talked with Harold Yoder and his mother. A fine lady, that. Her boy just got caught up in the web. I think maybe they're using a very mild wreaking around the schools, shot-gunning so to speak, hoping for a break. They've probably tried some things we haven't even glommed on to yet. I think we're lucky that they haven't narrowed it down already."

The other two men nodded in agreement. Bear continued his story: "Anyway, I cut Harold loose with a warning. But I was able to catch up with his contact at the arcade. A match made in heaven, or hell as it were. A right snot of a kid, he was." Sawyer related his encounter with George Polopolis, especially the part where the boy dented his pickup leaving the parking lot. "I have a good reading on the boy's voice and speech patterns. I think I can match it well enough on the telephone to entice someone to meet me. I've sent the phone numbers off to Research but I doubt we'll have any luck there. Probably prepaid cell phones that they ditch after so many incoming calls. Tomorrow I'll try and set a meeting with whomever answers the phone. Just in case I'd like a Watcher or two standing by."

"Okay, do it. Get with KatyJay and see who's available. But she's not to pull JohnPaul off Amy. I have no logical reason but somehow I feel she is part of this along with LaTisha Wood. Better she keep watch on LaTisha, too."

"Do ye hav' a strong feeling 'bout this then? Twas that the reason ye gifted them with the talismans?"

"Partly that, plus I felt that the Little One needed some friends. This bonded them faster than they normally would have. I don't regret it. Even without the jacks I think they would stick by her."

"Aye, that they would. Which is remindin' me. I got a phone call from my friend Big Martha today."

"Isn't she the local dealer you use to convert our older coins into ready cash?" asked Bear.

"Aye, that she is, and a good person in the bargain. She called me to tell me she were robbed." The other two men looked at Wolf as if to say *so what?* A smile leaked out from Wolf's eyes. "Seems the bugger was apprehended before he could make off with the loot." Again Wolf got the *so what?* looks. "And would ye believe it were our own darlin' girl in the next room what foiled the attempt, with a wee bit o' help from LaTisha?"

"You're kidding! Bear, did you know of this?"

"This is the first I've heard tell, Hawk. Bandy, you little sneak, why didn't you call and tell me! You're like a weasel with a duck egg not wanting to share!"

"Oh, it pains me to hear ye talk to me so, to think so little of me poor self. If it twill make ye sleep better, then know that I got the call not long before ye got here."

"Why," asked Hawk, "did she call you in the first place?"

"Two reasons I'm thinking. Firstly, she knows a little about me, and second, somehow she knows that the Little One is acquainted with meself. Martha had a problem, she did. It seems the girls saved her life, or so she's believing. But the Little One, God bless her, made Martha promise not to involve her. The girls skedaddled, and Martha was left with the culprit old cold in her store. She called me for help."

"I'm afraid to ask," said Bear.

"Doan look at me like I'm Ted Bundy ye big goof! I sent a pair o' Watchers over to the Mall and they collected the man in a laundry hamper."

"And where would he be now? The laundromat?" asked Hawk.

"Nae, they took him to be dry-cleaned. It had ta be done, Hawk. He woulda spilled his guts sooner or later. Probably not soon enou to affect the Little One, but in time he could have hurt Martha for sure. An' I hav' no doubt he was plannin' ta kill her befor' he left."

"And what did Big Martha think when the Watchers arrived? That you were her fairy god-mother?" asked Bear.

"Nae, I told her me cousins would scare the boyo to death and put his arse on a bus heading West. I were speaking half the truth, anyway."

"He was measured, Wolf?" asked The Hawk with intent.

'Aye, Hawk, and twice. He fell short, he did. His rap sheet was as long as me arm." Wolf spoke without humor, and there was no sympathy in his voice.

"So be it, then. Nice clean work, Wolf. Incredible maturity on the Little One's part. Men, our little girl is growing up."

"Yes, too fast I think. Wolf, do you have the details of the robbery or must I beat them out of you?" Bear asked with a smile.

"Details have I, and plenty! A tricky witch is our little girl. You'll never believe how she did it . . ."

* * *

Mary Feye set aside the wrappings to the package. Placed within the box was a simple audiocassette tape. She picked it up and looked at it intently. "Not a prerecorded tape. It looks to be homemade."

Elizabeth made the connection quickly and went to the bar. As Hawk had said, there was a portable tape player sitting there. She brought the machine over to her mother and placed it on the coffee table. With great trepidation Mary Feye inserted the cassette into the player and turned it on. At first all they heard was tape hiss, a bumping noise, then what sounded like a microphone hitting the floor followed by a muttered curse. The tape bumped again and for the first time in her life Elizabeth heard the sound of her father's voice.

"My dearest Mare. How strange this is to talk to you now, in this manner. I hope the experience isn't too painful for you. Having to hear my voice after I don't know how many years must be a bit of a shock. But if you are listening to this at all then I am surely in another realm, and lost to you. I am in Ireland at the moment, soon to be home with you. I must get this down now before it is too late. Mare, Darling, my time is short on this earth. I have foreseen what is to come and must do what I can to stop it. Funny, I'm talking about things yet to come and for you it is past history. You probably know more than I about these events. There is a force out in the world than means no good to me, to you, and especially to Aubrey. If I can

I will stop these people from doing you and the baby harm. You will know if I have succeeded." Here they could tell the tape was stopped and then restarted.

"*My biggest regret is that I did not tell you more of my work. I was forever shielding you from it in the vain hope that the Evil which I fight would pass you by. I was so very wrong in that, wasn't I? All I did was squander our time together. How many birthdays did I miss, how many dinners and weekends and vacations? Is it too late to say I'm sorry? I hope not.*

"*Since you have this tape things must be very tense in the world. I would guess that members of the Society have clued you in detail, and asked your help, or the help of our daughter. Knowing you, and having been on the receiving end of your temper a time or two I can guess you are balking at helping. I wonder who gave you the tape? If they still live I would guess Jackson Sawyer or Wolf Bandy, or maybe Clarissa Hurd. You can't miss Sawyer-big as a house, and Bandy, well, he has the worse accent known to man. Lady Clarissa you would like, too. I am giving this tape to a friend who will get it to a man named Nocknagle. He will safekeep it, and see that it is put in the correct hands if it is warranted. My love, by now you know that a strong enchantment was placed on you years ago, to keep you hidden from Darkness. I imagine that now the spell has been lifted, or, as is your want, you have split it asunder. Great strength is yours. Beware that you do not become your own worst enemy."* The tape paused again, then restarted:

"Mare, is Aubrey there with you? Aubrey, if you are then I send you my love. I know you must be as smart and beautiful as your mother. I hope you are old enough now to understand what and who you are, and what tremendous stakes we are playing for. My loves, you must listen to the Society! Mare, I know you. You will wish to protect our child above all else, especially after losing me at such a crucial time in your life. But you must, must look beyond that to the world and the generations yet unborn. Heed those that gave you this tape. This I ask of you." Again they heard the sound of the tape stopping.

"Aubrey, if you are there, would you humor the father you never met and let me talk to your mother alone for a minute? I'll pause the recording here." Mary stopped the tape. "Well, kiddo, I didn't see this coming at all. It's been sixteen years since I heard your father's voice. Now here he is talking to us like we just parted yesterday. It's a bit of a shock."

"He sounds very nice, Mom. You can tell how much he loved you just by his voice."

"Yes, there was never a doubt there. Honey, would you mind too much going into Mr. Bandy's bedroom for a minute while I listen to what your father has to say?"

"Of course not, Mom." Elizabeth got up and went into the bedroom. This was a place she had never seen before. She marveled at all the strange and eclectic things in the room, reflecting the owner's odd personality. As she looked around she could just barely hear the click of the tape recorder as it started up again.

"Beloved, there are a hundred ways you can love a person. I loved you each and every one. Sorry I am that you had to bring up our child by yourself. But I am confident you have done a great job. You are incapable of doing otherwise. Yet now you must decide what trail you will follow. Destiny has many paths. There is the high road with thin air and sharp rocks, the low road with swamp and miasma for company, and the middle ground where the road is paved and easy. Know that all roads lead to the same destination. It is the journey that is important. But you must decide which road you will take, and decide now. If you find you cannot bind yourself to the Society then so be it. Tell the people you are with and that will be the end of it. My love goes with you. Stop the tape now and return it to the one that gave it to you. Should you decide otherwise then pause this tape, then continue." The Artful Dodger stopped speaking. Mary Fey hit the pause key and leaned back in her chair. *It all boiled down to this, then. Possibly sacrifice her daughter for an indifferent world, or keep her safe and maybe that world goes to hell in a hand basket.* Mary sighed. *Well, evidently these AntiJacks have been hunting us forever. If they want Elizabeth they're going to have to fight me to get*

her. With more resolve than ever Mary Feye released the pause button.

"Thank you, my love. All will be well in the end. Now, I want you to place your left hand on this tape, or through whatever device you are using. Just your left hand. I am going to say some words, ancient words, words of power. There will be a wreaking on them. After you hear them you will forget them. This is for your own safety. No outsider will be able to access the words without great skill and cunning. If our daughter is involved, then I want you to grasp her left hand with yours, and speak her true name. You will automatically remember the words and speak them to her. Then you both will disremember them. But they will be stored within you. At great need either of you will be able to retrieve them without effort. Do not say them except in extreme circumstances! Now, please do as I ask." Mary flipped up the plastic cover of the tape player and touched the tape as instructed. As she listened *The Artful Dodger* quietly spoke three sentences in what seemed like Gaelic, or something of Celtic origin. She could repeat the words exactly but had no clue to their meaning. Then, as quickly as she had memorized the words, she forgot them. Her husband's voice returned: *"As with all words of power there is a quid pro quo. I-"* The tape stopped, then restarted. *"Mare, I must go. My . . . contact is at the door. I must give him what I have. When I get home I will make another tape and explain other*

things that really must be said. But now I have no time. I love you both dearly, Mare. Through all the time I have lived you have been my only love, and my only wife, as Aubrey is my only child. You were worth waiting for . . . and dying for. I shall love you always." The tape hissed until the spool was empty. Mary had expected to cry but her eyes were dry. She would cry later. Right now she felt absolved. She realized for the first time how she had resented Art for leaving her. She had been using the Ladder Society as a whipping boy to take out her frustrations instead of channeling her emotions in a more positive direction. That time was now over. Mary Fey called for her daughter.

Elizabeth hardly heard her mother so intent was she looking at the dim photographs in Wolf's bedroom. She was surprised to discover a very young, very slender Mrs. Hurd in one of them with Wolf's arm around her. On the dresser she had found a group picture with Bear, Mrs. Hurd, Wolf, and two other men she didn't recognize. They all looked much younger than they did now. Finally her mother's voice penetrated her thoughts. Elizabeth left the photos where she found them and went to her mother.

"Elizabeth, your father has convinced me to let you attempt this journey. He has told us to trust the LS, and these people. I think it is time we did."

Elizabeth grinned from ear to ear. "You won't be sorry, Mom. We can do it. I know we can!"

"I hope so, Honey. In the meantime your father has given us some insurance." Mary related what was told to her about the words of power. She held her daughter's left hand in hers, breathed deeply, and spoke her full name: "Elizabeth Aubrey de la Feye". In an instant the information was passed, memorized, and forgotten.

"That's it?" asked Elizabeth.

"Expecting lightning bolts, Honey? Big things in small packages, I think. Your father was forever hiding his light under a bushel. Now, go roust the menfolk while I grab a glass of wine from Mr. Bandy's excellent stock."

50

Jack Daws was feeling pleased with himself. Things seemed to be running true to form, with the exception of George's little escapade. He was halfway home when his mind was wrenched away. *So much for feeling good. A summoning was never good. It was like an IRS audit. They always found something wrong.* Daws hurried to the nearest place of dead power, in this case a local junkyard. Once inside among the dead vehicles his being was amplified, as was the voice that called him.

"How do things go with you, Crow?"

The voice was real but only Daws could hear it. "Well, my Lord. Very well."

"How have you arrayed my thralls? What battle name have you given them?"

"Sire, I have used the English names of the venomous snakes common to the land at this time. The local minions seem to embrace the symbols and like the rivalry. We are aligned in four sections. I have concentrated your forces from Fredericksburg in the South to the Mason-Dixon Line in the North. The Cottonmouths hold the South up to Alexandria. The Rattlers take the North from the Line to just south of Baltimore. The Corals cover the area between Alexandria and Baltimore, including the Capital and the lands to the east. The Copperheads are to the West, spread all along the South of our line to the North, with their backs to the mountains. They work their way to the sea, as those to the North and South tighten the web ever closer along the coast."

"How goes the search?"

"Great sums have been laid out, Sire. We blanket the entire area. We have had many false leads but the search narrows. I have Internet trolls sending mass emails in my name to all that meet the criteria in hope that one will lead us to another. Our strongest clues point to an area west of the city of Baltimore. Our people have already moved from Manassas, Hagerstown and Harrisburg and move toward the East. We are very close. But she is well hidden, or shielded. I have agents near almost every high school within the target area. Sooner or later a slip will be made."

What strength have you committed? Are they provisioned?"

"Master, there are nigh two battalions total strength numbering over sixteen hundred individuals. We have all that we need. Drug sales are up, with Ecstasy doing very well. We want for nothing."

"You may want for nothing, yet I still do not have the child contained! And what of my tool, Severin Antoniovich? Can you not keep him in line? He now leaves a trail that a blind mouse could follow."

Son of Satan! thought Daws. "Master, I have spoken to him. He will soon be aware of himself. In two day's time he will remember the location of the diary. With that we shall find the box. I am sure of it."

"You had better be. Should you fail me Death will be something to cherish. Remember that as you plod along like a snail in a salt mine. And what of the Jehovahs? Why have you not found the local nest and done away with them?"

"Master, they do not show themselves, in mundane or preternatural ways. We sense their presence yet they do not display themselves. Again, the area near Baltimore is our best hope."

"Tell me why."

"Sire, I have lost contact with some of my people in that area. It could be a coincidence but I think not."

"For once we agree. Look harder in that sector. Commit more resources. Find the Jacobs, these Jacks, and destroy them. Find them and you find the child.

*Turn or destroy the child and our plans will not fail.
Do not fail me, churl. My time grows short! Go!"*

Sweating like it was high summer, The Crow went out into the night.

51

Elizabeth returned to the living room with the three men in tow. Mary Feye had advised her daughter to keep silent on what they had heard, and learned, from The Artful Dodger. So it came to pass that none of the three knew which way the wind would blow. Mary Feye waited for everyone to find a seat–except for Bandy who came already equipped–before she spoke.

"I have something to say to you Mr. Sawyer, and Mr. Bandy, and especially to you, Mr. Hawkins." Just her tone of voice demanded attention. "I have heard many a tale in this room. Whether they are true or not remains to be seen. I can only tell you what I know. The essential fact is that you wish to put my child in harm's way. You want to set her on the trail of some hell-spawned piece of human garbage. As a mother, as *her* mother, it is my duty as a parent to refuse to lend her to your scheme." Elizabeth's mother paused for effect as she watched the three men in turn as their faces showed disappointment and resignation.

Then Mary Feye pulled her daughter to her side and held her hand and said: "However . . . as *An Bheannaigh Go Specisialta*, greatdaughter of the union of Meridrill, Lady of the Misted Forest and Eldriss Fenmaster, and widow of the slain Artful Dodger, know you this: If the *Barak Dymdik Ky* want a war with this family they have found one! We stand with you and we fight!"

The three men; The Wolf, The Bear, and The Hawk, looked at each other, smiled, and in unison said: *"YES!"*

END

Bad Moon Rising
The Second Book of the
Chronicles of The Ladder Society

The tale of An Bronntanas o Dhia continues in

The Gales of November
The Third Book of the
Chronicles of The Ladder Society

Visit www.tconnormichael.com
to keep up-to-date

Made in the USA
Middletown, DE
30 March 2021

35793293R10260